A Visit Home

BY

WILL AITKEN

SIMON & SCHUSTER
New York   London   Toronto   Sydney   Tokyo   Singapore

SIMON & SCHUSTER
Simon & Schuster Building
Rockefeller Center
1230 Avenue of the Americas
New York, New York 10020

Designed by Irving Perkins Association
Manufactured in the United States of America

1 3 5 7 9 10 8 6 4 2

Library of Congress Cataloging-in-Publication Data
Aitken, Will.
A visit home / Will Aitken.
p. ; cm.
I. Title
PS3551.I95V5   1993
813'.54—dc20   92-37241
CIP

ISBN 0-671-74707-X

The author would like to thank his editor and friend, Chuck Adams, for his support and patience.

For my sisters,
Janet Aitken & Anne Carson

in memoriam
Janet Tolosa

But how shall I speak a thing that appalls my speech?
—SOPHOCLES, *Ajax*

. . . keep open the wounds of possibility.
—KIERKEGAARD

PART ONE

The Memorial
Service

*T*he girl with brick-red lips tapped Daniel on the shoulder. "Excuse me, can I just snake this in here?"

Daniel smiled and leaned to one side as the girl used a strip of gaffer's tape to affix a small cylindrical mike to the larger speaker's microphone sprouting from the lectern.

He hadn't expected so much fuss, but then he hadn't expected much of anything—a short ceremony, a laminated plaque, wine and cheese after in the chairman's office. The speaker's microphone now had six, no, seven mikes of various sizes taped to or propped against it, and the girl with brick-red lips was talking to a rotund man with a TV news camera hoisted on one shoulder.

SRO, Daniel concluded, scanning the steeply raked auditorium. The ceremony must be required attendance for architecture students. He could think of no other reason why they should all be so closely ranged in rows on such a flawless spring day. The room was stuffy and yet no one thought to pole open a couple of the high sash windows.

He clasped his hands together and coughed. Nerves. Silly but undeniable. Queasy stomach, cotton mouth, the beginnings of a headache. Leslie said nerves were part of the process. Go with them, she counseled, you wouldn't be you without them. No, wouldn't be *good* without them.

Where was Leslie? She'd said she would come if she could get out of court in time.

Peter Olon, chairman of the school of architecture, rushed in through a low doorway to one side of the dais, conferred briefly with two of his colleagues and rushed out again.

Daniel leaned back in his chair, trying to get a better look at the woman sitting on the opposite side of the lectern. He hadn't caught her name during the jumbled introductions Peter Olon had made when Daniel first entered the auditorium. She leaned back too, peering at him over the top of the flattened octagonal lenses of her black-framed glasses. "Are they always this well organized?"

"This is pretty good for McGill," Daniel said. "Especially good for Peter Olon. I'm sorry but I didn't get your name."

"McCrory, Meredith McCrory." She reached out and gave his hand a sharp shake. Daniel couldn't make out if her accent was British or simply the mid-Atlantic drawl cultivated in academic circles throughout the Northeast.

"Daniel Kenning. Peter said you're from New Haven?"

"I was at Yale for six years but now I'm back at Oxford." She took off her glasses and buffed the thick lens with a gray silk handkerchief.

"I feel so thick," Daniel said. "Meredith McCrory. You wrote that wonderful book about architecture and Greek tragedy."

She smiled, careful not to show any teeth. "You know it?"

"Something about doors . . ."

"*He Who Controls the Door*. It looks at power, kinship and architecture in Greek drama, both comedy and tragedy."

"I remember it very clearly. The title slipped my mind. Extraordinary book. I have to admit I don't know as much as I should about Greek drama, but what you said about the symbolic use of space . . ."

Meredith McCrory's smile threatened to widen. She put one hand over her mouth. "And your work is . . ."

Peter Olon burst back into the room, carrying a large leather-bound volume and what looked like a pair of bronzed gyroscopes mounted on cubical wooden bases. He set the gyroscopes on the table next to the water pitcher and plastic cups and, thumping the book down on the lectern, leaned into the microphone. His normally mild voice shook the auditorium. "MAY we get started, PLEASE?"

A student at the top of the auditorium had succeeded in opening one of the tall windows with a hooked pole. Daniel could hear tentative bird song and the distant pong of tennis balls.

"Martins," Olon said, at last leaning away from the mike, "I would thank you to keep that window closed. The heat is still on in this building."

Five hundred student and faculty heads silently swiveled to watch as Martins carefully closed the window.

"Environment, after all," Olon said, opening the leatherbound book, "is one of the reasons we're assembled here today for this 1985 edition of the Helios awards." Daniel could see that Olon had inserted his speech, scrawled in pencil on lined looseleaf paper, between the vellum pages of the impressive volume.

"I don't have to remind you," Olon continued, "that the Helios awards are given in recognition not simply of fine architecture"—he inclined his head in Daniel's direction—"or of firstrate thinking and *écriture* about architecture"—he patted Meredith McCrory's shoulder—"but also of how architecture interfaces with the deep syntax of our ecosystem, becoming a veritable paradigm of the universe's undecidability curve . . ."

Daniel was glad to hear that, in the fifteen or sixteen years since he had sat in this same airless room as an undergraduate enrolled in Peter Olon's required course, the Semiotics of Architecture, the man had continued to add to his critical vocabulary. "Interface" and "paradigm" dated to Daniel's years at McGill, but "ecosystem" and "undecidability curve" were new. He scanned the crowd. Everyone—students and professors alike—looked utterly blank.

"Our first Helios," Olon said, "for the innovative reimagining of a preexisting structure goes to Pettigrew, Carstairs, Jacob's renovation—if that is not too dilute a word for such a bold venture—of the old Schlegel mansion. Slide, please."

The mechanical whirr of a slide projector issued from the projection booth window at the top of the auditorium. Daniel craned his neck to see the screen above and behind his head. He couldn't make out anything.

Olon leaned into the microphone. "LIGHTS, JULIA."

The lights dimmed. A professor got up from his aisle seat and pulled down the shades on the windows closest to the screen. The projector clacked twice. Giggling erupted among the upper tiers of students. Someone called out, "What're you on, Julia?"

Daniel looked up at the screen: the Schlegel mansion hung batlike from a grassy sky.

The invisible slide projector clicked and whirred. The slide reappeared, righted.

"As you can see here," Olon said, "the Schlegel mansion was half-destroyed by the wrecker's ball before the municipal authorities could get the preservationist gears turning. The structure was saved, but only just, and in the subsequent debate over turning the mansion into a community center, numerous *experts* suggested it would be cheaper to raze this treasure lode of Montreal history and start over from the ground up. Next slide, please."

Daniel was getting a stiff neck from looking over his shoulder.

"A bit fuzzy, Julia. That's better." Olon produced a small stainless-steel rod from the inner pocket of his suit jacket. He flicked the rod at the audience, like a man casting flies. The shiny rod telescoped into a four-foot-long pointer, which Olon moved across the image from the next slide, a three-quarter view of the completed Schlegel project. "You can see here, I think, how Pettigrew, Carstairs, Jacob succeeded in turning devastation into triumph, slicing away the damaged third of the mansard roof, augmenting and yet never detracting from the essentially classical lines of the building with the ziggurat configuration of the south wall. Notice too how playful the palette of color and texture is, the nearly musical arrangement of clerestory windows across the damaged end of the façade . . ."

The tribute was so fulsome, the Schlegel project so inadequate—in the end it had cost far more than starting from scratch—that Daniel felt embarrassed. He looked at the slide and all he could see were flaws, cut corners, flat-out mistakes.

". . . and so today we are gathered here to honor the supervising architect on the Schlegel project, a building that conclusively demonstrates that we can and must move beyond mere *façade-isme*. Ladies and gentlemen, I give you Daniel Kenning, one of our own."

The applause startled Daniel, it sounded so genuine and enthusiastic, punctuated by whistles and foot stamping. The TV cameraman went down on one knee before him and switched on his floodlight. This is too much, Daniel thought, getting to his feet.

Olon, shaking Daniel's hand and reaching for one of the bronzed gyroscopes at the same time, knocked over the first Helios, which knocked over the second, which fell with a thud to the dais, the wooden base splitting off, the bronze openwork sphere rolling off the dais and onto the floor. An eager undergrad scrambled from his front-row seat and retrieved both parts of the award. He handed them to Olon, who, flushed and grinning, passed them on to Daniel.

The applause mounted, the whistlers went wild. The television camera, panning upward, caught it all. The girl with brick-red lips flashed Daniel the peace sign—or was it for victory?—laughing hard.

Daniel clutched the two parts of the Helios to his chest, feeling proud and fraudulent. Then he thought, what the hell, and held the broken pieces above his head so his arms made a giant V. The crowd roared its approval, and Daniel, laughing, sat down.

The rest of the ceremony was a shambles. Daniel tried to listen to Olon's flustered tribute to Meredith McCrory but tuned out when it became clear Olon hadn't read the book he was praising.

As the applause for Meredith McCrory's award—which remained intact—died away, Peter Olon began mumbling through the school of architecture's calendar of coming events. Students bolted for the exits. The girl with brick-red lips came up to Daniel, followed by her cameraman. "Mr. Kenning, could we have just a few moments of your time?"

Daniel said, "Of course," hoping he sounded like someone who was accustomed to giving television interviews.

"If we could go someplace quieter . . ." the girl said, holding out her hand. "My name's Lindy Massey."

"The common room's right through there," Daniel said, taking her hand. "We could probably find a quiet corner."

"The quieter the better." Lindy squeezed his hand and then let it drop. He looked at her more closely. Not a girl after all. Late twenties at least, although the way she tossed her white-blond hair suggested a teenager.

He led her and the cameraman into the common room. A

handful of professors and what looked like graduate students had already gathered at a round table spread with canapés. At a smaller table a long-haired student in a motorcycle jacket poured wine into plastic cups.

"Maybe over by the fireplace," Lindy said. She had dragged a coffee table out of the way and pushed two red leather armchairs closer to the empty hearth before Daniel could offer to help.

"What do you think, Claude?" she said to the cameraman.

"You going to hold the mike?" Claude said.

Lindy took Daniel by the shoulders and pushed him down into one of the armchairs. "I think we'd better wire you. If I have my way, this is going to be a long item, so I need good quality."

"I'm game." Daniel felt relaxed, loose limbed, a bit light-headed. He thought it would be nice to be applauded every day. He liked Lindy's take-charge attitude. He also liked the pale down on her bare forearms.

The cameraman handed Lindy an alligator clip with a tiny microphone attached to it.

Lindy leaned in close, taking hold of the lapel of Daniel's jacket. To steady the clip she slipped her hand inside his jacket and held it against his chest. "Your heart is beating like mad," she said, looking into Daniel's eyes. "You've got a glow on too."

Daniel looked down reflexively before realizing he had misunderstood. "What do you mean?"

The mike in place, she withdrew her hand from inside his jacket, her fingertips grazing his nipple through his shirt. "You're all flushed. Like you've had too much to drink."

"I am feeling warm," Daniel said, sinking down into the soft red leather.

Lindy sat down opposite him. The cameraman lumbered over and pinned another lapel mike to the collar of her blouse. "We're supposed to be at the antique fair at four," the cameraman said.

"We'll get there when we get there," Lindy said. "It's not like the antiques are going anywhere." Daniel thought that when she frowned she looked like a sulky little girl. Lindy noticed he was studying her. The frown became a wide smile. "For a long piece," she said, "I like to do at least one cassette."

"How long is long?" Daniel said.

She looked into his eyes again. "You tell me." She giggled and ran her hands through her hair. "About three minutes."

Daniel sat up and crossed his legs.

Lindy lightly touched his knee. "Here's how it will go. I ask the questions, and when you answer you can look either at me or the camera, whichever you feel more comfortable with, okay? We'll do cutaways after."

"Cutaways?"

"Me nodding and looking enthralled while you talk, tight shots of your hands, that kind of thing." She put her hand over his, clasped on his knee.

The door to the auditorium opened and Leslie walked in, bulging briefcase in one hand, trench coat thrown over her shoulder. Daniel smiled and waved. She nodded, smiling, and headed for the leather-jacketed bartender.

"Who's that?" Lindy said.

"My wife."

"Maybe we should get started. *Ça roule, Claude?*"

Claude nodded and switched on the camera's floodlight.

Lindy's face seemed to change—the girlishness went, replaced by a smooth professional mask. "Would you say that what you've done with the Schlegel mansion is postmodern?"

Daniel smiled. "The new McDonald's is postmodern. What we've tried to do with the Schlegel mansion is something quite different."

The mask slipped for an instant, and Daniel glimpsed the angry girl behind it. Too late he realized that she had meant to impress him with her architectural knowledge.

When the cameraman finally switched off his floodlight, Lindy unclipped her mike and got up. "Give me the cassette," she said to Claude and walked out of the room.

Claude bent over Daniel and removed the lapel mike. "She's running in high gear today, eh?" he said. Daniel laughed.

Leslie crossed the room, carrying two brimming cups of white wine. "I'm so sorry I didn't get to see the ceremony." She kissed his lips. "The judge acted like he'd never even heard of the Youth Protection Act, let alone read it."

"It was actually pretty much of a disaster," Daniel said, slipping an arm around her waist. "You know McGill." He told her about the slides and the dropped award.

"Well, you look pretty terrific anyway."

"I feel pretty terrific."

"About time you got a little recognition. And on television too. Did they film the ceremony or just the celebrity interview? Porter and Alex will want to see it."

"I think they got it all."

Leslie kissed his cheek. "I'm so proud of you." She glanced at the door. "Who's she?"

"That's Lindy Massey."

"Oh, yes. I've seen her on 'Newswatch.' "

"Strange girl."

"You looked as though you were getting along quite nicely. She does have a kind of lean and hungry look about her." Leslie put her briefcase down and threw her trench coat over the back of a chair.

"She's not nearly as young as she looks, you know."

"Glad to hear it. Daddy's little girl. I know the type."

"I'm not old enough to be her daddy."

"I'm sure she'd adapt." Leslie put her empty cup on the chair arm. "I could use a real drink. Do you think they need you for any further adulation here?"

Daniel glanced over at the drinks table, where Peter Olon was demonstrating his telescoping pointer to several interested colleagues. He wanted to say goodbye to Meredith McCrory, but she was nowhere in sight. "You want to go out for a drink, or home?"

"Porter and Alex are sleeping over at Dimitri's."

"Home it is then." He held up her trench coat. She turned, tilting her head to one side. As he draped the coat over her shoulders, he smoothed aside her long hair and let his hand linger on the back of her neck. "If you're nice, I'll let you interview me," he said, picking up Leslie's briefcase.

"Only if you promise to wear a motorcycle jacket."

• • •

He was sitting in the window seat, reading the Sunday paper when the phone rang.

The voice at the other end of the line said, "Gillian's dead. Someone crashed into her car last night. At Roslyn and Sherbrooke. She wasn't actually hurt. I mean there were no apparent injuries. She had a massive stroke either on or shortly after impact. They disconnected the support machines early this morning. I thought you would want to know."

Daniel returned to the window seat. He picked up the arts section and held it in front of his eyes. He tried to think of what he ought to be feeling.

The phone rang again.

The voice at the other end of the line said, "Have you heard about Gillian?"

"Yes," Daniel said, "but I don't think I've taken it in yet."

Later that afternoon Daniel sat at his drafting table, working on preliminary sketches for a house he was due to present to clients in a few days' time. His thick black drawing pen moved across the oversized sheet of paper. Roughing in the ornamental trees and borders meant to suggest future landscaping, he abruptly remembered that he had last seen Gillian Bordeleau only the week before. He was walking through Westmount Park, not paying much attention to the elaborate plantings of spring flowers or the yellow ducks riding the dark green water of the ornamental pool, when a voice called out his name. He looked up, and there was Gillian only a few feet away but separated from him by a row of blossoming cherry trees.

"Aren't these divine?" she said, ducking under the branches sagging so low with blossom that as her shoulders brushed them hundreds of petals drifted to the grass like pink confectionery snow. "I always forget how beautiful they are from one spring to the next."

They stood and talked a few minutes, Daniel on the sidewalk, Gillian on the green verge that sloped up toward the cherry trees. Thick blossoms clustered behind her, and crescents of blue sky.

Daniel wondered if his ultimate encounter with Gillian had been in, say, Steinberg's meat section, would his memory have turned steak and rump roast into an image as consoling. He considered too whether this image of Gillian weren't overlaid by another, more distant one—of a Japanese film he had seen so many years before that he had forgotten the title, a film about an aging businessman. Stricken with stomach cancer, the man goes around the world on a kind of farewell tour. In nearly every city he visits he encounters the same beautiful and mysterious Japanese woman. Daniel thought there had been a scene in which this ebony-haired woman appeared to the businessman against a backdrop of cherry blossoms. Or perhaps it had been autumn leaves hung with mist. In any case, the beautiful woman turned out to be Death.

Gillian was middle-aged, closing on fifty, neither particularly beautiful nor stylish. Her clothes ran to nondescript trousers and cardigan sweaters with a hand-knit sag to them. Her face was pleasant but oddly clownlike: small black eyes surmounted by thick, high-arching black eyebrows; a sharp, upturned nose; a wide, often smiling—for Gillian was American—mouth; dark down on her upper lip like the slip of a grease pencil. She was short, with a low center of gravity, inclining to dumpiness, although that became less pronounced each spring as she made the transition from dark wool to pastel cotton trousers. A brisk walker and drawling talker, a giggler too, especially when she drank, and Daniel had the impression Gillian drank a fair amount. But wasn't there also—and here Daniel hesitated—wasn't there something faintly Japanese about Gillian? Her small size, the narrow obsidian eyes, the thick black coiffure that never quite seemed to fit her head, so that at times Gillian seemed weighed down by her own black hair.

At dinner—Alex and Porter were off somewhere—Daniel tried to explain to Leslie what he felt on hearing of Gillian's death, except he didn't get very far, perhaps because he wasn't sure he felt much of anything at all.

"She looked so . . . alive. There in the park, I mean."

"That's generally the way you do look until you die," Leslie said. "But I know what you mean. The body alive, the body dead—the same thing and yet completely different."

Daniel wasn't sure that was precisely what bothered him.

"Did you consider Gillian a close friend?" Leslie asked him later, bringing the coffee into the living room.

"No." Daniel studied her as she bent to pour the coffee, the light from the standard lamp bringing out the gray in her long hair, emphasizing too the pouches of fatigue beneath her eyes.

A flock of kids passed down the street, Alex and Porter towering among them. Although it was a warm evening, all of them —boys and girls alike—wore hooded army parkas emblazoned with badges, appliqués, felt-pen designs.

"Mods' night out," Leslie said, watching them pass.

Daniel followed their progress too, until they disappeared into the lane. Even then he could hear Alex's booming laugh, the high giggling of the girls carried on the evening breeze. He felt such a pang of desire, of envy and loneliness. He wanted to wander out into the night with them. A song ran through his head.

"That's an old one," Leslie said. She sang, " 'I'll be seeing you, in all the old familiar places . . .' "

Daniel hadn't realized he was humming. He glanced at his watch: almost time to take the dog out. Drinks at seven, dinner at eight, coffee in the living room after, walk the dog at nine-thirty, the news at ten and so to bed. Custom, ceremony, routine.

Leslie absently hummed a few more bars. His mind supplied the words: "In a small café, the park across the way, the children's carousel . . ."

"I love you even when you're off-key," he said, stroking Leslie's shoulder. She stopped humming.

Later, walking Beaver in Murray Hill Park as the night wind blew the new leaves silver, she noticed his silence. He had counted on her noticing. He always counted on it. She always noticed.

"Are you very upset?" She smoothed down Beaver's coat.

"I don't know. It doesn't make sense. It's not as though we were that close." Daniel took the fluorescent orange ball from his jacket pocket and flung it skyward so hard that for a moment he thought he had done his shoulder serious damage. Beaver tore across the playing field, paws thrumming against the close-cropped earth.

"Pain doesn't have to be logical." Leslie looked out over the reflecting pool at the city skyline, gray and silver against low-hanging indigo clouds.

"Who said anything about pain? I think it's more bewilderment. Trying to make sense of it. I've been thinking about it a lot, and the thing about Gillian . . ." Daniel paused, wondering what the thing about Gillian could be even as the words came out of his mouth. "The thing about Gillian is that she was so very involved in life."

"Oh?" Leslie swung her gaze from the skyline to Daniel.

"She had this vitality. Political action, that sort of thing—a long history of it. I remember her telling me once that she dropped out of college for a year and went down South to volunteer when blacks organized that big bus boycott in Alabama—was it Birmingham?—back in the fifties. She was always very keen on those touchy-feely things too. Gestalt, I think it was. I know she did some counseling."

"Yes?" Leslie smiled.

"I don't imagine she did any real harm."

"The question is," Leslie said, "do you think she did any good?"

"How can you tell with something like that? She was so intense. I think that must count for something in a therapeutic context. Even if you knew her only a little it was clear that Gillian was a wonderfully empathetic person."

"Daniel, I don't mean to criticize Gillian. It's just that I know so little about her. Obviously she means . . . she meant a lot to you. But I think that fact surprises you as much as it does me."

"She doesn't mean that much to me," Daniel said, trying to get Beaver to hand over the ball. "I simply find it all confusing. One minute she's alive and walking in the park, the next minute she's not. Maybe it's just mortality that gets me."

"Give me the ball, Beaver," Leslie said, and the panting dog trotted over, tail wagging, and plopped the ball at her feet. "I don't know what to say. I wish I could be of more help."

"I don't think I'm asking for help," Daniel said, his voice cracking. "It's something I can work out on my own." He wandered away from her, massaging his sore shoulder.

Leslie scooped up the orange ball and sent it spinning high into the air. Beaver hurtled across the playing field, grinning furiously through the dark.

The rat comes at night, into his bed. Daniel's asleep, dreaming. He wakes to the scrabbling of claws between his legs. No, he doesn't awaken at once. First he incorporates the feeling of the claws into his dream. Someone is scraping his inner thighs, combing the fine hair with a yellow ivory back scratcher, the kind with a little ivory hand at one end.

But the rat won't be reduced to harmlessness. It begins to bite at Daniel with sharp teeth. Little nips at first. Then it sinks its teeth into the soft white flesh, scooping out small chunks of skin, fat, muscle. Daniel's dream can't convert this new sensation into anything but pain and flowing blood. He throws off the covers. The rat sits up between Daniel's legs. Daniel is surprised by how large it is. He can see the muscles shifting in the rat's sleek gray flanks. The rat looks at Daniel and grins, bloody teeth dripping. Flailing with his legs Daniel knocks it to the floor.

Daniel is going downstairs to tell his mother about this rat. He crosses the parquet to the stairs, the rat nipping at his heels and ankles. Blood spatters the parquet. Daniel scrambles down the steep stairs, the rat keeping pace, leaping higher and higher into the air, taking chunks out of Daniel's calves and thighs. Blood runs down between his toes, smearing the stair runner.

By the time Daniel reaches the second flight of stairs the rat has grown smaller. Instead of crouching on its hind legs, the rat is down on all fours, naked tail darting out straight behind. Smaller now than Daniel's hand, the rat could be an escapee from a laboratory maze. Even its fur has lightened. It's almost white. As Daniel descends the second flight, the rat still follows, but hesi-

tantly, fading perceptibly step by step until it is finally a tiny ghost
rat.

"Mother." Daniel bursts into the kitchen. She's bent over the
sink, slicing hard-boiled eggs with a serrated knife. "Mother."

"What is it?" She doesn't turn her head.

"There's a rat in my bed."

She turns around. Her watery gray eyes are full of reproach.
"Oh, Daniel, I can't believe that's true."

Daniel could scream. "It is true. It is. Look at the blood running down my legs." They both look down. His bare legs are
white and spotless.

Daniel runs out of the kitchen, heading for his father's den. His
father's playing the piano, "I'll Be Seeing You," upbeat, slightly
jazzy. He nods to Daniel over the top of his sheet music. "Hello,
Son." His head's too big, too heavy for the rest of him, nodding
in time to the music.

Daniel goes to the piano and slams the lid down on his father's
hands. The lid severs his father's fingers at the first joint and yet
there's no blood, just four disc-shaped wounds the slick kidney
color of medical textbook illustrations. Daniel's father raises his
fingerless hands and holds them in front of his face.

"What seems to be the problem, Son?"

Daniel tries to compose himself. "There's a rat in my bed. I
woke up, it was between my legs, clawing and biting. I was
bleeding all over the sheets."

His father smiles. Daniel notices he has retained his thumbs.
They wiggle like porpoises. "A bad dream, Daniel," his father
says.

"It wasn't a dream. The rat was there."

His father slowly raises the keyboard lid again. "Then where's
the rat now?" His eight amputated fingers lie aligned on the white
keys, pink and squirming. In place of a nail each finger has a pair
of eyes, black and shiny as jet.

"It was there, in my bed," Daniel says. "It followed me downstairs, except it got smaller and smaller until finally it wasn't there
at all."

"Like your rat wounds?" Daniel's father pounds the keys with fingerless fists. The pink fingers fly up in the air, darkening as they rise. "How many times have I warned you about telling lies?"

The fingers are gray and furry now, growing longer, plumper in midair. They hit the ground running, teeth jutting out beneath twitching noses. Their tiny, sharp claws scrape at Daniel's naked toes.

"Stop," Daniel's father says. The rats disappear. His fingers caress the keys. He sings, " 'I'll be seeing you, in all the old familiar places . . .' "

Another line or two and he stops, although his fingers continue to play over the keys. He looks up at Daniel and smiles. "You've got to get over this, Son. You can't go around telling people your dreams. They'll think you're crazy."

Daniel hurried along Sherbrooke, sure he must look a ridiculous figure to the evening strollers he rushed past, the jacket of his pale linen suit ballooning to the wind. He suspected he was a caricature: Young Man in a Hurry. Except, the voice inside his head chided, you're no longer a young man. Youthful, perhaps, though after a day like today no longer even that. You will be thirty-six soon. You are growing old. You can fool some of the people some of the time, at a distance or in a good light; you can dress, exercise, eat carefully to hide or diminish unsightly bulges. But you are growing old. You can fool others, but you can't fool Time.

Or Death.

Daniel tried to banish these thoughts. He knew why he was entertaining them: Gillian's death. He hoped that, in a week or two, he would be able to put it behind him. The thought of Gillian, the image of her unsummoned in his mind, would cease to jar. Someday soon, he was certain, even these meddlesome echoes of his own mortality would fade.

By the time he reached the church the back of his shirt was damp with sweat. Such a humid, blustery day. The sanctuary was sure to be close. Small groups of people stood talking quietly on the wide front steps, the women in pale dresses or summer suits, the men in navy, black or dark gray suits or jackets. Daniel didn't see anyone he knew.

He mounted the steps and opened one of the heavy wooden doors. Four stocky men in dark suits huddled together in the dimly lit entry hall. Ushers. They had been murmuring together but broke off and turned in unison to survey Daniel's approach. All four held small stacks of pale yellow programs. Daniel extended his hand, expecting one of the men to offer him one. None did. They stood, frozen, baleful, staring. Daniel felt a rivulet of sweat course down his spine. He wanted to move on into the sanctuary, but the four bulky men blocked his way.

At last he said, "Excuse me." The four, as though waking from the same dull dream, broke apart, one thrusting a program into Daniel's damp palm.

The darkness of the entry hall had left him unprepared for the sanctuary's light. He had expected that for an evening service the room would be darkened, like a theater. Instead the wide, high-ceilinged sanctuary glowed, amber light from the half-dozen brass chandeliers pouring down over glossy wainscotting and pews. From the street First Unitarian had never made much of an impression on Daniel—gray stone with Gothic tracery, but a subdued, domesticated English Gothic, the simplicity of the building's façade overshadowed by the Romanesque clump of the Erskine and American United Church to the east and the massive yellowstone apartment building to the west.

Slipping into the last pew at the back of the sanctuary, Daniel wondered why he had never thought to come inside before. Such a nearly perfect room of its kind—plain style and yet elegant, an elegance that came more from graceful proportion than anything else. Even the big rectangles of stained glass on either side of the room were unostentatious, lozenges of rich, dark color—gold, ruby, amethyst, emerald—depicting not improbable patriarchs in implausible postures but, rather, the four seasons, a luminous window for each.

Gillian certainly had a lot of friends. He counted the rows down to the front of the church—there was no altar to speak of, just three ornately carved high-backed chairs set up on a dais

along with a matching lectern—and performed some hasty calcu-
lations. He concluded there must be close to five hundred people
crowding the long pews.

A sharp clatter from directly above his head, and suddenly the
whole room vibrated to the deep tremolo of a pipe organ. It
sounded like Bach, something meant to be soft and pensive with
occasional rumblings of sorrow, not bombast. Whoever was at
the keyboard, though, ripped through the piece as if it were a
riotous fanfare announcing the arrival of the Four Horsemen and
retinue. Daniel clenched his teeth: certain especially loud bass
notes made his fillings vibrate. At last the piece pounded to a
hyperventilating halt. Looking about him, Daniel saw a number
of older women with white-gloved hands pressed firmly against
their ears.

A door to the left of the dais opened, and three figures, two
men and a woman, filed in. The first, a lean, silver-haired man in
a pearl-gray bespoke suit, was Jonathan Pettigrew, head of Pettigrew, Carstairs, Jacob, the firm that Daniel worked for and
which had employed Gillian as chief landscape architect. Pettigrew's presence on the dais came as no surprise, but that the bond
between free-and-easy Gillian and this upright, cautious patrician
had been as strong as it was, seemed, to Daniel at least, inexplica-
ble. Following Pettigrew and deflecting all attention from him
came Kelley Athanatopoulos, the office's gofer, wearing what
could only be described as a cocktail dress—black chiffon with
silvery streaks, worn far enough off the shoulders to reveal a fair
amount of cleavage. The third figure was a man Daniel didn't
recognize, a dumpy, balding fellow in a shapeless moss-green
suit.

Kelley and the dumpy little man took their seats, Kelley making a great to-do of her sprawling skirt, while Pettigrew strode to
the lectern. Switching on the small green-shaded lamp affixed to
the lectern, he removed a stack of index cards from the inside
pocket of his suit jacket and placed them carefully before him,
sliding them back and forth with his index fingers until the cards
were perfectly aligned at lectern center. He kept his silver head
bowed, waiting for silence.

" 'There's a great spirit gone'!" Pettigrew delivered the line in a stage whisper. The rest was from—Daniel tried to keep a mental tally—Shakespeare *(Antony and Cleopatra* and *A Winter's Tale)*, Homer, Ovid, Catullus, both Brownings, Hardy, Yeats and Mies van der Rohe—larded with rhetorical tricks too numerous to catalogue, although "What can we say of a woman who . . ." figured prominently, as did "Ours is not to . . ." and "Let us then . . ." By the time Pettigrew had worked those assembled up to the final breathless hush that is the funereal equivalent of a standing ovation, Daniel was feeling restless.

He shifted about, trying to find a more yielding portion of the pew. At least, he told himself, Kelley will be unpredictable. But as Pettigrew subsided into his chair, Kelley did not make a move to rise. Instead the organ boomed out again. Daniel leapt in his seat. He remembered this piece from childhood—this one was definitely Bach, an Agnus Dei, yet the rate and force at which it was played suggested an entire flock of rabid, marauding sheep. The tune ended with a final blatt. Daniel's head was starting to throb.

Kelley rose and glided slowly toward the lectern. She carried a thick legal pad. She adjusted first the microphone and then the reading lamp's green glass shade, sending beseeching glances toward Pettigrew, who gave her a wintry, encouraging smile. Finally she raised her eyes to survey the crowd. Even from his distant pew, Daniel could see a war was going on within her. Lack of sleep had engraved deeply tiered semicircles beneath her large, dark eyes; her lower lip, which she bit repeatedly with small white teeth, trembled.

He had no firm sense of what she would say, but he knew it would be terrible and naked. Kelley wasn't just vulnerable. She was proud of her vulnerability, she paraded it—on the job, in the street, at parties. The last time he had seen her she had trapped him into watching a reel of short films she had made, projected onto the bare wall of the office's tiny AV room. Knowing his reputation as a film buff, she wanted his honest opinion. All the films—there were five or six, each only a few minutes long—starred Kelley. Her one directorial technique was to fix the camera to a tripod and perform before it. Instead of changing the camera's position, she moved toward or away from it to create close-ups or long shots. One of the super-8 films consisted entirely of her staring into the camera without blinking; in another, she clawed flaking paint off a wall while the tape-recorded sound track played Poulenc.

With a final thump of the microphone, Kelley began, her voice quavering with emotion. "Gillian was my friend, my teacher, my lover. She was all things to me, my Universal Donor. When I needed help or comfort, she was there. When I was down in the depths of despair, Gillian lifted me up. When I was flying sky-high, she shared my joy. Gillian wasn't like Some People"— Kelley looked about the sanctuary accusingly—"who are alarmed by strong emotion. No, Gillian reveled in it. She encouraged all those around her to express themselves in whatever way they could. She encouraged me in my own pursuit of the Muse. And that is why, instead of saying anything more about Gillian, I would like to read you a poem I wrote about her. Last night."

Kelley tossed her shiny hair and rustled back the first page of the thick yellow pad. Her neck elongated, the glowing oval of her face rose high above the lectern, her normally thin voice took on timbre and volume:

> O, *when I heard, Gillian,*
> *That you were dead, Gillian,*
> *The thoughts I had, a million,*
> *Went racing through my head.*
> *My heart bled, Gillian,*
> *In heavy drops vermillion . . .*

And so it unfurled, line after line, stanza upon stanza, canto following canto, yellow legal-pad pages crackling back one by one, the Gillian epic restricted in breadth and scope only by the number, admittedly limited, of words rhyming with "Gillian." Daniel sank lower and lower into his seat.

Toward the end, Kelley's pace quickened. Her breathing grew shallow, her face more pale as the poem's cadences became

richer, fuller. Her delivery grew, if possible, more insistent, a
demon wail of grief mixed with rage, until finally all—words,
voice, pain—came crashing down onto those assembled, like the
final great destroying wave on a much-battered shore:

> And now you are gone, Gillian,
> You are gone and I am left,
> A sad and tortured soul bereft,
> This heart grown cold, reptilian,
> My Gillian.

Kelley hung her head, glossy dark hair falling forward to conceal
her face. A stunned silence followed. Then the organist on high
cantered through the mud of a Buxtehude anthem.

By the time the rumpled little bald man attained the lectern, it
was clear to Daniel that the congregation was sated. Programs
employed as fans rustled noisily. Bursts of coughing erupted from
various parts of the room. People shifted about on the hard
wooden pews.

The rumpled bald man had little to say. It turned out he
worked in some capacity at the Westmount Park conservatory.
He offered a few tepid memories of Gillian at work on this garden
or that courtyard, a few lines of prose-poetry that sounded suspi-
ciously like Kahlil Gibran.

Daniel uncrossed his legs and flexed his shoulders, preparing to
stand. It would be good to leave this increasingly stuffy room,
with its smell of Hawes Lemon Oil, eau de cologne and genteel
perspiration, good to be out on the street with the rushing, blaring traffic, exhaust fumes mixing with the sweet incompatible
smells of night and summer and the mountain. In the far distance
he thought he heard a roll of thunder. Probably a jet, but the
weather lady on the evening news had mentioned precipitation.
Daniel thought he could use a little rain.

He was half out of his seat when the music struck. Not the
rampageous organ, but the lowest ripplings of a harp. Stunned by
the sudden sweet sound, he looked about, craning his neck to see.
How had he missed them? Discreetly to one side of the dais, two

women sat on folding chairs. One, a frail white-haired woman in a lilac-print dress, held a large gilt harp between her knees. The other, wraith-thin and sallow beneath a feathery cap of orange hair, lifted her violin and began to play.

What was that music? He was sure he knew it. But from where? He felt suddenly warm, as if the music were raising the temperature of the room. But it was a different kind of warmth, Daniel realized, an interior warmth rising up inside him as if he were a vessel slowly filling with liquid. It was not an entirely unpleasant sensation and yet so unusual that Daniel felt frightened. This clogging of his throat was especially worrisome, not to mention the constriction of his chest. Could these be the symptoms of that special heart attack that without warning strikes down only those in early middle age, the kind one reads about in the leisure section of the morning newspaper? As if in answer, there it was: the uncontrollable heaving of his chest, followed closely by a surge of pain jolting across his rib cage and on up the column of his neck, ending in a terrible pulsing behind his eyes. He twisted about helplessly in his pew. His throat was so tight he knew he couldn't cry out, even if he were capable of overcoming his aversion to making a scene. To have it end like this, he thought, eyes clouding—the worst sort of death, public and ignoble, with people standing about wringing their hands and saying, "Oh dear, someone really should call 911." His head throbbed, his eyes prickled, burned, stung . . .

Oh, hell, Daniel thought. Not here. He rested his head on the fingertips of one hand and felt the warm water slide over his palm and on down his wrist, wetting the sleeve of his linen jacket. He felt so ashamed. But there was nothing he could do. He couldn't stop the flow, even if he wanted to. Out of nowhere came the line—he thought it might be from the Bible: ". . . and my tears dissolved my couch."

The violin began a melancholy crescendo, and the organ came thundering in from above, sweeping simplicity aside. Daniel felt doubly ashamed. He did know that music: it was Massenet's "Méditation de Thaïs," used to pad the sound track of a hundred movie melodramas from the thirties and forties. He was not just falling apart, he was falling apart in public, to the tune of a piece of nineteenth-century French kitsch. Even that knowledge had no power to stanch his tears. The organ plunged onward, harp purling, violin soaring ever higher, sliding, oozing, double-bowing, coating the high, amber-lit sanctuary with the sweetest, sickliest lyrical honey. Daniel's shoulders shuddered, his nose ran freely. It was all out of his control. He was out of control. He realized that he felt, in the midst of spasms, mucus and tears, curiously at peace.

"White or red?"

It took Daniel a moment to understand that the young woman carrying the oval silver tray was addressing him.

"Red, please."

He took his glass and wandered about the long, clamorous room. The din and brightness of the stucco-walled hall made him long to leave, but he felt that, after what he could only think of as his "exhibition" at the memorial service, he must show that he could be relied upon to do the proper thing by offering his condolences to Gillian's husband, Jean-Claude. He could see him across the room, near the main entrance, surrounded by mourners politely pressing forward to shake his hand or kiss his cheeks.

Daniel made for the opposite end of the hall. He'd need repose and fortification before joining that crush. He sat down on the wide sill of one of the low casement windows. The half-open, dark-framed window gave onto a small unlit courtyard. Daniel could hear trickling water but could make out no fountain in the gloom. The heavy smell of lilacs drifted up to him.

He turned his attention back to the hall itself, which was as pleasant and calming in its simple, unadorned way as the sanctuary downstairs—beeswax glow of wide-planked pine floors, amber-washed walls, brass chandeliers suspended from heavy dark beams. Ensconced in the window embrasure, he was feeling better. Protected. In control, more or less. He casually ran a hand down over his cheek in what he hoped looked like an absent-minded gesture. No moisture. Good. He was almost certain that, apart from those seated in his pew, few others in the congregation had been aware of his unseemly outburst. At the end of the service he had remained in his seat, head bowed in apparent deep meditation, until the sanctuary emptied.

He signaled to the woman with the silver tray and exchanged his empty glass for a full one. It was surprisingly good wine, definitely not *plonk*. At his own memorial service, he wondered, what would they serve? The stuff that came over from France in the holds of converted oil tankers or a nice Mâcon-Lugny? He smiled to himself. Leslie was a pragmatic sort, unlikely to break the bank to slake the thirst of a few hundred friends. But would there be hundreds at his service? Would people come out in force, would orators pour out their hearts, remembering Daniel's warmth and tender deeds? The idea that people might not come, that they might find nothing warm and tender to remember, made him panicky. He thought perhaps he should slip out of the hall without paying his respects—his eyes were starting to burn again.

"Hello, stranger."

Sissy Cournoyer lightly touched his elbow. Daniel jumped, nearly spilling his wine.

He got up from the windowsill. They touched cheeks. Daniel could see the tracks that Sissy's now-dried tears had traced through her *maquillage*.

"Where's Leslie?"

"She didn't feel like coming. She barely knew Gillian."

"That was Lucien's excuse as well. Mine too, but I came anyway. I always feel so much better after a good memorial service. They don't get much better than this, do they? That violin. They might rein in the organ a bit, don't you think? But you know"—she laid one gray-gloved hand on Daniel's arm, her eyes suddenly aswim with tears—"I really don't feel all that much better."

Daniel glanced out the window. "You find it's hitting you rather hard?"

"That's what's so strange, Daniel. Gillian and I had little more than a nodding acquaintance. She did do our garden some years ago, so there was quite a lot of contact then, some of it rather sticky—she could be so pigheaded, and it was *our* garden, after all—and I would see her on Greene Avenue or at the symphony from time to time and we would usually stop to chat, but we weren't close. Never close." Sissy paused, as if not sure how or even whether to go on. She brushed back a stiff tendril of ash-blond hair. "What's truly odd is that this turns out to be the exact experience of practically everyone I've talked to tonight, and you know that sooner or later I do talk to everyone, even forbidding old you, hiding in your dark corner."

"I wasn't hiding. I just wanted to get away from the fray."

"The service got to you too?"

"Sorry?"

"Oh, don't be so coy, Daniel. It's nothing to be ashamed of. With the possible exception of her husband and, I suppose, Jonathan Pettigrew, almost no one here knew Gillian more than casually, but haven't you noticed, nearly everyone looks shaken. Unmoored. It was so sudden."

Daniel looked about the bustling hall. Now that people had had sufficient time, like Daniel, to finish off a few glasses of wine, they were loosening up, some of them talking too loudly, some braying with laughter, others weaving noticeably as they navigated the hall. But beneath the brightening atmosphere, people looked ashen and confused. The overhead light, soft though it was, seemed to turn their skin transparent. For a brief, sharp moment, Daniel surveyed a roomful of glittering, grinning skulls.

"But why Pettigrew?" he remembered to ask. "He was such an unlikely friend for Gillian to have. Do you think it was their shared interest in gardens?"

"Honestly, Daniel," Sissy rolled her eyes. "And you must have seen them every day of the week. I thought it was common knowledge. Jonathan and Gillian have been an item for, oh, years. Were an item," she corrected herself, nodding in Pettigrew's direction. He stood at almost the exact center of the room, talking quietly to a large-boned older woman in a pale blue dress. "Actually," Sissy said, "of all the people here tonight, he looks pretty good. That's his cousin, Henrietta Fine. The psychotherapist? I'm sure Leslie knows her. I thought Jonathan's speech was lovely."

"I found it incredibly pompous." This came out more force-fully than Daniel had intended, perhaps because he had been visited by an uncomfortably vivid image of Jonathan and Gillian in the clinch.

"It wouldn't have been Jonathan if it hadn't been pompous, Daniel. It made me cry."

"Oh?" Daniel carefully placed his empty wine glass on the windowsill and folded his arms across his chest.

"I'd be the first to admit it doesn't take much. I've been crying, off and on, ever since I heard."

"Really?"

Sissy grinned up at him. A single tear hung from the heavily mascaraed lower lashes of her right eye. "Men. Composure all the way—that's the watchword, isn't it? Although there was a fellow somewhere behind me at the service who was absolutely racked by sobs. Could you hear him? Poor man, I wanted to help him somehow. Last evening, after I'd burst into tears for about the twelfth time, Lucien said to me, 'I think you actually like dwelling on death and sadness.' That hurt me at the time but I think he may be right. I do like to stay with it, rehearsing the details until I'm fed up with them, till I've washed it all right out of my system. Even those commercials for long distance on televi-sion make me cry. All I have to see is a white-haired old actress in an apron standing at the screen door of a farmhouse and I'm crying for my mother. She died in 1972—we were never close—and as far as I remember, never put on an apron in her life.

"But there's something different about crying over Gillian and I've been trying to sort it out all day. You can't say the grief is particularly sharp because she was so young. Let's face it, past forty and you're fair game."

Daniel studied Sissy's face, wondering if she had passed forty yet. He caught her sidelong look: was she wondering the same about him?

"Maybe it was only the suddenness of it," Sissy said. "I saw her last Thursday at the florist. Did you know Muller & Aubin have opened a new shop on Victoria? So convenient. Or maybe it's just this—the sense of something left unfinished. I always liked Gil-lian, I always enjoyed bumping into her. She was so . . . so *accueillante.* Yet I never made any effort to know her better, although it was something I intended to do. I'm sure if she had lived to a hundred I'd never have gotten round to it. But still, it was nice to have the possibility open, don't you think?"

"I don't know what to think," Daniel said, hearing the thickening of his voice. He wondered if what Sissy was feeling, what he was feeling, had much to do with mourning Gillian. She had lived a full and apparently happy life. She had always seemed content, fulfilled, self-contained. Were he and Sissy mourning the incompleteness of their own lives rather than Gillian's sudden death? He didn't know how to say that to Sissy—he was afraid it might hurt her. He put his hand to his forehead and massaged his temples. "I feel like I've got a terrible headache coming on. Maybe I should pay my respects to Jean-Claude and go."

Sissy reached up with one gloved hand and touched his cheek. Her hand felt warm through the soft cloth. "You're sure you're all right, Daniel?"

"Of course I'm all right. It's just a headache. Blame it on the organist." He kissed her tear-stained cheeks. "We must have you and Lucien over."

"Let's do that. It's been ages since I've seen Leslie. The boys must be huge by now. You'll call?"

"I'll call. Or Leslie will."

Daniel got another glass of wine, downed it in one go and headed for the cluster of people that signaled Jean-Claude's position in the hall. Jean-Claude's back was to him, so Daniel could stand to one side and watch a moment, pulling himself together for the evening's final test. He cast about desperately, trying to think of appropriate words to murmur. He was near enough to hear benign and unaccented English, an exact mirror of Jean-Claude's precise, unemphatic French. "Yes, she was, wasn't she? . . . *Oui, la musique était superbe* . . . old friends of Gillian's . . . *Merci d'être venu—c'est trop gentil.*"

Daniel took a deep breath and reached out to touch Jean-Claude's shoulder—a gesture he hoped would both wordlessly convey his sympathy and briefly draw Jean-Claude away from the mourners gathered about him. But as Daniel reached out, his eyes rested on the back of Jean-Claude's suit jacket. It was gray worsted, too dark a gray and too heavy a fabric for May. What drew Daniel's attention was a small rent in the material at the seam joining the back of the jacket to the left sleeve. The tear was no more than an inch or two long, the broken gray threads of the stitching spoking out like sutures around a reopened wound. Peering closer, Daniel expected to see the white of Jean-Claude's shirt. But the rip was superficial. The black cloth of the lining was intact: Daniel looked down into darkness. He let his hand drop and bolted.

He flung open a heavy door, expecting it to lead to the main staircase. Instead he found himself at the top of a long stairway that was both steep and narrow, the slanting stairwell ceiling so low he had to incline his head to avoid scraping it on the rough stucco. The only light came from above and behind him—a bare bulb in a metal cage that threw out slender arching shadows like filaments of a giant spider's web. The wooden steps seemed to tilt beneath his feet. The railing he clung to felt too solid, too real, too thick. His hand encircled it easily enough, but the touch of the smoothly polished wood, soft as skin against his palm, made Daniel cringe. He wanted to let go, yet he knew that if he did he would tumble headlong. The ceiling seemed to be pressing down on him as though the entire staircase were a set from some German Expressionist film. He listened to the sound of his own shallow breathing. Sweat ran down his brow. With his free hand he tried to wipe the moisture away, only to discover his brow wasn't simply damp, it was bathed in sweat. The more he wiped away, the more poured in to take its place.

I must calm down, he thought. This is all psychosomatic, like my "heart attack" down in the sanctuary. He stood, head bent, one hand grasping the railing, the other on his chest, willing his breathing to return to normal.

"I've heard of being lost in thought, Kenning, but this is absurd." Daniel swung his head around to see Pettigrew behind him, filling the doorway. Pettigrew's perfectly groomed head was so close it seemed to float above Daniel, disembodied. Daniel could make out every detail: the short black hairs poking out of

Pettigrew's elongated nostrils, the gold inlays in his big, smiling mouth, the tiny scar slashing across his tufty silver eyebrow. Daniel knew he should make some response, but all he could do was stand where he was, mouth open, clinging to the bannister, bile rising fast in his throat.

"I say, Daniel, are you all right?" Pettigrew's face swam closer. Daniel could feel the man's warm, vinous breath on his cheek. "You look completely chalky, my boy. Come back inside; we'll get you something for it."

Daniel swallowed hard. "No. Fine. About to do same thing. Downstairs. Too many people. Please. Got to get out." He could feel his body swaying, the railing moist and sticky beneath his palm.

"Nonsense." Pettigrew grasped Daniel's biceps with one long-fingered hand. "Come along with me. There's sure to be some brandy around somewhere. That will just do the trick."

Daniel wrenched his arm away. "Let me go. I've got to get some air."

Pettigrew's head shrank back, like a balloon deflating. Pale now himself, he disappeared from the doorway. Letting go of the railing, Daniel clattered down the narrow steps and slammed out a fire door. He found himself in a small darkened courtyard— water was flowing somewhere, but he could see no fountain— where he was promptly, violently sick at the foot of an immense flowering lilac.

PART TWO

Shift: Retrieve

*D*aniel scooped the putty knife into the can and spread careful arcs of grainy brown glue across the backsplash. He hadn't laid tile since he was a boy, helping his father remodel the third-floor bathroom. At home. Odd how he could summon up every detail of that hot summer afternoon—the square plastic tiles in mint green, with narrow black tiles for the shoulder-high border. Plastic tiles were brittle and hard to split properly to fit corners. He could hear his father cursing in that small heat-baked room as he broke and wasted tile after tile—"Godammit, I can't get this right"—sweat streaming down through the curling black hair on his chest and belly. Ten-year-old Daniel worked along quietly in the opposite corner of the room, setting the green squares into the thick brown glue.

Now here he was, a grown-up himself, doing much the same job. The tiles were different—ceramic squares from Ecuador, with an aquamarine glaze. Leslie hadn't been sure she wanted tile that vivid for the kitchen—she wasn't sure about barn-wood cabinets stained slate gray either—but she usually yielded to Daniel on questions of taste.

Having laid almost a full yard of backsplash tile, Daniel found he was no longer sure himself. The glaze seemed far gaudier than when the tiles had first caught his eye at the wholesaler's. He had chosen to finish the tiling today, at a time when so much else about the house demanded immediate attention, because he wanted a task that was simple, repetitive, mindless, one that would allow him to shut out the world so he could go blank and numb in peace.

Half an hour's steady work and he had achieved numb. Blank was harder to do. He was willing to settle for the next best thing to blankness: a mind that drifted, alighting now in the past, now the present, the voices in his head—his father's, his own—more distinct than the single words or phrases floating in from the garden, where Leslie was having coffee with a woman from the next crescent. What was remarkable about his current free-floating state, Daniel thought, was that no matter how pleasantly each memory or thought began—the cool green tiles from childhood, the present satisfaction of at last putting the final touches on the kitchen—all quickly spiraled down into anger, self-hatred, despair. His father cursing himself, Daniel lying on the newspaper-covered countertop, pressing tile after tile into the gritty glue and wondering why he bothered—who would care if he finished, who would notice if he didn't?

Angling himself down off the counter to open another box of tiles, he noticed that the wallpaper covering the lower third of the kitchen walls, hung in a burst of midwinter energy, was already speckled with dirt, evidently from Beaver shaking off the spring mud after his walks. Daniel dampened a sponge and wiped down the worst part, the wall by the door to the deck. But what was the use? Change was inevitable, decay constant. Sooner or later everything went to rot. He could spend the rest of the day in the kitchen, wiping down walls, rooting out dog hair from under the baseboards, scouring paint flecks from the wall telephone, and by next week the room would be filthy again. Filthy. Why bother? Everything in this old house, this late-Victorian that he and Leslie had hungered after for years before it finally came on the market at a price they could more or less afford, everything was running to ruin. He would never catch up with it all. Their friends and neighbors thought what he and Leslie had done was "just lovely"—the inventive renovations outside and in, the opening up of rooms, the big windows punched into the wall of his attic workroom overlooking the St. Lawrence. But friends and neighbors only came to visit, only glanced about while there. They didn't notice patches of damp and minute fissures, loose boards and crud in dark corners, dust bunnies under every bed, dresser and armoire, the faint smell of dog piss in the clammy basement.

Daniel stood for a moment, looking at the kitchen with its subtle pin-striped wallpaper, handcrafted slate-gray cabinets, the golden oak pegged floors and trim, and thought, This is not where I thought I would be at the age of thirty-six. Exactly where he thought he would be, Daniel couldn't remember. He eased himself back onto the countertop and lay there supine, the underside of the overhanging cabinets closing down on him like a lid.

He pressed another row of tiles into place, careful to maintain an eighth-of-an-inch gap for the grout he would lay in later. Almost a month since Gillian's death, and nothing had changed. He had assumed he would be over it by now—it made no sense that he should still be obsessed with her passing, obsessed with death itself. For all his thoughts came down to that, came down to an image of his own corpse in a coffin. A couple of nights before he had awakened in a sweat, having dreamed he was lugging his cadaver about from room to room in a vast empty house, trying to figure out how to dispose of this ungainly carcass.

Escape was what he needed. A week or two of the blissful illusion of freedom. Somewhere by himself. Paris, Mar del Plata, Istanbul, Bali. Why not? He could afford it. With all the frequent-flyer points he had racked up traveling for the firm, he could go anyplace he wanted for practically nothing.

And what if he went and didn't come back? What if he stayed away? Chucked it all, with no notice, just disappeared. What if he hiked down to the autoroute, clambered over the chain-link fence, stuck out his thumb and hopped into the first car that came along? He could do that. In his mind he watched as a car drove up, a big old bottle-green Chevy, bulbous and chrome streaked— from the early fifties, he supposed. Hop in, hop in, the driver beckoned. The red-plaid plastic seat covers hot from the sun, but good hot, a hot that seeps into your bones. How roomy and enveloping, these old cars, so wide and comfortable. Just look at that felt-upholstered ceiling. Don't make them like that anymore. Where you going, Son? the driver asks, his smile wide, encouraging. Anywhere you want, Daniel smiles back, liking the warmth on his bare legs, the warmth of the stranger's smile.

The whole house shuddered. Daniel glanced at his watch. Now, there's a life, he thought: rolling out of bed at two in the afternoon. Some Sundays it was four or even five. Well, Leslie didn't mind, and they were, after all, her sons. She didn't mind either that they stayed out until dawn at clubs on Stanley or St-Denis that didn't seem to notice if their clientele had proof of age or not. If Leslie didn't mind and the owners didn't care, who was Daniel to say a fifteen-year-old and a sixteen-year-old shouldn't be trusted with so much freedom? Daniel accidentally scraped his arm against the glue-covered backsplash and silently cursed himself.

Alex stomped into the kitchen. Stomping wasn't an expression of anything particular, that was just the way Alex walked, everywhere he went. At fifteen he was already well over six-four and, thanks to hours and hours of weight training, heavily muscled, if not highly coordinated. He had on his martial arts pajamas, the ones he wore everywhere except to martial arts, which he had dropped after the first week. They were already too small, and he'd had them only since December.

Alex headed for the fridge, flinging open the door and surveying the contents before drinking from the spout of the plastic orange juice pitcher. Replacing the pitcher, he wiped his mouth on his sleeve and turned around, half gallon of milk in one hand, cantaloupe in the other.

"Hey, Daniel. I didn't see you. What are you doing?"

"I'm milking a cow. What's it look like?"

"Looks neat. They're really beautiful. It's a pretty green. Has Leslie seen what you've done? Where is Leslie?"

"Not green. Aquamarine. She's out in the garden, talking with Hilary Longman."

"Tory's mom?"

"The very same."

"Then I guess I'd better stay in here." He opened one of the cabinets above Daniel's head.

"I thought you liked Tory." Daniel used his putty knife to nudge a tile slightly to the left.

"I do, but last night she had this party . . ."

"Hungry. Hungry. Hungry." Porter goose-stepped into the room, stringy legs and arms pumping. He had on a pair of mud-spattered rugby shorts, black hightops and a camouflage-net

T-shirt cut off a good two inches above his navel. "What are you doing under there?"

"Milking a cow."

"Oh, Daniel. I bet they thought that was really funny back when you were a kid."

"Actually, it's something my father always said to me when I asked a dumb question."

"Where's the old woman?"

Daniel didn't like it when Porter called her that, but Leslie didn't seem to mind.

Alex answered for him. "Out in the garden. With Mrs. Longman."

"Oh shit." Porter slammed the cabinet door so hard that Daniel's teeth rattled.

"Can you fucking believe it?" Alex hit the tabletop with his fist, his bowl and cutlery jumping, his face going red right up to the roots of his *Hitlerjugend* brush cut.

The boys whooped in unison and slapped hands.

Daniel sensed they were waiting for him to ask what was so awful-funny about Mrs. Longman being out in the garden with Leslie, but he wasn't going to give them that satisfaction. He fitted in another tile.

"You mind if I get some music?" Alex switched on the radio. At first Daniel couldn't place the song that was playing. Mellow, even sad. Thank God Leslie kept the kitchen radio tuned to a nostalgia station. Oh yes, "Try a Little Tenderness," by what's-his-name—died in a plane crash. Or was it drugs?

"You think Mrs. Longman's here to talk to us?" Alex said to Porter—he was trying to sound unconcerned, but Daniel could hear an edge of anxiety in his voice.

"Nah." Porter wedged six slices of bread into the toaster oven. "Besides, it wasn't us."

It never is, Daniel thought.

"You hear what happened, Daniel?" Alex couldn't hold back.

"What?" Daniel's neck was beginning to stiffen from lying on the hard counter so long.

"At Tory's party last night some Skins tore the porch off the front of their house."

"The whole porch?"

"Not the whole porch. Most of it's stone. But the railing and all that stuff."

"Where was Mrs. Longman?"

"I don't know," Alex said, as though the thought of an adult being bodily present at a teenage party had never occurred to him. Porter removed his charred toast from the toaster oven, letting the metal door spring back with a clang.

"So anyway," Alex said, trying not to shout at the excitement of it all, "there were all these Skins and they wanted to come in the house, but Tory said they couldn't because they weren't invited, so they just grabbed onto the railing—you know, that kind of twisty metal . . ."

"Wrought iron?" Daniel said.

"Right, so they ripped it off and threw it out in the street so cars couldn't get by and everything, and Tory called Westmount Security, but by the time they got there, the Skins had completely taken off."

"It was so fucking unbelievable," Porter said. "So totally sick. Tory worked half the night trying to fix it before Mrs. Longman got back."

"Can you stand it?" Alex waved his glass of milk in the air. "She tried to put it back together with electrical tape."

Porter laughed. "Since it was black, she thought maybe the tape wouldn't show."

"And then this big wind came along and knocked everything down." Alex used his glass to show the sweep of the wind. Milk splashed onto the floor. Alex smeared it around a little with one bare foot.

"That's when we left," Porter said.

They whooped and slapped hands once more.

The door to the deck opened. Leslie and Hilary Longman came in, Hilary looking, Daniel thought, preoccupied.

"What's all this shouting?" Leslie said. "Isn't it a bit early in the day for such animal high spirits?"

Hilary looked at her watch at the same moment Daniel glanced at the wall clock. Both refrained from commenting on the fact that it was going on three.

"Goodness, Daniel," Hilary said, "you don't look very happy jammed in there like that."

"On the contrary. I've never been happier in my life. Hello, Hilary."

"He's milking a cow," Alex said.

"Really, Daniel," Hilary said, "you look like you're stretched out on your bier."

"Thanks, Hilary. Exactly the words of encouragement I needed to see me through this difficult time."

"When you're through there maybe you could come over and look at our porch."

"I heard that was quite a storm you had last night."

"What storm?" Leslie said.

"The one that blew the porch off Hilary's house," Daniel said.

"I'm sure you two know nothing about it," Hilary said, turning to Alex and Porter.

"That's right," Porter said, stretching out his long skinny legs until they nearly bisected the kitchen.

"We left early," Alex said.

Beaver, who had most likely been dozing in some cool basement corner, wandered into the kitchen, tags clinking, and promptly buried his long nose deep in the crotch of Hilary's walking shorts.

"Beaver," Alex said.

"Pervert," Porter shouted, whacking Beaver's flank.

"It's okay, Beaver," Hilary said, stroking his nose. "Best offer I've had all week."

Leslie laughed. "Come upstairs. I'm sure those books are around somewhere. Daniel, have you seen that Jeffrey Masson book I got last week?"

"What Jeffrey Masson book?"

"*The Assault on Truth,*" Leslie said.

"I haven't seen it. Who's Jeffrey Masson?"

"It's up in my room," Alex said.

"How'd it get up there?" Leslie asked.

"I was reading it," Alex said, blushing.

"Oh," Leslie said, looking closely at Alex. "Have you finished it?"

"Yeah." Alex turned away and opened the refrigerator.

Leslie and Hilary filed out of the kitchen, closely followed by Beaver. Porter grabbed Beaver by the collar and dragged him back. "You stay here, you deviant."

With a maximum of clatter, Porter rooted out the omelette skillet from under the sink. "Alex, how many eggs you want?"

"Four."

"There are only seven in the carton."

"So?"

"So I get four, you get three."

"Fuck you, man."

"No, fuck you. I'm cooking, dickhead."

"No, fuck you."

Daniel could block them out, no problem. Their breakfast conversations ran on automatic. Born barely fourteen months apart, they argued incessantly, reflexively and, for the most part, without animus.

In the right mood, Daniel enjoyed their raillery and irreverence, their high-voltage energy no matter what time of day or night, their insouciance in the face of authority, parental or otherwise. Considering their real father's behavior toward them— Frank, a chronic alcoholic, had left home when they were still toddlers—they seemed to Daniel remarkably well adjusted. Happy, even.

You could see that happiness in their long, healthy bodies, in the way they flung their limbs about, the way they gleefully farted and belched and smelled rank armpits to see if they could put off showering one more day. Daniel couldn't fault Leslie as a mother. She was indulgent, to be sure, permissive by the standards of most, and yet the boys were nearly through high school and had never been in any serious trouble. On weekends they stayed out all night but rarely seemed to come home drunk, probably—as Leslie pointed out—because they never had enough money to get pissed in a downtown bar. They had experimented with drugs too, in the casual way kids seemed to have these days, and decided they didn't much care for them.

Deep down, Daniel wondered if it was all somehow too good to be true. Something must be lurking, something must be off about them, but he had always thought that, from the very beginning had looked for the telltale flaw. The first time he had stayed over at Leslie's tiny apartment in the McGill ghetto, the boys— they must have been four and five at the time—had come tumbling into Leslie's bedroom the next morning, pink and naked, climbing into bed and under the covers, crawling all over Leslie, who was naked as well, hugging her and kissing her cheeks and crying, "Lessy, Lessy, Mama, Lessy." Leslie had carefully introduced him—she hardly could not have; he was lying at her side, tightly wrapped in an Indian print bedspread. Their response to him had been complete indifference.

Their reaction—or lack of one—had wounded him, for from the moment the previous night that he learned Leslie had children, without realizing it, he had begun fantasizing, not only about moving in with Leslie, but also about endearing himself to her sons, becoming a second father to them, playing with them, taking them to movies and museums, teaching them how to ride bikes, put together models, ski. Daniel, who until that moment had never considered having children—had, in fact, rejected that possibility while barely more than a child himself—suddenly pictured himself with a ready-made family of his own. An ideal family.

This ideal family did exist. Except now he wondered if it didn't exist apart from him, parallel to his own existence. The loving relationship between Leslie and the boys was both ideal and real. They loved her deeply, and she them. Daniel loved Leslie, she loved him. But the formula was not transitive: Daniel felt that he stood off to one side, in a space all his own. He was pretty sure that the boys didn't love him, and he had never learned how to show his love for the boys, no matter how much he longed to. They called up in him impulses he didn't know how to deal with or express.

He coated the final section of backsplash with arcs of glue, then scored the glue diagonally with the putty knife, just as his father had shown him years ago.

The problem was that even when he observed it in the very solid flesh, Daniel did not understand or even believe in strong, demonstrative love between parent and child. As a child himself, when he saw parents and their children behaving happily on television shows, he knew it was a put-up job. They were behaving like that only because the camera was on, because that's what the script said to do. They didn't really feel it. No one did. Now he felt much the same way when Alex came home from school depressed from doing less well than he'd anticipated on a math exam and Leslie would take him in her arms and hold him for minutes at a time. Even prickly Porter would sometimes lie on the end of Leslie's bed in the morning, pouring out his troubled love life while she held his big, grimy-nailed hand. Coming upon these scenes, walking into them by accident, intruding on them by design, Daniel immediately would feel two things: that what he was observing was somehow false—playacting, really—and that he longed to be a part of that pretense.

The odor of frying bacon filled the room. The smell made Daniel slightly nauseous. He hadn't eaten since breakfast. Either the radio station had changed its format midbroadcast or one of the boys had changed the station, for the kitchen now pulsed with African tribal drumming and high banshee shrieks.

Block it out, Daniel told himself, get back into your groove. Ride the despair train down to the ever-receding horizon. These days he felt better when he was really down. When he was up he felt brittle and unsure: he knew that, sooner or later, it was all going to collapse. But down—he knew where he was then.

Four more rows of tile and he would be finished. Where was he in his brooding, his silent fulminations? He hated it when he was interrupted, when the other world made him lose his place. Something about the boys. Yes, their happiness. He glanced over his shoulder. Porter stood at the stove, spatula in hand. Alex stood at his side, running orange halves through the juicer. The afternoon sun lit Alex's pale hair, Porter's brown skin. Towering there side by side, they both looked so self-contained and perfect in their youth that Daniel felt a sudden sharp pang of love. He wanted to get down from the countertop, go over to them and hold them close to him, the way Leslie held them close.

"Hey, Daniel, you want some pancakes?" Alex asked. "I think I made too many."

"No thanks." Daniel edged the last tile into place.

"What's the matter," Porter said, hunched over the chopping board. "Afraid you'll get fat?"

"Something like that." Daniel eased down off the countertop. The smell of onions made his eyes water.

"You don't have to worry about that," Porter said.

"Why not?"

"Because it's too fucking late, fat man."

Daniel sucked in his belly and rushed at Porter's back, meaning to grab him. "I'll get you for that," he said.

"Watch out, Porter," Alex said.

Porter turned around as Daniel was about to grab him. Daniel reached for Porter's hand, noticing too late that it held a long white-handled knife. Daniel's hand closed on the flashing serrated blade. Porter pulled back. Daniel felt sharp cold streak across his palm, then something moist, stinging.

Daniel screamed in pain. Beaver leapt high in the air, barking. Porter knocked the carving board to the floor, chopped onions flying everywhere.

Alex said, "Down, Beaver, down."

Porter stood leaning against the sink, pale, chin trembling.

"Daniel, are you okay?" Alex said, touching Daniel's shoulder.

"Leave me alone," Daniel said. Then he screamed again. At first he thought his voice was something else, like the smoke detector going off. Beaver growled and snapped at his ankles.

"Let me see your hand," Alex said. He held out a dirty tea towel as though he meant to bind Daniel's wound.

Daniel ran out of the kitchen and up the stairs, shrieking as he went. Leslie and Hilary stood on the second-floor landing, each holding a stack of books.

Leslie stepped forward. "What on earth . . ."

Daniel ran past her, the strange piercing sound of his screams as mortifying as it was uncontrollable.

He gained the safety of his third-floor workroom, slamming the door behind him. He sank down on the daybed. He was shaking all over. He had stopped screaming—his jaw was clamped so tightly closed his teeth ached. Suddenly he cried, great racking sobs that shuddered his back and emptied his lungs until he felt so light-headed he put his quaking head between his knees.

Clink, clink, clink on the stairs. Beaver nosed open the workroom door. The dog, big as he was, climbed into Daniel's lap and licked his chin.

Daniel could hear Leslie on the stairs. "What happened, Daniel? Are you all right?" she called.

"I don't think so," he said. He saw that he had opened his fist. A faint red line ran diagonally across his palm, more a scrape than a cut. Beaver inspected his open palm as well, then licked that too.

Not a thing about the room pleased Daniel. Not the low-slung corduroy-upholstered sofa, not the parchment-shaded lamps made from old milk cans, not the glass-and-brass coffee table and certainly not the art. That hulking Inuit sculpture—either a large woman or a small walrus in the throes of labor—and the large silver-framed poster of Hockney's ubiquitous irises made him cringe. He was certain he had seen the same soapstone carving and the identical Hockney print in the waiting rooms of his dentist, his GP and his accountant.

He rummaged through the neat stack of magazines on the coffee table. *The Atlantic, Harper's, Maclean's,* two copies of *Saturday Night* and one *Arts Canada Arts*. He picked up the *Arts Canada Arts* and leafed through it. A long article on what makes Canadian art so distinctive. Followed by an even longer piece on a Toronto painter whose works adorned the corporate boardrooms of the nation. He turned to the full-color centerspread: Mom and Dad barbecuing a large fish out on the patio, sister looking on entranced, while at the center of the picture a skinny boy in sagging swim trunks swallows a fiery sword, unnoticed by the others.

Daniel turned back a page to read the accompanying article. He thought he'd recognized the style—the painting was the work of a young American artist who had spent several years working and teaching in Nova Scotia. He flipped back to the painting. Classical triangular composition, with the boy's tousled blue-black hair at the triangle's apex. His head was tilted back to receive the flaming sword, narrow rib cage shining through his skin. Daniel didn't get it, this little miracle worker at pool's edge. What would he do for an encore—walk across the chlorinated water? If he did, would the rest of the family notice, or were they too preoccupied with the fish? The fish. Fisher of men, maybe, but more likely just a pun on the painter's name.

The door to the inner office opened a crack. Voices, both female. Backlit darting silhouettes. The sound of women laughing. When the door closed again, Daniel relaxed. He glanced at his watch. Three-ten. Already running late. Would he be allowed to run ten minutes over as well? And what about the woman who, presumably, would be leaving shortly? What should his attitude toward her be? Should he affect to be so absorbed by *Arts Canada Arts* as not to notice her passage through the waiting room— difficult for her to manage without brushing within inches of his crossed legs—or should he give up all pretense of reading, toss the magazine back on the coffee table and regard her frankly, with the suggestion of a complicit smile playing across his face?

He consulted his watch again. Three-thirteen. If the door didn't open by three-fifteen he was going to leave. At work he never kept anyone waiting more than fifteen minutes and he expected to be treated with the same respect. This tardiness, this complete disregard for his own schedule, made Daniel begin to question how things were run here. He tried to concentrate on the centerspread—the bilious semitropical colors, the boy with the fiery sword, the barbecuing fish, whose curve echoed the sword's—except the picture's power had vanished now.

The door opened wide. The magazine slipped from Daniel's fingers and landed splayed open on the gold broadloom, clearly

visible through the coffee table's glass top. A young woman
emerged. Her white-blond hair was cut in a style that was known,
when Daniel was a boy, as a burr—so short it required no groom-
ing at all. Ordinarily such a cut tended to emphasize the ears, but
this woman's were tiny, like pink butterfly shells found at the
beach. As she drew closer—Daniel uncrossed his legs and drew
in his feet—he saw that she was wearing unmatched earrings.
One was a lizard in beaten silver, the other, also silver, a miniature bunch of bananas.

The woman halted at the coffee table and stood staring down
at it. Daniel wondered if she might be mad. She gave him a
tentative smile and rummaged through the magazine pile.
Straightening up, she looked about nonplussed, then glanced
down through the coffee table's glass top. "There it is. Would you
hand me that magazine that's under the table? Henrietta said I
could borrow it."

Daniel looked down at the magazine spread open in front of
his wing tips as though noticing it for the first time. He bent down
and retrieved it, carefully closing it.

"Were you looking at it too?"

Daniel looked down as he handed the magazine up to her.
"Not really. I mean, I flipped through it."

She rifled through the slick pages, thumbing past and then
returning to the centerspread. She held the magazine open in
front of his eyes. "I don't care what anyone says, I think that's
absolutely amazing, don't you?"

Daniel looked slightly to the left of the open magazine. "It's
quite nice."

The young woman called over her shoulder, "You're sure it's
all right if I take it, Henrietta?"

A voice came from the inner office, low and mellifluous, "As
long as you bring it back."

"I will. Thanks, Henrietta." The young woman closed the
magazine, stuck it into her canvas knapsack, smiled at Daniel and
went out the door.

A figure stood in the doorway to the inner office. "You may
come in now, Daniel."

At first he registered only that Henrietta Fine was a large woman—tall, gaunt, rawboned. Hard to guess her age—a thick streak of white ran down the center of her haphazardly cut black hair. Her face, bejowled and heavily creased, struck him as mannish.

"Sit wherever you like." She waved a bony hand at the bright, oblong room. "Sorry for the delay, but some days I get behind and it seems there's nothing I can do to catch up. Do you ever have days like that?"

Daniel nodded eagerly, feeling like one of those bobbing objects on the dashboard of a poor person's car. The moment he saw her he knew he wanted to please this woman more than anyone else on earth. For he knew that if he pleased her she would, eventually, take him in her arms and hold him close, his cheek against the pendulous breasts he could guess at from the scoop neck of her seersucker sundress.

He couldn't decide whether to take the lavender striped-velvet club chair or the high-backed black leather chair with bentwood armrests. On a table between the leather chair and the club chair—closer to the leather chair—stood a small brass carriage clock and a pale blue box of tissues. Daniel concluded that the black leather chair must be Henrietta's, so he promptly sat in it, feeling sure that this stately, self-assured woman would prefer a client who asserted himself from the start.

She sat down in the club chair, reaching to retrieve a gray stenographer's pad half-concealed by the chair's velvet skirting. Daniel felt he had been subtly outfoxed. Instead of opening the pad she held it in her lap, a tortoiseshell fountain pen poised in her right hand.

"So tell me, Daniel, why have you come to see me?"

He tried to avoid her eyes, but she stared at him so intently he felt he had no choice in the matter. Her eyes, beneath slightly sagging lids, were a blue so pale as to seem almost colorless.

"I've been having some problems lately. A lot of crying. And I'm depressed a lot. In fact I don't feel like I'm very much in control these days. I guess you could say I'm not very happy." He paused, sure he saw a skeptical glint in her pale eyes. "I'm, er, unhappy."

Henrietta scratched the back of her head. "And how did you come to see me?"

"My wife said you were the best psychotherapist in town. Actually, what she said was that you are the only intelligent psychotherapist in town."

Henrietta smiled at the compliment. "And how did your wife come to hear of me?"

"Perhaps you know her? Leslie Seaforth?"

"The only other intelligent psychotherapist in town." Henrietta smiled more broadly this time, showing a protuberant crescent of large, widely spaced teeth. "To start off, Daniel, so I can get a better sense of who you are and where we should be heading, why don't you tell me a little about yourself and your family, not just you and Leslie but also your own siblings and your parents and their parents too, if you know anything about them."

For the next forty-five minutes Daniel talked, tentatively at first, then with increasing fluency, urgency. To his own surprise he spent little time on Leslie and the boys. Instead he gravitated almost immediately to his parents and their parents as well, describing, as clinically and unemotionally as possible, his hatred of his father, his distance from his mother, the recent protracted deaths of his grandparents. As he talked, Henrietta made brief notes on her pad from time to time. Daniel assumed she was writing down symptoms so that eventually she would be able to reach an accurate diagnosis. He knew he was sick, he just didn't know what the proper label for his sickness might be. He was sure Henrietta would know. She looked so competent and dignified, despite the badly cut hair and the sacklike sundress that showed one yellowed strap of her brassiere. The strongest sense he had of her was that she was a woman who didn't care what people thought of her—she was going to live her life to suit herself. Daniel admired and resented that attitude more than he could say.

The longer he talked, the worse he felt. It was as though with each member of his family that he described he was constructing, bar by thick black bar, an enormous cage about himself. The more he revealed, the more he was sure his case was hopeless—there would be no way out of this cage. Built up from generation to generation—he did not know what cumulative misery lay beyond his grandparents, what great-grandparents and great-great-grandparents had helped lay the foundations of anger and frustration—this family cage was his legacy, his identity too. He knew no other, deserved no better. Besides, wasn't the saga he was relating essentially, fatally skewed and subjective? Simply his own bleak, unforgiving view? All the other members of his family seemed, if not quite happy with their lot, at least resigned to it. Only he caused problems, only he failed to fit in. He was and always had been the misfit and troublemaker, the malcontent. Without him, he reflected, his family might have achieved a muted happiness. But he had come along, trailing his bitterness and neuroticism behind him like a surly circus cat's flea-bitten tail. Perhaps it was worse than neuroticism, that truth had to be faced: maybe he was crazy. The notion had been bruited about in his family for as long as he could remember.

Mad. He thought he might welcome that. He saw himself shut away from the world. Of course they didn't do that much anymore, did they. More likely he would end up doped to the gills, whistling while he worked. Oh well, a change is as good as a rest, or was it a rest is as good as a change? Daniel knew he surely would go mad if he couldn't shut off this voice inside him, this insistent, yammering, lunatic voice that had been haunting him since Gillian's death. Strange how this voice could go on, rising in intensity and decibels even while his speaking voice—he was going to say his real voice except he feared the yammering was his real voice—grew softer, thinner, weaker as he spun out the tale of his family's woes to this attentive woman slumped down in her striped-velvet chair.

He sensed he was winding down. There was much more to tell, but he had no stomach for it. His limbs felt heavy, his throat dry, his neck stiff from holding up a head that longed to subside into forgetful slumber. He could sleep here, he thought, even with the inner voice rampaging through his head: now she knows it all, you've told her everything, even the worst, or almost the worst. She has seen you naked, she has judged you and found you wanting. You come in here, wasting her time with your petty problems, while out in the waiting room this very minute there is undoubtedly someone with real problems, not some self-indulgent, self-pitying fraud like yourself.

Abruptly Daniel stopped speaking, midsentence, even as he wondered if that was permissible—to sit silently while taking up valuable therapeutic time. Henrietta sat very still, looking down at her pad, the tortoiseshell pen suspended a few inches above the blue-lined paper. Finally she looked up.

"That's a very sad story, Daniel."

"It is?" Daniel said, and burst into tears.

"No. Not those. These." Daniel pointed at the glass top of the display case, while the Korean woman's hand hovered over rows of sunglasses.

"These?"

"No, to the right. Sorry, your left. Right. No, I meant, that's right. Those are the ones, yes. Also"—he cleared his throat so he could finish the sentence—"a packet of tissues, please."

Daniel paid for his purchases and walked out of the pharmacy. He threw the small plastic bag into a trash can, put the package of tissues in his jacket pocket, peeled the price sticker off the sunglasses and put them on. Much better.

He felt . . . he didn't know what he felt. Different, that was clear. He had the sensation that his body had faded away and he was a pair of eyes behind blue-tinted lenses, floating down the street, taking everything in—the sky, the rich purple-and-gold pansies encircling the cabbage clock at the corner of Westmount Park. Faces drifted by, he studied them all. He thought he could see right into the passersby, see the pain lurking behind their daily masks.

He reached the corner of his street. It tilted up before him, warm wind stirring the massed crowns of the maples running up either side, late afternoon sun angling in from the west. He thought the street had never looked so lovely or unreal. A few hundred steps and he would be home. Even from the corner he could make out the blue blur of the delphiniums Leslie had planted to line the curving front walk. Daniel turned to regard the thick rush-hour traffic at his back. He could hop a cab, go back to the office, make up for the time he'd missed, catch up on—but no, not today. He had a much more pressing demand to attend to, although for the moment he couldn't think what. Then it came to him: he had to lie down.

Home was out as well—he wanted complete isolation. No interruptions, no telephone, no Leslie, no Alex and Porter. Westmount Park was just across the street but somehow too parklike, every square inch designed, shaped, pruned. Without thinking much about it he followed Sherbrooke to Greene Avenue and then headed up Greene, slowly mounting the series of stone or wooden staircases and switchback streets that led him to the tree-enclosed campus of Marianopolis and on up the stone staircase marking the Côte-des-Neiges entrance to Mont-Royal Park. He had a specific spot in mind, even if he wasn't aware of this until he came to it—an overgrown promontory overlooking the city.

He took off his jacket, folding it neatly on the ground, and lay down next to it in the long, pale grass. He could feel the contours of the cool earth beneath his body, as if he were sinking into the ground. He wasn't exactly sleepy—the lassitude creeping over him was unlike anything he had ever known. He wasn't simply slowing down, he was stopping. Dead halt, everything—mind and body. Nothing stirred within him but the sluggish beating of his heart. He thought he had never felt so comfortable, so at ease with himself and the world. Even the tears leaking from his eyes caused no alarm. He felt them running down his cheeks, his neck, imagined them seeping into the ground. His mind drifted on to put the world together, as if for the first time; piece by living piece, the cycle of beginning, ending and beginning again, warm liquid penetrating dry earth to engender new life, which in turn would burgeon, wither and die. The withering and dying bothered Daniel not at all, now that he finally was seeing the world and seeing it whole. For a moment he wanted to leap up and tell the world of his discovery. But not just now. For the moment he would just lie here on the side of the mountain, taking in the sky.

"I don't know why," Leslie said, a lump of heavily sauced eggplant between raised chopsticks, "when they call it Szechuan, they have to make it so sweet."

Daniel hadn't noticed, but then this evening he wasn't noticing much. Or rather was noticing everything but minding very little. Tonight everything about the Jade Garden was endearing—the dime store–chinoiserie decor, the scarlet-jacketed waiters with their barely comprehensible English and worse French, even the food, heavy though it was with MSG, sugar and who knows what else. It was all so poignant, somehow, so alive with promise and emotion.

"You look like you're running on high tonight," Leslie said.

Daniel laughed. "Sorry, were you saying something? I'm having trouble attending."

"I wasn't saying anything. I was sitting here watching you. All of a sudden you look so young. It's as if ten years had dropped away overnight."

Her compliment made him shy. He looked down at his plate. Tonight was going to be good, he could tell that, when they got home. "I feel . . . I wish it weren't so hard to explain. I feel better than I've felt in my entire life. Really, no exaggeration."

Leslie signaled the waiter and asked for another pot of jasmine tea. "That's pretty dramatic. Simply from unburdening yourself to Henrietta? I mean, I assume you've told me most of the things you told her, and it never had this effect."

Daniel picked up his small ceramic teacup and admired the pink-and-gold border, the shiny glaze. He wanted to put the cup to his brow, let the warmth seep in. "Talking to Henrietta isn't the same as talking to you, Leslie. You're too sympathetic, you're on my side. With Henrietta it's more like having an objective witness who synthesizes all the memories and impressions I bring her. And I like the fact that she doesn't say all that much. I thought I would find that intimidating, but it's not. Those long stretches of silence make her comments, when they come, all the more valuable. When I'd spilled out the whole sordid story of my family and she finally said how sad it was, it was as if someone had at last confirmed my existence. Someone had seen that it wasn't only me who was miserable—it was my entire miserable family."

Leslie held her rice bowl under her chin, Chinese style, using chopsticks to push the shiny grains into her mouth. Her long russet hair fell down over one eye. Daniel noticed he had the beginnings of an erection. Over Leslie's shoulder he could see a beautiful dark-haired boy dining with his attentive, attractive parents. Well-off, well dressed, they looked like an ad in some glossy magazine devoted to stylish familial bliss. The woman caught Daniel's eye. Instead of looking away, as he ordinarily would have done, he gave the woman a quick approving smile.

"But I've told you again and again how awful I always thought your father was," Leslie said. "What are you smiling at?"

"Nothing. Myself. It's not only my father. Just as it's not only me. That's what Henrietta emphasized. It's the whole system. The family unit, everybody united to deny the pain with silence. Eternal silence, generation to generation."

Leslie put down her chopsticks and slowly smoothed the table-cloth as though she were absentmindedly patting Beaver. "But deny what? What's the source of the pain?"

Daniel felt she was catching him up short. "We haven't gotten that far yet."

Leslie laughed. "At the rate you're going you'll be halfway through transference by the end of next week."

"Right." He stood up. "Back in a minute."

Was there an unwritten rule that said Chinese restaurateurs were required to provide awful bathrooms? The Jade Garden men's room was covered, floor, ceiling, walls, with peanut but-ter–colored plastic tiles emblazoned with scarlet sunbursts. Dan-iel locked himself into the single wooden cubicle so he wouldn't have to look at them. It was good to be alone for a moment, pleasant—away from Leslie's voice and the dining room hubbub—to escape back to the silence of this afternoon, to regain the sense of drifting harmoniously with the universe.

The outer door swung open, banging against the sink. In the gap below the cubicle door, Daniel glimpsed two small navy-blue lace-up shoes and a pair of spotless white socks with navy piping. The door was so ill fitting that Daniel could see it was the beautiful little boy from the next table. Daniel smiled to himself. The little boy was humming, a tune he evidently made up as he went along. He walked over to the urinals and stood there a long time. What could be taking him so long, Daniel wondered. Why doesn't he finish and leave so I can have the room to myself? Doesn't he know it's dangerous to hang about in men's rooms? Haven't his parents warned him, a boy as cute as that? Here I am, for instance, sitting in this tight, foul-smelling cubicle, attuned to every move the child makes, listening for the sound of his urine splashing against the porcelain trough, waiting for the noise of his small zipper ascending notch by notch.

At last the boy stepped down from the urinal and walked slowly over to the sink. Daniel could hear him turning on one tap, then the other. How long, he wondered, does it take to scrub thoroughly two four-year-old hands? Who did this little boy think he was, Lady Macbeth?

The boy turned the crank on the paper-towel dispenser several times, stuffing the result in the trash can. Then he cranked some more, stuffed some more.

The outer door opened and shut. Before it did, Daniel caught a glimpse of the boy's tiny, perfect shoes.

Daniel stood up, straightened his clothes and flushed, even though there was no reason to do so.

He looked up from his drawing board. The door was half open, although he clearly remembered shutting it. He sensed her presence before he saw her, waiting in the dark. She had tucked her hair up under the gray flannel cap. The gray flannel shorts ended just above her knees. The crested navy blazer broadened her shoulders, narrowed her hips.

He switched off the light that illuminated his drawing board.
Moonlight through the tall windows gave the workroom a silvery, ghostly glow.

He went to the door and opened it wide.

"What is it?" he said.

"Am I disturbing you, sir?"

"As a matter of fact you are."

"Is that why you turned out the light, sir?"

"Don't be impudent, boy." He grabbed her rep tie and pulled
her into the room.

"I've made a chart," Henrietta said, holding out her steno pad.
"I find it helps me to understand how your family works if I make
a diagram of how they relate to one another."

He couldn't make much of the diagram—her drafting skills left
a lot to be desired.

"Up here at the top are your grandparents," she said, indicating with her fountain pen. "They're just scribbles"—Daniel
thought they looked like clouds a four-year-old might scrawl—
"because I know relatively little about them and because your
experience of them is at one remove."

He was starting to make sense of it. The big block letters F and
M below the clouds stood for Father and Mother. A thin wobbly
line ran between F and M. More thin lines branched upward from
F and M to the grandparent clouds. Thin lines also extended
down to a smaller block letter E. His sister, Elspeth. A thick
purple line—Henrietta had gone over it so many times the paper
had pilled—ran from F to the small block letter D.

D is for Daniel, he thought, his identity diminished to a letter
in a child's alphabet book. He had the sensation that he was
growing smaller, his chair larger, as he sat listening to Henrietta.

"The lines between the letters," she said, "are the lines of
emotion running throughout your family. You can see that no
one's unconnected, but all the other connections pale next to the
one running between you and your father. From what you told
me last session—how much you hated him, how preoccupied he

seemed to be with you and your 'badness' when you were young—it's easy to conclude that the strongest emotional link in your family was between you and your father. That seems to have been the one"—Henrietta scratched the back of her head—"*passionate* relationship in your family. In a family grouping you describe as very WASP and cold, this is the one place where emotion flowed freely."

Daniel nodded, not sure he was following. If he had drawn a diagram, the lines would have been thick between his father and mother, between his father and Elspeth, between his mother and Elspeth. And, off to one side, D is for Daniel, alone, unlinked.

"So can we perhaps conclude," Henrietta said, "that your father loved you very deeply but that the proper expression of that love was"—she scratched the back of her head again—"difficult for him?"

She rested the pad in her lap and handed Daniel the pale blue tissue box. He dried his cheeks. His father loved him. That would take some getting used to. Loved him passionately. Right. Loved you so much he screamed at you, belittled you, beat you. What kind of love was that? Was she trying to tell him that he should be grateful for that love? Daniel had the oddest feeling in his legs and feet, as though they wanted to twitch about, maybe even violently kick out. Crossing his legs, he sat back in his chair, clamping his hands together in his lap.

Henrietta sat back too. She placed the pad on the floor at the side of her chair. "What you emphasized to me last session, Daniel, was how much you hated your father. Yet much of what you told me about your life suggests something different. Hiding from him as a child, begging to go away to boarding school when you were only nine, coming all the way to Montreal to university when there was a perfectly good architecture school in Vancouver. And then staying on here after, keeping almost a whole continent between you and him. And your younger sister, Elspeth, following a similar course—boarding school, away to England to university, then settling there after. To me that sounds more like fear than anger."

The room seemed to be dropping away, and he was falling. He

saw a small boy hiding under a bed, heard the boy's father calling up the stairs, "Come on, Son, you've got to learn to ride a bike sometime." He saw the small boy high up a tree in an orchard, the boy's father far away in a white gravel driveway, holding a wooden bat, two mitts and a white softball. He saw a small boy, so young and far away he seemed to be viewed through the wrong end of a telescope, riding in an old green Chevy on a road running alongside a river. The boy suddenly opening the door and trying to jump out of the moving car, the boy's father seizing him at the last moment and dragging him back.

"What are you thinking, Daniel—what's going through your mind?"

"I was thinking of all the times I tried to get away from him."

"What happened when you couldn't get away from him? What happened when he caught you?"

That was easy. "I got hurt."

"He beat you?"

"There was that, yes. But usually the beatings were more formal. By appointment. You knew when they were coming. The other is more difficult to explain. He had this idea that because he was my father and I was his son we should do things together, even though we could hardly bear to be in each other's company. Manly things. Sporting things."

Henrietta nodded, her face serious.

"I never wanted to—I was always such a klutz at sports. I think he must have had this image of how it should be—father and son having a wonderful time out in the open air—but then I'd some-how contrive to ruin it, dropping the ball or tripping over my own feet. Then he'd make fun of me, or scream at me. He was such a jock when he was young—hockey, soccer, football."

"He ridiculed you? Is that what you mean when you say you always got hurt?"

Daniel slowly shook his head. "There were a lot of accidents. I'd pitch and he'd bat. His favorite thing was to slam the ball right in my face. Then he'd laugh as though he was surprised at what had happened. He'd say, 'I about rammed that one right down your throat.' He also insisted on teaching me to ride a bike. He'd take me to the neighbors' driveway and he'd run alongside me, holding onto the seat. He'd get really furious because I couldn't get the hang of it, and I'd end up crashing into rose bushes or a fence."

"You think he did these things deliberately?"

Daniel sensed her skepticism. He was used to no one believing him. When he ran home to his mother, bruised and bleeding, she never believed him either. "I can't prove it, but it felt intentional. Even if he always started out nice, or at least mock-nice."

"Mock-nice?" Daniel opened his mouth and his father's voice came out. " 'Come on, Son, let's go out and knock the ball around.' There was always an ironic edge, as though he felt the falseness of what we were doing too. He did it because he felt he ought to—that's what fathers were supposed to do—and I did it because he gave me no choice. When we played together it was always as though we were performing for an invisible audience."

"Where did these accidents tend to occur?"

"Where?"

"Where was your mother when they occurred?"

"Not there. Never there. I'd go running to her afterward, until I figured out she was never going to help me."

"Where did your father take you so that she wasn't there?"

"We'd take the bike and go to a neighbor's driveway."

"What was wrong with your own driveway?"

"It was . . . I don't remember. Both drives were pretty much the same, I suppose—long and gravel and sloping."

"Where did you play softball?"

Daniel thought for a moment. "On the front lawn."

"Never the back?"

"No."

"Your mother never watched while you played?"

"No."

"When you were growing up, where in the house did she spend most of her time?"

"In the kitchen or the morning room. The library."

"Where are those rooms in relation to the front of the house?"

"They're at the back of the house. They look onto the garden and the orchards."

"Was there enough room in the garden to play baseball?"

"It was quite large. We did practically everything there. Lawn parties, badminton, croquet—it used to drive Keiji crazy. He was our yardman when I was little. Half the time he couldn't work on the garden because there was a party or something."

"Is it fair to say that when your father wanted to mistreat you he would first have to get you away from your mother?"

Daniel had never thought of it like that before.

Henrietta shifted about in her chair and softly clapped her hands together. "I'd like you to tell me about the whippings he gave you."

"What's to tell? He whipped me. That's what fathers did back then. All my friends' fathers took belts to them too."

"All their fathers?"

"I assume they did. We weren't much different from any other family, I don't imagine."

"I'd still like to know more about the specifics of the whippings. When would they happen—in the daytime, at night? Where?"

Daniel was feeling calm now, although his left knee trembled slightly. "Not during the day, at least not that I can remember. They always came at night, after he got home from the city."

"You would do something wrong while he was at work, and your mother would say, 'Wait till your father gets home—you're really going to get it'?"

"No, it never had much to do with her. I don't think she ever suggested to him that he whip me. That was always his decision, I believe. He'd send me to my room and then he'd come, but never right away. I always assumed that part of the punishment was not knowing when he'd come."

"It would be dark out? When he finally came?"

"Yes."

"It always happened in your bedroom? Never anywhere else?"

"The bedroom's a logical place for that sort of thing, don't you think?"

"Where in your bedroom would the whippings take place?"

Daniel had to laugh. Was she being deliberately thick? "On the bed. Where else?"

"He used a belt on you?"

Daniel tried to read her solemn, inquisitive face, searching for some sympathy there. "Yes."

"Did you leave your pants on?"

He had to smile at this woman's ignorance. "What would be the point of that? You wouldn't feel anything if you left your pants on."

"Underpants?"

"No."

She resettled her long body in the velvet chair, leaning forward, shoulders hunched.

"Would you say"—she paused and looked off to one side— "that there was the quality of an orgy about these punishments?"

"No, not that I'm aware of." He could feel his toes tingling painfully inside his shoes. He had to concentrate hard to keep from kicking out.

"What happened afterward, when he had finished with the belt?"

That was the part Daniel wanted to tell, he found it so confusing. "It was strange, as if a storm had passed. All his rage would be gone and he'd lie down next to me on the bed. Sometimes he'd even hold me. Those are the only times I can remember him touching me. With affection, I mean. Once or twice he cried."

"He would cry after he whipped you with a belt?"

"I think he hated having to whip me, except I didn't give him any choice because I was so bad."

Henrietta's pale eyes widened, as if she found it hard to believe him. "Do you think it's possible, Daniel, that you did bad things because you wanted to be punished, because that was the only time your father showed any tenderness to you, when he held you afterward?"

Daniel could see that there might be some logic in that. As a bad boy he had been singularly inept—stealing, lying, and always managing to get caught. "I was pretty perverse, eh?" he laughed, shaking his head at his own self-betraying ingenuity.

"Pretty desperate for love."

That too maybe, but "orgy"? He couldn't get the word out of

his head. His father and he, the night, the dark, the bed, pants, underpants, belt hissing through darkness, anger, release, tears, tenderness. No, whipping pure and simple. An act of punishment. Well deserved.

He tried to study Henrietta without her catching him at it. What was she up to? What kind of secret therapeutic game was she playing, trying to trap him, trick him into revealing things that weren't true? He didn't trust her, not really. Everything he said, she turned around until it was impossible to separate what he had told her from what she repeated back to him in slightly altered form. Strange too how much he hated and feared his father and yet how defensive he felt whenever she suggested his father's behavior had been less than satisfactory. But his father, after all—and she seemed reluctant to take this into consideration—had had a hard life, had never been happy or satisfied, never content with himself or those around him. Saddled with a son who gave him nothing but disappointment and grief, was it any wonder that he was so angry and bitter, that he sometimes got carried away?

"Did your father flirt with women?"

"What?"

"Were you ever aware of your father flirting with women? Do you know if he ever was unfaithful to your mother?"

Daniel paused—the question had never occurred to him before. "My father is completely faithful to my mother. I'm sure of that, even though he was, he still is, a very handsome man. Vigorous too, virile even. Women flirted with him a lot. I remember that. Clerks in stores, nurses at the hospital. He responded in a jokey sort of way, but underneath the joking he always looked bashful, almost like a little boy."

"Do you think women were attracted by that bashfulness?" A smile played across her face.

"Probably."

"Can you think of any other reason why women would flirt so much with your father, even though he never seems to have responded in more than a boyish, playful way?"

Daniel had a flash of inspiration. "Could it be because he didn't respond? Because women sensed he was safe?"

Henrietta laughed. "That's certainly a possibility. So as far as you know he never cheated on your mother?"

He shook his head. "Never. It just wasn't part of his makeup."

"Is it part of yours, Daniel?"

He coughed. "It has been known to happen. Occasionally. Never anything really serious. Mainly when I'm away. Traveling."

"Would you say as well that you like to flirt?"

He couldn't help smiling. "I've been known to."

Henrietta massaged her left knee. "When would you say the bulk of the whippings occurred?"

Daniel felt impatient. She was so flighty, never sticking to one topic for more than a minute or two before doubling back or jumping forward to another unrelated one. "I don't know. I guess the worst of them came when I was twelve, thirteen, fourteen."

"What was going on in your life then that caused you to be beaten so often?"

Daniel tried to remember. "I guess you could say I was pretty wild then."

"Wild?"

"Sneaking out of the house late at night, drinking, running around with older, kind of hoody guys, that sort of thing."

"What about sex?"

"Yes."

Henrietta smiled. "Would you say you were fairly sexually active then?"

"Yes." Daniel felt warm inside, recalling the hot summer nights, the cheap, sweet brandy.

"With girls?"

He shook his head. He was surprised to feel so relieved that she had asked. "At that age they were pretty inaccessible. Girls came later. After I got my license. When I was thirteen or fourteen it was mainly other guys."

"Older guys?"

"Yes, but my age too."

"Did your father know about this?"

"He caught me in the act quite a lot. I was a fairly active kid."

"Would it be fair to say that your father tried to catch you in the act?"

"What do you mean?"

"Did you ever have the feeling that your father was spying on you?"

He didn't have to think. "All the time."

"About sex?"

"About everything. He was always watching me, waiting for me to do something wrong. But yes, mostly about sex. Even when I was alone, he'd manage to catch me masturbating. There was a time too when I wasn't allowed to shut the bathroom door or even the shower curtain when I took a bath or shower. He said he didn't want me 'playing' with myself because I was already 'too worked up' as it was."

"What would he do when he caught you with another guy?"

"Whip me."

"I see. Is that what most of the whippings were about? At that age, at around puberty?"

"Yes."

Henrietta reached down at the side of her chair and retrieved her steno pad and fountain pen.

"What's wrong?"

She looked at him. "Wrong?"

"The pad."

"Nothing's wrong, Daniel. I wanted to make a note to myself."

"I'm not gay." He was trembling, close to tears. She was just like his father—watching him, spying on him, trying to catch him out.

"Is that what you thought I was going to write in my notebook?"

He nodded.

"How long did these experiences continue?"

"Until I was fifteen or sixteen. It seemed to be a pretty common thing. You know how horny adolescent guys can be—any port in a storm."

"So no gay experiences after that?"

He studied his nails. "A couple of times at university."

"Would you say that's a part of you that you've deliberately repressed?"

He thought about that. The boy from the Chinese restaurant ran through his mind, little legs kicking. "Not really. It was exciting when I was a teenager—anything connected with sex was. Those two or three times later, yes, they were exciting too, but more because they were daring, risky. That was the late sixties, early seventies—sleeping with another guy was a kind of cool thing to do as long as you didn't make a habit of it. When it comes down to pure pleasure though, it's never been much of a contest. I prefer women. Sexually, emotionally."

"And your father?"

He felt as though she had slapped him across the face. "Do I prefer my father?"

She blinked rapidly several times. "No, no, Daniel. Do you think your father preferred women too?"

Why bring his father into it. Why couldn't she stick with one topic and explore it thoroughly? It was getting so confusing, this leaping back and forth, this turning and twisting in the wind. What was the point? He knew he could never be completely honest with Henrietta. Not even she was ready for the things he had to tell. She was taking the wrong path, a path that he had diverted her along. She was going after his father. But Daniel knew his father wasn't the problem. He was the problem. How could she be so blinkered as to not see that? What an untenable position he had placed himself in. He wanted Henrietta's help so much, craved her sympathy and comprehension, longed for her forgiveness. But he knew that in order to secure and retain all, he would eventually have to reveal all. She was not a stupid woman—surely she must get a whiff of the underlying stench from time to time. Revealing all would lose him all. Her professional interest, her neutral compassion. He was stuck, trapped. Out of the old cage, into this new one, the bars thrusting up hard around him, each one untouchable, unencompassable.

"What's going on now, Daniel?" Henrietta tugged at the collar of her suit jacket. It occurred to him that she looked different today. Something about her hair. Softer, with a definite shape to it. The suit wasn't bad either, jade green with a lighter green pinstripe. All session she had been tugging at various parts of the suit, pulling at the shoulders, smoothing the skirt, stroking the lapels.

"Is that new?" He smiled, not wanting to overdo it.

She looked down, as though surprised at what she had on. "Why yes, it is. Do you like it?"

"It's a good color for you."

"Really?" She smiled back. He sensed she didn't believe a word he was saying. He was beginning to see that there was going to be no pleasing this woman. She patted at the back of her hair. "When I think of all you've told me over the past two sessions, I get the sense that you must have felt fairly hemmed in as a child. Nothing you did, no matter how hard you tried, could make your father happy. And from what I can tell, your mother was, for reasons we don't yet know, unreachable. So you were caught between a rock and a hard place." She beamed at having produced such an apt cliché. "You couldn't move. But little kids have a lot of energy. If you let them, most of them will run and run until they drop. What about you, Daniel? Caught the way you were, what did you do with all your energy?"

What did it matter now? It wasn't as though he could get any of it back. "I wasn't much like other kids. I was pretty sluggish, in fact. I liked to lie around a lot, reading, daydreaming, pretending I was someone else, somewhere else. From my bedroom window I could see the tops of the big trees that lined the road at the foot of our drive. The crown of one big elm reminded me of a knight's plumed helmet and another, a great spreading willow, looked like a lady's veiled face. I used to lie in the window seat, dreaming about the knight and his lady—how kind and chivalrous they were. Isn't that weird?" He laughed, waiting for Henrietta to join in. Her humorlessness was beginning to wear on his nerves.

"I'd like to stay with that sluggishness for a while. Could you describe it for me?"

"A lot of the time I had no energy at all. I'd be playing and then all at once I'd feel weak, used up, as though all the strength was draining out of me and there was nothing I could do to stop it. I remember standing at the edge of the orchard—I must have been four or five—looking out at a field of grain. At the far edge of the field was a stream. I loved going there to play in the water, building dams, dredging canals, catching box turtles, frogs, minnows. Anyway, I was standing there looking across the field and I knew I didn't have the strength to carry me across it—the distance must have been no more than a few hundred yards. But I would get this feeling of weakness in my arms and legs, they'd go all rubbery, and I'd have to drag myself back to the house, back up to my room."

A long silence followed. Daniel could feel the room, Henrietta's room, as though it were a living thing, breathing along with him. Sunlight came through the miniblinds in hard diagonal shafts that seemed to vibrate slightly in time with his breathing. He felt he could reach out and grasp the shafts of light, hold their bright thickness in his hand. The thought made him queasy.

Finally Henrietta said, "You must have been a very depressed little boy."

He nodded. "I'd lie in the window seat for hours or, if I was feeling really bad and couldn't stand the light, I'd climb into the upper bunk of my bunk bed. I'd feel so strange—sometimes I worried I would never be able to get up again. I'd just lie there, hands clenched at my sides so they wouldn't touch the bunk railing. At times like that there were things I couldn't bear to touch. Touching them made me feel worse. Sick."

"What things?"

"Things. I don't know." What was happening to his voice? It seemed thick and low, far away. "There were some things that seemed too big to touch. Too real. Too thick and hard. Too smooth. It's difficult to explain." He could feel his nose crinkling up as though he were smelling a noisome odor. His upper lip rode up in disgust. A flash of pain behind his eyes, and the room went dark. He could hear Henrietta but he could no longer see her.

"Daniel, where are you now?"

He didn't know. Inside. He could see her again, although the light was soupy. The room seemed huge, and Henrietta was a long way away. He saw that his body was an upright husk and he had shrunk deep down inside it, waiting for a sign that it was safe to come out.

"Daniel, I think we've hit a wall. Perhaps we should talk about something else now."

Daniel slowly came back from where he had been hiding, and they spoke of other things.

He closed the door to his workroom and pushed open the wide double windows over his drawing table. Night air rushed in, warm and damp. Layers of high-backed inky clouds hung, unreal as stage flats, over the St. Lawrence. Daniel hoped it would rain. The garden was starting to droop, the front lawn going copper at the edges.

Sitting down at the drawing table, he opened the ebony domino box in which he kept his drawing paraphernalia. He felt a twinge of guilt on lifting the brass-hinged lid, for the box belonged to his father, purchased back in the fifties on one of his annual African safaris. Like most of the objects acquired on those hunting expeditions—wooden masks, Benin tribal figures, thick ivory bracelets, necklaces of strung beads, semiprecious stones and animal teeth or claws—his father bragged that the domino box had cost him next to nothing. He had gotten it, like the other booty, for a ballpoint pen, a dimestore watch, a Zippo lighter. Daniel had felt no qualms about taking the ebony box with him when he went away to school. Certainly his parents' house held far too many such objects. They seemed to spill over every available surface and wall of the library and especially of his father's den, although his mother had managed to stem the exotic tide at the portals of the dining and living rooms, preserves of pale wallpaper, paler trim and discreetly framed British oils and watercolors. It had taken his parents a year or so to miss the ebony box—it was his mother who finally asked if he had seen it. Daniel lied, claiming not only not to have the box but also saying he had no memory of ever having seen it in the first place.

The ebony dominos were long gone, dispersed among Alex and

Porter's toys, the toys themselves now either in crates and trunks in the basement or in the possession of younger cousins or the neighbors' children. Tonight, in addition to his usual drawing pens and pencils, the oblong box held a pack of Rothmans, bought on impulse at the Korean pharmacy after this afternoon's session with Henrietta.

He quit smoking in the late seventies, along with nearly everyone he knew, but this afternoon the thought of a cigarette seemed golden with promise—not the taking up again of an old and dangerous habit but rather a one-time-only pleasure that would calm his flayed nerves. His upper lip especially seemed in need of something to close on. When he wasn't thinking about it, his lip would ride up until it quivered in a double sneer beneath his reflexively crinkled nostrils. Tonight at dinner Alex had said, "What's the matter, Daniel, something stink?" Before Daniel could wrestle the lip down into its proper position, Porter had chimed in, "You look just like the rabbit in *Bambi,* with your nose all scrunched up. What was his name?"

"Thumper," Alex said, and both boys thumped the table with open palms until Leslie, bringing in the salad, made them stop.

"Une bonne cigarette," Daniel thought, examining the pack. Had Rothmans used that slogan, or du Maurier? He almost laughed out loud, abruptly recalling an old French catchphrase for Peter Jackson cigarettes: *"Une Peter sur toute lèvre."* The slogan had been the object of many off-color jokes in the English community. Daniel could feel his lip curling up once again. He had never had a tic before. He hoped it wouldn't prove permanent.

Carefully unpeeling the gold band, he tore off the cellophane wrapper, tilted back the cardboard lid, folded back the silver foil. Reaching into the pocket of his Bermudas, he produced a book of matches lifted from the junk drawer in the kitchen while he helped Leslie load the dishwasher after dinner. Looking about the long workroom, his eyes rested on the Twinings Prince of Wales tin that held his watercolor brushes—the perfect ashtray. He spilled the brushes out onto the sill, opened the north window wide and turned on the small floor fan just to be safe. Leslie would be asleep by now. It was doubtful, even should she awaken and smell smoke, that she would climb the stairs to his workroom, but Daniel realized that cigarette smoking had become again what it once had been in his adolescence: a furtive pleasure. Like sex.

Back at his worktable he tapped the bottom of the pack. Three cigarettes popped up, as neatly as in an old television commercial. He chose one and lit it, feeling slightly awkward. His smoking had always lacked the elegant insouciance displayed by men smoking in old movies or men of his father's generation, for whom lighting up was automatic and yet stylized too, right down to the plucking away of the tobacco flake that adhered to the tongue after that first blissful drag on an unfiltered Player's or Craven "A." When they were still at university, his friend Press had told Daniel that each time he lit up it looked as though he was doing it for the first time.

He inhaled deeply and felt the giddiness that a first puff after long abstention always engendered in him. He resolved to smoke the two remaining cigarettes that poked out from the pack. The rest he would crumble into the wastebasket. He thought he had that much willpower.

Taking up his drawing pen—twin of the one he kept at work, jet black, thick, with real heft to it—he slid the T square to the bottom of the drawing board and taped a fresh sheet of drafting paper in place. He knew he ought to do some detail work on the ski resort for Val Blanc—first presentation was less than a month away—but tonight wasn't the night. Tonight he simply wanted to let his pen go, follow where it led him. He found this was often the best way of discovering new ideas, new directions, especially when he was stuck. Not that he felt stuck, at least not in terms of work, but he did feel keyed up, sure that if he tried to sleep, sleep wouldn't come, at least not until he had soothed his jangled mind with a cigarette or two and the dark, slick feel of his pen gliding across the white sheet.

He made a series of elongated attached O's, a warm-up exercise dimly remembered from grade-two penmanship class. In the upper right-hand corner of the page he tentatively sketched a candle, flame guttering, wax pouring down one side. The candle suggested columns and so he watched as his hand drew a small classical temple with five fluted pillars resting on a shallow staired dish. It turned out to be a ruined temple—he became so preoccupied with the columns themselves, so caught up in articulating the tendriled intricacies of their capitals that in the end he couldn't imagine putting a lid on these Corinthian eruptions with some prosaic dome or pediment.

Without thinking much about it he lit another cigarette. Wind whipped in through the double windows. The cooling air smelled of distant rain and of garbage waiting to be collected in the laneway below. Daniel considered switching off the floor fan, but the steady purring soothed him. Watching his hand as it moved automatically across the page led him to begin sketching the hand and the drawing pen it held—an exercise remembered from introductory drawing classes at school. What better, more accessible life model than oneself?

He had never been much good at hands, or faces for that matter. Live flesh was too changeable, hard to fix. Even with one's own hand, the slightest shift of sinew or bone, the subtle lengthening of light or shadow, and either one had to start all over again or try to incorporate the incessant changes. He inevitably ended up with a drawing of a hand so bloated or palsied looking as to belong in a medical textbook. Tonight he simply suggested his hand with a few deft curves and light crosshatching.

The pen itself gave less trouble, was in fact a pleasure to get down on paper. The bulbous cap inlaid with four narrow gold bands, the sleek, hard shaft angling downward between thumb and forefinger, the delicate, almost needle-fine nib pouring forth black ink in a smooth, steady stream. Daniel paused, sitting back to gain perspective on his effort. A clean job, he decided, inhaling deeply and absently tipping ash into the Twinings tin. But neat and precise as the outline was, it didn't give the full, almost ominous effect of the pen itself when viewed close up. He had often fantasized that, with the proper special-effects work, his pen would make an excellent spacecraft for a sci-fi picture—a villain's vessel, darkly pulsing, probing the deepest recesses of the universe. What was missing in the drawing, he decided, was the quality of blackness itself, the silent, menacing, satiny sheen of the shaft. He began to fill in the pen's contours, running the nib back and forth along the pen's length in smooth, even strokes so the blackness was uniform.

Some whiteness shone through, the ghost of the paper still faintly glowing. He pressed down hard, feeling the cramp in his hand but not caring, pushing the nib back and forth until the ghosts of whiteness gave way. This was what he was after, the full shaft glowing like obsidian. The nib caught on something. It looked like soggy leavings of a gum eraser. He hunched down to blow them away and saw that they were tiny curls of ink-stained paper. The nib had worked through, leaving a black tubular stain on the white surface of his drawing table.

He ripped the sheet of paper from its moorings, crumpled it, threw it across the room. Examining the oblong stain on the drawing board's smooth surface, he saw that ink had pooled slightly at the nether end of the stain. His hand, the hand holding the pen, was shaking. Something about the stain itself, the shape of it, bothered him—the dark blot of ink poised at the end as though about to fall.

The clouds layered over the St. Lawrence lit up for an instant. Daniel waited for the sound of thunder but none came. The lamp suspended over his drawing board cast a bright circle of light, but the room seemed to darken about him. His hand gripped the pen so tightly that the blood had left it, leaving the skin blanched, unreal. He forced himself to relax his grip. The shaft of the pen rolled between finger and thumb, feeling unnaturally warm and hard. If he held the pen a second longer he was sure he would vomit. He flung it at the opposite wall. The pen clattered to the floor, apparently unharmed, a testament to the durability of Swiss design. Daniel felt no better. His head ached, as if dark clouds had massed behind his eyes and were fast expanding. His head was shaking too. He clenched his jaw in an attempt to halt the trembling. His upper lip shot up in a double sneer, his nose twitched. Gagging sounds issued from deep in his throat.

In the next instant he knew—simultaneously knew and won-

dered how he could not have known for so long. He knew what
the pen was, the columns, the guttering candle, the bunk-bed
railing in his attic bedroom at home, the stair rail at Gillian's
memorial service, the rain and thunder and feeling trapped, his
father's footsteps on the stairs, coming up to close the windows.
Daniel wanted to laugh at his own stupidity, the willed denseness
that kept him from understanding what hand, lips, body had been
trying to tell him for so many years. Too long, too smooth, too
thick, too hard. Too much to encompass. Too much to handle.
Of course it was, for such a small boy. But he had handled it all,
had curled his lip, wrinkled his nose. In his crib, he knew it was
his crib, in that darkened room, the wooden cage around him, the
nightly teasing, prodding and taunting, the thrusting through the
bars.

He looked down at his hand, as if it were another's lying
against the drawing board, clenching and unclenching, and yet
each time never completely closing, always leaving a space, a
thick tube of air waiting to be filled. He could feel the absent
smoothness, the columnar length of it.

He was crying now, shuddering and gasping for air, tears
streaming, his neck seized up, head trembling. I know, I know, I
know, I know. The knowledge terrified him—this sudden rent in
the surface of his existence.

He must tell Leslie. On the narrow stairs down to the second
floor it was like a childhood dream of flying upright, his feet
skimming along a few inches above the stair runner. He was
about to throw open the door to their room when he stopped. He
glanced at his watch. Almost one-thirty. He ached to tell her, and
yet . . . He imagined her face pressed into the pillow, her hair
fanning out. What could he say at this point that would make
sense to another person? It barely made sense to him.

He would wait to tell her. First he had to marshal all these
shadowy impressions and sensations, steel himself for the doubts
and objections that were sure to come. Would anyone believe
him? Worse than anything the others could come up with, he also
could feel his own objections stirring. You're making this up, this
is crazy, this can't be real, you always were a horrible little liar,

crazy as they come. Your father, of all people. Your father with his handsome smiling face, his prosperous practice, lovely family, beautiful home, his circle of admiring friends—why, he was a pillar of the community. Daniel almost shouted with laughter at this last, inadvertently horrific image—saw his father rise up before him, broadly grinning, saw him swell with strength and power.

I've got to get out of here, he thought, out into the air, the night. This house can't hold me tonight. Leslie can't help me or hold me either. Tonight I won't be held, touched, helped. Tonight I will be, for once in my life, inviolate.

He sat on the low granite bench between the reflecting pool and the wading pond. He had no sense of how long he had been sitting there. He had gotten only as far as Murray Hill Park at the top of the street, struggling up the steep grassy slope to the water, fighting to catch his breath in the panic of the climb. No one else was around, not even any cars in sight as he crossed Côte-St-Antoine, yet Daniel felt frightened, threatened, pursued. People at his back, voices in his head, equally unreal, equally real. The night itself was watching him, conspiring against him. Every second minute he thought about turning around and going back home, to safety. But that was impossible. That would be far worse than sitting out here alone in the night, at the mercy of the elements.

Well, the elements of Murray Hill Park. The carefully clipped shrubs; the grass smooth, green and unblemished; the gracefully curving, carefully edged asphalt paths, the brightly lighted tennis courts within their chain-link enclosure. He knew he was not Lear on the blasted heath. Still, the blustery old man kept coming to mind even as Daniel struggled to reject such a self-dramatizing parallel. He had never felt so naked or vulnerable in his life.

The night was cooling but still close. Humpbacked clouds floated thick and low. The wind had dropped and with it the promise of rain. He felt cold even as his polo shirt stuck to his sweat-damp back.

He sat on the granite bench because he could think of nothing else to do. His mind insisted he must do something—he couldn't just sit there, wasting invaluable time. Yet he couldn't imagine getting up from the bench either, for that would mean leaving the water, the sound of it ceaselessly pouring from the semicircular reflecting pool into the oblong wading pond, the sight of it pouring, a miniature waterfall no more than a dozen feet wide, falling only a foot or so, continuously, smoothly, a cool, glassy arc.

He had to stay near the water, it made him feel less crazed. Otherwise he thought he might scream, shriek, tear out his hair, uproot small decorative plants. Every gesture was both too great and too small; his mind, teeming with images, words, half-articulate sensations, seemed eager to entertain all possibilities. No more picking and choosing, censoring and denying—the floodgates had lifted, and the only way to survive, now, was to agree to be swept along.

Underneath this intensity ran a wide seam of exhaustion, mental as much as physical. He knew sleep was out of the question, but he stretched out on the bench, feeling the hard, prickly surface through the thin cloth of his shirt and shorts. In the distance he heard a car. He lifted his head to see a police cruiser prowling along Côte-St-Antoine at the foot of the park. He knew the police couldn't see him, stretched out on a bench several hundred yards above them, but their presence made him uneasy. What if one of the houses looking onto the park had called Westmount Security to complain that someone was loitering after midnight, with intent? Once the cruiser crawled out of sight, Daniel got up from the bench and left the two shallow pools.

By the time he reached the western flank of Mont-Royal he felt not more himself, for he didn't think he any longer knew who he was, but more at ease with the body that carried him, more acquainted with the night. The sense that he was being followed, the voices that pursued him, had faded, although he still felt wary. The *grande allée* to the lake stretched out before him like the nave of a great nocturnal cathedral. Daniel moved along almost effortlessly now, legs striding, arms swinging. The clarity with which he viewed the night amazed and frightened him. He thought he had never so fully absorbed the texture and color of the world. From the crest of the hill he saw the lake itself, still and shining. He headed down to the walk edging the lake but, once there, realized that this wasn't what he wanted. Water alone was not enough to calm him now.

He climbed on up to the Chalet, where he sat on a stone parapet overlooking the city. He thought if he could stay in this one place, he would be all right for a while.

Sometime later headlights flashed and a silver sports car wheeled onto the Chalet's wide terrace. The car came to a halt at the far side, ruby taillights glowing. Daniel waited for the doors to open, for the sports car's occupants to step out and admire the view. But no one emerged. Probably a necking couple, he thought, admiring their temerity—cars weren't allowed in the park.

Not long after, a blue-and-white police cruiser nosed its way onto the terrace, pulling up next to the sports car. A cop got out, walked over to the sports car and, with his silver flashlight, tapped on the driver's window. The second cop, the driver, got out as well. He looked about the terrace, his eyes finally resting on Daniel. Daniel wasn't concerned: he knew the cop wouldn't bother him. Tonight he was invisible.

He could hear voices on the breeze. He concentrated on the skyline, the dark mirror strip of the St. Lawrence beyond. Eventually the silver sports car crept across the terrace and disappeared. The two cops stood at the parapet. Daniel could make out the glow of a cigarette. They stood quietly for a while, one of them looking out at the drifting clouds, the other at Daniel or simply at the illuminated office towers beyond him. The first cop turned to go. The other cop stared hard in Daniel's direction, then raised his arm. Daniel thought he was waving goodbye and lifted his arm in response. Then he saw the red ember of the cop's cigarette arc across the violet dark.

The air seemed less heavy. A strong wind blew in from the east. The mountain was giving up its heat. Daniel looked down at the houses laid out in crescents on the mountain's lower slopes. Great solid fieldstone or brick houses with steep slate or tile roofs and multiple chimneys. Some completely dark, others with a lighted upper-story window, the biggest places with gardens floodlit to ward off prowlers. Safe as houses—the phrase came to his mind—and houses as safes, the stout-walled repositories of the rich. Sealing out danger, sealing in privilege, status . . . what else? Sealing in secrets. All at once Daniel had a vision. He knew it was inside his head and yet he saw it as clearly as if it were unfolding before him. The roof of each house was hinged, and, suddenly, as though released by some secret spring, the roofs tilted back, like treasure chests opening, and he could see into all the rooms of all the houses, see cubical bedrooms with striped wallpaper and Persian rugs, brass lamps and glossy commodes, sleeping parents in their wide beds, sleeping children in their narrow ones. And Daniel saw that at the heart of every sleeping house, instead of treasure, was a festering secret—the sleepers' tortured dreams. They slept for those dreams, awakened to deny them.

He got up from the parapet and made his way slowly down the three flights of steep wooden stairs to the dirt road that wound round the mountain. He stopped at the foot of the stairs, uncertain which way to turn. A sudden crack and a heavy leafy shifting in the branches just above his head. The hair on the back of his neck stood. He thought of a mountain cat poised to spring. He looked up. A man was sleeping in the crook of the three central branches of a large maple. Perhaps not sleeping. Daniel felt watched. He stared up into the tree, trying to make out the man's face. For a moment he thought he could see him grinning like the Cheshire cat, but no, the leaves were too thick, the night too dark. He was briefly angry at the man for disturbing the peace of his journey. Once the initial shock had passed, though, he felt unthreatened by the man's presence. Just another of the increasing army of the homeless. A poor, bare forked animal. He would do Daniel no harm. Nothing could this night, this dark early morning, now that his life was finally getting under way. Daniel glanced back one last time at the man wedged between the branches of the spreading maple. "I have taken too little care of this," he said quietly to himself.

. . .

It was after eleven when he jolted awake. Breakfast was out of the question, no time for that. He must tell Leslie everything. He phoned her office. The secretary told him she was with a client. No, he wouldn't care to leave a message. Talking to Leslie's secretary reminded him of obligations of his own. He called the office to say he was ill and wouldn't be in. He wanted to get out of the house at once and yet he was afraid. The sun was too bright, the colors of summer too vivid. He would be over-whelmed. Everyone he passed would know what had occurred during the night: on the mountain he was invisible, now he felt transparent.

He picked up the phone and dialed.

"Press?"

"Yes? Daniel. My God, Daniel. Of course. Who else would call in the middle of the night?"

In his haste to make contact, Daniel had forgotten Press's aversion to morning light. Too bad for Press. "Look, I've got to see you. Right away. I need to talk to you. It's important."

He could feel the slow shift in Press's consciousness. "Give me half an hour. Make that an hour and I'll give you breakfast."

"I've already eaten," Daniel lied.

"I haven't," Press said and rang off.

Daniel wandered from the kitchen into the dining room and then the living room, righting picture frames, subtly re-placing pieces of furniture. He tried to work out the easiest way to get to Press's loft without being seen. He could call a taxi, except that would entail engaging in small talk with the driver, and Daniel was sure that any talk at all on his part would lead to sudden truth telling, naked divulgence. Public transit was out too—he felt self-conscious in the Métro at the best of times. He thought about walking, but no matter how unpopulated the route he was bound to pass scores of curious strangers with probing eyes. He couldn't do it. He could not leave the house. He would call Press and cancel.

He sank down onto the sofa, knowing it was absurd to be defeated by such insubstantial fears and yet knowing too they were real enough that without some special protection he wouldn't be able to venture beyond the front door. Absentmindedly he reached over and flicked on the amp and CD player, thinking he would put on a disc, something calming. The radio blasted on. Alex and Porter obviously had been listening last—it was set to their favorite station, cranked up. He was about to change the setting so that he could put on a disc, when a song came on that he recognized. He couldn't put a name to it or to the group that played it, but it was something the boys played on their own sound system quite often. As music went these days it wasn't bad at all, quite melodic in fact, with a loose, lilting beat and wisps of woozy synthesizer. The male singer sounded like a Brit. Daniel got up from the sofa and swayed to the music, even sang along when the chorus came: " 'This is the day, This is the day, This is the day, My life will surely change . . .' " He began to cry but didn't stop dancing. How crazy I must look, he thought. Chink, chink, chink. Beaver paused, midway down the stairs, brow furrowed. "Beaver," Daniel said, seeing a way out of his dilemma, and Beaver, thinking he was being called, bounded the rest of the way down the stairs and performed great springing leaps about Daniel as he danced and wept.

Press opened the heavy, tin-covered door. Beaver, straining at the leash, lunged toward him.

"Beaver. What a pleasant surprise." Press stepped back to protect his black silk kimono.

"I'm sorry, Press, but I couldn't think of how to get here without him." Daniel took off his dark glasses.

Press seemed to accept this explanation. "Why don't you take him off his lead. There's not much he can harm here."

Daniel unhooked the leash. Beaver skittered across the wide-plank floor and through the open doors to the terrace.

"Beaver." Daniel ran after him. Beaver already had his front paws up on the low balustrade and was looking down at the ten-story drop to the street, tail wagging, tongue dripping. Daniel dragged him back.

"I thought we would have breakfast out here. It's pretty much a disaster inside." Daniel, pulling Beaver along, followed Press back into the cavernous loft, which actually didn't look much worse than usual. Clothes were strewn across the sailcloth-covered sofas that formed a V in front of seven high windows framing a cloudless sky. The top two shelves of one of the bookcases running along the west wall had collapsed, spilling books and magazines across the waxed floor. The Plexiglas sheet covering a black-and-white photomontage over the dining room table looked as if it had been struck by a high-caliber bullet—a pinwheel of cracks radiated from the jagged hole in the Plexiglas.

"Like it?" Press said, yawning. "I think I may leave it that way."

"What happened?"

"Ethan and I had a bit of a dustup last night. Late last night."

"I'll say." Daniel took in the jade ashtray on the floor beneath the photomontage. Beaver nosed through the cigarette butts and burnt matches.

"Said I had bourgeois taste in art. Said I condescended to his art." Press nodded in the direction of a large canvas on the opposite wall that looked like a Rouault gone wrong, putrid, smeared-on colors barely hemmed in by black impasto outlining. Looking closer, Daniel saw it was a portrait, a nude, a youngish-looking man with a thickening body and an enormous blood-engorged erection.

"Why, it's you, Press."

"My more tactful friends affect not to notice. Ethan hung it last weekend while I was down in New York. That's one of the things we were fighting about. I told him I wasn't comfortable facing that every morning at breakfast."

Daniel laughed. "I didn't remember you being that, er, large." He blushed—he'd never referred to that one drunken night at university when he and Press had ended up in each other's arms. Neither had Press, as far as he could remember.

"Eye of the beholder, don't you know. I suppose I should be flattered, except for the fact that, as Ethan was careful to explain to me, the phallus in his *oeuvre* is more about power than sexuality. My perky organ isn't so much a sign of desire as of the brutal domination of the patriarchy. I believe 'phallocratic' is the word he used."

"Oh." Daniel had never cared much for Ethan, never really

approved of the yawning gap in age between him and Press either. But then Press was always getting involved with unsuitable types. Boys, or at least near-boys—wan, languid, artistic boys who seemed to stay twenty forever until one morning they woke up looking thirty and Press gently persuaded them they would be better off without him. Ethan was brighter than most of his predecessors, nastier too, at the boozy, drugged-out dinner parties that Daniel and Leslie frequented less and less. Daniel—trying not to stare at the scarlet erection on the wall—now realized it wasn't the age difference that bothered him so much as the father-son roles that Press and his minions acted out. Press sustained, supported (morally, financially), jollied them along; each one at first looked up to Press, aping his mannerisms, taste, accent, then turned against him. On more than one occasion, it ended in a physical attack on him. Daniel looked at Press's long, handsome face, jowls just beginning to soften the broad jaw, tiny broken blood vessels across the cheeks and at the tip of the nose, wispy blond hair that up close was as much gray as blond. The shoulders, beneath the thin silk of the kimono, were still wide and powerful, the body too was, apart from a slight inevitable sagging about the waistline, remarkably lean and solid, considering the fact that, with the exception of a few midwinter bursts of energy on the ski slopes or in the hockey rink (loudly regretted for days afterward), Press avoided exercise as strenuously as he avoided work. Yes, in many ways, physical ways especially, Daniel thought, Press made an ideal Daddy—handsome, masculine, strong, big. Daniel realized his gaze had rested on Press's thick thighs, on the triangle where they joined.

"What's wrong, Daniel," Press said, smiling.

Daniel jerked his gaze away, only to find he was staring at the thrusting painted erection. "Excuse me," he said, and ran for the bathroom.

Press ran with him and was now holding his shoulders as he heaved and gasped. "That's it," Press said. "Get it all out. Much better that way."

At last Daniel sat back on his heels. Press soaked a face flannel in cold water and spread it across Daniel's sweat-filmed brow.

"I'm sorry," Press said, leading Daniel back into the large room. "Going on like that about my troubles when it was clear from the look on your very pale face as you came in the door that something was drastically wrong. Even poor Beaver looked distraught. I suppose that's why I did go on about myself. But what is it, Daniel? Surely not something with Leslie?"

They went out onto the wide terrace, where Daniel told Press about Gillian's death, Henrietta, last night at his drawing table, the walk on the mountain, his vision of the hinged roofs. He found he could not talk without tears running down his cheeks—he wasn't sobbing, there was just this constant salty flow. It didn't seem to bother Press.

When Daniel had at last recounted everything, Press got up from his chaise longue. "Be right back," he said.

He returned bearing a round teak tray. On it were half a baguette, a third of a wheel of some soft cheese—Brie, Daniel assumed—two small crystal glasses and a bottle of Hine and a small gold lacquer bowl of Fig Newtons. "After you phoned I fell right back asleep, so I didn't really have time to do anything about breakfast." Press tore off a hunk of bread, scooped up some cheese and fed it to Beaver, stretched out on the flagstones at Press's feet. Daniel tore off some bread, dabbed it in the runny cheese and took a tentative bite—he could still taste the bile in his throat. Not Brie—something lighter, more fragrant too. He wolfed it down.

"Not so fast," Press said, handing him a glass of cognac. "Taken in the right proportions, I believe Hine and very ripe Brillat-Savarin are the only cure for a hangover, with Fig Newtons of course. Absolutely essential." He fished in the deep pockets of his kimono and produced a joint and a yellow cloisonné cigarette lighter.

"I don't know, Press," Daniel said. "You know me and marijuana. It makes me terribly paranoid."

"Or terribly amorous." Press grinned. "Don't worry, old dear. I'm not going to try to seduce you. You're far too old for me."

Taking the proffered joint, Daniel felt vaguely offended. He wasn't that old. Then he laughed. "I was worried you were going

to try something and now I'm irritated you're not." He was
surprised to find himself speaking so freely. Even with old friends
like Press he usually said far less than he thought.

Press inhaled deeply and somehow managed to talk without
letting smoke escape. "I would imagine you must have all sorts
of complicated feelings this morning. And not just about your
father." He exhaled. "This is bound to affect every aspect of your
life in one way or another, don't you think? The way you relate
to Leslie and the boys, for one. It's already affecting the way we
interact, isn't it?"

Daniel nodded. The movement of his head made him dizzy.
"Then you believe me?"

Press took another pull on the joint and handed it back to
Daniel. "Why wouldn't I?"

"You're a lawyer. It's all so"—Daniel waved the joint about—
"so nebulous, impressionistic. I mean it's things I remember, or
think I remember. Physical memories, sensations, as much as
anything. Nothing I could prove."

Press leaned forward and poured more cognac into their
glasses. "It's not as though you'll ever have to go into a court of
law with your evidence marshaled and the other side chipping
mercilessly away at it."

"That's what I was doing on my way here, tearing down all my
best arguments. I'd lose for sure."

"I'm not convinced. Besides, why would you make up something like that? And why wait so long? Why put yourself through
so much pain? And Henrietta—she believes you, right?"

"She doesn't know. My next appointment isn't till Monday."

"But from everything you've said, it sounds as if she's known
from practically the first day you walked into her office. That
thick line you say she drew on the diagram between you and your
father. Can't get much more graphic than that."

"I suppose not."

"I think it's out." Press flicked the remains of the joint over the
balustrade. "It all makes sense, you know. From everything I
know about you, and that's quite a lot, and from everything I
know about your father, which is admittedly very little. It was

never any secret that you hated him, and yet I could never figure out why. The few times I met him he seemed quite charming. You always claimed that was only one side of him, and of course I never saw the other. He was always wonderfully kind and, well, attentive to me. Remember that time he came through town when we were still at McGill and he took us to—where was it?—Chez Martin, it must have been. I seem to remember flocked wallpaper and a white piano. He ordered champagne and I forget what else. Got me happily snookered in no time flat and made me feel like I was the most intelligent, attractive, witty person in the world. When he turned on his thousand-watt smile . . ."

"And I got so angry at you afterward."

Press laughed. "I couldn't understand why, except you said he was never like that with you. Never easy, confiding."

Daniel saw that the amber cognac was sloshing about in his glass, his hand was shaking so. "That night at Chez Martin he didn't say more than a dozen words to me. All my life he was angry, scornful, critical, brutal. I can't remember a comfortable moment in his presence, a second I wasn't on my guard. The few times he seemed happy were the scariest, because you knew they weren't going to last. He was always worst after those, as if he in some way had to pay for them. Or rather I had to pay."

"You both had to pay."

"Yes." Daniel looked out over the industrial rooftops. In the blue distance the mountain reared up lush and green. The cognac glow was upon him, the marijuana appeared to be helping too. He felt that if only he could stop trembling he would be able to stand back and look at the relationship between his father and himself, if not dispassionately, at least with a certain detachment.

"It's odd, but all these years we've been friends . . . it's going on twenty years now, isn't it"—Press shuddered slightly, whether at the creep of mortality or the cool breeze coming off the mountain Daniel couldn't tell—"I never felt I truly knew you. At least not completely. There was always so much held in reserve, so many dark moods and blank spots when we talked, so much about your behavior I couldn't comprehend."

"Like what?" Daniel said, with an uneasy mixture of dread and curiosity—he wasn't sure he liked being told things about himself.

"Like your relationship with Alex and Porter. They're such good kids, yet you were always barking at them, especially when they were little, never satisfied with them, especially not Alex. You seemed uncomfortable when they were around."

Daniel thought for a moment. "I've always been afraid of them."

Press laughed. "Of Alex and Porter?"

"Afraid of what I might do to them."

Press looked at Daniel intently. Daniel met his gaze—he had never noticed that Press's brown eyes were flecked with green. "I don't doubt for a minute the things you've told me. It's like the last piece of a puzzle falling into place. Finally Daniel Kenning makes sense to me."

Daniel lay back in the chaise longue and looked up at the sky. He wanted to tell Press about the sense of relief flooding through him, but opening his mouth seemed too great an effort.

The head loomed big, big as a breakaway from Mount Rushmore, coming up over the blank horizon and hovering ever nearer. A smiling head, cheerfully bobbing in the empty blue air, eyes crinkling with delight. As it grew closer, larger, the bright eyes fluttered shut, the glistening lips parted. Two walls of teeth, gold inlays glittering, lolling pink tongue. He made to move back, but he was trapped, sealed somehow in this high wooden chair. The ground was far below his dangling feet in their small navy-blue shoes. Now all he could see was the vast, toothy mouth. The great tongue stiffened, darted out. He turned his head, but too late: warm wetness rasped down his cheek. He sank back into his chair as the muscular tongue sworled over his face, down his neck and shoulder, along his arm, coating the palm of his hand with warm saliva. How pleasurable it was, once he closed his eyes to shut out the huge grinning face. Relaxing, really. Made him feel quite strange inside, warm and . . . something else.

Daniel jerked into awareness. Press had tucked a quilt around him so he was muffled as a mummy, except that his left arm, having worked free, dangled over the side of the chaise longue.

Beaver was enthusiastically licking his palm. Daniel had an erection.

"Sweet dreams?" Press was standing over him, arms crossed over his broad chest. In the black silk kimono with the wide sleeves hanging down, he looked like some running-to-seed samurai.

"Pretty awful, actually." Daniel rolled over onto his side, hoping his erection beneath the thin quilt would be less obvious.

"Nightmare?"

"Sort of."

"About your father?"

"Him and me. Me in a very high chair."

"A highchair? Want to talk about it?"

"I don't think so." Daniel looked up at Press. He had never noticed what kind eyes he had—slightly sad, but warm and full of understanding. No wonder boys flocked to him. "I feel all talked out."

"I don't wonder. It's been a big day for you. Or a big night. Whatever."

"Press?"

"What?"

"What keeps you going?"

Press looked off into the far distance, at the emerald mountain and beyond. "I don't know. Sometimes it gets pretty awful, like last night with Ethan. I'm not a philosophical person. You know that. Basically I just like life, how you never know what's going to come next. Even when you're sure you do know, that's almost never what happens. I wouldn't miss it for anything."

"And love?" Daniel hoped he wasn't being too intrusive.

Press smiled. "Oh well, love. You're thinking about Ethan and Sebastian and Colin and whoever came before Colin? Truth be told, I've never put much stock in love. I like meeting new people. I like the excitement of it and the growing intimacy, learning all about a person, or as much as one ever can learn. And the endless little power games. But love itself—no, the deep, abiding, enduring, consuming kind, that's never interested me much. It makes sense for you and Leslie, what with the kids, continuing the race, that sort of thing. But for me . . . there are too many people out there, too many surprises waiting to be had, as it were."

"You don't think . . . as you grow older . . ."

"That I'll want someone to enter the Golden Years with, hand in hand? When the time comes"—Press reached down to stroke Beaver's muzzle—"I'll get a dog."

At the door, Daniel glanced back at the black-and-white photomontage with its shattered Plexiglas covering. "It does have a certain intensity like that."

"I'll probably have it fixed. Eventually. The photos are quite nice. Not especially good as photos, but I like the story they tell." Daniel followed him back over to the montage, careful not to step on the scattered cigarette butts.

"French girl did them. French from France, I mean. Not a girl, but youngish. Our age. Not old. Anyway, the photos aren't really the art, as far as I can make out. They're a record of the art. The dealer told me the name for what she does, but I forgot it. Neo-Irredentist or something like that. She invents these rather elaborate scenarios for herself and her friends and then acts them out. From what I can see, pretty much all her work involves invading other people's privacy in some way or another."

Daniel studied the photos behind the spidery fissures in the Plexiglas. Half a dozen pictures of a room in a European-looking *pension*. A brass bedstead with flowered wallpaper behind it. A table on which were neatly arranged a pocket diary, an opened white envelope, a much-folded itemized bill of some sort and a black fountain pen, uncapped. A brass bowl of plums on a gleaming windowsill. Two white shirts and a dark blazer hanging forlornly in a large armoire. And a silky peignoir carefully draped over a chair back. This last photo alone had a certain formal beauty to it, especially in the undulant balance of shadow and sheen on the nightgown.

"Read the bit at the bottom."

Daniel squatted down to read the typed paragraph on the manila card at the bottom of the montage.

"She somehow managed to get a job as a chambermaid in a small *pensione* in Venice," Press said, "and while the guests were out she took photos of their rooms. This is one from a series of six different rooms, I believe."

The paragraph explained that the bill on the table was for a night spent in that same room on a date that was, to the day, two years before the day on which the photograph was taken—the charge on the bill was for a double rather than a single room.

Daniel straightened up. "It's a very romantic photo for you to have, Press."

Press smiled. "Isn't it? Poor devil going back to Venice to remember his dead wife."

"It would make it more interesting if she weren't dead."

"You mean like in a Buñuel film? You are sick, dear. That's what I like about the piece: the more you look at it the more stories you make up about it. Or around it, at least. In that way, it's just like other people."

Daniel bent over again to pry a cigarette butt from between Beaver's clenched jaws. "Also, everything looks so composed, especially that nightgown so artfully arranged over the lyre-backed chair. What if your artist is just a brilliant set dresser? What if she never worked as a chambermaid? What if she just rented one room after another and then brought along a trunkful of props that would add up to a touching story for each room?"

"That occurred to me too. I'm not sure I like the idea."

"I do," Daniel said. "It adds another layer."

"I'd rather think it takes one away."

"That depends on whether you think art's to do with reality or artifice."

"I think art's about covering these endless walls." Press surveyed the room. "Sometimes I think about moving back to a regular place—one that makes fewer demands on me. Of course then what would I do with my art?"

"I really had better go," Daniel said.

They stood face to face at the door, Beaver eyeing it expectantly.

Press lightly touched Daniel's cheek. "You've got lots more color than when you came in."

He opened his arms, and Daniel fell into them. Press held him close, and Daniel began to cry. Press pulled him closer still. Daniel felt a stirring against his thigh. He stepped back.

"Sorry," Press said. "I find vulnerability so arousing. Even in an old thing like you."

When he opened his eyes, Leslie was standing over the daybed, holding a wooden tray. She had switched on the light over his drawing table.

"I didn't want to wake you, but I didn't imagine you'd want to sleep straight through either." She set the tray down on the battered olive-green steamer trunk that served as the workroom coffee table.

Daniel peered out the window. The streetlight shone through translucent leaves. "What time is it?"

Leslie looked at her watch. "Almost ten. I came up before supper, but you were out cold. Snoring. I can't ever remember you snoring. Rough time?"

He started to cry. Leslie sat down beside him, smoothing back his sweat-dampened hair. For an hour or so he wept in her arms, explaining the events of his night. She said little, stroking his shoulders and back. He cried so much that the front of her camisole was soon soaked through. He cried so much that he wondered what would be left of him once he was done with crying. He started to laugh.

"What's wrong?"

"I don't know. If I don't stop crying I feel like I'm going to disappear. Float away."

"You're worried there won't be anything left of you once you've cried it all out?"

"Something like that. A pretty common syndrome?" He felt crestfallen—he liked the idea that what was happening to him was unique. "Do you hear that from all your clients?"

"I was thinking about me. When my mother died. I was so angry at her when she died. I was already angry at her anyway— show me a sixteen-year-old girl who isn't angry at her mother— and then she had the gall to go and die on me. I was so furious

I couldn't mourn. I didn't shed a tear at her funeral or for a long time after. Not until I left home. I remember my first year at McGill I kept having the same dream over and over again. About this enormous iceberg suddenly melting, sweeping me and everyone I knew away."

"Is that what you'd call an anxiety dream or a wish-fulfillment one?"

"What?" She looked perplexed.

"I thought Freud said that all dreams were either expressions of anxiety or secret wishes."

"Oh, Freud. In my case, probably both. I wouldn't have admitted it at the time, but I was so angry about her dying and leaving me that I often fantasized about destroying the entire world."

"Just like that?"

"Just like that."

"I've always felt that," he said quietly.

"Wanting to destroy the world?"

"Yes. Or just him. Either alternative would have satisfied me."

"I'm sure."

"Do you think I'm crazy?"

She looked at him in surprise. "Because you hate him so much? Are you kidding, after what he did to you?"

"Not to hate him. Am I crazy to . . . to . . ."

"What, Daniel?"

"To say what I said."

"I'm not sure I follow."

He found it hard to say the words, they seemed both too much and inadequate. "To say he abused me sexually."

She took his hand. "Why's that crazy? I always thought there was something off about him. Remember the last time we stayed with them? He came to practically every meal in his swimming trunks."

"It was hot."

"That's what you said at the time. For someone who purports to hate him so much, you certainly rush to your father's defense whenever anyone says anything remotely critical about him. No one else came to meals dressed like that. And I never liked the way he was always watching Alex. Not just on that visit but any time he was around Alex. I couldn't put my finger on it then, but now it makes more sense. I always thought it was because he was waiting for Alex to do something wrong."

"That's probably true. That's the way he always was with me."

"There was more to it than that. The look he always had whenever Alex was around, it was more than simply the look of a censorious grandparent."

"What do you mean?" Daniel sat up abruptly.

"It was a hungry look. I've dealt with enough hungry fathers in family therapy to know the look, except usually it's directed at their adolescent daughters or stepdaughters. I guess that's what threw me off with your father. It never occurred to me that his look was lust."

He began to shiver.

"What's that sound?"

"My teeth."

"Oh, God. Hold on a second." She left the room and came back carrying a worn patchwork quilt, which she tucked around him. She felt his hands. "They're like ice. It's so warm in here I was going to turn on the fan. You want me to close the window?"

He shook his head. "I'll be fine." He tried to clamp his teeth together to keep them from chattering but then his whole head shook.

When the shivering subsided, he turned to her again. "You really believe me then?"

"Why would you make something like that up?"

He thought for a moment. "I don't know. Because I hated him so much, because I wanted some kind of revenge, because I'm unbalanced, a lunatic, a bad person unfit for human society."

"Even if all that were true, why would it take you this long to formulate the accusation?"

"Maybe I'm slow and bad."

"You look a little better now." She felt his brow. "Think you have a fever?"

"No."

"Somehow I don't think you're that worried about whether other people believe you."

"No?"

"I think it's more a question of whether you can allow yourself to believe what you know."

He leaned back against the wall, letting the quilt fall away from his shoulders. "I've been seesawing since last night. First I'm absolutely convinced that what I know is true, then I'm sure I've lost my mind. But even at the moment when I doubt myself most all I have to do is think of that instant of knowing, last night when I felt him in my hand, in my mouth, and I . . ." He noticed that Leslie was looking down. The fingers and thumb of his right hand had curved as though to grasp a tube of some sort. He could feel his upper lip riding up into a double sneer, the bile rising in his throat.

The next he knew, his head was between his knees. He could feel Leslie's hands pressing against the back of his neck. "Better now?"

He stared at his bare feet. His toenails needed clipping. "I think so. What happened?"

"You went really white and your eyes rolled up."

"Oh."

"You feel like sitting up?"

"Yes."

He lifted his head. The room seemed to slide to one side.

"You want to stay like that a bit longer?"

"Yes."

At last he sat up.

"Better?"

"Famished."

"Really? You're certainly all over the place tonight." She lifted the blue woven napkin that half covered the wooden tray. "How do you feel about cold grilled cheese?"

"Sounds great." He grabbed the slightly soggy sandwich and gobbled it down.

"The milk's not cold anymore either."

"I don't care," he said, draining the glass.

"Could you eat another?"

"Two more. Maybe three. And something sweet. Is there any ice cream? I'm dying for something cold and sweet."

"I think so." She stood up. "You want to come down with me, or should I bring it back up?"

"Don't go," he said.

She sat back down next to him and held him close, whispering in his ear.

"What?"

"I'm so sorry." She no longer whispered.

"It's not your fault."

"I know. But I feel so helpless, watching you like this."

"You do?"

She nodded.

"It's pretty awful," he said slowly. "But not just awful. If it were only awful I think it would be unendurable. But it feels like something new as well. It's hard to explain."

She kissed his cheek. "I don't know if you're interested. This probably isn't even a good thing to suggest. I'm not sure Henrietta would think it the proper thing to do . . ."

"What?"

"I've got a lot of material on sexual abuse at the office. You can't imagine how much. It's all about women though—father-daughter abuse, mainly. I know the literature fairly well and I don't think there's much of anything at all about father-son abuse. I believe the assumption is that it's quite rare."

"I'd like to see whatever you've got."

"Let me check at the library too. If you're sure it's all right."

"I don't think Henrietta would mind. How different can it be—father-daughter, father-son? It's all abuse."

"I don't know," Leslie said. "Instinct tells me father-son abuse could be doubly problematical."

"Why?"

"The double taboo involved. Not just incest but homosexuality too."

"Oh."

"Anyway, I'll see what there is." She stood up, picking up the tray. "So, two grilled cheese and a large bowl of chocolate mint? Shall I bring it here?"

Daniel got up from the daybed. "No, I'm coming with you."

He spent most of the weekend holed up in his workroom, reading. Leslie had brought him a thick stack of photocopied articles, inexpensively produced pamphlets and information sheets as well as four slim paperbacks and one cloth-bound textbook called *Patterns in Deviant Behavior.* He rapidly worked his way through them all, reading with more fascination and urgency than discrimination and critical detachment. The pamphlets and paperbacks tended to have lurid titles, like *Kiss Daddy Goodnight,* or *Now He Lays Me Down to Sleep.* They also were jargon packed, full of self-help homilies, twelve-step programs for quick recovery—he even came across something called "The Incest Survivor's Prayer." The paperbacks in particular seemed to make the same points and repeat the same catchphrases again and again— "healing the wounds of sexual abuse" occurred most often and most vividly—as though truth were established through incantatory reiteration. After a few hours of steady reading it occurred to him that the repetitiousness might mask profound hysteria and panic, and there Daniel thought he could find a mirror for his own behavior and emotions of the last few days: the obsessions, denials, recriminations that swirled through his mind during every waking moment. All the paperbacks and brochures, no matter how clumsily written or incompletely argued, how fanciful the leaps of logic or wildly flailing the rhetoric, seemed to have their source in truth, whether the author admitted she was writing from personal experience or not. There was no way of verifying this assumption, but he sensed that the rage and pain underlying every run-on sentence, every jerry-built paragraph, were genuine. These women writers—for they were without exception women—appeared to be united by an anger that, however inarticulate and extreme, had nothing to do with madness. Their outrage was often uncontrolled, only rarely framed by reason or objectivity, but whatever else it might be their fury struck him as pure and fierce. As just. They all of them hit the same crashing notes, again and again, about male power and dominance, about exploitation of the weak, about generations —no, millennia—of victimization, and in a way, Daniel found he envied them their anvil chorus because these women at least had each other, while he had only their books and pamphlets, their purple prose and exhaustive checklists.

Checklists. Every book and pamphlet had one. "How to Tell If You Have Been Sexually Abused," "Telltale Symptoms of Sexual Abuse," "Twenty Signs of Sexual Abuse." Some of the lists included indicators so vague and all-inclusive as to be meaningless—"victim has difficulty with sexual intimacy or exhibits sexually addictive behavior," "abused child feels alienated as adolescent," "object of abuse often feels depressed and hopeless or, on the other hand, anxious and manic." But certain indicators or "symptoms" seemed to recur on every list and set off alarms in his memory. These centered especially on the behavior of sexually abused children as they approached puberty and entered adolescence. "Child sinks into deep depression, manifested by sudden weight gain or loss or other eating disorders . . . victim who was previously a strong student suddenly loses interest in school, her grades plummet . . . self-mutilation is common, often focusing on hands, hair or genitalia . . . victim exhibits suicidal tendencies, often attempts to take own life . . ." And Daniel had thought he was the only one. A skinny, nervous kid, at eleven he had suddenly ballooned out, feasting compulsively on sweets. The after-school orgies he held in the privacy of his room, gulping down Caramilk bars, bagsful of Smarties and, at Christmastime, entire three-tiered boxes of chocolate-covered cherries. At about the same time, his grades dropped so precipitously and inexplicably that the school authorities called his mother in for A Talk. At twelve he picked at his toes until they bled, stripped down the big toenail on his right foot until there was no nail left, just a thin membrane so painful that he limped about for weeks. When questioned about his bloody-toed socks, he said he had a hangnail. As for suicide attempts . . . Daniel didn't want to think about those now.

He found the cool objectivity of the clinical articles a relief after the needy insistence of the self-help tracts. In one he read, "In families where sexual abuse occurs, mothers frequently play a diminished role. These mothers often present as passive, dependent personalities with a low sense of self-esteem . . . who are deprived of self-fulfillment within the family. Generally, the domineering husband minimizes or actively denigrates the spouse's role as mother and wife." Daniel remembered from childhood the jokes his father had lobbed at his mother: "Pass the tea, bag" . . . "Hand me the baseball, bat" . . . "When you hit forty, I'm going to trade you in for two twenties." He could see his mother's flinching smile. Although she majored in classics at university and briefly taught Greek and Latin at a Vancouver girls' school, after their marriage his father had forbidden her to work, saying it would make people think he was incapable of providing for his family. "In this way," the article continued, "children come to view their mothers as powerless and incapable of protecting them." The article also claimed that abuse victims felt contemptuous of their mothers' weaknesses and ended up identifying with their fathers' omnipotence. That is, the victims took on their fathers' belittling attitudes toward their mothers. In short, victims either consciously or unwittingly sided with their oppressors, right down to replicating the characteristics and behavior of the men who abused them. Thus the abused sometimes ended up abusers themselves.

Daniel wasn't sure he followed all this. He thought he had always hated his father too much ever to consider identifying with him. Suddenly the beautiful little boy from the Chinese restaurant ran through his mind. He threw the article aside and picked up the next slightly blurred photocopy, the last article in the stack.

"Characteristics, Pathology and Etiology of Father-Son Sexual Abuse." He stared at the title. At last an article that referred directly to him. He read the first line with a feeling of rising despair. "Very little is known about father-son sexual abuse . . ." He scanned the page. A lot of information already covered in the articles about father-daughter abuse. Then his eyes rested on the subhead, "The Tyrant":

These fathers use aggression, force, threats, intimidation and fear to assure compliance. They do not develop close or loving friendships within or outside the family unit, and may in fact become extremely jealous and possessive if other family members develop external relationships. These fathers may attempt to forbid or undermine such relationships.

It occurred to Daniel that his father had no close male friends. It occurred to him that when he was an adolescent his father had despised or ridiculed any close friend Daniel happened to cultivate. This one was too wild, that one too effeminate, a third was Jewish.

"Boys who are sexually involved with their fathers," the article went on, "often experience extreme emotional dislocation as they enter adolescence . . . these boys experience overwhelming guilt . . . this guilt metamorphoses into deep feelings of self-hatred . . . abused, the boys take on the blame for the abuse; they were abused because they were bad to begin with . . . such boys also manifest a deep sense of hostility toward their father . . . over the long term, it is as though the boys have been 'psychologically murdered,' and the murderer is the father." Daniel read that paragraph again: "Overwhelming guilt . . . deep feelings of self-hatred . . . 'psychologically murdered,' and the murderer is the father."

That sounded about right to him. He thought of what Leslie had said about the double taboo of father-son incest. He considered his father's attitude toward homosexuality, the attitude of his father's generation toward homosexuality. Could it be that, in father-son incest, the father projects what he most fears and loathes within himself—his own homosexual desires—onto his son? And then, because the son comes to embody that despised homosexuality, does the father attempt to obliterate the desire by destroying the child, emotionally or otherwise? He saw the softball driving into his face, the rose trellis rushing toward his bike.

He laid the article aside, then picked it up again, slowly turning back the photocopied pages one by one. Even as a small child, especially as a small child, he had been obsessed by the thought that his parents—not just his father but his mother too—wanted to kill him. As he grew older it was merely that "someone" wanted to kill him: a vague and faceless stranger who chased him up every stair he climbed, who lurked in corners, hid in the basement. When he reached adolescence he had the same nightmare again and again—he was in his parents' house and someone was shooting at him. Windows, lamps, bibelots shattered all about him. In the dream the shots came from outside the house, but when he went away to school he stopped having the dreams.

"Psychological murder." He wondered if a parent's unarticulated desire for a child's obliteration could cause the child to comprehend that desire. Did the child, ever helpful, ever loyal, translate that desire into its own death wish? Did the son become suicidal in order to accommodate, oblige the father? Not only going willingly to the slaughter, did the child also become Abraham and Isaac in one?

So many questions, Daniel thought, and a single photocopied article with only the most unsettling answers. He put the article aside and lay back on the daybed, immobile. Except, he noticed, his hand was picking at the skin of his big toe. He thought he could write his own pamphlet, compose his own endless checklist, full of ranting propositions and half-baked hypotheses, clumsily crying out his horror, rage and despair.

He stayed for a long time in the small blue-tiled shower off the workroom, setting the nozzle for massage and letting the jets of water pulse against the back of his neck. The water calmed him, washing away the words, the hectic mumble of colloquial and clinical voices.

At last he turned off the shower and opened the marbled glass door. Leslie stood at the sink, a large mint green bath towel wrapped around her. She had laid out a number of small tubes and bottles on the narrow countertop.

"Hi," she said without turning.

"Hi."

"Hope you don't mind—the boys have taken over the downstairs bathroom. Heavy night on the town."

"Oh." He reached for his towel.

"Anything wrong?" She smeared a strong-scented white cream onto her cheeks.

"Why do you ask?" He carefully toweled himself down.

"You just look—I don't know—distant."

"Oh?" He could see her watching him in the medicine cabinet mirror.

"How are you getting along with the reading?"

"All right. Excuse me, please." He reached round her to open the medicine cabinet and took out his deodorant.

"If I have time, Monday I'll stop by the library at Concordia and see if they have anything beyond what I turned up at McGill."

"Don't bother." He carefully ran the deodorant ball under each arm and then reached round her again to put the deodorant back in the medicine cabinet.

"But I thought you said—"

"I said don't bother." He slammed the medicine cabinet door. The mirror split horizontally in two, the bottom half splintering into the sink.

"Daniel, what on earth . . ." He saw half her face in the remaining mirror, watched her spin around. Her face was gray except for two shiny streaks of white cream across her cheekbones.

"Get out of my bathroom." Fists shook in front of him. It took him a moment to realize they were his.

Leslie stepped back against the sink. He stared at his trembling fists, clenched so tight they'd gone pale as her face.

"Daniel," she said in a low voice, "it's all right. Really it is." Slowly she reached out and grasped his trembling wrists. "Let's go into your workroom."

She slowly backed him out of the bathroom.

A light breeze off the St. Lawrence came into the workroom through the big double window. The evening sky was fading from gold to rose. Leslie steered him to the high stool before the drawing table. She let go his wrists and wiped his brow with both hands. "You're bathed in sweat."

He started to cry. "I'm so sorry."

She held him to her. "It's all right."

"I could have hurt you. The mirror. I was going to hit you."

"I don't think so. Is that what you were thinking—that you were going to smash my face?"

"No. I don't know."

She looked into his eyes. "That's not what it felt like. You looked more like you were trying to ward off blows than give them."

He shook his head. "All I could think was that I wanted you out of there. I would have hit you in order to achieve that. You don't know what I'm capable of."

"I think I have a pretty good idea by now. You haven't hit me, or even tried to, in the ten years we've been together—there's no reason why you would start now. I'm not sure it was a good idea for you to read all that material, not so soon. It's too much to digest all at once. You've spent practically the whole weekend up here, as if you were preparing for an exam or something."

He got up from the stool and retrieved the box of tissues from atop the steamer trunk. "It's just that it's all coming out now—all the things I've hidden for so long, hidden from myself, you, from everyone. All the evil's finally pouring out."

"Give me one too." He handed her a tissue. She wiped the white smears from her cheeks. "What you neglect to mention is that it's not your evil. You're remembering things that were done to you, not things you did."

"I know. It all sounds so logical when you say it, but when I'm alone with my thoughts . . ."

"How much more do you have to go?"

"With the reading? I finished."

"Everything?"

He nodded.

"But that was a week's worth of stuff at least."

"You know I've always been a quick study."

"No wonder you're having such a tough time of it."

"The worst was the last one I read. About victims becoming abusers."

"But that's not true in your case. You know it's not true."

He turned to her. He could feel the anger rising again. "You don't have to protect me anymore. I can handle the truth about myself. I don't need two therapists. You know as well as I do what the games we play mean."

She looked mystified. "What games?"

"The sex games."

She started to laugh. "Really, Daniel. Is that what's bothering you? Do you think what we do together makes you a child molester? Do I look like a child to you?"

A faint film of sweat had formed on her breasts. "It's the scenario we play out that bothers me," he said. "We wouldn't be playing it at all if it didn't have some basis in reality."

"Its basis is in fantasy. No one says you're forbidden to dream. Scratch any couple who've been together any time at all and I'm sure you'd find all sorts of kinky behavior."

"You know that for a fact? From your clients?"

"Not just from my clients. Sissy Cournoyer told me that she and Lucien have some quite detailed scenarios."

"Really? Like what?"

"I promised I wouldn't tell."

"I won't either. I promise."

For a moment Leslie looked doubtful. "Well, it's basically a rape fantasy."

Daniel couldn't help laughing. "Somehow Lucien doesn't strike me as the macho type."

"Precisely," Leslie said.

"What do you mean?"

"Sissy dresses up in their oldest son's high school letter jacket, with a hooded sweatshirt and tight jeans. I gather her costume is unvarying."

"And Lucien?"

"He's allowed a little more fashion leeway, except it's always something fairly frilly."

Daniel wasn't sure he followed. "But how . . ."

"With a dildo, I assume."

"I don't believe it. I can't believe Sissy actually told you that." He thought for a moment. "What did you tell her?"

"Nothing, really."

"Leslie . . ."

"Not about the school uniform. But I may have mentioned the clothesline and the Ping-Pong paddle."

"You didn't."

"Who's she going to tell, other than Lucien?"

"That's true."

She glanced at her watch. "I have to get ready to go. You're sure you don't want to come? Hilary said it would be just a few people for drinks. Come and have one drink. No one's going to mind if you leave early."

He shook his head. "I really don't feel much like being around people."

"I know. Do you want me to stay here?"

Daniel glanced at the darkening sky. "No, I'll be okay."

"Sure?"

"Sure. Give my love to Hilary."

"And my love to you." She kissed his lips. "I won't be late."

He watched the dark triangle of her bare back as she ran down the stairs. Then he went back into the bathroom and began gingerly picking pieces of mirror out of the sink.

"Apart from the bathroom mirror, no real damage was done?" Henrietta turned in her chair to glance at the carriage clock. She picked it up and slowly wound it. The brass clock flashed parallelograms of light onto the wall above her head.

"No." He was surprised to see that it was only three-thirty— he felt he had been talking for at least an hour.

"But you didn't actually hit her, or even touch her?"

He shook his head.

"Did you want to?"

"I don't know. It all happened so fast—I went completely out of control."

"Not completely."

"I didn't know what I was doing."

"The fact remains that you didn't hit Leslie."

"True."

She set the clock down, studying it intently. "The second hand seems to stick an instant every time it passes the hour hand."

"Maybe you should have it looked at."

"Maybe." She draped one sunburned arm over the back of her chair and leaned forward. "I'd like you to tell me more about the places where you think the abuse occurred."

He sat back in his chair and crossed his ankles. "It isn't very clear to me. I remember physical sensations, but to associate them with a specific place . . ."

"Try closing your eyes."

His eyelids became translucent screens that bright colors floated or flashed across. He felt drowsy.

"Don't work at it." Her voice seemed to come from inside his head. "Just let go and see what comes to the surface."

"Okay." He heard faint music, the buzz of flies, cicadas throbbing. "His workroom."

"Where was that? In the house?"

"No, above the old stables. Behind the house. He would have me sand and paint, for the models he made. He had this old radio with a big glowing dial. I remember Hawaiian music for some reason."

"Did you like to help?"

He shook his head. "He made me. He said I spent too much time with Mother. Said I was turning into a real sissy."

"How old would you have been?"

"Three or four."

"Not older?"

"I don't think so."

"Other places?"

Tires on a gravel road, the taste of dust in his mouth, warmth on the back of his legs. "His car. An old Chevy—1950 model, I think. Dark green. Red plaid seat covers. Remember I told you when I first came to you about trying to jump out of it while it was still moving?" He looked at her from under his lashes. She was nodding, but he was sure she didn't remember.

"Anywhere else?"

He didn't have to think. "My crib."

"Your crib?"

She didn't believe him. He opened his eyes. She looked angry.

"My crib."

"Surely not."

He uncrossed his ankles and flexed his shoulders. "First you tell me to relax and let my mind go, see what surfaces. Then you don't believe me when I name the one place I'm sure of."

For a moment he thought she was going to reach out and touch his knee, but then she evidently thought better of it. "Daniel, if what you see on my face is a look of disbelief, it has nothing to do with not believing you. Do you understand that? It's simply that no matter how often I hear it—and you'd be surprised how often I do—I can never get accustomed to the thought of someone molesting a child in its crib."

"Those are the first memories I have—the bars of my crib and him pushing through them. I dream about that."

She nodded slowly.

"I even . . ." He stopped. It seemed too ridiculous to say.

"What?"

"I keep dreaming about being in my highchair."

She winced. He knew he ought to have kept quiet.

"What else do you associate with your highchair?"

What was the point? "Nothing."

"Not necessarily abuse. Do you have other memories concerning it?"

He laughed softly. "It was a family joke."

"What?"

"That I was always falling out of my highchair. I had to go to the hospital for stitches a couple of times." He pointed to the small white scar on his forehead.

"How did you fall out of your highchair?"

"I think they always said I rocked it so much that it tipped right over."

"But surely highchairs are built to be so stable they won't tip over."

"You would have thought so. But you know, I'm not really

sure any of this is worth pursuing. Now that I've read all the material Leslie gave me, not to mention coming here to see you, my whole childhood seems to be nothing but abuse of one kind or another. Every memory I have now is tainted, I'm that obsessed. How do you know that what I'm telling you isn't completely distorted?"

"Let's stick with the memories for now. See what comes up. We can sort them out later. Can you live with that for now?"

"I guess."

"Do you want a glass of water?"

The question startled him. "Why do you ask?"

"You keep licking your lips."

He ran his tongue over his upper lip. "I was thinking . . . you know this really is becoming ridiculous, a kind of monomania . . ."

"What were you thinking?"

"He used to tape my mouth shut at night."

"What?" Her eyes seemed paler than usual, almost silver in the light.

"I was a mouth breather. Still am. He was concerned that this would somehow deform my palate and that eventually I would have to have corrective surgery. So when I went to bed he would come and tape my mouth shut."

"Every night?"

"It seemed to go in cycles. There were times when he did it every night and then long periods when he forgot all about it."

"And how old were you at this time?"

"I think it started when I was quite young—two or three—and continued, I don't know, until I was eight or nine."

"What kind of tape?"

"Cellotape at first, except when it got wet it would fall off. He tried black electrical tape for a while before settling on that kind of adhesive tape that's used for bandaging—he'd bring it home from the hospital. It really hurts when you tear it off."

"But if you ordinarily breathed through your mouth it must have been uncomfortable for you to breathe through your nose, especially if your mouth was taped shut."

"I remember feeling pretty panicky. I would lie there worrying

I was going to suffocate. Usually sometime during the night I'd manage to rip it off."

"Where was your mother during all this?"

"There."

"He taped your mouth shut night after night and she never said a word?"

"Well, there was a good medical reason for it, wasn't there? And he was—is—a doctor."

Henrietta clasped her hands together. "Yes, I suppose it must have been hard for your mother to argue with a real medical doctor."

Was that sarcasm he heard? And if so, was it aimed at his mother or his father? Or at both?

"Do you find you're dreaming a lot, Daniel?"

"Yes."

"Different dreams or the same one over and over?"

"Two or three different dreams, but over and over."

"You've already told me about the crib and the highchair. What's the third?"

He didn't know how to talk about the third. It wasn't, to be absolutely truthful, like the crib and highchair dreams. It wasn't new—he'd been dreaming it for a long time. "I have to go to the bathroom. I'm away at school. I must be thirteen or fourteen. I go down to the locker room, this vast underground room with rows and rows of lockers, benches and stalls. I go from stall to stall, pushing open door after door, but every toilet is coated in shit, thick yellow-brown shit. And then I notice that the floor's ankle-deep in shit and piss and the benches and lockers are smeared with it. The whole locker room's so swimming in shit that there isn't a single clean place where I can go to the bathroom. Isn't that a bizarre dream?"

"Not that bizarre."

"Why not?"

"It sounds to me like a dream about shame."

"Shame?" That had never occurred to him. He thought he remembered from psychology lectures at university that shit was associated with death.

"Perhaps your sense of shame for having participated, however unwillingly, in the abuse. Or perhaps even more than that. Is it possible that you experienced pleasure during the abuse? That wouldn't be unusual, especially for a small child, one who would do almost anything for love and tenderness. But remembering now, dreaming about what happened so long ago, maybe you're remembering pleasure as well. Dreaming about pleasure. That could be very frightening for you because it suggests complicity. Do you feel you're so foul that there's no place dirty enough for you to shit, not even a bathroom covered in it?"

He glanced at the little clock. Two minutes past four. Should he remind her that the session was over? "I don't know. Maybe. It's a lot to take in."

She leaned forward with a suddenness that made him jump and rested her sun-mottled hands on her bare white knees. "I just had a thought. You know what I wish we could do?"

"What?"

"I wish we could bring your mother and father here. Wouldn't it be something if we could all sit down together and thrash this thing out? Just think, Daniel, if your father was sitting right here in front of you. What would you say to him, what sort of questions would you ask him?"

He couldn't seem to catch his breath. He could hear air whistling in and out of his nostrils but none of it seemed to be reaching his lungs. If he didn't take a deep breath he thought he was going to pass out, but if he did open his mouth he was afraid he might scream at her. With all his strength he held on to the arms of his chair—he would remain frozen in that position until it was safe to move. Sunlight seemed to come through the blinds in hungry waves.

"What is it, Daniel?" He sensed that she had stopped moving too. "Where are you now?"

"Nowhere."

"I didn't mean to frighten you."

"I don't want him to come here."

"I'm sorry, Daniel. I'm afraid I wasn't very clear. When I say things like that—'I wish your parents were here' or 'What would you say to your father if he was sitting right there?'—I'm asking you to fantasize. Like a lot of what we do here, it's a kind of exercise, allowing you to step out of the old established patterns for a moment or two and enter the realm of possibility and change."

He thought he followed that. "But you sprang it on me so suddenly. I guess I got scared."

"Of him sitting across from you?"

He shook his head. "No. I could handle that. You'd be here, for one thing. I was thinking about the last time they came to visit. The guest room's on the third floor, off my workroom, which means they have to go through my workroom to get to the shower."

"This is the bathroom where you and Leslie had your run-in?"

"Yes. It was no real problem having them use it when they got up in the morning or before they went to bed—I just wouldn't go to my workroom then. But Dad . . . during the day, rather than use the powder room downstairs or the full bathroom on the second floor, would climb two flights of stairs to use my bathroom."

"Perhaps the others were occupied?"

Why was she suddenly siding with him? "That's not the point. He would come in while I was working, and he would leave the door to the bathroom open. He would sit on the toilet and talk to me."

"I see. What would he talk about?"

"He's been having prostate problems, so he would sit there for ten or fifteen minutes, straining and sighing, talking about how hard it was for him to pee. 'Micturate' was the word he used."

"All this with the door wide open?"

"You think I'm being overly fastidious, don't you?"

"I was thinking that in abusive families the boundaries are always a little loose."

"What do you mean?"

"That behind closed doors a lot of behavior goes on that would never be tolerated in an ordinary household. That the usual rules of privacy don't obtain in a family like yours."

"In warm weather he always parades around with his shirt off, his belt unbuckled and his fly a third of the way open. In winter too, when he's just hacking around in his work clothes, he never bothers to zip up."

"And no one ever says anything about this loose behavior?"

"What would you say? He'd just get angry or make fun of you for being a prude."

"What about when you were still living at home? Did he do things like that then?"

Daniel shuddered in spite of himself. He stood up. "Do you mind if I shut the blinds? The sun's right in my eyes."

"Be my guest."

He could feel her eyes follow him as he crossed the room. He cranked the miniblinds half shut, then all the way. "At home my room was in the attic. I had my own bathroom, sort of. Mum and Dad's bedroom was on the second floor, with a bathroom en suite. But before I went away to school—when I was eleven, twelve—every morning my father would climb the stairs to my room and use the bathroom there."

"Did he give any reason for doing that?"

"He said Mum was monopolizing theirs."

"He would wait until you were finished, or would he come in while you were still there?"

"What do you think?" He ran one finger down the blinds so they pinged like a tinny xylophone. "I tried getting up early, or waiting till the last minute, but it was as though he was downstairs, listening, waiting for me to stir. Then he'd barge in and throw off his robe. He was always naked, never with even a towel around his waist. He'd sit on the toilet while I was washing or showering and talk about his bowel movements while they were occurring. It was so disgusting." He glanced at his watch and cranked the blinds open again. "It's really late, you know. Almost four-thirty. We've gone way over."

"I know. You're my last client today. So what happened on the weekend between you and Leslie is beginning to make more sense to me."

He turned and looked down into her eyes. "To me too."

"Do you think you could tell Leslie about all this?"

"I think so." He went back to his chair and stood behind it, grasping the chair back.

"At the beginning of the session you said that you thought the sexual abuse stopped rather abruptly."

"That's the impression I have—I don't have any way of verifying it."

"And how old would you have been when it stopped?"

"Four or five—it's hard to be sure."

"But it seems to me that the abusive atmosphere continued as long as you were living at home. Continues, in fact, when he comes to visit, when you go there. Even though you're an adult now and he's an old man."

"When it happens, when he bursts in on me, I feel like a kid. I want to scream at him, tell him to get the fuck out of my bathroom."

"But why act like a kid when you're capable of acting like an adult? What would happen if you told your father, the next time he visited, to close the bathroom door when he came up to your workroom?"

"He'd probably act hurt. Or angry. Or both."

"Do you think you could deal with a hurt and angry old man?"

He thought for a long time before answering. "I think it would be a real pleasure."

He was supposed to meet the ski resort developers for drinks at the Ritz at five-thirty, so he had a full hour to kill. He was glad of that, for he always felt so vague, even drowsy, after a session. Instead of following Sherbrooke downtown to the Ritz, he crossed the street and entered Westmount Park.

It was surprisingly empty for an August afternoon. But then it was Friday and most people had headed off to their places in the Laurentians or the Townships, at least those who weren't away on actual vacations. Daniel, who refused to own a car, could see no point in owning a country place either—just another bother when you came right down to it, a weekend commute in hot, honking traffic in order to sit beside some polluted lake and stare at pines and maples browned and filigreed by acid rain. Besides, though he had grown up in the country, he was now a city boy at heart—Mont-Royal, Murray Hill, Westmount Park were enough for him.

Today the Westmount Park playground was nearly empty. Two West Indian nannies in pastel uniforms murmured together on a green wooden bench while their infant charges crawled back and forth over their white-shod feet. Daniel followed the curving path past the ornamental pond. He saw that the municipal authorities had finally seen fit to buy new ducks. One morning in June a groundsman had discovered the corpses of eight ducks— mother, father and six little ones—their severed heads scattered about them in the grass. The outcry was immediate and strong. VANDALISM! the headline in the Westmount *Examiner* screamed. Assorted Mods and Skinheads, who each summer night occupied different corners of the small park, were hauled in by Westmount Security and interrogated, according to Alex and Porter, mercilessly and at length. So many letters of outrage at "today's youth" poured in to the *Examiner* that two full pages were given over to them. Almost as an afterthought an SPCA vet was called in to inspect the feathered cadavers. "Raccoons," he quickly pronounced. "Often they do it just for the hell of it. They tend to hate loud noises—the quacking just seems to set them off."

The big circular flower bed at the intersection of three walkways was starting to look beaten down by the hard August sun. Asters and zinnias sagged slightly, outer petals paling and sere. Red-hot pokers were going purple with death. Only the sharp-scented marigolds seemed sure of holding their color much longer.

Ahead of him, on the elementary school playing field that abutted the park, Daniel could see a heavyset middle-aged man in ill-fitting white gym shorts and a red rugby jersey watching a small boy steer his bike across the sun-parched grass. The bike was obviously too big for the boy, who was surely no more than five. The handlebars were of the rakish V-shaped sort, not the sensible parallel-to-the-ground kind a child needs on his first bike. The blue seat, made of some plastic material that sparkled like glitter in the hot sun, was set far too high. But the little boy, in soiled yellow T-shirt and faded green shorts, pedaled along heroically, the bike pitching wildly back and forth. The father stood impassively watching, hands on hips, big gut hanging over the sagging elastic waistband of his shorts.

Daniel halted in his tracks, not knowing what to do next. He wanted to retreat, avoid this scene, but he knew he couldn't. He had to walk by it—pass, in fact, within ten feet of the father if he followed the curving walk. He thought it was somehow important to keep walking, to be a witness.

He drew near enough to the father to see his sun-splotched face, the walruslike drooping mustache, the same angry orange color as the sparse hair raked across his reddened pate. Daniel could see the cold blue eyes, the full, liverish lips. The man was breathing hard. Damp patches of sweat spread out from under his arms, which were freckled and thick with orange hair. By contrast his legs were pale beneath their reddish pelt, which ended abruptly six or seven inches below the knee, leaving a gleaming white shank.

The little boy pedaled valiantly toward his father and, finally, a few yards short of reaching him, the handlebars wrenched out of the boy's hands, the bike falling one way, the boy the other. He lay facedown, motionless, in the short dry grass. Daniel almost cried out in alarm. The man lumbered toward the boy, heavy dugs and belly flopping. With one arm he picked the boy up and set him right, brushing grass and twigs from his shirt and shorts. He remained stooping over, one meaty hand on the boy's shoulder. "I thought the seat was too high for you."

The boy cried softly, rubbing his eyes.

"That's clearly what the problem is," the man said. "You did fine on Zachary's bike the other day. But Daddy set the seat too high. No wonder you couldn't manage it."

The boy stopped crying. He leaned into his father's soft, sagging body. "I was okay, but then it flipped me. I think I hit something in the grass."

The man smiled and shook his head, hugging the boy to him. "No, it was Daddy's fault. Come on, let's go back to the house and get a wrench. I'm sorry. I always forget what a little guy you are."

"Then can we come back and try again?"

"If you feel like it. That was a pretty big fall you took. Knocked the wind right out of you."

"I'm okay now."

The father righted the fallen bike and with one hand guided it across the playing field. His other hand completely enveloped his son's small hand.

Daniel thought he might follow them home, at a discreet distance, just to listen to them talk. So this was how it was done—it looked so easy. But the tears were running so fast behind his dark glasses he had to sit down under a tree.

"Daniel, may I see you for a moment?"

He turned around impatiently, his elbow toppling a stack of slides onto the floor. He specifically had asked the receptionist to keep everyone out of the presentation room until after lunch.

Glancing up he saw a figure silhouetted in the doorway. "I'm sorry," he said, fumbling with the rheostat on the rosewood console. "I can't see a thing." The recessed lighting along the ceiling's perimeter came up to a soft amber glow. "Good Christ, Kelley."

"I can come back later if this isn't a good time for you." Kelley Athanatopoulos shrank back in the doorway, one hand on the door handle.

"Of course not, Kelley. Come in, come in." He bent to retrieve the spilled slides. He hadn't seen Kelley around the office for so long he had assumed she was gone for good.

Kelley made her way slowly down the narrow carpeted stairs that bisected the curving rows of thickly upholstered theater seats, demurely holding her clutch purse before her. Daniel saw she had exercised remarkable restraint in her dress: she had on a simple linen sheath cinched at the waist with a braided leather thong, beige cloth gloves that nearly reached her elbows and a becoming—perhaps on her alone—leopard-skin pillbox hat with a short bronze-colored veil.

"Nice outfit, Kelley."

"Thanks, Daniel." She paused at the foot of the three steps leading up to the dais and looked at him expectantly, her big dark eyes glowing. "Can you believe, I got the whole thing at a *marché aux puces* in Dijon for, let me see, just under thirty dollars. Isn't that extraordinary?"

Daniel agreed it was. And she looked extraordinary in the dim light, perfectly turned out for a warm September day. A warm September day in 1962. The clothes called attention to her, but not in the insistent way of the cocktail dress she had worn to poor Gillian's memorial service. Besides, he was beginning to see that Kelley, even drably dressed (although he couldn't quite imagine that), would draw attention all by herself—the nut-brown skin, narrow waist and high, full breasts, the gleaming hair pulled back into a tight chignon, the warmth radiating from her slightly hyperthyroid eyes. Somehow over the summer she had turned into a beautiful, rather than just beautifully eccentric, young woman.

"You look splendid, Kelley. You can come up."

She stepped up to the console and took both his hands, offering her cheek to be kissed. Daniel, leaning forward from the waist, brushed her left cheek, then her right with his lips. "You look pretty good yourself, Daniel. It's amazing—you seem so rested and happy. And your face is different, as though years have fallen away."

He didn't know what to say.

"You're sure I'm not interrupting?" She looked at the slide projected on the screen over his shoulder.

"Big presentation this afternoon. I'm afraid I'm a bit rattled."

She studied the image more closely. "It looks like a cloister of some kind."

Daniel laughed. "Actually it's a shopping arcade for a ski resort we're doing at Val Blanc."

"It's really beautiful—there's a real classical feel to it."

"I'm worried the clients may find it a bit too restrained for their taste."

"I'm sure they'll love it." She stood gazing at him intently.

He felt suddenly warm, as though a current of some sort were coursing between them. "What can I do for you, Kelley?"

She started, as if suddenly aware she had been staring at him. "Do? I don't think there's anything you can do for me. I know this is going to sound silly to you, but I'm here because of a dream."

"A dream."

"I know you think I'm strange . . ."

He shook his head to indicate such a thought had never crossed his mind.

". . . and I freely admit I am. I took the summer off to bum around Europe . . ."

That explained why he hadn't seen her around the firm.

". . . and it was a truly mind-opening experience for me. I met so many fascinating people. In a way I felt like I was returning to my roots, especially during my stay in Ireland . . ."

He tried to picture the Athanatopoulos clan, quaffing retsina with shamrocks in their hair.

". . . but why I wanted to talk to you, to see you, really, is that I had the most troubling dream about you, it must have been sometime in June. I was staying with some feminist druids in Somerset—they were squatting in the ruins of a fourteenth-century abbey. It was gorgeous, thick stone walls going up only so far and then sky and stars. I was lying there with Christabel in our sleeping bag . . ."

He felt crestfallen, not that he had ever seriously entertained the idea of trying to seduce someone as young as Kelley. Or as crazy.

". . . half-awake and half-asleep, when I had this shockingly vivid dream about you."

"Me?" Daniel registered that he was experiencing a spontaneous erection. He casually sidled to the far end of the console.

" 'Dream' isn't very exact. More like a vision, but it was so troubling that the second I got back I knew I had to come and see how you were getting along."

"As you can see," he said, leaning into the console, "I'm perfectly fine."

Kelley withdrew two long topaz-tipped pins from her hat and, with both hands, removed it. "I hope you don't mind, but I've been wearing this ever since I got in this morning, and it's starting to make me feel like a pagoda."

"You've only just arrived?"

"Didn't I tell you? Jeremy and I got a last-minute deal on a charter."

Jeremy?

She removed the black elastic band that held her chignon in place. Her glossy hair tumbled down about her face. "It wasn't your typical narrative dream. More like a series of separate symbolic pictures. I can't remember them all now—I wrote them down in my dream book, except I think I must have left it at a herbalist collective outside Barcelona—but in one of them you were trapped naked inside this small wooden cage and someone was poking at you through the bars with a big stick. In another, it was like a Madonna and child, maybe because I'd just come back from Italy, and you were clearly the child. It was a baby's body but with your grown-up face. The Madonna was holding a bowl of milk so the milk poured over your face. You had stigmata all over—blood was spilling everywhere in little ruby-colored streams. It was very disturbing. I almost forgot, the Madonna had a beard. I don't know what that means."

His erection had gone. He said quietly, "Can you remember any others?"

She shook her head. "There was another, I'm sure of that, but all I can remember are green mountains, a balsamy smell and water gushing from a snake's mouth. I'm not sure why that's related to you. The other two . . . I thought and thought about them, all the time I was traveling around, and I got the sense that something happened to you when you were very young. Something to do with your parents, maybe." Kelley bit her lower lip.

"I don't know how," Daniel said, stacking and restacking a small pile of slides, "but you're dead-on."

She gently put her arms around him, pressing her warm cheek against his. His erection came surging back. Her arms seemed to press through his slightly damp shirt right into his skin. He began to shake. For a moment he thought her arms were going to pass through him.

"I'm so relieved to see that you're all right," she said, lips brushing the stubble on his jaw. "Better than all right."

She stood back and surveyed him carefully. "You have a kind of transparency now, like an angel. You'll make it through. Even the pain in your stomach will go away."

He hadn't been aware there was a pain in his stomach until she named it. Then he realized it had been gnawing there since Gillian's memorial service. "How soon?"

"Oh, I don't know that. But soon." She took her purse, hat and gloves from the rosewood console. "I have to go now," she said, rewinding her chignon and settling the pillbox hat into place. "I'm supposed to meet Jeremy and Christabel for lunch at Sans-Souci. Care to join us?"

"I'd like to, Kelley, but I can't. Thank you for dropping by to check up on me. It means a lot."

"I can see that, Daniel," Kelley said and, with a valedictory flick of one gloved hand, slowly mounted the stairs to the bright doorway.

They trooped into the Taureau d'Or, Alex and Porter first, then Leslie and finally Daniel, bringing up the rear. As Alex, Porter and Leslie followed the maître d' across the room, Daniel watched the other diners looking up in surprise at this striking woman and her two handsome sons. They formed such an aloof and self-contained trio, so sure of themselves and their right to walk out into the world. Daniel wondered if they ever experienced the same insecurities he did, the same sense of being in some way inadequate to the world's demands. The confidence of their stately progress suggested otherwise, the boys looking oddly dignified in the three-button suits they had unearthed at a *vieux stock* shop in St-Henri. Leslie, still brown from working in the garden, was nearly as tall as her towering sons. She never gave much thought to clothes, buying her blue button-down shirts by the half dozen in the men's department of Howarth's. Her trousers, run up for her by a Polish tailor on the Main, were invariably the same cut: tweed, gabardine or poplin, depending on the season, high-waisted, baggy and cuffed, held up by a cracked alligator belt filched from Daniel's closet, a belt he in turn had once filched from his father. Daniel couldn't think of the last time he had seen Leslie in a dress, although three or four hung in her armoire, waiting to do service at a wedding or a funeral. Tonight her one concession to femininity was a double strand of pearls, a gift from Daniel's great-aunt Hortense, who doted on Leslie— pearls so rarely worn they had gone gray as an old woman's teeth in Leslie's quilted jewelry case.

Daniel stood awkwardly at attention as the maître d' seated Leslie. The boys dragged back their high-backed wooden chairs, oblivious to the grating of the chair legs on the terrazzo floor. He wrestled down the temptation to murmur a word of reproach: if the scraping didn't bother Leslie, who was he to say anything? He settled in at her side. Porter sat across from Leslie, Alex faced Daniel.

The waiter, a dark ponytailed fellow whose French was so accented it slid over into Spanish, took their drink orders. Daniel was going to have a dry vermouth on the rocks, but when Leslie ordered a martini, straight up, he followed suit, telling the waiter to bring them a pitcher. He thought a martini might take the edge off—he felt jittery, and sitting across from Alex wasn't helping matters.

Porter was telling a story that Daniel only half attended to, something about Skinheads trying to take over a downtown club Porter and Alex frequented. Alex chimed in every few seconds with an encouraging word or booming laughter.

". . . and so this Skin goes up to Katrina and goes, 'Sit on my face, Westmount cunt' "—Porter was turning red—"and Katrina goes 'No thanks, I have a toilet at home.' "

Alex crowed with laughter, his boxy blond head bobbing up and down with glee. Diners at adjoining tables turned to look, their faces showing a mixture of amusement and irritation. Daniel looked pointedly at Leslie, willing her to tell Alex, as she occasionally did, to turn it down a bit, but she didn't seem to notice his look. Daniel knocked back his martini and poured another, more generous one. That, she noticed.

The three of them—approving mother, indulged sons—were having such a wonderful time they hadn't so much as glanced at their menus, even though the waiter was due to return any minute. Daniel had chosen what he wanted only moments after the waiter had handed round the menus, had even chosen a fall-back position should the kitchen be out of salmon, always a popular offering at Taureau d'Or. If there was one thing Daniel hated, it was keeping a waiter waiting. But Alex and Porter chattered happily on, unconcerned by the approaching deadline, Alex pink faced and practically shouting now that he was feeling his first beer.

When the waiter returned to take their order, Daniel sat with his fists clenched under the table. It occurred to him that he could tolerate anything but Alex and Porter's happiness—it reminded him too forcefully of all he had missed out on as a child, an adolescent. Henrietta often suggested that he needed to mourn his blighted youth, but all he could feel was rage. Why should he have been denied what seemed to have been offered so freely to so many others? Never mind a happy childhood—he would have settled for an ordinary one, a childhood he could look back on without feeling overwhelmed by pain and fear.

Leslie set the tone for ordering by asking innumerable questions, in her best boarding-school French, about the freshness of one dish, the preparation of another, shaking her head at the variety of choices. In the end she settled on what she always ordered at Taureau d'Or: *ris de veau* in a nest of black pasta. Porter, ordering in English, surprised everyone by asking for *cailles en sarcophage* as entrée—usually he was conservative in his food choices, not even sure he wanted to come to Taureau d'Or for his birthday dinner. He retreated to the safe plateau of *entrecôte au roquefort* for his *plat principal*.

When Alex's turn came he frowned at the menu opened between his hands as though noticing it for the first time. In imitation of Leslie he asked, in French, if the scallops were fresh and then ended up settling on three entrées: chicken livers *en brochette*, tortellini *à l'aubergine* and an endive salad.

"You're sure you want three entrées?" Leslie asked as the waiter sent her a quizzical look.

"You said we could order what we wanted," Alex reminded her.

Porter held up his large, long-fingered hands. "It's my birthday, and I say Alex can have as many entrées as he wants."

The waiter smiled at Porter and turned to Daniel. Daniel gave his order, in French, in a low, clear voice that the waiter affected not to hear. Daniel had to repeat his order three times. When the waiter finally moved off, Daniel realized he had forgotten to order the wine. He called the waiter back.

"*Oui, monsieur?*"

"*On va prendre le Mâcon-Lugny, s'il vous plaît.*"

"*Pardonnez-moi, monsieur?*"

"*Le Mâcon-Lugny.*"

"I'm sorry, sir," the waiter said, switching to Spanish-accented English, "the noise in here, very bad."

"I said we'll have the bloody Mâcon-Lugny," Daniel shouted in the man's ear. Diners from tables flanking their own turned to stare. Daniel flushed.

"*Très bien, monsieur.*" With a flick of his ponytail the waiter turned on his heel.

Leslie reached over and touched Daniel's arm. He patted her hand and reached for the martini pitcher. He filled his glass, watching Alex out of the corner of his eye. The boy sat with one arm slung over his chair back, his long legs thrust out into the aisle where anyone could trip over them. The tablecloth in front of him was already littered with bread crumbs, his butter-smeared knife lay on the peach-colored cloth. Leslie had always been lax about instructing her sons in etiquette. She didn't seem concerned whether they were acquainted with even the most basic rules of dining out, from the proper time to unfold one's napkin to which fork to use. Daniel was grateful that his own mother had been punctilious about such matters. Leslie's solution was to avoid or simply ignore the problem. He realized that it was hardly a burning issue: they took the boys to good restaurants only on special occasions. Otherwise Alex and Porter were perfectly content with pizza joints or the Bar-B Barn.

Daniel watched as Alex and Porter teamed up to tease Leslie about how many martinis she had drunk. For a teenager, Alex had remarkably clear, soft skin—nearly sixteen and his beard still hadn't come in. Rigorous weight training and school sports had melted away the puppy fat, revealing a classical profile. His short-cropped hair still shone white from the summer sun. It struck Daniel, not for the first time, that Alex and Porter were so attractive and personable that their comportment probably didn't matter much. Even now people were attracted to them—peers and grown-ups alike—and wanted to be in their company, wanted to share their glow of contentment and high spirits.

The waiter brought the wine. Daniel rolled the cork between his fingers. As unostentatiously as possible, he held the glass up to the light. Taking a sip, he rolled the wine back and forth across his tongue. He frowned slightly and took another sip before pronouncing the wine drinkable.

"You do that so well," Leslie said.

"Yeah, Daniel, you're a real connoisseur," Porter said.

"A real lush," Alex said, and everyone laughed.

By the time he had finished his entrée, Daniel was feeling better—almost expansive. He was about to signal the waiter to pour more wine, when Alex reached over to the ice bucket and dragged out the bottle without bothering to wrap it in its cloth. With not the steadiest hand he replenished Daniel's glass and then his own, the bottle dripping ice chips across the tablecloth. "Leslie? Porter?"

Leslie and Porter shook their heads. Alex plunked the bottle back into the ice bucket, nearly knocking it over.

"Alex," Daniel said.

Alex looked up, blue eyes startled. "What?"

"You know, in a restaurant like this, it's customary to ask the waiter to pour the wine. For one thing, that way you don't run the risk of overturning the ice bucket, as you nearly did. Of course if we had a decent waiter to begin with, we wouldn't have to ask to have the wine poured at all."

Alex's eyes darkened, his smile faded.

"They seem seriously understaffed tonight," Leslie said.

"Why do you always pick on Alex?" Porter said to Daniel. "What kind of thrill does it give you?"

"I'm not always picking on Alex. I just think that if we're going to bring the two of you to good restaurants, you need to learn what's acceptable behavior and what isn't."

Porter's chin went up as he cast a cold eye over the room. "I never wanted to come here in the first place. It was your idea. You just can't stand it when we're having a good time."

"That's not true. I . . ."

"It's okay, Porter," Alex said, fingering the stem of his wine glass. He looked calm. He looked, Daniel noticed, almost like an adult. "I'm used to it." Alex let his eyes meet Daniel's. "Anyway, anything Daniel says to me he gets from Leslie."

Daniel glanced at Leslie, who had been observing this exchange with a certain detachment, quietly waiting to jump in to separate and soothe the wrangling parties. She couldn't quite hide her shock at Alex's words. "What does Daniel get from me?"

"Everything he says to me," Alex said. "All the stuff about how loud I am and messy and clumsy—they're all things you're thinking. Only you don't have to say them because Daniel does it for you."

Daniel looked at Alex in astonishment.

"I really don't know what you're talking about," Leslie said, smiling, hands palm down on the tablecloth. "You're not making any sense. Things. What things?"

"You never liked me when I was little. You were embarrassed to have a son like me. I was fat and loud and ugly—everything you're not and never were."

Leslie's voice went low. Daniel sensed she was shifting into her therapeutic mode. "Alex, you know that's not true. I admit that it was a difficult situation when you were little. Your father's drinking and his terrible rages, and when he left—"

"You leave our father out of it," Alex said. "He's got nothing to do with it. He never did. He's beside the point."

Daniel watched Leslie. She seemed to be moving to a place where she couldn't be reached. He suspected that what was sitting palms down at the table was merely her upright shell.

"I don't blame you for not liking me," Alex said. "It was my fault. It wasn't just you. Nobody liked me. Remember when I was in kindergarten and nobody gave me a Valentine? Who could like me? I screamed all the time and was sick a lot. I think I was a pain from the very beginning. I think that's why our father left."

"Alex, Frank's leaving had nothing to do with you." Leslie fixed her eyes, which to Daniel looked abnormally large and sincere, on Alex's own.

"Of course it did. Things were okay until I came along. You had Porter, and then because you were so happy with him you decided to have another baby, except you hadn't counted on it being me. When he saw what I was like, Frank left, and you were stuck with me."

Leslie sipped at her wine. Daniel could tell she was marshaling all her persuasive forces. "It was hard for you then, Alex. It was hard for all of us." She sent Porter a meaningful look. "You were a difficult baby, right from the start. There's no getting around that. Squalling, colicky, always sick. There was never a moment I didn't love you, but there were times when I have to admit that you weren't very likable."

Daniel turned to Leslie. "How can you say that? How can you say you didn't like a little baby? That doesn't make any sense."

Leslie regarded him steadily. "Of course it does. Babies are just like older people—there are times when they're not all that likable."

"Whether people are likable or not depends on how they were reared and what life has done to them. Babies come into the world *tabula rasa*. How can a baby not be likable?"

Leslie smiled at him tolerantly. "I don't think you're hearing what I'm saying. I didn't say Alex was an unlikable baby—I said there were times he wasn't very likable. Can you hear the difference? And only a person who has never had a child of his own would have difficulty with the proposition that babies aren't always likable."

"Leslie's right," Alex said, looking fierce. "I was a bad baby. I'm okay now. I'm not fat anymore, I've got contact lenses. Now everybody likes me."

Leslie looked dismayed. "Nobody said you were a bad baby . . ."

"I can't accept that, Alex," Daniel said, realizing his eyes were full of tears. "I don't believe you were a bad baby. I do believe that Leslie and Frank may have treated you like one, for reasons of their own, reasons they probably weren't even aware of."

Leslie laughed. "Oh, Daniel, sometimes I think you've been in therapy too long. What reasons, and why wasn't I aware of them?"

"This is what I was trying to say a minute ago," Alex broke in. "You don't realize that other people do stuff for you. You hardly ever get mad, you hardly ever yell, you never do anything radical. You don't have to. I can tell when I'm out of line and you don't approve, because Daniel starts getting edgy and mean. He knows when you're upset because he knows you better than anyone. Sometimes he watches me, or Porter, but he's always watching you."

"I don't see why we have to go into this now. It's supposed to be my birthday party, and now everyone's trying to ruin it." Porter looked around the table accusingly.

Daniel saw that Leslie was returning from wherever she had retreated to. "Porter's right," she said, smiling. "This is his special night. We can talk about this later."

"But we won't," Daniel said.

Leslie and Porter exchanged exasperated looks.

"It doesn't make any difference if we talk about it or not," Alex said. Daniel noticed he suddenly looked pale and exhausted. "It's not like it's going to change stuff that happened a long time ago."

Daniel reached for the wine bottle, and without bothering to wrap it in its cloth, poured out what remained of the wine into their four glasses. "I think we should finish this here and now. We never do. Anytime anything like this comes up, you put the lid on it." He looked at Leslie. "Then you talk to the kids about it. Then you talk to me. Separately. Why do you get all the power?"

Porter looked at Daniel like he was being cretinous. "Because she's our mother."

"She's not my mother," Daniel said, immediately seeing that Alex and Porter didn't buy that disclaimer for one second.

"Why don't you give it a rest?" Porter said.

"Why don't you order another bottle of wine?" Leslie said. "This one's lovely."

Daniel signaled to the waiter. "I think Alex is right. I know why he was a bad baby."

"And why was that?" Leslie's tone just avoided the supercilious.

The waiter arrived, and Daniel asked quietly, in English, for another bottle. When the man had nodded and gone, Daniel continued. "You can say this is just something I picked up in therapy, but I think it makes sense. You and Frank were about to split up. You're a very reserved person. From all accounts so was Frank, at least when he wasn't drinking. There was all that anger and, presumably, sadness over breaking up. And neither of you knew how to express it. So it all fell to poor Alex."

"I'm not poor." Alex was making tracks on the tablecloth with his dessert fork.

"That's a very nice theory," Leslie said. "Except like so many theories it collapses when you apply it to reality. Frank and I didn't break up until Alex was three. And Alex was hard to handle from the word go. He was even a difficult pregnancy."

"Could he have been a difficult pregnancy because you and Frank weren't getting on? Did you decide to have Alex in order to shore up your marriage?"

"If you guys don't stop, I'm leaving." Porter carefully folded his napkin.

"Me too," Alex said, but he left his napkin in his lap.

The waiter returned bearing the new bottle like a precious infant in his outstretched arms.

"Madame will do the honors," Daniel said. The waiter flashed a broad gap-toothed grin, as if to say he understood completely.

Daniel watched his shoes planing along the rain-washed pavement. They were good shoes—his favorite oxblood cordovan wing tips. He'd had them made seven or eight years ago when he'd visited his sister, Elspeth, while she was still at Oxford. Cast-iron shoes—so far they hadn't needed so much as resoling—

keeping his feet dry even in this unexpected October downpour. Running his hands through his hair, he slicked it back flat across his skull. Moisture streamed down his brow, hung from the tip of his nose.

People splashed by, some adequately prepared with umbrellas swaying, but most, like Daniel, unequipped for anything more than a crisp Indian summer day. Two or three women with magazines or purses hoisted above bent heads scurried past. One potbellied man, corduroy jacket hiked up over his bald head, nearly collided with Daniel.

A door swung open on Daniel's right, a few steps ahead of him. He slowed his pace as a figure stepped uncertainly out onto the sidewalk. An old woman, sparse white hair covered with a pleated clear-plastic rain bonnet. He was close enough to see faint pink patches of scalp through the rain-beaded plastic. Instead of walking on, the old woman stood in the center of the sidewalk, looking about her absently as the rain slid down the lenses of her glasses.

For a moment he stared at the deep tracery of wrinkles on the back of her neck. He determined to pass her on the left, but a legion of shrilling schoolgirls, shiny yellow macs thrown over blue jumpers, advanced on him, clogging the sidewalk. He thought he might be able to squeeze between the old woman and the shop windows to her right, but as he moved to do so, she tottered rightward, murmuring to herself. He dodged back to the left, intending to plunge into the breach left by the passing schoolgirls, but a car whisked up to the curb, the passenger door opening to disgorge a robust woman in a deerstalker cap and forest-green cape. Daniel saw he was trapped. He also saw what he must do. The woman in the clear-plastic rain bonnet was old, she was frail. One quick push and she would fall face-first onto the wet pavement.

The robust woman in the green cape sailed past, and Daniel saw that the way was clear at last. Glancing over his shoulder as he charged past, he noticed that the old woman's glasses were so fogged over as to make it impossible for her to see much of anything at all. He felt a brief pang of sympathy and then its contrary: she had no business obstructing a public thoroughfare on a day like this in the first place. She would be—it was plain to anyone who encountered her disorientated gropings and mutterings—better off in a home. Or dead.

And so, Daniel thought, would I. He immediately tried to banish this thought, along with the image of the old woman, facedown and bloodied on the pavement, from his mind. He didn't know where such ideas, images, impulses, came from. These days they sprang up unbidden, indelible reminders of how useless it was for him to continue seeing Henrietta. Beneath his well-polished public persona he was brutal, remorseless, corrupt at the core. And the odor was beginning to appall him. The perfumes of therapy, self-examination, self-improvement, would never sweeten this stench. Better, instead of standing at this corner waiting for the light to change, that he should step off the curb and into the path of that oncoming cement truck. The hitch was, in addition to his other unspeakable qualities, he was a coward. He would sooner maim or kill a pathetic old woman than risk the slightest pain to his own well-tended body.

"Peppermint?" Henrietta said. Daniel shook his head. He wasn't going to play that game any longer. Or any of the others for that matter. The time had come to strip off the mask. Stop pretending. Fly his true colors. He saw a pirate flag snapping in the wind, emblazoned with a grisly death's head.

Henrietta slowly unwrapped her peppermint, affecting not to be aware of his poisonous mood. But he knew she knew. Maybe it was time for her to stop pretending too. Wouldn't she feel better for it, if she could at last confess that she didn't like Daniel any more than he liked himself? Wouldn't such new and valuable frankness clear the air between them?

"So," she said, popping the red-and-white-striped lozenge into her wide mouth, "what's going on with you today?"

As if she couldn't see. As if someone had poked out her pale blue eyes with a sharp stick.

"Not much," Daniel said. "What about you?"

She tilted her head to one side and smiled. A distant look came into her eyes, as though she were savoring the sweet peppermint taste flooding the cavern of her mouth. He couldn't stand her air of self-satisfaction. Someone, he thought, should wipe that smile off her sweetly condescending face.

"I was just thinking," she said, rolling the peppermint slowly around in her mouth, "that today might be a good day for reviewing your progress. I think it's valuable to do that every so often, don't you? For you to sum up what you feel you've experienced over the course of your therapy. Could you do that for me?" She shifted about in her chair, trying to get comfortable, her gray pleated skirt riding up so Daniel could see the brown bands at the top of her nylons.

He thought she should know better than to sit like that. Who knows what thoughts such a posture might incite in one of her less stable clients. He knew she had clients like that—he had seen the silver panic button set into the wall behind her chair, the one that communicated directly with the police.

He opened his mouth to warn her of the danger she might be placing herself in. "You know," he said, his voice little more than a croak, "I don't see the point anymore."

"The point of what, Daniel?"

"Of anything. Of coming here. Walking down the street. Getting up in the morning. Going to the office. It's all so useless."

"Why do you think that is?"

"Because nothing's going to change. I'm the way I am. You're the way you are. It's a fixed thing. You can't change me into something I'm not."

As he talked he watched the glow of self-approval fade from Henrietta's face. He felt a certain satisfaction at so quickly destroying her good humor. At the same time he resented the look of studied concern she was putting on now.

"Is that what you think I'm trying to do—mold you into something you're not?"

"It's not your fault," he said. "That's why I came here to start with. I hoped you could turn me into an acceptable person."

"As I recall, you came here because you were in great pain."

"That's what I told you. It's not so hard to figure out how to get your sympathy."

"Would you say, then, that you've been playing me for a sap?"

He looked up, surprised at her choice of words. "That's exactly what I'd say."

"Who else do you play for a sap? In your life outside this room?"

"Everyone."

"How do you manage that?"

"It's ridiculously easy. People are eager to be fooled. They sense what's going on underneath but they don't really want to know. If you put up even the most transparent false front, they're more than willing to accept it."

"Is this a recent feeling you've been having, this feeling of being false?"

"No."

"How long would you say this has been going on?"

Daniel stuck out his chin defiantly. "All my life."

"Yet it's something I don't remember you saying much about before."

How would she know? She couldn't remember how long he'd been in therapy. Last week she had called Leslie "Lila." "I didn't think it worth mentioning."

Henrietta pleated the clear-cellophane peppermint wrapper so it resembled a tiny plastic rain bonnet. "Would you say, though, that your awareness of this feeling of falseness has intensified recently?"

"I don't know. Maybe."

"Could you narrow it down for me? Over the last month, the last two weeks, the last few days?"

He thought for a moment. He saw an expanse of crisp, peach-colored linen. "Two weeks."

"Was there something that happened two weeks ago that might have accentuated this feeling?"

"Yes, except it doesn't make any sense." He told her about Porter's birthday party, about Alex accusing Leslie of not liking him as a baby, about how quickly Leslie put the lid on the subject.

When he had finished, Henrietta shook her head. "That Alex is quite something, isn't he. How could he have so much insight at seventeen?"

"Fifteen," Daniel said wearily. "I know he reads a lot of Leslie's books on psychology."

"Does he? At this rate he'll be writing them soon."

"You think Alex is right?"

"That he was a bad baby from the start? No. But he could be right in sensing that Leslie didn't like him much when he was a baby. Kids, even tiny babies, have feelings. They pick up on that sort of thing. It's not unusual either, when a marriage is breaking down and the partners haven't quite admitted it to themselves, for them to project their anger, disappointment and sadness on the very child they've brought into the world in order to shore up their relationship."

"But that's exactly what I said. Why can't Leslie see that? I couldn't believe it when she said Alex was a bad baby."

Henrietta leaned back in her chair. "Are you sure that's what she said?"

"Yes. No. I don't know what anyone's saying anymore—whether it's just what they say, or what I want them to say, or what my mother or father said to me thirty years ago. What happens—what we believe is happening—at any given moment is so subjective."

"Isn't it though?" Henrietta beamed at him as though she wanted to congratulate him for something. "And you don't believe there's such a thing as a bad baby?"

"No. Do you?"

"No." She laid the cellophane wrapper aside. "But I sense there's something else bothering you about Peter's birthday party."

"Porter."

Henrietta laughed briefly. "I've always found it funny how, when families go out intent on having a good time, it nearly always ends in disaster."

"That's what bothers me most."

"The best laid plans of mice and men?"

"No. What Alex said about me helping Leslie keep him down. I've always felt so ashamed of how I've treated Alex and Porter, always criticizing and berating them, never comfortable in their presence. Porter's birthday dinner made me see not just what I've done but also a much larger and more pernicious pattern: the family I'm in now is just as sick as the family I'm coming from."

"Because you've belatedly discovered you're not the only one who's not in control around Porter and Alex?"

"I've never seen Leslie out of control with either of them."

"As Alex put it so well, with you around she doesn't need to be. Her first husband was a gentle man prone to alcoholic rages. Were those rages directed at her or the kids?"

"Mainly at the kids, from what I can gather."

"Don't you think that's an interesting pattern, especially since it so closely parallels what happens with you and Leslie in terms of the boys?"

He considered this for a moment. Then he said, "I want out."

"Yes?"

He had assumed she would be more surprised. "There's really no point, is there? No matter what family unit I'm in, it's inevitably corrupt."

"Correct me if I'm wrong, but in that statement I hear the assumption that it's your presence that causes the corruption."

He smiled. No matter which way he dodged and feinted, Henrietta always managed to get there ahead of him.

"There are obviously some problems with you and Leslie and the boys that need working out," Henrietta said, "but unless it's a really pressing matter, as Porter's birthday dinner surely was, I'd like to stay away from your relationship with Leslie for the time being. We can stir that one up later. We have enough on our plates right now, just dealing with what happened to you as a child. So can you hold off on leaving your present home for the time being? We've got to get you out of your original one first."

Daniel nodded, in disappointment and relief.

"There is one additional thing. This anger you feel at Leslie—is that in some way related to the anger you feel at your mother?"

Anger. That wasn't precisely the word he would have used to describe what he felt toward Leslie. As for his mother . . . "You always keep harping on this—that I've somehow got this deep-seated anger toward my mother. It must be incredibly deep, because I'm certainly not aware of it. Why should I be angry at her? It's not as though she did anything."

"That's precisely my point. That's why I keep"—Henrietta paused, smiling—"harping on it. You always maintain it would have been worse for you as a child if she hadn't been there to protect you, but she still doesn't seem to have protected you nearly enough."

"You mean because the sexual abuse occurred at all?"

"Not just that, but also the abusive atmosphere that seems to have continued long after the explicitly sexual acts ended—the whippings, your father's preoccupation with your sexuality, the whole family focused on your behavior, everyone constantly monitoring your 'badness.' Where was your mother while all this was going on? Whose side was she on?"

"That's easy. His." Tears spurted from Daniel's eyes. Even as they trailed down his cheeks, he resented them, these predictable-as-clockwork tears. Arriving every session about three quarters of the way in, they provided momentary relief; then, next session, he had to start all over again.

"That's why I keep coming back to your mother and your feelings toward her. I see what she did or didn't do, and I think, Daniel must have a great store of anger toward this woman who failed to protect him on so many levels. You seem to have worked through your anger at your father, for now at least, because you've been aware of that anger your whole life long. But your mother is more problematic, for you and for me. I can't really get a sense of her. Not at all. Even when you do manage to say a few words about her, she remains a complete enigma to me."

"To me too," Daniel said, irritated that they should be going back over the same ground they had already covered so many times before.

"One thing I don't think I've asked you about. We've talked about your father's depressions—perhaps we should say his life-long depression—but what about your mother?"

"What about her?" Why, he wondered, did everything Henrietta said have to be in the form of a question? Why couldn't she simply say what was on her mind instead of always recasting into the cautiously interrogative what were most probably ironclad therapeutic observations?

"Is your mother ever depressed?"

As if he hadn't made that clear innumerable times before. "Are you?"

She didn't flinch. "From time to time."

"You never show it."

"I would if I thought it was appropriate to what was going on in this room. But actually I haven't had any real bouts of depression recently. They usually hit at Christmastime."

"Oh really?"

"Really." She slowly massaged her left shoulder. Daniel could see that rubbing her shoulder was just a ruse to distract him from the fact that she was glancing over her shoulder at the small brass carriage clock on the windowsill. "Does your mother ever show her depression?"

"There's nothing to show. My mother has never been depressed a day in her life."

"You're certain about that?"

"That's what she has always maintained. She never gets depressed, never suffers from insomnia"—Daniel paused, trying to recall the rest of his mother's tranquil mantra—"oh yes, and she never dreams."

"Never dreams?"

"That's what I said."

"I suppose she doesn't have to do any of those things so long as your father is there to do them for her."

"You mean he protects her too?"

"It's usually fairly mutual in a couple, isn't it? Leslie protects you by keeping the boys away from you, because she knows they upset you. You protect her by expressing anger and all the other strong emotions she's uncomfortable with."

"I guess." It was all so neat. Henrietta had everything nailed down. There was nothing he could say that would surprise her, no paradox or emotional knot so complex that she couldn't hack through it with her sure professional sword.

"Do you think you could describe your mother for me?"

"I've done that before."

"I know. But would you be willing to try one more time? I promise not to ask you again."

Right. He sighed and rested his face in his hands. This was the part he hated. Most of the time he couldn't see his mother's face. Even when he could see it, what was there to say? He knew from old photographs that she had been conventionally pretty as a girl and young woman. Brief memories from his childhood flickered: his mother in a rustling cocktail dress, bare shoulders fragrant with powder, mouth transformed by a smile, eyes shining with excitement. But now, twenty or thirty years later, what was left of that beauty, that vivacity?

"You look as though you're stuck."

"I am."

"Would you say there is one physical trait that stands out more than any other?"

He sighed again. This was useless. They would never get anywhere with her. There was nothing to describe. His mother was a nonentity. Couldn't they just leave it at that? She had devoted her entire life to coddling and protecting her precious child-molesting husband, and the effort had worn her down to a colorless ghost of a woman. What was there to say about someone like that? Nothing at all. For one thing, his mother wouldn't allow him to say it. He could see her silent look of disapproval. The warning look that never failed to shut him up. Eyes opaque, lips pressed tightly together: the wordless demand for perpetual silence, perpetually obeyed.

Finally he said, "All I can see is her mouth."

"Could you tell me more about your mother's mouth?"

"What's there to tell?" God, but he hated this. The slowness of it. Time no longer existed. The room darkening, walls narrowing in. He couldn't look at Henrietta, couldn't stand the sight of her kindly probing face. He concentrated instead on the Inuit sculpture from the waiting room, perched heavily next to the carriage clock on the windowsill behind her.

"What kind of mouth is it?"

"A mouth's a mouth. They're all pretty much the same—lips, tongue, teeth." Just like my mouth, this mouth that can barely open. Just like your mouth, smiling that insipid, encouraging smile, wrinkled lips slightly parted.

"I was thinking, Daniel, not so much of an exact physical description as a sense of what her mouth suggests to you. I know I'm expressing it badly. Would you say your mother has a forgiving mouth?"

He laughed deep in his throat. It came out louder than he had intended. "No, I wouldn't say that." He stared at the Inuit sculpture until he thought his head would split open.

"Would you say it's a happy mouth? A contented mouth?"

Christ, this was like some demented party game, played in slow motion, underwater. He wanted to stretch his arms, fling them about in the darkening weighted air. He wanted to leap to his feet, shout, scream, tear the silence in two. He wanted to rage about the room, rip the tasteful salmon miniblinds from their sockets, with his bare fists shatter the windows in a hail of glass and blood, tear down the sickening silver-framed print of a gull in flight. But his hands were locked between his crossed knees.

"No, I wouldn't say it was a happy mouth. Or an especially contented one."

Henrietta leaned forward in her chair, resting her hands on her knees. "What would you say, Daniel. About your mother's mouth?"

I would say, why don't you leave me alone? I would say, what pleasure does it give you to torture me like this day after day, week after week? What kind of thrill does it give you? You don't care about me. Nobody does. You're doing this only because I'm paying you. If you weren't getting the money you'd turf me out of here in about ten seconds. You can't stand me any more than anyone else can.

She leaned closer, her face swimming up through the dense air, rising up so close to him. "What's going on now, Daniel? Where are you now?"

I'm right here, he thought. Come any closer and you'll know where I am. I'm fine. Nothing's going on. We've just come to the end, that's all. There's nothing more to say. You can't help me.

No one can. I don't want to be helped. This is crazy. We're not getting anywhere. We never will.

He noticed the tingling sensation in his feet. He wasn't sure how much longer he could keep them still. Or his arms for that matter. He couldn't breathe. The big toad was too close, sitting so complacently on her velvet lily pad, sucking up all the air. She was suffocating him. What do you think? What are you feeling? Where are you now? Shit. It was all shit. He was shit.

He sprang to his feet.

Henrietta looked up.

"I've got to get out of here."

"I can see that, Daniel."

"I'm leaving," he said, but still he stood there, immobile, staring at the Inuit carving. The bloated stone woman—or walrus—giving birth. Henrietta had obviously moved it in from the waiting room to taunt him. He glanced down at his feet: one of his oxblood wing tips was untied.

Henrietta's head bobbed up and down. She struggled to her feet, hands waving about uselessly. The dark air rippled. She was coming at him, lips moving. She was saying something he couldn't hear. They looked like wooden lips, a puppet's lips. "Shut up," they said, "shut up, shut up." But the voice he heard wasn't Henrietta's.

He stepped away from her and darted to the windowsill behind her chair. He had to touch the stone carving, its cool sea-green contours. He needed their smooth hardness. And something else, something else. Something to do with blood and power. His damned shoe. Take care of that first. He crouched down to tie the dangling laces. He saw the oblong silver panic button set into the wall, just above the baseboard, EMERGENCY engraved in tiny silver letters. He pressed the button, expecting a siren, an alarm. Nothing. He pressed again.

"What are you doing, Daniel?" Henrietta's voice, her real voice now, not his mother's, came soft and low, behind him.

"Pressing the panic button."

"Do you think that will help?" She had crouched down beside him.

"I was going to kill you."

"I'm sorry, Daniel. I got too close."

"I was going to kill you."

"When that happens, when I'm probing too deeply, you've got to tell me. You've got to be able to say, 'Back off.' You have the right to do that. You've got to have the right to protect yourself. No one else is going to do it for you. You know that by now, if you know anything at all. Coming from where you're coming from, you've got to be able to slam the door and say, 'Stay out' and have that wish respected."

"I was going to smash your face in, smash it with the . . ."

"But you didn't, did you? You protected me instead. I got too close, my finger was in the wound. No wonder you wanted to kill me. It's when you're most vulnerable that you react defensively. But even then you didn't do it. Even when you were most threatened, you protected me instead of you."

Daniel sat down on the floor, feeling brave and stupid. In the distance he heard a siren wailing.

"That will be the police," Henrietta said, sitting down on the carpet at his side. "They're usually not that quick. We'll have to think of something plausible to tell them."

PART THREE

A Visit Home

*D*aniel was trying to avoid his own reflection. He studied the prickly leaves of holly ringing the mirror. Bits of Cellotape held the leaves to the glass, the clusters of red berries so glossily false he assumed they must be real. In the mirror he watched the other clients floating up and down the freestanding staircase behind him, the women looking comfortable on display, the men sheepish and out of place in this pastel, strong-scented world. Beyond the stair he could make out the crimson smocks of three other clients—two women, one man— sitting impassive before their image.

A boy's face materialized in his mirror, blond head directly above his own. Choirboy face. Daniel's eyes caught the boy's, then darted away. Clearly a mistake had been made.

"Hello, Mr. Kenning. I'm Barnaby." The voice was precise, the delivery matter-of-fact.

Daniel glanced at his own reflection in an attempt to avoid the boy's and was horrified at what he saw: chalky skin, lank damp hair, dents of exhaustion beneath dead eyes, swirls of gray in the hair curling across his chest. He pulled the lapels of his smock together. "Someone must have gotten his wires crossed," he said. "I'm here for Sylvie."

"Didn't they tell you at the desk? Honestly, they're so disorganized upstairs. Sylvie's not feeling terribly well this morning. Last night was our Christmas party."

"I see." If he had known Sylvie was indisposed he would have rebooked for another day. He certainly didn't want this cherub-faced boy cutting his hair. Barnaby. The image confronting him in the mirror was too much like a study for a Victorian allegorical painting: Youth and Age maybe, or Beauty and Despair. He was trying to think of a tactful way of saying he would come back another day when Barnaby rested his pink, delicate-fingered hands on Daniel's brow and then slowly combed his fingers back through his hair.

"So," Barnaby addressed him in the mirror, "what did you have in mind today?"

"I thought a haircut might be nice," Daniel said.

Barnaby grinned and with one hand flipped the wet hair that trailed halfway down Daniel's neck. "Is that what you call what Sylvie gave you?"

The last thing Daniel needed was a cheeky haircutter. That's why he liked Sylvie so much—she never gave any lip, for that matter rarely said anything at all, just stood behind him, making regular, comforting snipping noises. "What's wrong with it?"

Barnaby grinned again. "Nothing's wrong with it. Sylvie's a perfectly competent cutter. It's just that it doesn't suit you very well."

Daniel turned his head to look Barnaby in the eye. "It's the way I've always had it cut."

"Precisely," Barnaby said, picking up his scissors. "I can do it that way, if you like. Give you at least a semblance of The Sylvie Look."

Since when did haircutters go about saying "semblance"? "What did you have in mind, Barnaby?"

"Oh, nothing, really. When I first saw you sitting there it struck me that you looked like someone who wanted a major change."

"I do?"

"Not necessarily a radical change, although we could do that too of course. But at least much shorter, more in tune with the times. And with the shape of your face."

Daniel looked at himself more closely in the mirror. "What's wrong with the shape of my face?"

Barnaby leaned down so that his face was level in the glass with Daniel's own. "Nothing's wrong with your face. It's a good face, actually. Long and narrow—a very English face—with good bones. Wearing your hair like that makes your face look even longer. And those bangs—if I had a high, noble forehead you couldn't make me hide it."

"So you would cut it shorter and chop off the bangs?" Daniel said.

"Right, if that's what you want too," Barnaby said, a teasing half smile playing across his face.

Daniel glared at his own reflection. He hated what he saw. "What if that isn't what I want? What if I were to opt for a radical change?"

Barnaby paused and looked him in the eye, in the mirror. "I would be happy to accommodate you there as well."

"Hey, Daniel, when did you turn Skinhead?" Porter said.

Daniel walked into the dining room, head held high.

Leslie looked up from the soup tureen, ladle suspended in midair. "Daniel, whatever . . ."

Alex shouted, "Let me touch, let me touch." Daniel bowed his head. Alex rubbed his big hand back and forth across Daniel's sheared scalp. "Neat," he said, "it's even shorter than mine."

Leslie handed Daniel a bowl of soup. "You know, if I had passed you on the street I'm not sure I would have recognized you."

"You like it?" He watched her closely.

"It's very . . . different."

"You look like a German artist," Porter said.

"A German artist?" Leslie said.

"Like they have on TV Ontario all the time. 'My art is a synthesis of the concrete and the absurd.' Except they usually have these little metal-framed glasses too. And an earring."

"Actually, I was thinking about getting an earring."

"You're not." Leslie glanced at Daniel to see if he was joking.

"I don't know. Maybe. I feel like doing something . . . radical. I've looked the same way practically all my life."

"Yeah," Porter said, "like a Ken doll."

Daniel laughed. "Not anymore."

"I know what you look like," Alex said.

"What?" Leslie said.

"A guy from a concentration camp."

Daniel remembered his reflection in the mirror when Barnaby had finished and knew that Alex was, as usual, dead-on.

. . .

He was lying back in the big claw-foot bath, separating and ushering together again the mountains of bubbles he had made, when Leslie knocked on the door and entered carrying two *ballons* of cognac.

"It's lovely in here," she said, eyeing the pair of lighted candles on the shelf over the bath, their brightness doubled by the small oval ormolu mirror behind them. She handed Daniel a *ballon* and sat on the bath's porcelain rim. "So warm. Are Decembers getting colder or is it just my imagination? Or my advanced age?"

Daniel took a healthy sip of his cognac. "They are getting colder. Saw an article about it in the *Gazette* just the other day. The frigidaire effect, scientists are calling it. Something to do with the ozone layer and changing permafrost conditions. Nothing to be overly alarmed about. At least not for you and me. Of course the boys will die."

"Of course." Leslie eyed him speculatively. "Now I'm growing used to it I think I actually like your hair that way. It suits you. Although each time you're out of the room for five minutes and I see you again, it's a terrible shock."

"It's hideous, isn't it?"

"Hideous? I wouldn't say that. Not at all. But Alex was right, you do look like you just got out of Dachau or something."

"Funny he would say that."

"Why?"

"I don't know. I'm not sure why, but getting my hair cut this way has something to do with going home."

"Are you very worked up about it?"

"Wouldn't you be?"

"I'm not convinced it's something you should do at all."

"I haven't spent Christmas with them for years and years."

"I don't mean you shouldn't go. I'm quite happy to put off our Christmas till New Year's Eve. I'd be willing to put it off indefinitely if it weren't for Porter and Alex. No, I'm simply concerned about why you're going home."

Daniel hated it when Leslie expressed doubts and fears that echoed his own suppressed ones. "You don't think I'm ready to face them?"

"I agree with Henrietta that it's important for you to make some kind of contact with them, but does she think this is the right time to confront them?"

Daniel pulled himself up and rested his arms on the cool porcelain rim. "I'm not going to confront them. I'm going there to 'break the silence.'"

"Is that what she calls it? How are you going to do that without confronting them?"

"I'm not sure. I'll know when it happens."

"I admire your courage," Leslie said, dabbling in the suds with one finger.

"I don't feel particularly courageous. I feel eaten up with anxiety—it's all I think about, every moment of the day. I'm having some pretty graphic dreams as well. But I feel this has to be done if I'm going to go on from here."

"You don't have to answer this if you don't want to."

"All right."

"Do you ever feel that Henrietta is pushing you to do this?"

"Obviously you do."

"I don't know what to think."

"Look, what she says, at least the way I understand it—I could be getting it wrong, God knows I do that often enough with the things she says or I think she says—but what she claims is that all I have to do is tell one person in my family: Elspeth, my mother, him, God forbid, and the bubble of silence is burst. Everything will change, instantaneously."

"And then your father will shoot everyone."

"There is that to consider."

Leslie stared into her glass. "I really do find it all pretty terrifying."

"Me too. Henrietta has me under orders to proceed with extreme caution. My main goal, I believe, is to let him know, either by indirection or by telling him outright, that the rules have changed. That I'm onto him."

"How do you think he'll react?"

"I try not to think too much about that."

"I get these horrendous flashes."

"You know, you're not making it any easier for me."

"I know. I'm sorry."

"It's important we talk about it, it's just that I'm extremely keyed up. It's impossible to predict what will happen, how he'll react. How anyone will. I really don't think I'll talk to him, at least not about the sexual stuff. The one solid piece of advice Henrietta offered was, Don't be alone with him."

"Very sound advice too." Leslie submerged her hand beneath the bubbles and then ran it over the top of Daniel's head. "It's so short. Do you intend it as a kind of signal?"

"Signal?"

"Letting them see right from the start that there have been some dramatic changes on your side of the family equation."

"Could be that. What Alex said seems right too. I didn't see it when the fellow was cutting it, but I do look like a victim, don't I?"

"A very sexy victim."

"Press said something about that. Back when I first told him what had happened. I forget his exact words. Something about complete vulnerability giving him a hard-on."

"Sounds like Press." She trailed her hand down his chest. "Makes you look like a very young victim as well. You really do look about twenty-five."

"Great. I always wanted to look like a hideous twenty-five-year-old."

"Don't complain. When you reach my great age you'll see the wisdom in settling for that. I've never much minded being older than you, mainly because people have always told me I look young for my age, and you've always looked old for yours."

"Is that what they say?" Daniel said, feeling hurt.

"But over the past few months, that's changed. It's not just the haircut. I feel I'm aging a lot these days, and you have the ill grace to start looking younger."

"You really shouldn't complain. I hope I have the good luck to look as young as you do when I'm forty-five."

Leslie ducked her head. She hated compliments so much that Daniel rarely gave them. Once, not long after they had met, he told her she was "a lovely woman." That made her so angry that he had learned his lesson—Leslie said she found such talk dishonest and embarrassing.

"It's true, you know," Daniel said, pushing his luck.

"And what's this?" she said, changing the subject.

"A little friend."

"Not so little."

"Not so friendly either."

"No?"

"No."

"Let's see if your little friend bites back."

"Leslie . . ."

He arched his back in the warm water as Leslie's hair trailed across his chest and into the foam. Water splashed over the sides of the bath. She scraped him lightly with her teeth. It had been a long time since they had made love—each time they tried recently had turned out wrong, stale, complicated—but tonight Daniel felt free and sure of himself. Nothing was going to interfere with tonight.

He sat up abruptly. "I can't see you down there," he said. "I can't touch you down there." He stroked her warm cheeks, brushing back her damp, heavy hair. He touched her nipples through her shirt, leaving two wet stars. Leaning forward he kissed the stars, searching with his tongue for first one erect nipple, then the other. He slipped one hand inside her shirt. Her skin was warm. He could feel her heart beating. He rolled one nipple back and forth between thumb and forefinger, his mouth fastening on the other. Leslie pulled him to her, running her hands over his close-cropped head.

He eased his other hand inside the waistband of her trousers until his middle finger found her through the thin cloth of her panties. He pressed hard, the thin cloth soaked through at once.

"Stand up," Leslie said, gasping.

Daniel stood, water streaming down his thighs.

"You look great like that," she said.

"Yeah?"

"Like a hungry boy."

"I am hungry."

"I can see that. You've lost so much weight too. I can count your ribs."

Daniel looked into the wide mirror over the basin. She was right. Never before had he stood unclothed in front of a mirror and liked what he saw—the fleshly animal, naked, wet, aroused. Now it was as if he were seeing someone else, someone new.

He stepped out of the bath, grabbing one of the big plush towels.

"On the floor?" Leslie said.

Daniel shook his head and spread the towel on the marble counter.

"Will it work?" she said, wiping the steam from the mirror.

"We'll make it work."

She lay back on the counter, head against the mirror, legs splayed.

Unfastening her belt, he tugged off her trousers and panties. He left her shirt on, unbuttoning it all the way down. The blue oxford cloth emphasized the creamy white of her skin. He looked up and glimpsed himself watching her.

"You know what?" Leslie said, craning back her head. "I can see you too. In the mirror, I mean."

"Perfect."

The angle was perfect too. He watched as he disappeared inside her, millimeter by millimeter. The wet, curling hair of her sex glistened—glistened in the mirror as well. He thought he never had felt so aroused, never had wanted to fuck so slowly, gliding in to the farthest limit and then slowly, slowly pulling back. He felt enveloped in wet, coursing warmth. Leaning forward, he rested his hands on her breasts, then bore down, crushing them till she moaned. He heard that he was moaning too—he hoped the boys were nowhere near, eavesdropping on this steamy bathroom duet.

Leslie reached between his legs and, cupping his balls with one warm hand, made them play back and forth in the silky sack. He was trying to hold off, to prolong the pleasure, to concentrate on her body in both its manifestations, trying to watch himself too, the sweaty pallor of his flesh, the heaving rib cage; bony, lurching shoulders. He could see it all—her body, his, the crimson of her open mouth, the silver trail of saliva running from his parted lips to her taut throat. He could see this act, their love, stretching on forever, facing mirrors doubling down to eternity.

In that instant of vision it all exploded, a flash inside his head, a burst and a heaving, Leslie's eyelids fluttered closed.

The next he knew he was lying with his head on Leslie's breast. He felt himself shrinking, shriveling, becoming only himself again, the steamy air cool now on his sweaty back.

Leslie's eyes were still closed when she started to laugh, softly at first and then full force. "I think you're going to have one hell of a Christmas, Daniel."

The empty carousel continued to revolve, mightily creaking. Daniel looked down at the pile of unmatched bags at his side— the scuffed gray leather duffel he'd borrowed from Alex, his own battered gladstone with black electrical tape on one handle, Leslie's fashionable calfskin knapsack, the burgundy cordovan portfolio that held his preliminary notes and sketches for the Steinmetz house, the brown suede satchel he'd bought at a flea market in Florence in the early seventies. Briefly he wondered why he had brought so much for a five-day visit and then remembered his favorite line from Cocteau—in *Les Enfants terribles,* when Paul and Elisabeth are invited for a day-trip to the seashore, Elisabeth promptly announces, *"Il faut beaucoup, beaucoup de bagages."*

Five minutes before the gray-carpeted baggage area had seen a melee of dangerously pivoting nylon-encased skis, runaway squeaky-wheeled trolleys laden with wrapped and beribboned packages, screaming snowsuited infants in strollers and one dazed old woman in a wheelchair, a glen plaid throw over her shrunken lap—three hundred people united only by the dry, hygienic jumbo-jet scent wafting sourly from the pores of their slowly uncramping bodies. Now the low-ceilinged, fluorescent-lit room was virtually empty, although across an acre or so of gray tile Daniel could see a row of blond women sitting behind a segmented length of rent-a-car counters.

For their benefit he tried to look unconcerned. He knew he

hadn't been forgotten. He had phoned his mother just two nights ago to relay his arrival time; she had indicated that "someone" would be dispatched to pick him up. He was not surprised that no one was at the airport to meet him—that was frequently the case when he came home on a visit. He asked himself if there were perhaps a message for him in that, an unspoken reluctance to have him home at all, or whether his family put off going to the airport until the last moment because they secretly hoped to avoid witnessing the public displays of emotion and affection that arrival and departure call forth in other people.

At the far end of the rent-a-car counters the smoked-glass electric doors glided open and Elspeth made her entrance, at a trot. The blondes behind their counters swiveled leftward in unison. She looked almost too elegant, in a narrow black velvet suit, black hair cut in a careless Eton crop. She spotted Daniel immediately and loped across the terminal.

Halfway to him she called out, "It's not my fault." The blondes behind their counters started at the basso voice. "I was on time but then he made me late. Quite intentionally, it seemed to me."

Daniel moved forward uncertainly to hug his sister. She raised her arms and hung them gingerly about his neck, leaning forward from the waist so their lower bodies did not touch. Her lips brushed the skin in front of his right ear, then his left. Daniel wondered why they were always so physically awkward on meeting, why she always held back from him. What did she remember?

"You look terrific with your hair like that," he said.

"And you look like . . ."

"Everyone has a take on it."

"I'm sure. I was going to say like a political prisoner fresh back from the gulag, but on further reflection I think I'll go with St. Francis. You remember the Bellini at the Frick, all that pink-gold light streaming down?"

Daniel held up his hands. "No stigmata."

"Early days yet." She looked down at his feet. "This your gear? My God, are you moving back home?"

"I thought I might. I so miss the warmth and comfort, the smell of fresh-baked bread."

"Please. What we talk about when we talk about yeast."

"Elspeth, it's so good to see you. What a suit!"

"Like it?" She sucked in her cheeks and performed a mannequin's half turn. "You'd better. Set me back four hundred quid. My bags are in Amsterdam or Singapore, no one's sure which. British Airways strikes again, so I've been wearing this and only this ever since I arrived—to the grocery on last-minute errands for Mother, to the home to visit Tante Hortense. She told me I looked like a *croque-mort.*"

"What's that?"

"I had to ask too. An undertaker."

"How is Tante Hortense?"

"Fading fast, according to her. Says her eyes are going, can't hear, no appetite. She wolfed down her dinner while I was there, complaining all the while that nothing tastes anymore. She is terribly shrunken—the hump's more pronounced than ever. I'm sure she could survive in the desert for weeks and weeks. Her eyes are so bad she could see I still bite my nails from all the way across the room. Don't let's stand here talking." She grabbed the big duffel and slung it over her shoulder. "Come on."

"How's London?" he asked, following her through the electric doors.

"Gray, gray and more gray. Not all that different from here."

She led him to a midnight-blue Cadillac of ancient vintage, illegally parked at curbside.

"Where did you get that?" Daniel said.

"Don't you recognize it? It's Tante Hortense's. Mum and Daddy are storing it for her in the stables. Till she's able to drive again, which seems unlikely, not to mention dangerous, but Hortense has accomplished stranger things."

"It's an antique."

"Yes, 1965, I believe. See? They were starting to tone down the fins. Remember how everyone mocked her when she bought it?"

"Grandfather Morton always called it 'the Jew Canoe.' "

Elspeth grimaced. "Christ, but he was a vile old man. I was all set to whip over here in Daddy's new Jag, pick you up in the style you're accustomed to, impress the natives and all that. I got as far as heading out to the garage when he waylaid me. He simply had to have it to deliver Christmas gifts to all the tenants. Tried to convince me to go with him."

"Little Miss and her father the Squire. Sure to be lots of tugging of forelocks all round. How is he?" Daniel tossed his bags into the cavernous blue-carpeted trunk.

"How is he ever? Distant. Critical. Nasty, given the occasion. His usual genial self. I've been concentrating on avoiding him, which isn't easy—he keeps tracking me down. I think he's lonely. No wonder."

Daniel slid into the passenger seat and sank deep into dove-gray leather. "I can't believe it. It still has that new-car smell."

"Open the glove box and inhale," Elspeth said, turning on the ignition.

Daniel opened the glove compartment, which contained only a flat box of facial tissues. He leaned close and sniffed. "Jicky."

"Hortense still wears it. Every day. Guerlain should feature her in an ad: 'Les anciennes odeurs.' You know, I asked her yesterday if she ever regretted marrying into an Anglo family and leaving Montreal forever. She thought about it for a moment and said, 'Every day of my life' and then cackled loudly."

"I'm eager to see her," Daniel said.

Elspeth smoothly piloted the big boat of a car over the draw-bridge and onto the highway. In the distance, Daniel could make out the Vancouver skyline, festooned with mist like a ghostly galleon.

Once they left the city behind them the road was nearly deserted. Mist gave way to steady rain. Daniel felt his spirits sag. Elspeth chattered on, about London, about the horrid Margaret Thatcher, about the "comic"—the fashion magazine where Elspeth worked as assistant art director—while Daniel subsided into silence.

Eventually Elspeth turned to him. "Don't you do it too."

"What?"

"What they do. I arrive home for the first time in almost two years, there's this tremendous burst of excitement, kisses all around, everyone talking at once. An hour later, it's as though I've never been away. They're both sunk back into their usual primordial funk."

"I'm sorry, Elspeth." For a moment he thought he might force himself into cheerfulness, just for her, but then he said, "Could we stop somewhere for a cup of coffee? I need reviving, and I need to talk to you. Face to face."

Elspeth sat across from him, looking down at the Band-Aid on her left thumb. "I wish I could say I was shocked or surprised or horrified, but everything you say seems right. It's as though all the things I've always wondered about in a vague sort of way are suddenly making sense. Converging, one might say. At a dizzying speed."

Daniel sighed heavily and sat back in his banquette. The maroon marbleized plastic upholstery creaked. "I'm sorry to dump this on you all at once, but I had to get it out. You have no idea how relieved I feel."

"I'm not sure how I feel. Whoops, yes I do. I feel like a cigarette. If I buy a pack, will you help me smoke them?"

Daniel nodded.

"Be right back."

Purchase made, she sauntered toward the booth, ducking to miss the gold tinsel crisscrossing the diner, and tossed a small, forest-green packet onto the Formica tabletop.

"Export 'A,' " Daniel said. "You're a real man, Elspeth."

"You said it, baby." Elspeth opened the pack and offered him one of the stubby cigarettes. She produced a box of kitchen matches from her jacket pocket. "Wasn't I smart to bring these along? I knew we'd end up smoking together. Have to remember to buy gum before we get home."

"No point. Mum will smell it in our hair, on our clothes."

"In our every orifice."

"God, this tastes marvelous." He reached across and lightly touched Elspeth's hand. She jumped. He withdrew his hand. "Sorry."

"No, it's all right. It's just that I feel a bit weird."

"It takes some getting used to. I'm not sure I am, even now. Sometimes it feels so completely unreal. I tell myself I must have made it up. Then I remember the night I actually remembered. That couldn't have been more real."

Elspeth wrinkled her nose in disgust. Her upper lip rode up to reveal her front teeth and a narrow band of gum. "It makes me feel kind of queasy."

"There's something else I should tell you."

"I'm not sure I can stand much more."

Daniel saw that she was joking and not joking. "I don't know how to say this. I think I may have done it to you. Sexually abused you. Once."

She looked at him calmly, blowing smoke out through her nose. "You mean once upon a time, or one time?"

"One time. I'm not even sure about that. How much I did or didn't do, I mean."

"If it's any comfort to you, I have no memory of it." She slumped down in her seat and closely examined the Band-Aid on her thumb. She tried unsuccessfully to smooth out the wrinkles in the flesh-colored plastic tape.

Daniel knew she didn't want to hear any more. But his need to unburden himself was more powerful than any desire to protect her from pain. "I think I was eleven. Maybe twelve. Old enough to have an erection. That means you were three or four. It was afternoon. I went into your room, and you were taking a nap. It was hot out—all you had on were underpants."

Elspeth ground out her cigarette in the red tin ashtray. "You know, you really don't have to tell me this, not if it makes you so sad."

"I'm pretty much used to feeling sad. I was wearing a yellow terry robe. I must have just come up from the pool. I think I climbed onto the bed next to you. I think I"—Daniel exhaled a plume of smoke and coughed—"I think I pressed my erection against your bare back."

Elspeth wriggled her shoulders. "Maybe that's why I have all this lower back pain. Instead of wasting my time with a chiropractor I ought to have been deep in analysis."

"Elspeth, could we be serious, just this once?"

"I'm not sure how to be serious. With you. It doesn't seem to work like that."

"I know. Irony's a groove we automatically slip into."

"Especially if we're trying to deal with something awful. Remember how outrageous we were at Grandmother Morton's funeral?"

Daniel reached out and touched her wrist. "You honestly don't remember me doing anything?"

This time she barely flinched at his touch. "I don't remember a thing. I don't think you traumatized me for life. Not doing that, not one time. When I was asleep."

"I'm not absolutely sure you were asleep."

"Daniel, please. You're torturing yourself over that?"

"These days I'm torturing myself over pretty much anything. I thought I should bring it up, so we could start out with a clean slate. Also because you always seem so uncomfortable when I touch you."

"Relax. I'm that way with everyone. Even Graham. He's this bloke I'm seeing? I like sex well enough. Adore it with him. But after, when he goes to stroke me? I can't tolerate it. And it's so hard to make him understand that it's more irritating than anything else. Like being rubbed the wrong way all over."

The waitress, a middle-aged Japanese woman in a canary-yellow nylon shift that whisked when she walked, came to their table, carrying two slabs of dark cake.

"I'm sorry," Elspeth said, "but we didn't order that."

"This on a house," the woman said. "My fruitcake. Special recipe. Lots of brandy. Merry Christmas."

"Merry Christmas," Elspeth and Daniel said, in unison. Then they laughed like a couple of kids.

Mrs. Hansel opened the door, wiping her hands on her poinsettia "company" apron. "Did you go and join the army, or what?" she said to Daniel and then reached up and kissed him on the cheek. Her pink lipstick felt thick as paste. "And you're as wasted away as your sister. Go see your mum and then come out to the kitchen. I'll fix you a little something to hold you over till dinner."

"We're fine, Mrs. Hansel," Elspeth said. "We stopped for a bite on the way home."

Mrs. Hansel scowled. "At some greasy spoon, I'm sure. Don't know what you'll pick up in places like that."

"It was actually quite nice," Daniel said. "Run by a Japanese lady. She gave us fruitcake. Very good too."

Mrs. Hansel primped the tight white bun at the top of her head. "Better hope that's all she gave you. Never know what those people are thinking, all that hissing and sucking their teeth."

"Is Daddy back yet?"

"I don't believe the doctor's back from seeing the tenants yet. Poor man, as if he doesn't do enough for the world the rest of the year. Your mum's in the morning room, I believe. Better knock before you go in. She's wrapping presents."

Daniel always forgot his mother was old. In her letters, during their monthly phone calls, in his mind, she was always thirty-five or forty, roughly the age he was now.

She looked up from the glass-topped wrought-iron table, gray eyes big behind the oval magnifying lenses of her "designer" glasses. Her hair was grayer than he remembered, a gunmetal, dyed gray. It didn't move much as she got up and briskly crossed the morning room, the long tweed hostess skirt emphasizing her thinness and her height. "Hello there," she said, licking a finger and then rubbing his cheek before lightly kissing it. "I see someone got here before me." She stepped back and studied his hair closely. "Is that the fashion in Montreal?"

"You like it, Mum?"

She tilted her head to one side. "Let me tell you in a day or so, once I've had time to get used to it." She leaned forward and sniffed at the shoulder of his corduroy jacket. "Have you been smoking?"

"That's from the plane, Mum. It was terrible."

Mrs. Kenning nodded absently. "Elspeth, would you go tell Mrs. Hansel we're ready for tea? Or perhaps you two would prefer something stronger?"

"A drink would be nice," Daniel said. Elspeth nodded vigorously behind their mother's back.

"I might join you," their mother said, "even if it isn't quite five. Jonathan should be back from the tenants soon."

"Does he shout 'Ho-ho-ho' as he hands them their turkey baskets, or is it a more restrained affair than that?" Elspeth said.

"I'm not sure why, Elspeth, you always want to cast your father's affairs in such a cynical light."

"Mum, I'm only kidding."

"I know, dear, but it always sounds, to my ears at least, a bit harsh."

"Shall we go to the den," Daniel said, "or do you want me to bring a tray in here?"

"Let's go to the den—that way we can surprise your father when he comes in."

"Surprise doesn't begin to describe it."

"What's that, Elspeth?"

"Nothing, Mother. After you." Daniel and Elspeth followed their mother across the hall and into their father's den.

The rest of the house had changed over the years, rooms gradually lightened and made airier in keeping with the times, a conservatory added here, French windows put in there, woodwork stripped and given a paler stain, dark floors taken up and replaced with terrazzo, marble, oak. But in the den the floor was nearly black with age, what bits of it could be seen beneath animal skins stretching every which way. Daniel looked up at the double-coved and coffered ceiling. When he was a child this big mock-Tudor house of sturdy between-the-wars construction had seemed to him the height of fine design and good taste. Now this, the last unrenovated room in the place, reminded him of everything he despised about Anglo-Canadian, slavishly colonial architecture. A mangy lion's head, flanked by a zebra and a lyre-antlered antelope, looked down from above the mantelpiece, big topaz eyes more pathetic than threatening.

His mother followed his gaze. "I've tried and tried to get your father to do something about this room. I'm ashamed to bring anyone in here anymore. Especially younger people. Practically all the young set at the hospital belong to the Sierra Club now, or that other one—Greensleeves, is it? But Jonathan says it's perfectly all right to display them since he shot them so long ago, back when it didn't matter."

"One suspects it may have mattered to the animals," Elspeth said.

Their mother clasped her hands together in perfect hostess form. "Now what will you both have?"

"This room always makes me feel like a Bloody Mary," Elspeth said.

"Surely not on Christmas Eve," their mother said, laughing a little to show she could be a good sport.

"Martinis?" Daniel said, and his mother and sister smiled in relief. It wasn't a drink either would have thought to suggest, but coming from Daniel it sounded just the thing.

"Will you do the honors, Daniel?" their mother said.

"What's that doing there?" Daniel pointed toward the refectory table, which had been pushed up against the gun case.

"Don't you remember it?" Mrs. Kenning said. "Your father lugged it up from his workroom this morning."

"Of course I remember it," Daniel said softly. "I didn't know it was still around."

"Your father spent all morning cleaning it up. You should have seen the dust."

Daniel stared at the model that nearly covered the table's surface. A perfect replica of their house. One of the first models his father had attempted, when Daniel was a small child. He remembered playing with it for hours on end, until the day his father decided it wasn't a fit plaything for a boy. The next time Daniel went looking for it, the house had disappeared, no one knew where.

Even for an early effort it was quite accomplished. The half-timbering was balsa wood stained dark; the stuccowork, white-washed sandpaper; the roof tiles, the orange-painted ends of tongue depressors. Carefully carved sponges made convincing decorative shrubs, hedgerows and trees, the contours of the garden were simulated by a green fiberglass shell. Even the rock pool, the swimming pool and the summerhouse were there—the blue-painted fiberglass was the least successful element of the model. The blue, a fifties turquoise, was too garish to represent water. And in the turnaround behind the stables, his father's 1950 Chevy, bulbous and bottle green.

"Bet you'd forgotten all about that." His father was standing behind him.

Daniel turned around slowly. "No, I remember it quite clearly. Hello, Dad."

"I didn't know if you and Elspeth would have made it back yet." He gave Daniel a manly hug. This was the physical contact Daniel had been dreading for weeks, and yet when it came it was so automatic and impersonal that it carried no special charge. His father stepped back, holding him at arm's length, smiling broadly. "Say, Son—what happened to your hair?"

"I got it cut," Daniel said.

His father reached up and rubbed his hand back and forth across the top of Daniel's head. Daniel jerked his head back. "That's a real brush cut, isn't it? Reminds me of my Navy days. You look young enough to be called up."

Daniel could feel his face reddening. He looked down and saw that his fists were tightly clenched.

"How were the tenants?" Elspeth said, her eyes moving from Daniel's hands to his face.

"Oh, fine, fine. Mrs. Farkey's pregnant again."

"Would you care for a drink, Jonathan?" their mother broke in.

"What are you having?" he said, glancing at his gold wristwatch. "I guess it's not too early."

"Daniel was about to make us martinis."

"Martoonis!" Dr. Kenning said.

"And it is a special occasion," Mrs. Kenning prompted.

"Christmas Eve," Dr. Kenning said with a sigh, as though testing to see if the words still had some magic in them.

"And Elspeth and Daniel both home together for the first time in . . . how long has it been, Daniel?"

"I think I was here for Christmas in '79, Mum," Daniel said, pouring gin into the heavy crystal pitcher.

"Seven years. Well, it's a real treat for us, isn't it, Jonathan?"

"It's a damned shame Leslie and the boys couldn't have come as well."

"Leslie wanted to," Daniel lied—it amazed him how quickly he got back in the habit, almost the minute he entered this house. "And the boys—well, you know how they are at that age. They don't want to have anything to do with anyone old." He could see the pained expression on his father's face. "I don't mean you and Mum. Anyone over eighteen is old for them. They're going down to Vermont to do some skiing."

"They must be big fellows by now," Dr. Kenning said. "Still growing, are they?"

"Porter just hit six-five and Alex isn't far behind."

"That Alex," Dr. Kenning said, shaking his silver head in amazement. "Shoulders like a linebacker even when he was only twelve or thirteen. Remember, Margaret, romping around the garden like a young colt?"

Mrs. Kenning made an assenting noise deep in her throat.

"You tell those boys any time they want to come out here for a visit, we're more than happy to have them. They're old enough to come on their own, and we've certainly got plenty of room. The skiing's pretty good in this part of the world too, you know."

"I'll tell them," Daniel said, gulping down his drink.

Later that night, after Mrs. Hansel had served a light supper in the morning room, Daniel found Elspeth and his mother in the living room, sitting as far apart as they possibly could. Half the room was "sunken" in the dramatic style of the thirties. Mrs. Kenning sat reading a *Smithsonian,* feet curled under her, on a love seat next to the fireplace in the raised part of the room. The fire popped as Daniel walked by, making him jump. Elspeth sat on the floor at the sunken end of the room, rummaging through the packages piled around the white-flocked tree.

"Where's Dad?" he said.

"I think he must be out in his workshop," Mrs. Kenning said without looking up from her magazine. "He usually heads out there directly after supper."

"What's he working on now?" Elspeth said, holding up a large package wrapped in red-and-gold foil and shaking it vigorously.

"Something new. He finished that Palladian villa he'd been working on for so long. Then for months and months he couldn't think of what else to do." She pursed her lips. "You know how it can't be just anything—he has to be inspired. Finally he settled on an Elizabethan manor house. You must know it, Elspeth, it's quite famous, I believe. Hellfield Hall? Something like that."

"Hatfield House?" Elspeth said.

"I'm so forgetful anymore. Perhaps that's it. Elizabeth I stayed there or was held prisoner there or something. I can't keep up with him. You two really should go out and let him show you what he's up to. He would be so pleased."

"I will," Elspeth said. "Later."

"Have you got any playing cards?" Daniel said.

"In the drawer of the drum table. Would you feel like a hand or two of something?" Mrs. Kenning said, looking up from her magazine expectantly.

"I thought I'd play a few hands of solitaire. I find it calms me down," Daniel said.

"Oh, yes."

The double pack was covered in moss-green felt. The back of each card, within a narrow gilt border, featured a polychrome photo of a King Charles spaniel. Daniel shuffled and turned the first four cards face up. Elspeth got up from sorting through the packages and wandered over.

She watched for a few moments as he went through the deck by threes, alternating black and red cards in descending order under each of the four original cards. "I've never seen solitaire played like that before."

"You don't have to watch."

"Not just the cards bark." She moved away, finally settling into Grandmother Morton's wing chair in the bow window, where she sat picking at the Band-Aid on her thumb.

Daniel quickly lost the first hand, shuffled and laid out four more cards.

Mrs. Kenning cleared her throat several times. She laid the *Smithsonian* aside and produced an emery board from the pocket of her long skirt.

"Is everything all right with you, Daniel?"

Daniel paused, holding the ace of diamonds midair. Elspeth looked up from her thumb, startled.

"Why do you ask?" he said.

"You did mention you needed calming down."

"That's true." He looked at his mother carefully. "To be perfectly frank, I'm not doing very well."

Mrs. Kenning gazed at him through thick oval lenses. "No?"

"This summer I had a sort of breakdown. A friend of mine died and . . ."

"I'm sorry to hear that."

"She wasn't a very close friend, but for some reason her death, the suddenness of it, I suppose, seemed to set me off. I was crying all the time and having terrible dreams too."

Mrs. Kenning ran her emery board back and forth over an especially rough patch of nail. "Really?"

"So finally I went to see a psychotherapist."

"That's a good thing to do, I would imagine." Mrs. Kenning cleared her throat once more. "And are you feeling better now?"

"No, actually I'm not. Or in some ways I am but in others, not at all."

"Perhaps you have the wrong psychotherapist. I know they say that can make all the difference in the world."

"She's an excellent therapist. She's done wonders for me. That may not be immediately apparent, but if you had seen me last summer you would notice the difference."

Mrs. Kenning put down her emery board and checked to see if her garnet earrings were still in place. "It's probably simply a question of time."

Daniel began to cry. "Aren't you even going to ask me why I went to a therapist?"

Mrs. Kenning's eyes widened. The rings of cartilage in her

throat rippled up and down, as though she were having difficulty swallowing. "You said your friend died."

Although his tears were flowing fast, Daniel found he could see through them perfectly—this room, his mother's face with the fire reflected in the lenses of her glasses, Elspeth across the way, looking on with her mouth open. "Mother, I hardly knew her. She was someone I worked with. She was nice, I liked her. That's all. Can't you hear me?" He kept wiping tears away from his cheeks but found he couldn't make them dry.

"Perhaps you should run and get Daniel a handkerchief, Elspeth."

Elspeth bounded up eagerly, but Daniel said, "I'll be fine. Just let me finish. My friend's death made me start remembering things. Things about Daddy." Daniel hiccoughed loudly. "Excuse me."

Mrs. Kenning picked up her emery board again and began pushing back a cuticle. "I'm not sure I see the connection."

"There isn't a direct connection. I'm trying to explain to you what happened. You know that he and I never had a very good relationship."

Mrs. Kenning glanced sharply at him, lips compressed. "I know the two of you have had your problems, but I thought— now that you're a grown man with a family of your own—that things were getting better between you."

"They're never going to get better unless"—Daniel hiccoughed again—"we talk about what happened between us while I was growing up."

Mrs. Kenning sat perfectly still. "You certainly had your differences."

"He beat me. He slapped me so hard he broke my glasses and my face was bruised for a week. When I was ten. He whipped me with a belt repeatedly. There were all those 'accidents' when he and I were alone together. You must remember those—I'd come home scraped and bruised and crying."

"You know that standards of child rearing have changed so much since the two of you were growing up," Mrs. Kenning said, casting a look of appeal toward Elspeth. "Whippings were what one did when a child got out of hand back then."

"Mum," Elspeth said, "Daniel's not talking about whippings. He's talking about being hit and beaten and hurt."

A faint pleading tone came into Mrs. Kenning's voice. "That wasn't your experience of your father, was it, Elspeth?"

Elspeth shook her head. "No, he never laid a hand on me. But I remember how he was with Daniel. How mean and crazy he could get. I remember him behaving like a wild man, chasing Daniel up the stairs to his room. And not just once."

Mrs. Kenning slowly shook her head, as though trying to recall an old story, one not very closely connected with herself. "But those two, they were always at loggerheads. There was something about Daniel that just seemed to set your father off, Elspeth. Right from the start. I don't know what it was. Almost as if it was something chemical."

Daniel felt another hiccough coming on. He tried to stifle it. It came out a resounding belch. "Sorry." He belched again, even louder this time. "Sorry. It was more than that. He was on my back the whole time I was growing up. He spied on me. He never allowed me any privacy. He was always bursting in on me—in the bathroom, my bedroom, always lurking around whenever I had friends over. Always trying to catch me out."

"Your father was trying to do the best he could for you," Mrs. Kenning said with some heat. "You know how difficult you were. And now you know how hard it is to be a parent yourself. Even the best intentions go astray. He was only trying to protect you."

"No." Daniel hadn't meant to shout. Elspeth jumped in her chair. Their mother remained motionless. "I won't listen to this shit."

Mrs. Kenning ran her tongue over her upper lip. "I don't see the need for that kind of language, Daniel."

Elspeth sat with one hand, the Band-Aid one, over her mouth.

"Perhaps," Daniel said quietly, "if you had been through what I have, you would feel the need."

"But you said you were getting help." Mrs. Kenning looked perplexed.

"You must see that this isn't simply my problem. It's something that involves, has always involved, all of us."

"You know we'd do anything we can to help you, but I'm not sure what we can do for you with you living so far away." Mrs. Kenning found a loose thread in her skirt and carefully snapped it off.

"You can help me by talking about it with me."

"Isn't that what we're doing this very minute?"

"I mean all of us talking."

Mrs. Kenning looked at him blankly. "Don't you think this is something you and Jonathan should discuss together? In private?"

"We're a family. We're all adults now. I want to talk about this as a family."

"If you think that's really necessary. But I can't answer for your father. You know how he is. This could be very upsetting for him."

"We certainly wouldn't want to upset him," Elspeth said in a low voice.

Mrs. Kenning either missed or chose to ignore the irony. "You both know how he gets."

"There's more, Mother," Daniel said.

"Yes?" The fire had died down. Daniel could see her eyes, bright and blank behind thick oval lenses.

"The dreams I had. They were about Daddy. They were sexual dreams."

Mrs. Kenning looked confused. "Isn't that within the realm of normal behavior? People can't really control what they dream about. At least that's how I understand it. You know I don't dream. But didn't Freud say something along those lines?"

"Mum, these were dreams about Daddy doing things to me. Sexual things."

Mrs. Kenning looked down at her clasped hands. "I'm not sure what that has to do with anything we've been discussing. That's surely a matter to take up with your psychotherapist."

Daniel's tears had dried, even his hiccoughs seemed to have abated. In a flat voice he said, "It's not just dreams. They came first. Then I started remembering. Mum, I think he abused me sexually. Over a period of several years, as far as I can tell."

His mother's lower lip trembled for a moment and then was still. The fire popped loudly. Elspeth seemed to have stopped breathing.

Finally Mrs. Kenning said, "I can't believe your father would do such a thing."

That wasn't the answer Daniel had expected. In rehearsing this moment over and over, Daniel had imagined his mother devastated by this new knowledge, had pictured her protesting, crying, denying—even turning on Daniel and ordering him out of the house. All these scenarios, he saw now, ignored his mother's essential nature. She had been preternaturally calm and unemotional for as long as he had known her. A sudden allegation, however startling or sordid, wasn't going to alter her character, change the way she met the world. What surprised him most was how mild her denial was. Not "How dare you accuse your father of such a thing," not "Your father never would have done that," but rather, "I can't believe your father would do such a thing."

Mrs. Kenning turned to Elspeth. "I suppose you're *au courant* about all this?"

Elspeth nodded.

"What do you make of it?"

Elspeth gnawed at her thumb. Daniel saw that the Band-Aid was no longer in place. "I . . . I don't know what to make of it. But Daniel's right—we need to talk about it. All of us."

Daniel felt both the stab of betrayal and the balm applied to the still-fresh wound. His sister would support him in one way, but not in another. He knew she had her reasons. Not for the first time, he wondered what her relationship with their father had been like.

Mrs. Kenning politely swallowed a yawn. "I suppose I can see the sense in that. I will talk to your father."

"About everything?" Daniel said.

"Not about everything. I think that's for you to do, after your own fashion. The most I can do is convey to him that you need to talk." There was something new in her tone, Daniel thought, something colder and more distant than he ever had heard before.

"We need to talk," Daniel said. He wasn't sure she caught the nuance.

. . .

The gentle tapping at the door seemed to have been going on forever. Daniel called out, "Who is it?" only to discover he had no voice. The tapping continued. He threw back the covers, struggled into his yellow terry robe and went to the door.

Mrs. Hansel stood with her fist raised. "Your sister's waiting for you down in the car, young man. You're supposed to go with her to collect the old folks."

Daniel opened his mouth to protest that he knew nothing about such a plan, but no sound came out.

"What's the matter—cat got your tongue?" Mrs. Hansel giggled, covering her mouth, and made her way down the narrow stairs.

In the bathroom, Daniel picked up the uncapped toothpaste tube. A long white coil spilled out into the basin. He hadn't even squeezed, yet it kept on coming. "Who left the lid off the toothpaste?" he shouted, but the shout stayed inside his head. He could hear a horn blaring down in the turnaround behind the stables.

"No time for breakfast?" Mrs. Hansel called after him as he dashed out through the sliding glass doors of the morning room. She teetered after him on spindly heels across the spongy lawn. "Here," she said, handing him a small package bound in gold tinsel. "Some fruitcake to tide you along. Velly good, velly good."

Elspeth sat at the wheel of the Jaguar. She was wearing an oversized blouse. One side of it, back and front, was black, the other, pure white. Down the middle, where buttons ought to have been, ran a bright crimson stripe.

"I didn't realize we were so late," Daniel said, climbing into the car. His laryngitis had disappeared. "Nice blouse."

"Graham gave it to me."

"Graham?"

"My new bloke. I told you about him. The one who makes me come."

"How'd you convince Daddy to let you use the Jag?"

Elspeth smiled dreamily. "Didn't you know? Daddy and I have a special relationship."

Once they were on the highway, Daniel couldn't keep his eyes open. He pressed a silver button. His window descended.

"If you get the upholstery wet, Daddy will kill you," Elspeth said.

Daniel tossed the tinsel-strung fruitcake out the window and pressed the silver button again. The window slowly rose, sealing out the rain. He felt so sleepy.

"Daniel, Daniel, we're here." Elspeth shook his shoulder. Her nails, long and sharp, were painted ruby red.

"You had a transplant?" he said.

"They've always been like that," Elspeth said, throwing back her head and laughing. "I'll run up and get Grandfather Morton. You go out to the conservatory and find Grandmother."

"What about Tante Hortense?"

"Didn't I tell you? She phoned this morning to say she preferred to take the bus."

Elspeth ran on ahead across the blue marble floor of the wide portico. Daniel held back. The big Corinthian columns frightened him. A Beefeater stepped out from behind the fourth column on the left. "So, the young gentleman. I thought I saw your lovely sister fly by." The Beefeater tugged at his forelock.

The mahogany-paneled lobby was crowded with Boy Scouts and Girl Guides. They pointed and giggled at Daniel's yellow terry robe. He was having trouble keeping it shut. Leaving the house in such a hurry, he had left the sash behind.

Grandmother Morton was sitting in her wing chair in the conservatory.

"I knew you were coming," she said. "I told all the nurses. They just said, 'So's Christmas' and laughed at me."

"This is Christmas, Grandmother."

"I know that. I'm not such an old lady I don't know that."

He helped her out of the chair. "Do you want your shawl, Grandmother?"

"Of course I do. What a question." He let go of her for a moment to reach for her peacock shawl. She listed abruptly to the left. "Whoa, Grandmother." He grabbed her arm.

"What do you think I am, the Derby winner?"

He led his grandmother slowly along the colonnade, the eyes of her shawl blinking dimly in the thin, gray light.

The brass elevator doors were just opening as the two of them lurched into the lobby. Elspeth backed out of the elevator, pulling Grandfather Morton in a wood-and-cane bath chair. Daniel rushed over to greet the old man. He had on his best linen suit, his "ice cream" suit. The jacket was open. His big distended belly hung down between his knees. The trousers had yellowed about the fly.

"Hello, Grandfather Morton," Daniel said.

"Who's this? Who's this? Who's this?"

"Don't you recognize your only grandson?" Elspeth said.

"Where's that old woman?" Grandfather Morton's blubbery face went red. "Where is she?"

Daniel glanced over his shoulder. Grandmother Morton stood in the exact center of the pie-sectioned marble floor of the lobby. She swayed first to the left, then the right, then to the front, then the rear, with each sway reaching a forty-five-degree angle to the marble floor. Daniel rushed over to lend her support. He got her upright only to realize his robe had fallen open. Boy Scouts and Girl Guides circled about, pointing at his arching penis and snickering.

With much coaxing and prodding, Daniel and Elspeth managed to get the old folks settled into the back of the Jag.

"What about the bath chair?" Daniel said.

Elspeth climbed into the driver's seat and started the engine. "Sod it. We'll use a wheelbarrow."

"There's no need to use that kind of language, Elspeth," Grandmother called from the backseat.

Everyone was already at table by the time they got back. Daniel thought he had never felt so hungry.

"Aren't you going to greet all our guests?" his mother prompted as Daniel slipped into his chair.

"I'm too hungry," Daniel said, nodding politely to Tante Hortense and Pierre Elliott Trudeau, who were already wearing their foil party hats in anticipation of New Year's Eve. Daniel reached for his milk. Tante Hortense and Pierre Elliott Trudeau pulled a

Christmas cracker between them. The explosion startled Daniel. He dropped his goblet of milk. White liquid poured everywhere, flowing in thick, sluggish streams across the peach-colored damask and onto the balding Aubusson.

"For shame, Daniel, for shame," his father called from the far end of the table. "Can't you be more careful than that? Is this how we raised you? Aren't you even going to apologize?"

"For shame, for shame," the rest of the table murmured, except for Tante Hortense and Pierre Elliott Trudeau, who were engaged, tongues intertwined, in a passionate kiss.

"I think you should apologize to everyone here," Mrs. Kenning said to Daniel, her mouth hinged like a puppet's.

Daniel picked up his gold-bordered dinner plate, milk running off it, and examined the stamp on the back. "Spode Ganymede," he read aloud. "I don't give a fuck about this family," he shouted. "I want out." He smashed the plate down on the table. It broke in two, right down the middle. Crimson stained the broken edges. Daniel saw he had cut his thumb.

"Do you have an extra Band-Aid?" he called to Elspeth, who was sitting at a separate table all the way out in the morning room. She shook her head sorrowfully and held up both hands. A tattered Band-Aid fluttered from every finger.

"I don't care if you are bleeding, you're going to clean up this mess right now," his father called from the far end of the table.

"Fuck you," Daniel said and jumped up from his chair, knocking it into the glass doors of the china cabinet. Satinwood splintered, beveled glass shattered. Daniel ran from the room.

"Such language," Grandmother Morton said.

Behind him, Daniel could hear a chair overturning and the sound of thudding feet. He ran up one flight of stairs and then another and another and another. Blood was dripping everywhere, and milk—milk came gushing down each new flight of stairs. He could hardly breathe. His nose squinched shut, his lip rode up until it touched his nose. He knew he had to hurry or he would never make it. The thundering on the steps behind him came louder and louder.

The final flight loomed up before him. Only a hundred steps or so and he would reach the big cherry door at the top, half open. Haven. He knew he could make it. It wasn't as though he hadn't done this a thousand times before. He was the younger, the swifter. Then—it must have been overconfidence, or longing, that did him in—he slipped on the ninety-eighth stair. His head and shoulders fell through the open doorway, but a hand clamped round his ankle and dragged him down.

The gentle tapping at his door seemed to have been going on forever.

"Yes," he called.

"May I come in?"

"Yes."

Elspeth peered around the door.

"You can come all the way in."

She was wearing a pair of magenta-striped silk pajamas. "You're not angry with me?"

"What would I be angry about?"

"You are angry."

" 'Hurt' is more like it."

"You can understand my position."

"No."

"I mean if you knew my position you would understand it."

"Where'd you get those pajamas?"

"They're an old pair of Daddy's."

"I thought so."

"Honestly, Daniel, you don't have to take everything as a personal affront. My bags still haven't arrived. I can't put on my *croque-mort* suit every time I need to go to the loo."

Daniel sat up in bed. "What I don't understand is how on the one hand you say what I told you made everything fall into place, and then you turn around and tell Mum you don't know what to think."

Elspeth parted the heavy green velvet drapes and took what Daniel considered an inordinate interest in the lightly falling rain. "I don't see any contradiction in those two statements." She turned to look at him. "I like your jammies better than his jammies."

Daniel slept naked. "The point is, you didn't support me when I most needed it."

"I agreed with you when you suggested we all sit down and talk. Although now I'm wondering whether I might not be busy washing my hair when the time comes."

"I hate to say this, Elspeth, but that's just like you, caving in at the last moment."

"Fuck off. You love saying it, and I didn't cave in. I didn't support you. That's different. And I don't intend to."

Daniel put his hands behind his head. He felt as if he hadn't slept at all, but the clock radio said 11:32. "I don't understand you at all."

"If it makes you feel any better, I'm not going to support him either. You're my brother and I love you. He's my father and I love him. In my fashion. Got it?"

"Got it."

"If I believe what you say about him, it means reexamining my whole life in a new light, and I'm not sure I'm up for that at the moment. Things are confused enough as it is." She leaned against the door frame, arms crossed over her breasts, as though waiting for him to tell her to get out. "Can you understand that?"

"I suppose so."

"You suppose so. Why should I support you or him? What have any of you done for me? It was always you and him, or you and Mum, or you and him and Mum. I was an afterthought in every sense of the word. By the time they got through with keeping you in line, they were too exhausted for me. 'Mum, can I go next door and play with the rabid dog?' 'That's nice, Elspeth, but don't overstay your welcome.' "

All at once Daniel saw the chart Henrietta had made months before, with the big F and M at the top, and the smaller D and E at the bottom. The thickly drawn line ran from "Father" to "Daniel." The line between "Mother" and "Daniel" was thinner, but not nearly so thin as the filaments connecting "Elspeth" with "Father," "Mother" and "Daniel."

"I'm sorry, Elspeth."

Elspeth hung her head. "Me too. I'd like to have been the center of attention once in a while." She looked up and smiled. "Not all the time, mind you. One sees rather a lot from the sidelines. But occasionally, only occasionally, I would like to have had everyone fussing over me."

"Don't be too sure."

"I know, I know." She stuck out her tongue. "It's lonely in the limelight. Laaaa-da-da-da-la-da-daaa." Elspeth hummed, but because she was tone deaf, Daniel couldn't begin to say what. "Don't you remember that?" she said.

"First you have to tell me what it is."

She flushed. "It was your favorite song when you were a kid. You even taught it to me. It's the first song I ever got by heart. 'Smile though your heart is breaking, smile even though it's aching . . .' "

"That's the wrong movie, Elspeth."

"What do you mean?"

"That's *Modern Times,* not *Limelight.* You know, where they toddle up the road at the end with 'Smile' on the soundtrack."

"Really, Daniel, you can be so pedantic. Does Leslie ever just haul off and sock you one?"

"Why would she want to do that?"

"You really should get up, you know. Mrs. Hansel was sure you had died in your sleep, but in the unlikely event you hadn't, your breakfast is neatly arrayed in the microwave. You want to come with me to fetch Tante Hortense?"

Daniel sank back into his pillows. "Do I have to?"

"Of course not. You should be taking it easy your first day back. You can greet the other guests as they arrive, handing out vats of eggnog to all and sundry. Or you could have a nice heart-to-heart with Daddy in his den."

"You think she's told him yet?" Daniel felt a sudden gnawing at the bottom of his stomach.

"I know she hasn't." Elspeth opened the door and turned to go.

"How do you know that?"

"Mum told me she wasn't going to deal with any of this until Christmas was cleared away."

"She's so sane, isn't she?"

"Pathologically so. Ciao, bébé." Elspeth shut the door behind her.

Daniel went to the drinks cabinet and poured himself a large brandy. He felt he deserved a reward. He had survived the regulation three-hour Christmas dinner without exchanging direct words with his father and without arguing with or insulting any of his parents' guests, although it had been touch and go at times.

Christmas dinners had once been such animated affairs, when Grandmother and Grandfather Morton were still alive; Grandma Kenning too, although she added little to the festivities except in those years when her paranoia was cycling especially high. His father's two brothers used to fly in from wherever they happened to be as well. The elder, Byron, was dead now, while Malcolm and Father had had a falling out some years before. Not that dour, taciturn Byron had ever added much seasonal charm. But Daniel had always liked sweet-natured Malcolm, who, as far as he knew, still lived with his "young friend" César on Central Park West. It occurred to Daniel that by now César must be pushing fifty. When Daniel was young the Christmas table was also crowded with three or four great aunts in addition to Tante Hortense, as well as a handful of other adults—Father's colleagues from the hospital who for one reason or another had no other place to go for Christmas cheer, old school chums of Mother's, weathering second divorces or first widowhoods. Always too a scattering of ill-defined cousins and their various offspring, including—Daniel recalled with a sigh—Agathe from Trois-Rivières, who gave him his first blow-job out in the orchard one especially warm Christmas Day. He wondered whatever had happened to the lovely Agathe. Then he realized with a start that she must be closing on forty.

Christmas dinner now was such a different story. Of the surviving oldest generations of the Morton and Kenning families, Tante

Hortense was the only one who could or cared to attend. Who could say what had happened to the various cousins, English or French? In place of hospital colleagues came a pair of retired doctors, Dr. Partiger and Dr. Rance. Daniel hadn't bothered to discover which was which—their looks and opinions seemed perfectly congruent, running to hale and balding on the first count and to typical Western bigotry on the second. The Jews, the blacks, the Sikhs, the Chinese—especially those vulgar rich ones from Hong Kong who were buying up Vancouver as fast as Vancouverites could sell it—were ruining the province. Elspeth and Daniel exchanged looks and silent toasts throughout the meal, in the process managing to put back a fair amount of burgundy. Daniel sensed that, as the only relatively young people at table, he and Elspeth were being not very subtly baited, especially when one of the doctors quoted an Alberta judge who had said, from the bench, that "regulations were like women—made to be violated." Daniel wasn't particularly shocked by the doctors' sympathies: long experience with his father and his father's colleagues had taught him that the medical profession had more than its share of practiced sadists.

Just as Mrs. Hansel was bringing in the pudding, Tante Hortense, who had been remarkably quiet throughout the meal, chewing each mouthful with great deliberation, slowly raised her head, thrust out her downy chin and addressed the doctors. "I think you missed one," she said.

"I beg your pardon?" the doctors said in unison.

"You missed a group."

The doctors exchanged humor-the-old-dear glances. "Group of what, Mrs. Morton?"

"Another group that's ruining the country," Tante Hortense said levelly. "French Canadians."

"Now, Tante Hortense," Dr. Kenning broke in with his best bedside manner, "these fellows are all in good fun. They aren't really against other races."

"Goodness no, Mrs. Morton," Dr. Rance or Dr. Partiger said, "we were just joshing, you know."

"That's right," Dr. Partiger or Dr. Rance added, "we make

jokes about everyone, regardless of race, color or creed. We're equal opportunity discriminators."

"I can think of another word for what you are," Tante Hortense said, picking up her wine glass and drinking deeply from it.

"I'll just see how Mrs. Hansel's doing with the coffee," Mrs. Kenning said, getting up from her chair as the leather-covered door to the kitchen swung open and Mrs. Hansel came in carrying the big pewter pot.

Now the doctors snored harmlessly in the Knole chairs flanking the library fireplace. Daniel assumed his father had fled to his workshop directly after coffee. Elspeth had disappeared as well. He wandered back through the empty dining room. All that remained of the afternoon's feast was the stained and becrumbed damask cloth. Rain streamed down the three sets of French windows. Daniel pushed open the door to the kitchen.

"Can I be of any help in here?"

The kitchen was already spotless, the dishwasher grinding away. His mother and Mrs. Hansel were drying the crystal with soft towels. Daniel suspected both women had been working side by side in the hour or so since dinner without uttering a word. His mother gave him a thin-lipped smile. "I think Mrs. Hansel and I have everything under control."

"It was very good."

His mother held a water goblet up to the light. "The credit for that goes to Mrs. Hansel."

Mrs. Hansel looked horrified. "Mrs. Kenning, you know that's not true. I did what I always do—the stuffing, dessert and the rolls. That goose and everything else was your mother's, Daniel. Don't let anyone tell you different."

Daniel sounded his big, hollow holiday laugh for the nth time that day. "It certainly was an excellent meal and a credit to you both." He looked closely at his mother, trying to read her face. Was she angry at him—hurt, devastated, in turmoil? It was impossible to tell.

Tante Hortense was curled up on the settee in the morning room, a white fur throw over her legs. Her head was turned to stare out the window at the fog slowly enveloping the orchard.

"Can I get you anything, Tante Hortense?"

She turned to see who had spoken. Her eyes were full of tears. Poor Hortense, he thought, her husband dead so long ago, her only child, Elise, killed in a car accident not long after.

"You startled me, my boy." She patted the settee cushion. "Come sit by me. If you don't mind the tears of an old woman." She produced a lace-trimmed handkerchief from the sleeve of her quilted Chanel suit, one Daniel was certain he remembered from his childhood. She dried her deep-set eyes and delicately blew her nose.

"Is Christmas a difficult time for you, Tante Hortense?"

She looked at him with red, swollen eyes. "What? Oh, Christmas. No, no. Christmas has no meaning for me. *Réveillon,* as you know, is the important holiday at home. No, I was only looking at the rain and making myself blue. I fear I may never drive again."

Like the rest of the family, Daniel thought that might not be such a bad thing. Tante Hortense, even on the very high heels she favored, stood no more than five feet tall. At the helm of her midnight-blue Cadillac, she didn't so much look over the steering wheel as through it. Before she moved to the convalescent home, she had had three fender-benders and two speeding tickets between her eightieth and her eighty-fifth birthdays. The fender-benders, miraculously, never turned out to be quite her fault, and she had gotten out of the speeding tickets by charming the presiding judge, who ended up taking her out to dinner. But now that she was nearing ninety, her spine was so brittle she could do herself serious damage just trying to open the Cadillac's heavy doors. Until this moment he hadn't been aware she was so eager to hop back into the driver's seat.

"Aren't taxis almost as convenient as driving yourself?"

"Oh, taxis," Tante Hortense said, making a dismissive moue. "Taxis are fine for around here." She grabbed on to Daniel's arm with a strength and urgency that startled him. "I must get to the city, Daniel. No one dances around here."

Daniel didn't know what to say, so he simply nodded his sympathy. Tante Hortense was always so intense.

"You don't know how I miss it. I'd just ordered two new gowns from New York—lovely, lovely ones, especially the full-skirted aquamarine. You know what a *pouf* is?"

Daniel nodded uncertainly.

"The skirt resembles a tulip turned upside down, and it's quite short. *Très osé.* Then I had this terrible, terrible accident."

"I heard." She had fallen in her bath at home and lain there, with three badly damaged vertebrae, naked and shivering in the cooling water, for twenty-four hours before her cleaning woman discovered her. That was when the family insisted she move to a home. "It must have been horrible for you."

She shook her head emphatically. "You will understand when you are my age. It's not only the pain. It's being trapped—unable to move."

"I'm sure. In a cold bath—"

"No, no," she said impatiently. "Being trapped in that home. Nothing but old people everywhere one looks. All my friends are in the city. All my dancing partners." She crossed her arms and stroked her shoulders. "But this is just *un échec.* I have been through worse and come back. I will come back from this. I promise you that." She glanced at her tiny diamond wristwatch. "I really must be getting back soon. My hydrotherapy is at six." She leaned close and murmured in his ear. "There isn't supposed to be therapy of any sort on Christmas Day, but Ernie is coming in especially for me. Such a nice young man. Native boy from Yellowknife."

"I'm sure you'll be better soon, Tante Hortense," Daniel said, although he couldn't imagine her slight, frangible body turning even the power steering of her mammoth car, let alone twirling across the parquet of a hotel ballroom. He reached out and stroked the knotted joints of her diamond-encrusted hand. Her spotted skin was smooth and cool, like a reptile's. He ran his hand over the fur throw. "It's so soft."

"Ermine. Morton gave it to me for our fifth anniversary."

"It's beautiful."

"I had it resewn—back in the sixties, I believe it was. They did a wonderful job." She stroked the sleek fur herself. "Morton was so good to me. We had seven years of perfect happiness together.

If you're granted that much in this life, why tempt fate? That's why I never remarried. Not that I wasn't asked." She squeezed Daniel's hand. Her rings were almost the same cool temperature as her skin. "But I also have always valued my independence. *La liberté*. Most people never understand how important that is." She looked at him sharply. "How are Leslie and the boys?"

Daniel was caught off guard. That often happened with Tante Hortense. "They're fine."

"And you, Daniel?"

"I'm fine too."

He felt her steady gaze but couldn't bring himself to meet it. "Excuse a nosy old woman, but I had the impression at dinner today that you are much troubled."

Daniel considered telling her everything, in one great outpouring. What would she make of it all? "I have been having some problems, Tante Hortense. With Mum and Daddy."

"They're wonderful people, your mother and father. What sort of problems?"

"Just . . . I don't know how much you'd like to know. Personal problems." He could feel the sweat breaking out on his brow.

"Excuse me, Daniel. You must stop me when I'm being *envahissante*." She laughed and reached up to touch the top of his head. "I must tell you, before I forget, how much I like this hair. It reminds me so much of a boy I once knew. Before I met your Uncle Morton. A doughboy. An English. That's how he looked when he went off to war."

Daniel looked down at her and smiled.

"Now go tell Elspeth," she said, gathering up the fur throw, "that Tante Hortense wants to be carried home."

The microwave was empty. Two days home and they'd forgotten his existence. Then Daniel remembered that Mrs. Hansel always got Boxing Day off.

In the bread bin he found half a loaf of Mrs. Hansel's cinnamon bread. He sawed off two thick slices and put them in the toaster oven.

He was just taking his first bite when the door to the dining room swung open and his father walked in. He was wearing his work clothes: a slouch-brimmed gray hat with a bristly yellow feather cocked in the band and a suede bomber jacket that once must have been moleskin, now streaked with grease and paint and tacky with dried glue; the tails of an age-yellowed white T-shirt and a lime-green UBC sweatshirt swagged like bunting below the jacket's unraveling knit waistband. His baggy brown gabardine trousers needed a belt—fly gaping half open, they hung down below his slight paunch.

"I was wondering if you were up yet," his father said in his false-hearty voice.

Daniel nodded. In an instant his mouth had gone dry. It was all he could do not to choke.

"Why don't you come out to the den when you're through here?" his father said, noticing the toast cooling on the bread-board. "Is that what you call breakfast?"

Daniel nodded again.

"Your mother told me you have a problem, Son."

Daniel managed to shake his head and say, "No."

His father clapped his hands together silently. "I'm sure that's what Margaret told me."

Daniel coughed. He watched a fleck of toast fly out of his mouth and arc onto the counter. "We have a problem," he said.

"That's not the way Margaret had it."

"I'll be there in a second."

The door swung twice, and his father was gone.

Daniel opened the door to the pantry and scraped both pieces of toast off the breadboard and into the dustbin.

His mother and Elspeth were sitting on the sofa before the fire-place. The chintz slipcovers were so old and faded that on the armrests the flowers gave way to oblong bleached patches. Mrs. Kenning and Elspeth sat at either end of the long sofa, neither of them affecting to do anything more than wait.

"Where's Dad?" he said.

"He couldn't remember if he'd shut off the heater in his workroom," Mrs. Kenning said. "Sometimes he's almost as absent-minded as I am."

"I do believe the sun's coming out," Elspeth said. She got up and went to the corner window. "I'd practically forgotten there were hills at all. Blue remembered hills."

Daniel wandered over to the refectory table and examined the model of their house. Each time he studied it he noticed something new. He bent down to inspect what looked like a tiny parasol at the edge of a flowering border in front of the summerhouse.

"Can't you tell what that is?" Daniel felt his father's breath on the back of his neck.

"It's too small for a beach umbrella," Daniel said, aware his voice was quavering.

"And what are those?" His father pointed to two small lumps of brown clay protruding from under the parasol's rim.

"I don't know," Daniel said.

"Shoes," his father said. "It's Keiji, weeding the flower bed. That's his straw hat."

"Who's Keiji?" Elspeth said.

"He was our yardman," Mrs. Kenning said. "Keiji died, oh, long before you were born."

"I'm glad you didn't throw this out," Daniel said to his father, brushing a bit of fluff off the roof tiles of the summerhouse.

"Why would I throw it out?" his father said.

"I don't know. For some reason I thought you had. That day you cleaned out the basement."

"What are you talking about, Son?"

"Do you remember seeing the house when you were small, Elspeth?" Mrs. Kenning broke in.

"No, Mother," Elspeth said, sounding tired. "That was before my time."

"Go ahead," Dr. Kenning said to Daniel, "lift up the roof."

Daniel stooped down to look under the eaves. The roof was hinged on one side. He carefully tilted it back, remembering, remembering. "God," he said.

Half the attic was a warren of box rooms and maids' quarters, the other half a wide open space with dormer windows at either end. When Daniel was eight or nine all the small rooms were torn out and the whole attic became his bedroom aerie, but when he was small the room with the two dormers was his nursery. In the model it was decorated to look like a circus. At the room's center stood a red-and-gold painted ring. Inside the ring were three hand-carved wooden figures—a whip-wielding ringmaster in crimson jacket and shiny black hat; a dancing bear, paws held high; and a little boy in a glittery white leotard, swallowing a tiny sword. Off to one side of the ring, a woman in a pink tutu walked a tightrope. Beneath the rope a Scottie dog barked. In the far corner of the room stood a tiny yellow crib with black-painted bars.

"Don't you remember helping me carve those figures?" his father said.

Daniel nodded slowly. He remembered the sharp-fumed, brilliant-hued model paint that came in small glass pots.

His father pointed into the attic with one soot-stained finger. "See, there you are, doing your act. And there's your mum trying to keep her balance on the high wire"—he chuckled—"I wanted to have her tongue sticking out the corner of her mouth to show how hard she was concentrating but I just couldn't manage it with the means I had. I could do it now, no problem. Better tools. I've been using a jeweler's loupe lately—makes all the difference in the world. And that's me"—he chuckled again—"cracking the whip."

"I told Daniel and Elspeth they should go out and see what you're working on now," Mrs. Kenning said.

"Makes this look like a kid's school project," Dr. Kenning said, grinning. He tilted the roof of the house back into place and brushed off his hands. He went over and sat in the tufted leather armchair next to the fireplace. Elspeth scurried from the window back to her place on the sofa, as though she were playing some private demented version of musical chairs. That left Daniel the Windsor chair on the other side of the fireplace, facing his father.

Dr. Kenning jumped up again. "I'll just run and get some wood for the fire."

Elspeth said impatiently, "Daddy, it must be seventy out today."

"When you get to be my age you feel the damp. Maybe you should open the window, Daniel."

"I'm quite comfortable myself," Mrs. Kenning said, readjusting her beige cashmere cardigan.

Dr. Kenning leaned forward, elbows resting on his knees, fingertips touching so his hands described a globe. "Now, the way I understand it, Son, you have the idea that we don't have a very good relationship."

Daniel nodded.

Dr. Kenning sat back abruptly in his chair, as though this revelation came as a physical blow to him. "I have to say that I was surprised when your mother told me that. Isn't that right, Margaret?"

"He was," Mrs. Kenning said, nodding.

"You actually think we had a good relationship?" Daniel said.

"I know we didn't get along very well when you were a teenager, but that's often the case between fathers and sons, isn't it? There's frequently a rivalry, an edginess there. I see it with some of my younger colleagues and their sons."

"It's not just a question of rivalry, Dad. Last spring I had a kind of breakdown."

"I'm very sorry to hear that. I'm just not sure why you're telling me. You're an adult now—what happens to you is your own business." Dr. Kenning spoke softly, reasonably, an understanding smile on his handsome lined face.

"I'm not asking for your sympathy. I just want to tell you what happened. That's all. I went to see a psychotherapist, and we started talking a lot about my childhood."

"That's pretty much the usual procedure when you go to see someone like that," Dr. Kenning said, nodding and crossing one leg over the other.

Daniel felt less panicky, now that he could make out his father's game. It was the one he had always played whenever Daniel had tried to reach him, to talk to him as an equal: the reasonable, compassionate physician carefully attending to the dubious complaints of a mildly unbalanced patient.

"There was one thing I discovered almost immediately, one thing that surprised me a lot. I always thought I hated you"—his father's shoulders twitched—"but it turns out I feared you more than anything else."

"Now, Son," Dr. Kenning said, slowly stroking his thigh, "this sounds a little extreme to me. What kind of doctor did you say you went to see?"

"I'm still seeing her. She's not a doctor."

"Oh? I hope you checked out her credentials beforehand. There are a lot of charlatans out there, ready to hang out a shingle that says 'Therapist' when all they really want is your money. I saw an article just the other day in the *Wall Street Journal*—"

"Daddy," Elspeth broke in, "Daniel's trying to tell you why he's been having such a hard time. Don't you want to hear?"

"What I can't accept, Elspeth, is that a complete stranger, who knows nothing about how things were between us, should have the right to influence Daniel in such a way, to try and turn him against his own family."

Daniel could feel a scream of frustration rising up inside him. Then an odd thing happened: he heard Henrietta's low, melodious voice deep inside his head. "If you let him make you angry," the voice said, "the game is up. If you throw a tantrum, you're that helpless little boy again, the one no one ever believed."

"Dad," Daniel said at last, "my therapist wasn't trying to turn me against you—she was trying to help me understand why our relationship has always been so bad, so I could try to change things. Before it's too late." He was amazed at how calm he felt. "We're both adults now—wouldn't you like us to be able to get along better, to be able to talk more openly with each other?"

His father slouched down in his chair, chin almost hidden by the neckband of his sweatshirt. "I don't like all this talk about how scared you were of me. That poisons the well for me right from the start. In exactly what ways was I such a bad father? I didn't hit you, did I?"

Was it possible that he didn't remember? "When you got angry you would slap me hard across the face."

"At least I hit you in anger. They say it's worse when you—"

"You hit me hard enough to leave marks. To break my glasses. I told my fourth-grade teacher the big bruise on my cheek came from falling off a horse."

"And who's to say it didn't? I think you're blowing this all out of proportion. Go to your friends and ask. Find me a father who never, in a moment of frustration, hit his kids."

Daniel said quietly, "There were also the beatings."

His father shook his head doubtfully. "I may have spanked you once or twice on the bum when you were little. But I never beat you. You mean with a belt?"

Daniel felt the conversation was becoming surreal, his father anticipating questions that hadn't been asked, denying accusations not yet made.

"You beat me a number of times with a belt."

"But never on your bare buttocks."

"On my bare buttocks. And not just when I was a little boy. You did it right up until I was fourteen or fifteen."

His father sat up in his chair. "I know I never left any marks."

"What difference does it make if you left any marks?"

Dr. Kenning turned to his wife. "Margaret, do you know what he's talking about?"

Mrs. Kenning's eyes darted back and forth between her husband and her son. "Yes," she said finally, staring into the empty fireplace. "I do remember that you would use a belt on him from time to time. I think I recall the time when you broke his glasses. Also I remember once when we were on vacation and Elspeth and Daniel were squabbling in the backseat. You were driving and you turned around to slap Daniel and nearly got us all killed."

Dr. Kenning shook his head in disbelief. "I just don't remember any of this. Here I've gone through my entire life not realizing I was the worst father who ever lived." He gave a short, bitter laugh. "Have you talked to your friends—the fellows you grew up with? Was I really that much worse than any of their fathers?"

"I don't know," Daniel said.

"I don't think that's Daniel's point," Elspeth said. "It's not a worst-father competition."

"Then I'll be damned if I know what his point is and why I should sit here one more minute listening to his accusations."

"He's not accusing you," Elspeth half shouted, face flushing. "He's trying to talk to you."

Dr. Kenning crossed his arms over his chest and looked up at the coffered ceiling. "Daniel, all I can say is, you were a problem child from day one. My mother always said, 'Problem children demand special measures,' and you're proof positive she was right."

"Would you say I was a bad baby?" Daniel said, hearing Henrietta in the phrasing of the question.

"Perhaps not 'bad.' You were a difficult baby, from the moment we brought you home from the hospital."

Elspeth turned to her mother. "You always told me Daniel was such a good baby. You said all the nurses doted on him."

Mrs. Kenning nodded absently. "Yes, that may be true. I—"

"He was fine at the hospital," Dr. Kenning said. "But something happened the instant we got him home. He changed completely. Screamed all the time. I had the 2:00 A.M. feeding, so I should know. I remember"—he chuckled sheepishly—"I took a diaper pin and made the hole in the nipple bigger so the milk would go down faster. Some nights it went down so fast I was terrified the little bugger would choke to death. Those feedings were a nightmare for me, a sheer nightmare."

Daniel said, "I don't think there's such a thing as a bad baby. It doesn't make sense."

"That's because you never had any children of your own."

"It doesn't make much sense to me either," Elspeth said. "A baby is pretty much an empty slate, isn't it?"

"Ah, the great expert on maternity speaks," Dr. Kenning said. "You seem to forget that I work in a hospital. I see babies every day. Miserable babies, deformed and scarred babies, babies whose faces and bodies I've spent months reconstructing. I think I know far more about the subject than either of you ever will, so don't try to tell me my business."

"Dad," Daniel said, "you're a cosmetic surgeon, not a pediatrician."

"We all go through the same training. You know that. As a

student I did my time in pediatrics. On the whole newborns were the sweetest bunch you could imagine, but"—he shook his head sadly—"there was always a black sheep, a bad apple in every bunch. Besides, it wasn't just as a baby that you were bad—think of how often you were in trouble when you were growing up."

"How could I not have been in trouble? You were always spying on me, trying to catch me out."

"I certainly didn't have to spy very long or hard to catch you at it. In any case, isn't that exactly what a father does? He watches over his children to make sure they don't get into serious trouble."

"You must admit I was never in serious trouble."

His father thrust out his jaw. "Only because I was there watching you every minute."

Daniel sighed in exasperation.

"And now you and this woman you're seeing are trying to turn it all into something sick."

Daniel stared at his father's face. Something was missing, he couldn't think what. Then it struck him: never in his life had he looked directly into his father's eyes. When his father spoke he looked down at the floor, up at the ceiling, off to one corner of the room. This very moment he was studying the lion's head over the mantelpiece.

"No one said anything about sickness," Daniel said, trying to will his father to look into his eyes.

Dr. Kenning reached up and stroked the lion's shiny muzzle. "You never could be trusted as a child. Always lying. Isn't that right, Margaret?"

Mrs. Kenning looked at her husband blankly.

"You must remember," he turned to look at his wife. "Dr. Van Houten called you in to talk about all the stories he was telling at school. We weren't his real parents, we were just taking care of him. His real parents lived in France and were royalty or something."

"Who was Dr. Van Houten?" Elspeth said.

"His elementary school principal," Dr. Kenning said. "She knew something about psychology."

Mrs. Kenning spoke haltingly, as though she were having dif-

ficulty recalling such a long-ago event. "Dr. Van Houten told me
. . . I can't remember exactly how she phrased it . . . she told me
she thought we needed to give Daniel a lot of love. She asked
me if I thought he was getting enough love at home."

Dr. Kenning slapped his hand down on the mantelpiece.
"That's crazy. How could we have given him any more love than
he already had? Would he even let us love him? Always off in
some dream world, making up lies and more lies. Did you ever
want for anything? Was anything ever denied you? Christ, when
I think what I went without as a boy, and then you, you . . ."

"That's not the point and you know it," Daniel said.

"You keep saying that. 'That's not the point, that's not the
point.' " Dr. Kenning screwed up his face to mimic Daniel. "But
we never seem to find out what the point is. I'm some kind of
monster—isn't that the point?"

"I thought you were, once. I don't anymore."

"Then what am I?"

"I don't know. All I can figure out is that, however you
behaved, it wasn't because you were evil or some kind of monster. Maybe you were so consumed by your own private pain that
it blinded you to the pain you inflicted."

"My own private pain?" His father's voice shot up an octave
and cracked like an adolescent's. "What in hell is that supposed
to mean? My pain. What pain is that? I don't have any pain in my
life. I have a wonderful wife, a profession I love, a beautiful
home. Why would there be pain in my life?" He stood over
Daniel, pointing down at him. "You don't know what you're
talking about, mister. I've spent my whole life trying to alleviate
pain. I've dedicated my life to taking people's pain away—that's
what a physician does, or tries his damnedest to do. And you
come along saying I'm full of pain, 'consumed by pain'—isn't
that the way you put it? You say I inflict pain instead of healing
it. I've got a pain all right. I've got about as much pain as you've
got. Made-up pain, that's what all this is, you dredging up the
past to make everyone miserable. You and your bloody unhappy
childhood. So who didn't have one? And what was so unhappy
about it? I remember you as a child, singing, always singing. It

was all we could do to get you to shut up. What was so unhappy about your childhood?"

"Dad," Daniel said, aware his head was trembling, "I tried to kill myself three times before I was seventeen."

"Right," Dr. Kenning said, shaking his head in disgust. "Real serious stuff, I'm willing to bet."

"Serious enough," Daniel said.

"What did you take?"

Daniel thought for a moment. "The first time, a bottle of aspirin."

His father snorted. "That won't do it."

"I didn't know that at the time. I was twelve years old. The second time I drank a bottle of cough syrup, the kind with codeine in it?"

Dr. Kenning tilted his head to one side, considering. "How old were you that time?"

"Fourteen."

Dr. Kenning shook his head. "No. Might make you a little groggy in the morning, maybe blur your vision for a day or two. Certainly wouldn't kill you."

"The third time I combined cough syrup with a bottle of sleeping pills."

"Where'd you ever get sleeping pills?" Dr. Kenning asked.

"At a pharmacy."

"Over the counter?"

Daniel nodded.

"That wouldn't do it either. Nothing over the counter would kill you, not unless maybe you mixed a lot of things together," Dr. Kenning said, glancing pointedly at his wife and daughter.

Without quite realizing what he was doing, Daniel leaned forward in his chair and reached his hand up toward his father. "Dad, I'm trying to tell you how much it hurt when I was a kid. Enough that I wanted to die, even if I didn't quite know how to go about accomplishing it."

His father looked down at the empty hearth. "You always were the dramatic one in the family. And I can tell you I've about had a bellyful of your accusations, your insinuations, your lies.

How can you seriously expect me to believe a word you say when as far as I can ascertain you've never told the truth in your life? I remember quite clearly, one time when you were home from McGill, I asked you if you were smoking marijuana and you had the gall to sit there and tell me no, when Mrs. Hansel had found three cigarettes of the stuff in your room. Do you remember that?"

"Of course I remember that. I don't see what that has to do with what we're talking about now. That was almost twenty years ago."

"As far as I can see, everything we're talking about today happened twenty or thirty years ago. Ancient history. But the marijuana thing is important for two reasons. Number one, it shows you can't be trusted. Number two, it shows you have a history of drug use, which would certainly account for a lot of your current psychological problems."

"Daddy, everyone smoked marijuana at university," Elspeth said, "even when I was at Oxford."

"I wouldn't say you were the stablest person around either, young lady. Just look at what you do to your nails, for one thing."

Elspeth clenched her hands and then, embarrassed by that reflexive action, opened them again, revealing a Band-Aid on her index finger and a small bloody scab at the edge of her thumbnail.

"It was when you went away to university that you started to change. Both of you. You just ran wild. That was the first time I noticed a profound change in your personalities. Not as extreme in your case, Elspeth—I always thought your hostility toward me was just a question of you following your brother's lead."

"Daddy, Daniel went away to boarding school when I was only six or seven. I hardly saw him after that."

"You were always thick as thieves when he did come home. Secret looks, private jokes—you think I didn't notice?"

"What are you talking about? Daniel and I hardly had a word to say to each other until we were both adults, until he came to visit me when I was still at Oxford. Where the fuck did you get the idea that . . ."

"Elspeth, please," Mrs. Kenning said levelly, shifting about uncomfortably at her end of the sofa.

"You got your language from your brother too," Dr. Kenning said.

"Oh, Christ," Elspeth said. "This is completely unreal."

"Blame that on your brother. This whole . . . this 'session' wasn't my idea." Dr. Kenning turned to Daniel. "Have you said all you've got to say? Are you satisfied—have you hurt your mother and me enough for the time being? Do you think, mister, that you've about shot your wad?"

The metaphor was so crude Daniel couldn't ignore it. "No, I haven't," he said, "but I don't know if there's any point in continuing, since on the one hand you have no memory, and on the other I'm a pathological liar."

Dr. Kenning waved a hand dismissively. A shock of white hair had fallen down over one eye. "Go ahead, go ahead. There's nothing you could say that would shock me."

"Since I've been in therapy I've started having all these dreams . . ."

Dr. Kenning bent down to untie and then retie his shoe. "Dreams? This should be good."

"First dreams, then more specific physical sensations and memories."

Dr. Kenning nodded. "Sounds like the scientific method to me."

"Dad, be quiet," Elspeth said.

Dr. Kenning set his jaw and tilted back his head so that he looked at his daughter through half-closed eyes.

Daniel was having difficulty finding his voice. He cleared his throat twice. "I think you abused me sexually."

There was no movement in the high paneled room. Daniel could hear the sound of his own breathing.

Dr. Kenning was the first to move. He turned his back to the room and said quietly, "I know what's going on here. You're trying to kill me."

Daniel clung to the arms of his chair. "I'm not trying to kill you. I'm trying to talk to you."

His mother sat with one hand over her mouth. Elspeth started to bite at her thumb, noticed what she was doing and put her hand down in her lap again.

"You're trying to kill me, and I'm telling you it won't work." The mangy lion's head hung just above him, mouth open to reveal curving, yellowed fangs. For a moment Daniel thought his father was going to insert his head into the lion's mouth, but he turned abruptly and stood staring down at Daniel, his half-open fly level with his son's chin. "When is this supposed to have happened?"

Daniel looked up at him steadily, trying to catch his eye. "When I was little. It continued till I was four or five. I think. From what I can remember I finally let Mum know what was going on, or she found out, I don't know. And then it stopped."

" 'You think,' 'you think,' 'you think,' 'you don't know.' That about settles it as far as I'm concerned. I think you need another therapist. I think you need a real professional. You need a psychiatrist. Why, you're crazy. You talk about dreams. You're dreaming in color, mister. You are a pathological liar. You're deeply sick, is what you are."

"Jonathan," Mrs. Kenning said, almost whispering, "it won't do any good to get all worked up."

He spun around to look at her. "Did you know anything about this? Were you in on this? Did he tell you all this?"

Mrs. Kenning shook her head slowly. "He talked to me about the whippings. This is the first I've heard about . . . the other."

"Mother," Elspeth said, "I was right there. Christmas Eve. Daniel told us everything."

"You keep out of this, young lady," Dr. Kenning said.

"I certainly don't recall Daniel saying anything about . . ." Mrs. Kenning trailed off in desperation.

"It's clear you've got your wires crossed," Dr. Kenning said, turning back to Daniel. "What you say may have happened to you. Considering the hijinks you got up to with other boys when you were a teenager, I'd say there are pretty good odds some kind of sexual thing did happen. You were pretty seductive. But not at my hands. You're dreaming there, boy." To Daniel's astonishment his father then rattled off the names of older men he had always suspected of having sexual designs on his young son: his own "flitty" brother, Malcolm; Daniel's grade-seven music instructor; Keiji, the Japanese yardman; the Vancouver architect who hired Daniel as a gofer the summer he was thirteen.

"Nothing happened with any of them," Daniel said, smiling at the thought of the architect, an indefatigable womanizer, making a play for a chubby, awkward, bespectacled adolescent boy.

"Where are these so-called events, these molestations, supposed to have occurred?"

"Dad," Daniel said uncertainly, "I don't know what else I can tell you. I don't know how we can discuss it at all, since you've already decided I'm a crazy liar."

"That's exactly what you are, and if I were you I'd get some real help and fast. But I want to know. I want details. Exactly what am I supposed to have done?"

"I can't tell you that—there's no point, since you've already decided that everything I say is a lie."

"Can you believe any of this, Margaret?"

Mrs. Kenning swallowed with evident difficulty and looked as though she was about to speak.

"And I hope," Dr. Kenning said, "that you don't harbor any ideas about any of this becoming yours." He made a sweeping gesture with his arm, indicating the stuffed animal heads on the walls, the balding animal skins on the floor, the sagging sofa, the fading slipcovers. It took Daniel a moment to realize his father was referring to his inheritance. "I hope," his father continued, "that you're not expecting to come into a fortune when I'm gone, because there isn't going to be one. We're going to spend it all while we're still around to enjoy it. Isn't that right, Margaret?"

Mrs. Kenning leaned forward. "Jonathan, I think we could . . ."

"And precisely when did you tell your mother about all this? When you were a child, I mean. When is she supposed to have discovered these terrible things I did to you?"

"I'm not sure," Daniel said, trying to pull together all the images that came rushing into his mind. "I remember sitting in

the summerhouse with Mother—I must have been four or five—
and we were drinking lime Kool-Aid. It was kind of tart because
you"—he looked at his mother—"never liked using too much
sugar. And I told you I thought you wanted to kill me."

Mrs. Kenning looked frightened. "I don't have any memory of
this. Why would you say something like that? Why would you
even think it? What did I answer? Why should I want to kill you?"

"I don't know," Daniel said, "maybe I imagined you'd want to
kill me because of what I was doing with your husband. Anyway,
the next thing I remember is that Daddy went into this rage. He
was cleaning out the basement, taking great armloads of stuff—
toys and papers and even some of his model airplanes—hauling
them out to the ashpit and throwing them on this enormous
bonfire. The flames were shooting high and there was all this
black smoke. And you"—he continued looking at his mother—
"you were in the living room, sobbing facedown on the old
fringed sofa. He kept yelling at you and you kept sobbing."
Daniel realized that was the last time he had seen his mother cry.
"Then he ran back down into the basement and grabbed this
really big model." Daniel nodded in the direction of the refectory
table. "I thought it was our house he charged out to the ashpit
with, holding it high above his head and then heaving it into the
flames. But obviously it wasn't."

His father sat down heavily in the leather armchair and rubbed
his eyes. "Obviously. Just one more example of your overheated
imagination, not to mention your faulty memory. Daniel, I'm
going to make a phone call to Dr. Morgenstern at the hospital.
You probably remember him from parties here at the house—
youngish chap, curly black hair. Graying a bit now. He's been
head of psychiatry since—"

"I can't recall what we were fighting about," Mrs. Kenning
said in a voice so low Daniel had to lean forward in order to hear,
"but I know what it was that you threw on the fire." She pointed
toward the refectory table. "That isn't the first model house you
made, Jonathan. I'd completely forgotten. When we were first
married and still living in Vancouver, you made a model of the
bungalow on Marlowe. Our honeymoon house, you called it.
Don't you remember?"

"At this point I don't know what I remember," Dr. Kenning said. "He thought it was one house, you say it was another. All it proves is that our son, as usual, can't get his facts straight. Overactive imagination, liar, dreamer, crazy—whatever you want to call it, Danny boy, you need help. The sooner the better. And I'm going to see that you get it." Dr. Kenning stood up and with great deliberation walked out of the room, leaving the double doors open behind him.

Mrs. Kenning got up from the sofa, carefully resettling her cardigan. "I'd better see if there's anything I can do." She followed her husband out the door.

Daniel and Elspeth sat staring at each other, speechless, across an expanse of zebra- and leopard-skin rugs.

"Daniel, my God, you haven't changed one bit. How irritating. And all I've done is gotten fat." The red-haired woman encased in a long emerald taffeta dress opened the door wide. "And this must be your lovely wife. I'm so glad you could come."

"Olivia, this is my sister, Elspeth. Elspeth, Olivia Glyde."

"Elspeth," Olivia cried, leaning forward to kiss Elspeth, who was leaning away from her. "I don't believe it. The last time I saw you, you were only a little thing. Don't just stand there. Come in, come in."

"It's a lovely house, Olivia," Daniel said, taking in the vast cathedral-ceilinged room, a vertiginous mixture of the rustic and the austerely modern, the ecclesiastical and the desert sere.

"Do you like it? Really and truly?" Olivia said, her already loud voice ascending the scale as well as escalating in decibel level so that the guests already thronging the big room turned to stare at the new arrivals. "I'm so pleased," she said to Elspeth, entwining her own bare, freckled arm with Elspeth's velvet-covered one, "that a real architect sees the value of what Douglas and I are struggling to create here. It's so hard for us, you know. People around here can be so provincial. Why, we scoured Vancouver for a designer who even knew what Mission style was. Eventually Douglas just said, 'If we're going to do it right we may as well go whole hog,' so we brought in this wonderful woman from Los Angeles. And I tell you, she was worth every penny."

Daniel said, "The blanched wood is beautifully done."

Elspeth nodded. "So much of it too. Like being in the middle of the desert."

Olivia squealed. "Around here they just think it's not finished yet. 'When you gonna get some stain on those boards, Olivia?' If I had a dollar for every time I heard that I would be a very rich woman."

"You don't look as though you're doing too badly as it is," Daniel said, eyeing the ice-green leather sectional that snaked its way about the room, the Southwestern antique sideboards and occasional tables in soft, weathered pastels, the bleached antlered animal skull over the adobe fireplace.

"It's like something out of Georgia O'Keeffe," Elspeth said, maintaining a straight face.

"Would you like to see the rest of the place? Now just say no if it sounds like too much of a busman's holiday, Daniel, but I'd really love your opinion on the various things we've accomplished here. The stories I could tell you about contractors and rake-offs and getting painters who know how to mix according to—"

The doorbell rang, an electronically simulated trumpet playing the first bars of the chorus of "Cielito Lindo." "Excuse me for just one second," Olivia said and pounded up the stairs to the entry landing.

"Are you sure coming here is such a good idea?" Elspeth whispered to Daniel.

"Less sure by the minute. I thought it might distract me from other, more traumatic issues."

"You look a bit pale, you know."

"I feel a bit pale."

"Maybe a drink would help."

"Sangre de Cristo would really hit the spot."

Elspeth led the way through the crowd to the drinks table. "I have no memory of meeting Olivia before. Ever. Somehow I'm sure I would have if I had."

"I didn't think you had. She was quite poor when we were kids. Well, not poor-poor, but her family lived in a little ranch house right on the highway out on the west side of town. She was always very ashamed of that, and of her parents too. Her father worked at some factory in Vancouver—as a foreman, I believe. Olivia was always very bright. Ambitious too. We were quite close at elementary school. We told each other the most fantastic stories. I was the love child of the Bourbon pretender and she was a fairy princess, enduring a long test of her mettle in the B.C. boondocks."

"Both of you plainly psychotic."

"Yes, but that didn't occur to us at the time. Nothing the estimable Dr. Morgenstern couldn't straighten out, I'm sure."

A bolero-jacketed waiter, black hair slicked behind his ears, speaking English with a strong Quebecois accent, offered them margaritas, sangria or bourbon.

"Even Western drinks. God is in the details," Elspeth said, clicking her margarita glass against Daniel's full tumbler of bourbon.

"Think of what Olivia might have accomplished in the real world, if elegant housewifery hadn't gotten her first."

"Don't make me shudder," Elspeth said. "This is quite a good margarita."

"I haven't had bourbon in years. Did I ever tell you about the time when Press and I hitchhiked to New Orleans and—"

"Do you think he really called Dr. Morgenstern?"

Daniel drank deeply. "I wouldn't put it past him."

"What will you do?"

"He can't make me see him."

"I was just wondering what British Columbia laws say about commitment."

Daniel laughed, feeling giddy. "That had entered my mind as well. Probably the father's word is sufficient."

"This afternoon I found myself thinking about the gun case rather a lot too."

"I'm glad to hear that, Elspeth," he said, touching her wrist. "I thought I was being paranoid."

"We probably are, you know, but I found him so scary this morning. Watch your drink."

Daniel's hand was shaking so much that bourbon was dribbling onto the blue flagstone floor. "Sorry, I don't feel quite in control."

"I shouldn't wonder," Elspeth said. "When I'm not thinking rationally about what happened today, my mind's raging all over the place. There was something so eerie about the way he responded. As though he had on this mask, and the more you said, the more deeply he hid himself behind it."

"I also had the sense"—Daniel found he had to clamp his teeth together to keep them from chattering—"of seeing him for the first time. In my dreams he's this enormous presence. In my mind too, I guess . . ."

"He's starting to look so old," Elspeth said. "Not frail-old— he's clearly strong as an ox—but old, as in petrified. Have you noticed how his face seems to have gone perfectly rigid? The professional smile has become a rictus."

"Sitting there beside the fireplace, he looked so small, like a frightened little boy."

A heavy hand came down on Daniel's shoulder. Half Daniel's bourbon went down the front of Elspeth's suit.

"What have I done?"

Daniel turned to look at his assailant. "Douglas. You startled me."

"I can see that," Douglas said, signaling to the barman, who dashed over to their corner of the room, brandishing a saffron-colored towel. Douglas wrenched the towel from the barman's hand and began to pat Elspeth down. She watched, bemused, as he knelt down before her, efficiently smoothing the towel down her thighs.

"There," he said, at last standing up. "I don't think it will stain. Not bourbon, and not velvet of that quality. It's European, is it?" he said, fingering the jacket sleeve.

"I got it in London."

"It's a stunning piece of work," Douglas said, looking her up and down. "Beautifully cut."

Elspeth was starting to blush. "You seem to know a lot about clothes."

He flashed a squadron of large white teeth. "I should. It's my business."

"I'm sorry. Elspeth, this is Douglas Glyde. The Glyde department stores?" Daniel said.

Elspeth laughed in embarrassment. "I don't know why I didn't make the connection."

"Olivia told me all about you," Douglas said, nodding his handsome head. Daniel thought he was nearly as lean and blond as he had been twenty years ago when he captained the St. Michael's College ski, hockey and tennis teams. "Daniel, it's so good to see you again. Are you home long?"

Daniel started to explain that he would be returning to Montreal the following day, but Douglas had stopped listening.

"What about you, Elspeth? You're not leaving tomorrow too?" he said, all his attention focused like a golden spotlight on her.

"I'm here till Saturday."

"But that's wonderful. You'll have to come over for a swim or something. Did Olivia show you the pool?"

Elspeth shook her head.

"Come on, you two," Douglas said, wrapping his sinewy arms across their shoulders. "You've got to see what we've done. Trying to make people around here understand you're serious when you say you want a black swimming pool—you wouldn't believe the resistance we've run into at every possible turn."

Daniel ducked out from under Douglas's arm. "Join you in a minute. Want to freshen my drink."

Elspeth gave him a beseeching look as Douglas carried her off.

Instead of heading for the drinks table, Daniel slipped out onto the terrace running the length of the house. He almost expected to find cactus and sagebrush. The moonless night was cool—cold enough by valley standards to keep the rest of the guests indoors. Daniel stared up at the deep violet sky. Living in the city for so long, he had gotten used to looking up and seeing nothing but haze or dark clouds. Tonight the stars looked so close at hand they made him dizzy.

He found an adobe staircase to the garden, which seemed to sweep down for acres toward a long declivity. The house was much larger than he had supposed. From the front it appeared to be two stories high, but from the garden he could see that, because of the site's steep incline, it was four. He walked along in the dark—the terrace lights had little effect here—pacing off the length of the house. He stopped counting when he reached an obliquely angled stretch of dark glass. Peering in he could make out an elliptical pool with what looked like a black slate surround. The only illumination came from underwater lights: the rest of the room was in shadow. Daniel was about to move on when Douglas, in a thong-like black bathing suit, made his way across the slate. He mounted the low diving board and performed a perfect somersault. When his head broke the surface again, Elspeth came forward from the shadows, applauding, half ironically, hands held high in the air.

Daniel turned away and headed for the ravine at the bottom of the garden. He felt the chill now but had no desire to return to the house.

The ground angled down sharply, and he came to a stream, no more than fifteen or twenty feet across. It was shallow enough that Daniel could see the stones shimmering on the streambed. He thought the rushing sound would calm him, but the water sounded harsh and cold as it spilled along. Daniel pictured it rushing through darkness, down to the sea. The thought came to him that if it had been a deeper stream he could have drowned himself in it. He began to shake all over. He wasn't sure if he was going to cry or vomit. In the end he did neither, just stood on the bank of the narrow stream, quaking with terror and relief.

Back inside he found Elspeth leaning against the natural-finish baby grand. A beaming Douglas was playing, effortlessly, a soft, jazzy version of "A Foggy Day (in London Town)." A group of young men had gathered round the piano and were laughing at practically every word Elspeth uttered.

"Are you serious?" one of them asked, just as Daniel caught Elspeth's eye.

"Excuse me for a moment," Elspeth said, "I'll be right back."

"Having fun?"

"Yes, actually. They're all so fresh-faced and *sportif*. Don't see a lot of that in London, let me tell you. Makes me feel like Tinker Bell. You don't look so hot."

"No. I think I'm going to go."

"Would you mind if I stayed on? I think we're going to throw Olivia to the crocodiles sometime later."

"Do you mind if I take the car?"

Elspeth glanced over her shoulder at her impatiently waiting new friends. "I'm sure I'll be able to hitch a ride home with someone."

"I feel odd about going home at all."

"That occurred to me too. What time is it?"

Daniel looked at his watch. "Going on eleven."

"That means it will be only eleven-thirty or so when you get home."

"You think he'll still be up?"

"Undoubtedly. I keep seeing the gun case in my mind and thinking silly things."

"Me too," Daniel said.

"I could go with you now . . ." Elspeth bit at the Band-Aid on her index finger.

"No, no, you stay here and enjoy yourself, and I'll go home and get my head blown off. I don't mind. Really."

"Oh, Daniel . . ."

"It's all right, Elspeth. I'm going to the Wampum Lounge at the Holiday Inn and get thoroughly pissed. Or something. May even rent a room."

"You're sure you don't mind?"

"Don't be silly. I'm a grown man. I can take care of myself. I just don't want to go home if there's any possibility he's still up and prowling about."

"I think that's wise. Tell you what. I'll make sure to be home by two at the latest. You can come home any time after. If Daddy's still up, I'll wait till you get home. How's that?"

"Perfect."

She leaned forward and kissed him gingerly on the cheek. "I love you."

She had never said that before. Then he realized he never had either. "I love you too," he said, feeling it sounded insufficient.

The tapping at his door was so faint, Daniel had to pause in his packing for a moment to make sure someone was actually there. "It's not locked," he called, expecting Elspeth.

His mother backed into the room, arms full, slightly breathless from climbing the stairs. "I didn't know if you and Leslie would want these or not. I thought you might, Daniel, as keepsakes." She eased her burden down onto the unmade bed.

Daniel felt uncomfortable having her in his room, having her so close. He didn't know what else there was to say, now that he had said everything, now that he was going away. He tossed a handful of dirty clothes into Alex's duffel bag and zipped it shut. "I think I can fit a few things in. What is all this?"

"Old things—things I'd forgotten about." Talking seemed a strain for her too. She kept licking her lips. He thought she must hate him for what he had done. Yet if that were true, why was she bringing him gifts? "You don't know when you'll be back this way again," she said, "so I thought I should offer them to you before it was too late."

Daniel went over to the bed and picked up a sepia photograph in a silver art nouveau frame. "Grandmother and Grandfather Morton. I don't think I've seen this before. When was it taken?"

"I'm not exactly sure." His mother stood close behind him, looking over his shoulder at the photograph. "From Mother's suit I would think it must be the twenties."

"Grandfather certainly looks prosperous."

"He still has quite a bit of hair too, so it must be the twenties. I always forget how fat he was. Of course he wasn't considered fat. I remember your Great-Grandmother McLeod always saying he was 'such a fine figure of a man.' Look on the wall behind them—don't those look like rivets? This must have been taken on shipboard during one of their crossings to England, don't you think?"

Daniel studied the picture. "You're probably right. That's why they look so relaxed and happy."

"It's odd, but an ocean liner was one of the few places in the world where Mother felt completely comfortable and secure. Even before we'd leave harbor a kind of serenity would settle over her."

Daniel laughed. "Maybe that's why Grandfather liked to travel so much." He picked up a smaller photo in a cheap wooden frame. "Who's that?"

"Can't you guess?"

The photo, apparently taken without the subject's knowledge, was of a fashionably dressed young woman walking down a city street, her face tilted slightly to one side as if she were deep in thought. The face was marked by fatigue or melancholy, it was difficult to say which. "I don't have any idea. She's very beautiful."

"It's your Grandmother Kenning."

He looked again, amazed. "I never realized Dad looked so much like her."

"That's always been my favorite picture of her. They hardly had enough money to get by on when your father was a boy, and yet look how elegantly turned out she is. She made all their clothes herself. My, but she was a proud woman."

There was so much Daniel wanted to ask, about Grandmother Kenning, about his father, about the entire family, and yet he felt that he had somehow forfeited the right to ask any further questions by asking the one that never should have been asked at all. "What's this?" he said, picking up a narrow plum-lacquer box with an inlaid golden tree on the lid.

"Open it and see." Mrs. Kenning covered her smile of anticipation with one hand.

Daniel slid the lid to one side and folded back layer after layer of yellowed tissue. "A shawl?" he said, staring at what looked like pleated ivory silk.

"Lift it out," his mother said, "but gently."

The fabric spilled out in a white rush, falling to the floor. "A nightgown?" Daniel said. He had never felt any cloth so thin and weightless.

"It's Mother's Fortuny," Mrs. Kenning said. "I don't imagine the name would mean anything to you, but they were all the rage when Mother was a young woman. I believe Father got it for her in Venice just after the First World War. She hardly ever wore it—thought it was far too revealing. Look, hold it up to the window."

The cloth shone, almost transparent.

"It's crepe de chine. The pleats are permanent—I'm not sure how they did it. I thought it would be perfect for Leslie—she has the height to carry it off."

"Yes," Daniel said, thinking it was the kind of garment Leslie would get into only at gunpoint and at the same time picturing her in it—the curve of her long thighs, her nipples visible through the soft clinging fabric. "I'm sure she'll love it, Mum."

"And these"—Mrs. Kenning picked up two small boxes, one of tortoiseshell, the other of battered black leather—"they're probably not Porter and Alex's style at all, but I thought they're old enough now that they might appreciate them anyway."

Daniel opened the tortoiseshell box. It contained a leather-banded gold wristwatch. The numerals were vaguely art deco. Instead of a sweep second hand there was a second small dial at the bottom of the watch face, with a single tiny hand. "This I remember very well," Daniel said. "Grandfather Morton's." He carefully wound the stem. "It still runs?"

"Oh yes. It's in perfect condition. It must be sixty or seventy years old."

Daniel opened the black leather box. "A pocket watch," he said. "Grandfather Kenning's?"

"It's only gold plate. See on the back where it has rubbed thin? I'm sure you could have it redone."

"Alex will love it just as it is, Mum. He's crazy about anything old. He has this three-piece bespoke suit he found at a church bazaar. It must be from the forties—big baggy pants and . . ."

His mother looked up. Her eyes behind the thick oval glasses were full of tears. She stood only a foot or so away from him and yet she seemed so isolated and alone. It struck Daniel that perhaps she had always looked like that—he had simply never noticed. He wanted to take her in his arms and comfort her, except he couldn't quite imagine acting on that impulse.

His mother stepped back, clasping her hands in front of her. "That's that then," she said. "I'm pleased you're taking all these . . . these things. They were just stuck away in cupboards here."

"Mum, are you all right?"

She paused, as if to consider the question from all possible angles. "Yes, I'm fine."

He wanted to apologize for bringing her grief and pain and then leaving her to handle it alone. He wanted to tell her how sorry he was, for everything. "Is there anything I can do?"

She regarded him steadily. "No, no. I don't see that there is anything more you could do."

"Do you think you could get Dad to see someone?"

"See someone?" She blinked rapidly several times.

"Someone he could talk to about all this. A therapist or something."

"I don't think he sees it as his problem."

"I see."

"And I don't feel it's my place to bring it up again. It would only upset him more."

Daniel found himself nodding in agreement: no, it wouldn't be fair to upset his father any further, he had surely been through enough this Christmas week. "Is he downstairs?"

"He's in bed. Didn't I tell you? He's picked up this horrible flu. Everyone has it. He was up half the night."

"Then I'll just stop in and say goodbye on my way downstairs."

His mother looked alarmed. "I'm fairly certain he's sleeping."

"I'll just look in for a second."

"Daniel, I really don't think he wants to be disturbed. He must be very contagious right now, and you don't want to take this awful bug back to Leslie and the boys."

"It's probably the same bug that ran through our house in November. I'll be all right, Mum," he said, laughing. "I'll just duck in and—"

"I think he wants you to leave him alone, Daniel."

Daniel turned back to his bags and the open dresser drawers. "All right, Mother. Then you'd better say goodbye for me."

"I think it would be better that way," Mrs. Kenning said and slipped out of the room.

"Whatever am I going to do around here for another three days?" Elspeth said, wheeling the Jag onto the highway.

"You could always go for a midnight swim with Douglas."

"That's the quality one values most in a brother: subtlety. How was the Holiday Inn?"

"Quite pleasant, actually. The pianist-singer accomplished the unexpected—a completely original rendition of 'Send in the Clowns.' "

"Our instincts were right, you know. He was waiting up when I got home. Wondered why you weren't with me. Gave me the third degree. He was sitting in the living room, of all places. He never sits in the living room. Mother sits in the living room— that's where she reads. He goes to the den or out to his workshop. That's the drill. Last night he was playing solitaire. I've never in my entire life seen him play solitaire."

"How strange."

"Creepy is what it was. It was so clear he was waiting— waiting for me to go to bed, for you to come home. Every fifteen minutes the grandfather clock would chime, and he'd jump a little. I'd had one too many margaritas with Douglas and the boys and could barely keep my head up, let alone read, but I sat there like a real trouper with a *Town & Country* propped in front of my eyes. I must have read the same paragraph about Viscount Linley three hundred times. I felt so valiant."

"I appreciate it, Elspeth. I don't think he would have done me any real physical harm . . ."

"I don't either, although last night the threat seemed real enough. I don't think I've ever seen solitaire played with such vehemence. When he shuffled it was like machine-gun fire."

"I think he just wanted to get me alone in order to bait me—get me to lose my temper, shout and scream—to prove to the world that I'm the loon."

"Not even to the world," Elspeth said. "To himself. If you're not the crazy one, where does that leave him? Those things he said in the den yesterday—you're mad, a pathological liar, deranged doper—that wasn't the first time I'd heard all that. That's been his line on you all along."

"He's always said those things to me. I didn't know he'd said them to you too."

"One way or another he was always warning me off you, especially once you left home. Usually it was said in a joking way—'Daniel can't tell the difference between fantasy and reality,' 'Daniel always has had an overheated imagination,' 'Daniel's lies are going to get him in a lot of trouble one day.'"

Daniel looked out the car window at the drenched orchards streaking past. "I wonder what will happen now. I hate leaving Mum alone with him."

"As far as I can tell they've been living together in silence ever since I left home for good. That was ten years ago. I doubt you've succeeded in interrupting that pattern. They don't talk about things that bother them. They never have. Why should they start now? Besides, she's not exactly blameless, you know. Everything he says, she sits there and nods. She can be a delight to be around, but never when she's with him." She turned the windshield wipers on high. "I keep thinking how convenient it would be if he would just die."

"Do you? Me too."

"I can't quite make out how we're all to go on after this. As a family, I mean."

Daniel opened Leslie's knapsack and took out the framed photographs and the watch boxes. "I got the distinct impression I'm not invited home again anytime soon."

"And these are your payoff, now that you've been disinherited?"

"I don't think it's as callous as that. Maybe this was her way of giving me part of the family—to tide me over now that I'm officially exiled from it."

"You really think that's it?" Elspeth said, glancing at him. "She doesn't want you coming home anymore?"

"I'm fairly certain."

Elspeth sighed. "Some people have all the luck."

On the first fine day of April, Daniel and Leslie took Beaver for a walk on the mountain. The trees weren't out yet, they weren't even in bud as far as Daniel could tell, but the main road that spiraled round the mountain was reasonably dry. Along its edges small patches of tiny fernlike growth had sprung up, shining neon green against the dull gray earth.

Daniel bent down to let Beaver off his leash.

"Do you think you should?" Leslie said.

"There's hardly anyone around."

"You know how he can be with joggers."

"*Sauve-qui-peut.* You'll be a good doggy, won't you, Beaver?" Beaver bounded down the side of the mountain, foraging for throwable sticks.

"I can't believe the road's dry this early," Leslie said. "At this rate the trees will be out full by mid-May."

"Tell me seriously—you really think I should go?"

Leslie looked at him in exasperation. "I already told you seriously. Of course you should go. I can't believe you're not jumping at the chance."

"I'll feel like such a fraud. I don't know the first thing about landscape architecture."

"No one expects you to. That was Gillian's province. The Japanese invited her, but they also seem to be keen on establishing closer ties with the firm. Pettigrew wouldn't have asked you to go in Gillian's place if he didn't think you could carry it off. Beaver, that's far too large a stick. Put it down. Down, Beaver."

Beaver was dragging a small uprooted tree up the mountainside. It kept catching on stumps and other small trees.

"There will be other regular architects there," Daniel said, trying to reassure himself. "After all, the title of the conference is Landscape and Architecture, not Landscape Architecture."

"And think of it: two weeks in Japan, all expenses paid."

"Still . . . you sound keener on it than I am. Why don't you come with me?"

"Daniel, you know I couldn't possibly on such short notice."

"No, I suppose not."

They walked along in silence for a way, Beaver running in wide arcs through the scrub below them.

Leslie brushed her hair back over her shoulders and looked off at the skyline, sharp and clear in the afternoon sun. To Daniel it looked like some improbable pop-up city.

"Besides," Leslie said with some deliberation, "I think it might be good for us to be apart for a while. Get some perspective on things."

"What things, specifically?"

"Like us, for one."

Daniel had known this was coming, although he had avoided bringing it up himself. He had felt, throughout their years together, that it was always he who had agitated for change, he who had announced that their conjugal life was growing stale or routine, he who had started the necessary quarrels and late-night mutual-criticism sessions. Lately he had decided to relax a little, let go his vigil over their connubial existence.

Curious reactions began occurring almost at once. For one thing, Leslie became even more detached than usual. He would glimpse her, standing alone in an otherwise empty room or working intently in the garden, and he would have the briefest, faintest impression that she looked depressed. He knew, however, that this was unlikely, for Leslie was rarely depressed—it just wasn't in her nature. The day he had finally ventured to ask if she was feeling low, she had answered shortly, wondering whatever had prompted him to ask such a question. Friday night they had made love. Sex, from Daniel's point of view, had never been better than over the past few weeks. After so many months of viewing it as an only sometimes pleasant obligation, or worse—a trial, an emotional obstacle course they triumphed over intermittently— he had begun to look forward to sex again, even to anticipate it eagerly and to create various scenarios and techniques in order to ensure its freshness. Friday night he felt especially aroused as they lay face to face in their wide bed, arms wrapped about each other. He felt he couldn't kiss her too deeply or too often, felt that nothing compared to the warm, wet taste of her mouth. He pushed into her, not looking for penetration just yet, but content to feel his erection rubbing against the softness of her naked belly, her breasts pressing against his chest. He was moaning, kissing, thrusting—feeling the release of it, delighting in all the sensations, tactile and emotional, that combine in a single act of love— when he realized with a start that Leslie was not moving with him, that his boundless enthusiasm was not shared. He pulled back from her and said, "What's wrong?"

She rolled over onto her back. "Nothing's wrong. I just can't seem to get into the mood."

"Oh."

"I think we're in a rut again," she said.

"And I thought we were doing so well."

They had talked for a while after that, although there wasn't much to talk about, just the two of them trying to assure each other that neither of them was feeling angry or hurt by this breakdown in their lovemaking. Then Daniel went up to his workroom, stared disconsolately at a floor plan for an hour or so and fell asleep on the daybed.

"What about us?" Daniel said, prying a stick from Beaver's jaws and flinging it down the mountainside.

Leslie glanced over her shoulder. They were about to be overtaken by a pair of speed walkers, evidently a husband-and-wife team, kitted out in identical yellow jerseys and black bicycle shorts. Leslie said, lowering her voice, "I just feel a bit unsettled. About us, I mean."

"What do you mean?"

The speed walkers charged by, arms pumping.

"Therapy has done wonders for you, Daniel. When I think of where you were a year ago and where you are now, I can hardly believe the difference. You seem so centered and sure of yourself, the mood swings have virtually gone, you're so much better around the boys too." She rubbed the side of her neck, as if it were stiff. "It's just that . . . I don't know how to put this . . . it sounds awful even when I say it to myself . . . I don't know where we're heading, now that you're a whole, integrated person."

Beaver bounded up again, a new and thicker stick between his jaws, his paws wet and muddy. He pranced at Daniel's side, trying to get him to take the stick, until Daniel pushed him away. "You mean now that I'm better you want to split up?"

"Who said anything about splitting up? That's so like you. The least sign of disagreement or contention and you assume it's all over. I don't understand what's going on between us, but something is gone, something that was very central. For me at least. You know how important it is for me to take care of people, to help them. Nothing satisfies me more than that. This wasn't clear at the time, of course, but looking back I think I was attracted to you initially because you seemed so needy, so hurt and confused. You wanted taking care of."

"And now that I don't, you don't want me anymore." Daniel felt disorientated for a moment, as if he were two places at once: here, walking in the park with Leslie, and at home, in B.C., in his bedroom, his mother laying out her "things" and bidding him a tacit farewell.

"Daniel, please," Leslie said. "Don't exaggerate. I'm not saying I don't want you. What I am saying is that for me there's now this hole at the center of our relationship. You can't expect me to adjust to that overnight. My work is very fulfilling, but at home, with you, I feel so useless. I feel I don't have a role in your life any longer. You don't need my help or protection anymore."

"Would it make you any happier if I went back to being the old nasty me?" Daniel said.

"Won't you please listen to what I'm saying? I'm not asking you to go back. I'm not saying it's over between us. All I'm saying is that I'm having a rough time of it right now." She shook her head several times, as if she were trying to clear it. "I guess you could say I'm fairly depressed these days."

Daniel felt vindicated that she was at last confessing what only days before she had hotly denied, but he also felt frightened and confused. "And your depression is my fault?"

"No one's talking about fault or blame," Leslie said. "These things happen with couples. I've seen it a thousand times. I simply think we need some time away from each other, to sort things out."

"You're sure that's all?"

"What do you mean?"

"You don't want me to move out?"

"Of course not."

"Have you talked to the boys about this?"

"Why would I do that? You'll only be gone two weeks."

Daniel kicked a small flat rock. It sailed through the air, going much farther than he'd intended. "I don't think that it would hurt for them to know we're having problems. They must sense something's wrong, especially with you being so depressed."

"I am not *so* depressed. I've been a little depressed, on and off, since Christmas."

"As long as that?"

She turned on him abruptly. "Don't go putting on a therapeutic voice with me, Daniel Kenning."

"What are you talking about?"

Leslie shoved her hands into the pockets of her baggy trousers. "I know Henrietta's voice when I hear it."

"I think three months, almost four months, is a long time to be depressed without saying anything about it to the people you're close to. I had a pretty good idea what was going on, being not unfamiliar with the signs of depression. I thought it was because of something I'd done and, in a way, that's true. All I'm saying is that the kids must find it disturbing too."

"If it's so noticeable," Leslie said slowly, as if she were trying to work out the difficult logic of what she wanted to say, "why should I talk to them about it?"

Daniel couldn't believe what he was hearing. "You know the answer to that as well as I do. You know how kids are—they think everything's their fault. You go around the house moody and distracted, I'm willing to bet Porter thinks it's because of his grades and Alex is sure it's because you never liked him much to begin with."

"That's another thing I don't much care for," Leslie said, "as long as we're on the subject. Lately you've been interfering with the way I handle the boys."

"What are you talking about?"

"You've criticized me in front of them. You've also told me you disapproved of the way I handled certain issues with them."

"My God, Leslie, we've only been living together as a family for ten years. You can't expect me to keep my mouth shut when I think you're handling something badly."

She stopped. "I don't like what you're doing. You're constantly critical. You question everything I do. You make me doubt myself, my own skills as a parent."

Daniel tried to put his arm around her waist, but she twisted away from him. "You know I think you're a very good parent. A wonderful parent in fact. They're great kids. I never realized how great, or how much I loved them, until I started seeing Henrietta. But don't you think it's good to doubt yourself, to hear other points of view?"

"Of course I do, *en principe*. It's the actual practice that I find hard to take. You make me feel like a failure with Porter and Alex."

"You know that's not true. All I'm saying is that you probably could afford to let them in on what you're feeling from time to time."

Beaver slunk up behind them, covered in burrs. Leslie squatted down to pick them from his flanks and tail. "Poor Beaver. Hold still. Stay, Beaver. Don't you snap at me. Good boy. You know that's Henrietta's particular jargon, her patented approach to everything. It works for some people, it worked amazingly well for you. You have strong feelings—sometimes they seem to come in torrents. It doesn't work that way for everyone. I'm not a particularly emotional person. I'm more logical-intellectual. Feelings come to me slowly, I'm slow to realize they're there. You can't expect me to change that. That's who I am."

He didn't know what to say. He knew he couldn't force Leslie to be someone she wasn't. "Couldn't you, when you're aware of some powerful emotion—when, say, you're depressed—couldn't you try to talk about it, with me and the boys?"

"With you? I'm doing that right now. I don't know about with the boys. They depend on me to be strong. I'm supposed to listen to their problems, not vice versa."

"I don't see why it couldn't be both, now that they're both nearly adults."

"How did I never notice before that you're such a utopian? It all looks so easy to you, doesn't it, now that Henrietta has given you all the answers?"

Daniel crouched down too and began carefully picking burrs from Beaver's ears. "Do you ever feel alone?"

Leslie looked at him over Beaver's back. "What do you mean?"

"I don't know. Some days I feel so completely alone. So isolated. Don't you ever feel that?"

Leslie plucked the last burr from Beaver's tail. "No. I really don't know what you're talking about. I've got too many responsibilities, too many people depending on me, for me to ever feel alone."

He suddenly felt so impotent, so incapable of conveying to Leslie what he meant. "Not physically alone. I don't mean physically alone."

"I know," Leslie snapped. "I know exactly what you mean. But no, I've never felt that, never in my life. Never. It's out of the question. That's a luxury permitted only to people who have too much time on their hands, too much time to think about themselves."

They walked in silence, Beaver trotting along between them. Daniel was stung by her remarks, stung by their truth. He was self-obsessed, insensitive to the damage he did to those around him. Leslie's anger, her pain, only made him feel that much more alone.

"What are you feeling now?"

"Depressed."

"Let's take it down then. Can you get more depressed?"

"Oh yeah."

"Go way, way down."

"I'm pretty far down."

"Can you go any further?"

"No problem."

"How far down are you now?"

"About all the way."

"What's wrong with all the way? What would happen if you touched bottom?"

"I'd kill myself."

"Is that all?"

"Or you."

"You don't think it's possible that you could go all the way down and just stay there a while, look around, become familiar with the territory, as if you were exploring, say, a vast cavern?"

"It's pretty scary down here."

"I know."

"And lonely."

"Have you touched bottom yet?"

"I think so."

"Is either of us in any danger?"

"For the moment?"

"It's all for the moment."

"No."

"Good. Is it possible that you scared Leslie?"

"Scared her?"

"By getting too close?"

"I don't get it."

"When you talked about how alone you sometimes feel. Is it possible you got too close to how alone she feels?"

"I hadn't thought about it."

"She certainly struck out at you, as though you had touched a very private wound."

"What do you mean?"

"When she told you you were self-obsessed and wasting your time in therapy."

"That's not quite what she said."

"Would you say I've inaccurately paraphrased it?"

"No. I just hadn't seen what she said in that light."

"No. But you got the message anyway."

"Yeah."

"How often would you say Leslie has been depressed over the course of your relationship?"

"Hardly ever. Once or twice."

"And how often were you depressed?"

"You know the answer to that."

"When you told me about what happened during your walk with Leslie, one element seemed to be missing, at least in terms of your reaction."

"What's that?"

"Where was your anger? Didn't you feel any anger when she told you, 'Now that you're a whole, integrated person I'm not sure how we can go on together'?"

"It didn't occur to me at the time."

"And now? Any anger now?"

"I'd like to kick your face in."

"Do you see any similarities between what happened with Leslie on the weekend and what happened at Christmas with your mother?"

"I believe so."

"Could you tell me about them?"

"Do I have a choice?"

"Yes."

"Okay. I go home. I finally get the courage to speak up. I find my voice. I tell them what I know about what went on when I was a kid. My father denies everything, says I'm crazy. My mother hints I should go away and stay away. I haven't heard from them since. I come back to Montreal incredibly depressed. You put me back together. Again."

"And with Leslie?"

"I grow up. I finally get the courage to talk to her as an equal. I tell her about what I see going on around me, in our little family unit. She gets angry. Suggests I should go away. I come to you incredibly depressed. You try to patch me up. Again."

"Common threads?"

"When I use my real adult voice to say what I see, people tell me to go away. Everyone gets angry, I get depressed."

"And guilty for using the power that belongs to you."

"And guilty. Yes."

"And angry, except you turn all that anger back on yourself. Because that's the only way you've learned how to direct it.

That's what your guilt is, isn't it—anger turned against yourself?
Any other parallels?"

"My mother tells me to go away. Leslie tells me to go away."

"Right this moment, what do you want to do?"

"I want to go away."

"To please them?"

"No, just to go away."

PART FOUR

The Mysteries of Mount Kurama

*O*ne pale green carpeted corridor poured into another pale green carpeted corridor, and that into another and another and another, like stream pouring into stream pouring into stream, down to an unseen sea. Daniel was trying to find the sliding glass doors that led to the Japanese gardens. The gardens. Silly to call them Japanese, since everything here was. Japanese hallways, Japanese elevators (Mitsubishi), Japanese bellboys, Japanese hotel rooms. On the way from the elevator to his room the maroon-jacketed bellboy had pointed out the doors to the gardens—Daniel glimpsed raked white gravel and stunted trees, a squat stone lantern. Now it all seemed to have vanished, in the time it had taken him to unpack his bags.

Japan was like that, he was beginning to discover. The world seemed to shimmer and disappear, shimmer and disappear before he properly could grasp it. At the Tokyo airport this morning—or was that yesterday morning? no, this morning—a beautiful girl in a navy polyester uniform had darted up to him the second he exited customs and pinned a yellow Happy Face button to his jacket lapel. He had looked down at it in groggy surprise; when he looked up, the beautiful girl was gone. A sleek-haired boy appeared next, grabbing Daniel's many bags and darting away. He was replaced by another girl in a buttercup-yellow pinafore. Her plastic sun visor was yellow as well, although not quite the same shade. She also carried a yellow pennant. She indicated that Daniel should follow her, and so he did, feeling conspicuous: they formed a parade of two, weaving in and out among piles of baggage and clutches of bewildered Western tourists scattered across the white-tiled floor of the international terminal, the girl waving her pennant. Once out the glass doors and into an atmosphere surprisingly hot and sticky for early May, the girl packed

him onto a bus. Daniel sat stupefied in his antimacassared, ve-
lour-upholstered seat, listening to a recording of a clingingly
feminine voice murmuring instructions, first in Japanese, then in
English, over the bus's public-address system, and wondering
why the bus driver, a burly fellow with a pumpkin-shaped head
who looked like an extra from a samurai film, wore little white
gloves. Did he have a skin disease?

At Tokyo Station, Daniel stepped off the bus; a new girl waved
a yellow pennant in his face. She rushed him across a vast green-
tiled concourse, up a flight of stairs and onto a concrete platform.
Scurrying along the platform, head down as though looking for
something dropped on a previous visit, she stopped abruptly and
pointed at the concrete floor. Daniel looked down and saw two
white-painted parallel lines running perpendicular to the platform edge. Between the white lines two numbers had been
painted: 16 11. The pennant girl, in elaborate pantomime, indicated that Daniel should stand exactly there, between the two
lines, his feet obscuring the numerals. She handed him his ticket
and rushed off, still holding her yellow pennant aloft.

Daniel stood between the two lines, vaguely wondering what
had happened to his luggage. The sleek-haired boy at the airport—perhaps he specialized in bilking unwary, discom-
bobulated tourists? Were Daniel's bags even now being sold on
the black market? his four summer-weight suits cut down to
apparel a score of Japanese men? Daniel looked along the
crowded platform. Good God, he thought, they're all Japanese.
He felt ungainly and conspicuous, although no one seemed to be
paying him any attention. At least he couldn't catch anyone at it.

A boy in a blue apron hurried up to him, stared at his lapel and
rushed away again. Thirty seconds later another aproned boy
wheeled up a cart containing Daniel's bags and unloaded them in
a precise ring around Daniel's feet. Daniel reached into his pocket
for some coins, but the boy had already gone. A pleasant pneu-
matic hum came from behind him. He turned to face the tracks
again, only to discover that a glistening white train had materialized while his back was turned. One of the train's doors was
exactly aligned with the white-painted parallel lines Daniel was
standing between. To the left of the door two numbers were

painted in black: 16 11. He looked at his ticket: 16 11 23a. He was beginning to feel that nothing bad could happen to him in Japan.

And now, he thought, rushing along yet another pale green corridor that jutted this way and jogged that and ran up and down short flights of stairs, if I can get from Montreal to Tokyo and from Tokyo to Kyoto with no serious mishaps, why can I not find my way to the fabled gardens of the Miyako Hotel? Just as he was considering returning to his room to collapse, the corridor opened out into a gallery. At the end of the gallery, a pair of sliding glass doors.

Ducking his head he stepped through the low doorway. A rich balsamy smell engulfed him, almost masking the omnipresent odor of soy sauce. Small flat stones formed a path across an expanse of white gravel. This didn't seem part of the same hotel at all—brick, mortar and glass gave way to white stucco, steel-blue roof tiles, rice-paper windows and doors. Daniel rounded a corner and nearly fell over a man in a simple kimono the same shade of blue as the roof tiles. The man, who was perfectly bald, knelt before a small wooden table, almost like a breakfast tray, set up on the gravel. He held a calligraphy pen in his left hand. Until Daniel's interruption, he had been covering a long strip of parchmentlike paper with Japanese characters. The man glowered at him briefly and returned to his strip of parchment. Daniel worried that he had intruded, that perhaps this garden was, after all, private. In his embarrassment he had somehow wandered off the stepping stones. He crunched across the white gravel as quietly as he could, feeling the kimonoed man's eyes boring into his back.

Eventually he found another path that wound around this curious compound. He came to a low wall. Unable to find a gate, he looked about to see if anyone was watching and then leapt the wall and scrambled up the mountainside. Light was beginning to fade. Even the trees seemed different in Japan—this was clearly a forest, yet all the foliage appeared to have been subtly pruned, arranged, tamed. The deciduous trees looked formal and un-real—clouds of leaves drifting over splaying branches as though across the fragile ribs of a painted fan.

Near the top of the mountain he stumbled across a cluster of what looked to be small gravestones within a low gray stone enclosure. Two of the gravestones wore small scarlet aprons. At the base of one someone had placed a porcelain bowl holding a pile of a white granular substance that had been molded to resemble a miniature Mount Fuji. He touched the granular cone and licked his finger: salt. He stood for a few moments, trying to figure out what all this could mean, until he realized that the hair on the back of his neck was standing on end.

He half ran down the mountainside. Bypassing the walled garden compound altogether, he found a proper Western-style doorway in the brick-and-mortar portion of the Miyako and hurried down cool corridors to his room, where he fell onto his bed and promptly fell asleep.

"Mr. Kenny?"

"Yes. Kenning."

"Mr. Kenny. My name is Iggy. I take you convention center."

"Igi?" Daniel said, trying out this unusual Japanese name.

"No, no. Iggy. Iggy Sato. Like Iggy Pop. You know Iggy Pop?"

"No, I don't know."

"He singer. Very big America. New-York-Lower-Eastside-CBGB. You know?"

"No, I don't think so."

"He make records Japan too. With Ryuichi Sakamoto. You know Ryuichi Sakamoto, of course?"

"Of course," Daniel said, shaking his head.

"He write music *Merry Christmas, Mr. Lawrence.*"

"Ah," Daniel said. "*Merry Christmas, Mr. Lawrence* I like very much." What, he wondered, was happening to his syntax?

Iggy Sato smiled for the first time. He looked to be sixteen or seventeen, but then practically everybody Daniel had met since arriving at the Tokyo airport looked sixteen or seventeen. He was very slight, surely not more than five-three, and although he wore a plain white dress shirt with a black knit tie and plain, cuffed navy trousers, he looked elegant, perhaps because both shirt and trousers were several sizes too large for him, their blousiness offset by the tightly cinched black belt that emphasized his narrow waist. On his small feet he wore outlandishly large black shoes, rounded and shiny as those Mickey Mouse wore in old cartoons, with inch-thick gum soles.

Iggy bowed, hands together. "Very good film. You like cinema?"

"Very much," Daniel said, bobbing his head.

"I saw film other night. Very old. Very good. *The Sad Man.*"

"*The Sad Man?*" Daniel racked his memory.

"Orson Welles and Joseph Cotten. Vienna after bombs."

"*The Third Man?*"

"That what I say," Iggy said. "My English disgusting."

"No, no, it's very good, Iggy. Should we get a taxi, or is the convention center close enough to walk?"

"Taxi waiting," Iggy said, ushering Daniel through the revolving door. A white-gloved driver sat at the wheel of a white Mercedes. The car's back door swung open as if by magic, catching Daniel in the kneecap.

"You okay, Mr. Kenny?" Iggy said.

"No, no, I'm fine," Daniel said, holding his knee and hopping about on one foot.

Daniel had assumed that, like all the other young workers he had encountered so far, Iggy too would disappear once they reached the convention center. Instead Iggy guided him into a half-darkened auditorium and sat down beside him, pointing out the earphones affixed to the back of the seat in front of Daniel. Daniel put them on and began listening to a translation of what the crisp-looking blonde who stood behind the free-form Lucite lectern at the front of the auditorium was saying. The Oxbridge voice in his earphones told about the use of silver birch and weeping ash in Finnish public parks.

Daniel looked about the hall. He had expected a more intimate gathering—there were two or three hundred people ranged about the windowless, wood-paneled room. The wood itself was unlike any he had seen before—golden as butterscotch and with a similar satiny glow. The delegates' seats were upholstered in a spongy aquamarine fabric that looked emerald green one moment, peacock blue the next. Even the lighting seemed unusual. Daniel looked up. The gently curving vault of the ceiling was covered in gold leaf. Recessed lighting around the vault's perimeter was angled so that the light bounced off the gold leaf, casting a golden glow over the entire room. Daniel thought he had never been in such a beautiful, calming place. He promptly fell asleep.

He awoke to find Iggy's hand on his shoulder. Not shaking it, just lightly resting there.

"Speeches over now. We go lunch."

"Where?" Daniel looked around groggily.

"Here. Restaurant downstairs. Very nice."

"Big restaurant?"

"Very big."

"Big lunch?"

"Everybody here there."

"Iggy, I have to get out of this place, otherwise I'll never wake up."

"Wake up?"

Daniel put his hands together, prayer-fashion, and laid one ear against them. Then he opened his eyes and abruptly sat up very straight.

"Ah. Awaken. 'Wake up' good too?"

Daniel nodded.

"We go outside. Speeches very boring. Disgusting."

Outside the conference center, Iggy rolled up his sleeves and produced a package of cigarettes. He offered the pack to Daniel.

"Mild Sevens," Daniel said, reading the label, and took one. He looked back doubtfully at the convention center doors. "You don't think I'll be missed?"

Iggy shook his head. "Dinner tonight, very important. Big guys there. Speeches, lunch—nobody know you not there."

"Great."

"Where we go?"

"This is your city. You show me."

"Kyoto not my city," Iggy said, making a scornful face. "I study in Tokyo. Come for conference only."

"What do you study, Iggy?"

"Architecture. Last year. Not study anymore. I work for Kawabata Company."

Daniel nodded. That was the company that organized the conference. "You do landscape architecture?"

"No, no," Iggy said, pulling on his cigarette. "Houses. Modern houses. Explode houses."

"I see," Daniel said, assuming something was missing in the translation again. "So where shall we go for lunch?"

"Japanese or American?"

"Japanese, of course."

Iggy looked serious for a moment. "I know place. Very cheap."

"Sounds good."

"After lunch?"

"Are you with me all day?"

"I with you all conference."

"Wonderful. I like see . . . I would like to see some temples."

The serious look passed across Iggy's face again. "Okay," he said finally, exhaling a plume of smoke. "No problem. Kyoto have five thousand temple."

The cheap restaurant Iggy knew turned out to be just down the street from the Miyako Hotel. The white Mercedes waited curbside while they ate. When they emerged from the restaurant, Iggy tapped on the Mercedes's window and conferred for several minutes with the driver, who kept shaking his head and loudly sucking his teeth. Then he drove off.

"Won't we need him to get to the temples?"

"We walk, Mr. Kenny. Temples everywhere."

They followed a trolley track that passed in front of the Miyako. A gaggle of schoolgirls in navy pleated skirts and pristine white blouses stared and yet seemed not to stare as Daniel and Iggy walked by. When they had passed, one of the girls said something and the rest giggled.

"What did she say?" Daniel said.

"She say you have eyes like stones."

"Like stones?"

"Maybe not good word. Women wear on ears, hands? Very blue."

"Sapphires?"

"Maybe," Iggy said, looking closely at Daniel's eyes. "Very blue."

He led Daniel into a short tunnel through a stone embankment. When they emerged from the tunnel, the Kyoto of trolley rails and crisscrossing trolley wires, rushing honking traffic and modern neon-trimmed storefronts had dropped away. Ahead of them stretched a wide cinder path, high stockade fences running on either side, rounded timbers weathered to a silvery sheen. It was starting to rain a little. Daniel looked up at the sky. A wedge of gray clouds was moving down from the mountains that ringed the city.

He turned to Iggy. "You think it will be all right?"

He caught Iggy stifling a yawn. "The hills are shrouded in mist," Iggy said, with perfect British inflection.

"What?"

"I learn in English class. Very beautiful."

"Yes. It looks like it's going to pour."

"Rain best time see Japanese gardens. They say."

"All right," Daniel said.

They came to an open gate. "You see?" Iggy said.

"Sure." Daniel paid six hundred yen to an ancient woman sitting in a bamboo booth. She handed him two slips of paper. He handed one to Iggy and scrutinized the other. Half the slip of paper showed an artist's rendering of the garden they were about to visit; the other half contained two paragraphs, one in Japanese, the other in English, explaining that this was a monastery garden.

"Where's the monastery itself?" Daniel said.

"This all monastery," Iggy said, opening his arms wide.

They tramped along the garden's carefully tended dirt paths. It seemed unremarkable to Daniel. No flowers to speak of, just a great variety of ground cover, from a spiky kind of ivy to stretches and hillocks of thick moss that seemed to grow greener as it soaked up the moisture hanging in veils in the air. Iggy walked along behind him, head bowed. He seemed depressed or

distracted, Daniel couldn't make out which. Perhaps it was simply the nature of his fine-boned face, which in repose became a
melancholy mask.

A small decorative pond curved through the garden. The foot-
path followed the pond's contours, more or less, sometimes wan-
dering away from it to take them up a low rise for an unan-
ticipated view, sometimes running right along the pond's edge so
that Daniel could see the dark shapes of fish jostling together at
the bottom of the pond.

"What kind of fish are those?" he said to Iggy.

Iggy held his hands out over the water and clapped twice. A
dozen or more long, plump fish rose to hover just below the
surface. One or two were ghostly white, the rest glistened orange
and gold in the pale green water. Some had diaphanous tails
wafting out behind them as they hung suspended in the still
water. It occurred to Daniel that these must be the carp that were
always cropping up in whatever clunkily translated Japanese
fiction he had tried to read over the years.

"They're beautiful," Daniel said.

"Hungry," Iggy said, turning away.

Another turn in the path and they were back at the old woman,
impassive in her bamboo booth. Daniel looked back at the garden, which had seemed to contain so many different vistas and
shifts in vegetation, so many topographical variations, and realized that it covered an area no greater than a city block.

They continued along the cinder lane. Gates appeared at regular intervals, some open, others closed.

Daniel looked longingly at the open ones, but Iggy trudged
ahead, murmuring, "All same."

The dirt road gave onto a wide, tree-lined grassy mall running
between stucco- and stone-walled monastery compounds. All the
compound walls sloped inward. Daniel was about to ask Iggy
why, but his closed face suggested it would be better not to
intrude. Daniel concluded that the walls were probably built that
way to better withstand earthquakes.

At the center of the mall stood a squat, solid-looking tower—
the exposed age-darkened piles looked a good five or six feet in

diameter. A mass of schoolboys in white shirts, black dress trousers and nautical-looking caps stood, hands linked, on the balustrade of the tower's wide stone terrace. Another schoolboy stood down on the grass, focusing an expensive-looking camera.

As Daniel and Iggy approached, the hand-holding boys started to giggle and chatter, then beckoned to Daniel and Iggy.

"What do they want?" Daniel said.

"They want *gaijin* in school picture."

"*Gaijin?*"

"Foreigner," Iggy said.

Daniel moved uncertainly toward the laughing, beckoning boys. When he reached the stone terrace, they clustered around him, each shaking his hand and saying, "Haro."

This accomplished, two of them took him by the hand and helped him up onto the balustrade. They stood there for a moment, thirty or so boys holding hands, Daniel looming very tall at their center, until the boy with the camera gave the signal and they leapt, hands still linked, off the balustrade. The boy with the camera clicked his shutter, catching them midair.

Another round of handshaking, and Daniel returned to Iggy's side, smiling sheepishly. He thought Iggy looked irritated, or bored, but with a face like that, who could tell for sure?

The mist kept turning into light rain, falling gently for a minute or two, then hanging again in midair. Daniel looked up the hillside: low white clouds stuck in tree branches like kites. They reached a long, rambling, thick-timbered structure covered by a series of high-gabled, wide-eaved roofs.

"Shall we go in?" Daniel said.

"Okay," Iggy said.

In the dingy entry hall they stepped onto a wide wooden pallet flanked by two stacks of open-ended wooden boxes, many of them containing neatly arranged pairs of shoes. Iggy pointed to the caramel-colored slippers lined up on the stone floor beside the pallet. Daniel slipped off his loafers and placed them on the shelf next to Iggy's Mickey Mouse shoes. He felt like one of Cinderella's wicked stepsisters: his heels hung over the edges of the caramel-colored slippers.

He clopped up the steps to the sales desk and paid six hundred yen for two entry tickets. Reading the paragraph printed on his ticket, he learned that there was more to this monastery than just a garden. The garden was called Nanzen-ji. The artist's rendering showed an otherwise empty boulder-strewn lot.

Ahead of him stretched a wide, plank-floored corridor, light streaming in milkily through rice-paper windows. To his right a door slid open. He saw a traditional Japanese room. Two women in pastel suits knelt on the grass matting. Before each woman stood a bowl of the kind he was used to seeing *café au lait* served in. Beyond the women another door gave onto a tiny, lush garden enveloping a cascading waterfall. The arc of the waterfall seemed calculated exactly to fill the doorway, as if the opening were not a doorway but a frame for a painting. He craned his neck to see more—the kneeling women, oblivious to him, seemed to be masticating great wads of chewing gum—when an unseen attendant slid the inner door closed.

Daniel and Iggy passed along more cloisterlike corridors, the plank floors creaking and popping under their feet. They looked into room after ill-lit room, the back walls of which were hung with panels on which gold-striped tigers lurked behind pale bamboo stalks or prepared to spring from spreading velvet-leafed trees.

"How old is this place, Iggy?"

"Maybe seventeen century?"

"Seventeenth century?"

Iggy nodded. "Some older. But all new. Burn down, they build again."

"The screens look very old."

"Always save screens."

"I see." Daniel wished Iggy could manage to be a little more enthusiastic. Between him and the rain, not to mention the dampness seeping into this murkily lit, rambling monastery, Daniel was beginning to feel a bit worn down. "Is there a toilet here?"

"Toilet?" Iggy pointed back along the corridor. "I wait here."

Daniel retraced his steps until he came to a narrow door with TOILET on it. He opened the door to a small vestibule fitted out with a narrow wooden pallet. On one side of the pallet were arranged two pairs of caramel-colored slippers exactly like his own. On the other side, a dozen pairs of maroon slippers with a gold Japanese character emblazoned on each toe. He slipped off his caramel-colored slippers, carefully aligning them with the other two pairs. Then he wedged his feet into the maroon-colored slippers and clogged into the bathroom proper, which contained four cubicles and four sinks. He tried the doors of two of the cubicles. Both were locked. The third door opened. He stepped in and shut the door behind him. Embedded in the mosaic floor was what looked like the top half of a small porcelain baby carriage, its yard-long trough fitted with a porcelain hood at one end. Daniel had no idea what to do. He unzipped his pants, squatted down at the unhooded end of the trough and peed into it, feeling fairly certain that this was not correct procedure.

Iggy was waiting where he had left him, looking with uninterest at yet another tiger in yet another stylized forest. As Daniel clip-clopped toward him, Iggy's black eyes brightened and he covered his mouth, shaking with laughter.

"What's wrong?" Daniel said.

Iggy pointed at Daniel's feet. *"Toileto."*

He looked down. He was still wearing the maroon-colored slippers from the bathroom. The gold character on the toe must stand for "toilet." He slunk back to the bathroom, sure that the other sightseers along the corridors were laughing behind their hands, behind his back.

When Daniel returned, Iggy flashed a grin at him and then retreated back into gloom.

They rounded a corner and found themselves on a long covered veranda looking onto the empty boulder-strewn lot pictured on the entry ticket. It was an oblong courtyard, bounded on two sides by bare masonry walls. The third side was a rice-paper-screened corridor and the fourth side, the gallery they were standing on. The courtyard was covered with fine white sand, carefully raked so that in places it looked like a vast music score waiting for the notes to arrive. Around the boulders themselves the sand was scored in concentric circles that seemed, on close inspection, to swirl round the boulders like rushing water.

"Famous Zen garden," Iggy said, with a noticeable curl of his lip.

Daniel's limbs felt heavy. "Do you suppose it would be all right if we sat down?"

"Nobody mind," Iggy said and squatted down on the bare boards, his back against a wooden pillar. Daniel sank down beside him.

The mist-rain had stopped. Feeble sunlight crept into the courtyard. As the sunlight grew stronger, the moisture on the boulders glistened, disappeared. Some of the boulders were one color all over, others were striated, still others flecked with chalky fossils. The masonry walls, which moments before had been a monotonous stretch of gray, now appeared to have cracked and been remended again and again, so that the wall had developed over time a fissured texture which suggested that, despite its apparent solidity, the wall might crumble at any moment. Above the roof tiles of the overhanging eaves, Daniel could see the tops of trees and, beyond them, the sky's new blue. He didn't feel sleepy, but thought he would be content to sit on this wide veranda, looking at sand and boulders, treetops and sky, for the rest of his life.

After what might have been half an hour—Daniel couldn't have said—he was aware that Iggy was watching him through half-closed eyes. Daniel turned to meet his covert gaze.

"You like garden?"

"More than anything I've ever seen," Daniel said, realizing from the pained look on Iggy's face that he had yet again done or said something gauche.

"What's wrong, Iggy?"

Iggy turned his head to look at the sky. "Nothing wrong."

"You've gotten so serious. I feel I've done something to offend you."

"Offend?" Iggy looked back over his shoulder at Daniel.

"Something . . . something that made you angry or sad."

"No, no," Iggy said with great vehemence. "I very happy. My awful face." He covered his chin with his hand and pulled as though he wanted to tear off his face and replace it with another, more pleasant one. "Always look like that."

"You've seemed a long way away, ever since lunch. You were so lively this morning"—Iggy's eyebrows shot up—"you were so *happy* this morning. But ever since we came to see the temples . . . You're sure I didn't say something wrong? Was it wearing the toilet slippers?"

Iggy's brow furrowed. "Slippers?" Then he laughed out loud, not bothering to cover his mouth, small hands slapping his thighs, shoulders bouncing against the wooden pillar. "Toilet shoes. That funny."

"Then what is it, Iggy? What's wrong?"

Iggy regarded him doubtfully. "I tell you, you promise tell nobody?"

"I promise," Daniel said, placing one hand over his heart and raising the other.

Iggy looked at this gesture and giggled again. This time he covered his mouth with both hands. When he took them away his face was solemn. "Okay, I tell. I hate garden. I hate temple. I hate monastery. I hate pagoda. I hate sushi. I hate kimono. Geisha. Cherry blossom. Green tea. Fan. Samurai. Sake. I hate Japan. All old. Disgusting. For me, prison."

Daniel was shocked. He felt like rushing to the defense of all they had seen today—jostling carp, hanging mist, leaping school-boys, tigers lurking in gilded gloom, this nearly featureless garden. It was all so extraordinary, so different from anything he had ever seen or experienced. "But why, Iggy? It's all so beautiful."

"All so old. Old and dead. You no understand. Impossible for you. Everything here dead. All old men. Look like modern place. Go fast, big building. But everything here same forever. Nothing change. Old men tell you what to do. Big prison for me. Everything the past, the past, the fucking past. Disgusting."

"Surely it's not that bad," Daniel said, but he could see the pain in Iggy's eyes.

"You no know. Everything decided here. Whole life. No freedom." He abruptly stopped talking, as though he felt he had said too much. He looked up at the steadily brightening sky. "You marry?

"Yes, I am. My wife's name is Leslie. She has two sons, Alex and Porter."

Iggy looked back at him in surprise. "Little boys?"

"Big boys. Fifteen and seventeen."

"You how old?"

"Thirty-seven."

His eyes widened. "Oh. You look so young. Japanese man, thirty-seven very old. Disgusting."

"How old are you, Iggy?"

"Twenty-five."

Even though he knew Iggy had finished his studies, Daniel was surprised. "And are you married?"

Iggy shook his head rapidly. "Not Iggy. Never marry."

"What will you do?" Daniel asked.

"I don't know. I go away. New York maybe. Paris maybe. Where people like me. Amsterdam." He giggled again, hunching his shoulders as though "Amsterdam" itself were a word rich in hilarity. "But very hard. Must have sponsor. Job. Money."

"Won't your parents help?"

"My father no help."

"Why not?"

"He hate me. I hate him. Always, always like that."

"I see."

"He rich. Rich, rich man but no give money. He say, 'You marry, then study Europe, New York.' I say, 'Fuck you, old man.'"

"You really said that to him?" Daniel said, laughing.

"We no talk long time. Twelve, no, two year. After my mother die."

"You stopped talking after your mother died?"

Iggy nodded vigorously.

"Did you like your mother?"

Iggy nodded again. "She very beautiful. Famous actress, twenty year ago."

"And she wanted you to go away?"

"Almost fix. She going to give me money. Then she die. Now he own all her money."

"And you're stuck in Japan."

"Fucking prison."

"That's a very sad story, Iggy."

Iggy slowly shook his head. "The Sad Man," he said, tapping his cheek with an index finger.

Daniel advanced uncertainly into the long, dark-paneled room. Middle-aged Japanese men in dark suits stood three-deep along the walls, observing Daniel's progress. None of them made any attempt to greet him, shake his hand or otherwise bid him welcome. When Daniel and Iggy entered the room, Iggy had suddenly dropped away from his side. He knew his pale linen suit was all wrong for a formal dinner, but he had sent his other three suits and his dinner jacket out to be pressed this morning before breakfast, assured by the bellboy that they would be back by five. Of course they weren't, and calls to the front desk, the laundry and the Miyako's manager had proved futile, not to mention incomprehensible.

At the far end of the room four older gentlemen in dark suits stood against a gilded six-paneled screen. As Daniel approached them, a beautiful woman in an orange-and-gold kimono materialized at his side, bowing so that he could see the cloisonné pins that held her elaborate black wig in place.

"Mr. Kenning," she said, startling Daniel by knowing his name, "please meet the governor of Kyoto."

Daniel shook hands with a beaming plump man whose teeth were edged in gold. "Welcome to Kyoto," the governor said. "And you are from . . ."

"Montreal," Daniel said.

"Ah, Canada," the governor said, beaming even more. "Montreal Olympic."

"That's right," Daniel said, nodding and bowing enthusiastically.

"And please meet," the beautiful woman said, gently steering Daniel onward, "Mr. Kawabata."

Mr. Kawabata was slender and slight, his neatly combed silver hair the same shade as his pearl-gray silk suit. He clutched Daniel's hand and bowed over it. "This is indeed a pleasure," Mr. Kawabata said, in perfect British-inflected English, his mouth turned down in the emblematic frown Daniel associated with two-hundred-year-old Japanese woodcuts. "I was saddened to hear of the death of Mrs. Bordeleau. She was a wonderful woman."

"I didn't realize the two of you had met," Daniel said quietly.

"Ah, several times," Mr. Kawabata said, still holding onto Daniel's hand, the corners of his mouth trying to turn up into a smile. "I first met Mrs. Bordeleau in 1975, I believe, at the *Jardins en fête* conference at Versailles. I must tell you that I am a timid man, Mr. Kenning, especially with Westerners. My English is so inadequate. But with Mrs. Bordeleau I felt immediately comfortable—and on the first meeting, as though we were old, old friends."

"Gillian had that quality," Daniel said, aware that his voice was thickening. "There are times I miss her terribly." A tear slid down his cheek. He was too embarrassed to wipe it away.

"And I as well, Mr. Kenning, even though I met Gillian only three times." Mr. Kawabata touched Daniel's wrist while still holding onto his hand. "But I think your Mr. Pettigrew has found an admirable replacement for her."

Daniel bowed his head.

"I hope we will have time to meet and talk more about Gillian," Mr. Kawabata said. "Perhaps over the coming days . . ."

"I would like that very much," Daniel said as the beautiful kimonoed woman propelled him onward.

Black-wigged women darted among the tables, glimmering like carp in their orange silken robes, distributing large tumblers of straight whiskey. In a distant corner of the room three more similarly dressed women played soft music on flat stringed instruments placed directly on the floor in front of the players.

"I can't drink all this," Daniel said to Iggy.

Iggy nodded. "Very important. Health drink."

"Health drink?" Daniel said. "Oh. For toasts?"

"Toast?" Iggy said, buttering an imaginary slice of bread with an imaginary knife.

"To drink people's health?"

"That what I say," Iggy said, gulping down half his whiskey. "Finish fast before health begin. Girl bring you another."

Daniel was well into his third whiskey when the governor of

Kyoto, Mr. Kawabata and a clutch of other worthies filed onto the dais. The toasts were long—speeches, really—made longer by their translation into English. From the table behind him, Daniel could hear the hygienic blonde's young woman translating the toasts into what he assumed was Finnish.

The meal, when it finally arrived—well after ten o'clock— turned out to be, to Daniel's disappointment, French, not Japanese. But it was such exquisitely prepared French cuisine, and accompanied by such carefully chosen wines—every few minutes a kimonoed woman came to replenish his glass—that Daniel's disappointment evaporated.

"Isn't this marvelous?" he said to Iggy. "I've never had a finer French dinner, in Montreal or Paris."

"Chef here very famous," Iggy said, gesturing with his fork.

"From France?"

"Japan."

"More wine?" a kimonoed woman said.

"More wine," Daniel agreed.

After dessert—simplicity itself, a spiral of raspberries in Devonshire cream—a wild-looking man in a short blue coat burst into the room, a wide wooden tray slung from his burly shoulders. When he came to their table, he shouted something guttural at Daniel and handed him and Iggy small wooden boxes with a tiny pile of salt on each box's narrow rim.

"What did he say?" Daniel said to Iggy.

"Big life," Iggy said, sipping at his wooden box.

Daniel drank from one corner of his box. Sake. Ordinarily he didn't much care for the taste, but this was superb. It was warm yet fresh and dry on his numb tongue. Each sip seemed to make him thirstier.

"Iggy, this is without a doubt the best night of my entire life," Daniel said. "Look, look, a slipper moon." He cast his arm wildly in the direction of the floor-to-ceiling windows. The other men at his table turned to follow Daniel's expansive gesture. They regarded the slender moon in silence for perhaps a full minute, faces solemn. Turning back to Daniel, they smiled broadly, clapping their hands and bowing. Daniel felt that, for once in his life, he had done the right thing, although he wasn't sure exactly what.

For a moment he thought a drum was pounding inside his head. The guttural-voiced sake server marched into the room once again, this time hefting a small wooden barrel on one shoulder and holding a large wooden mallet in one hand. He was followed by a young man in black-and-white plaid knee-length pajamas who pounded with his hands on a large bongo-like drum slung from his waist. A similarly attired boy wearing a conical straw hat accompanied the drummer on a small wooden flute.

Daniel swayed back and forth in his chair in time to the music. He felt that if it did not stop soon, he would be unable to control his urge to stand up and dance.

The burly sake server and his two attendants reached the front of the room. The governor of Kyoto, Mr. Kawabata and the rest of the speakers' table rose and bowed to this raucous trio.

Mr. Kawabata whispered something in the governor of Kyoto's ear. The governor of Kyoto signaled for the sake server to approach the dais. Leaning over, the governor of Kyoto, glancing in the direction of Daniel's table, whispered in the sake server's ear. The sake server looked over at Daniel's table, then whispered to the pajama-clad musicians.

The drum and flute began again, louder and more orgiastic than before. The men on the dais started clapping their hands in time with the music. Their faces, Daniel noted through the golden haze that seemed to have settled over the room, glowed red and were broadly grinning. Even Mr. Kawabata had managed to turn up the ends of his thin lips.

The trio stopped directly in front of Daniel. The burly man slammed his barrel down on the floor before Daniel and shouted something in his face. Daniel looked at Iggy.

"Stand up, stand up," Iggy shouted to him over the pounding drum, the shrieking flute.

Daniel stood. The room seemed to tilt subtly to the right, the lights dimmed a bit. He could see the silver slipper moon sprouting from the crown of Mr. Kawabata's pearly head.

The sake man grabbed Daniel by the lapels of his linen suit and roared in his face. From somewhere behind him, Daniel could hear Iggy's voice. "Take off jacket."

Daniel struggled out of his jacket. An unseen hand whisked it away. The sake man flexed his sweaty, meaty hands and picked up the big wooden mallet. He swung the mallet back over his head and brought it down hard on the lid of the small wooden barrel. Then he handed the mallet to Daniel. It was heavy. Daniel pushed back one shirt sleeve, then the other. The men at his table murmured appreciatively. Resting the mallet handle against his hip, he spat into one hand, then the other, and rubbed them together. The whole room seemed to be murmuring now. He picked up the heavy mallet and heaved it high above his head. He stood there, swaying. For a brief moment he thought he might fall over backward onto the table behind him. Then he brought the mallet down in one great rush. It hit the barrel head dead-on, the barrel jumped into the air, then fell over on its side.

All the men at the speakers' table, all the people in the room, clambered to their feet and shouted what sounded to Daniel like, "Bonsai. Bonsai."

Daniel collapsed into his chair, feeling dizzy. Iggy draped Daniel's linen jacket over his shoulders. The men at his table were seated again, but still applauding, holding their hands up in front of their flushed faces.

The white Mercedes nosed along a narrow, brightly lit street. Thousands of young people, all of them looking about as intoxicated as Daniel felt, swarmed about the Mercedes, waving at Daniel or tapping on his smoked-glass window. When the car could penetrate no farther, Daniel and Iggy got out. The driver lowered his window and growled something at Iggy. Iggy pulled down the lower lid of his left eye at him. The driver, enraged, pushed a button, and his window purred shut.

"Fucking-fucking," Daniel heard Iggy say under his breath as the driver began to back the Mercedes out of the congested street.

Iggy wrenched off his navy-blue suit jacket and slung it over his shoulder. Daniel did the same with his jacket. Iggy ran his hands through his neatly combed hair until it stood out at every possible angle. Daniel tried to do the same with his short hair. He followed Iggy through the smiling crowd. Above them tropical-colored neon signs were stacked one on top of the other, forming garish pagodas. Each sign advertised a different restaurant or bar. Many had English names: Hysteric Glamour, Scotch and Cakes, Dirty Whistle, Breast Waltz.

Iggy turned into a narrower street where the crowds were denser still, the stacked signs more vibrantly colorful. With his coat over his shoulder, the sleeves of his white shirt folded back, his oversized trousers cinched at the waist, Iggy looked like a photo Daniel had once seen of the very young Frank Sinatra—wiry, antic, grinning.

He followed Iggy through a low arched doorway into a small courtyard that contained a swan-shaped fountain spouting pink-tinted water from its beak and an elevator with harlequin doors, J-Trip Bar spray-painted across them. Iggy pressed a button, the doors glided open and Daniel found himself inside a mirrored box. He could see Iggy and himself, grinning madly, faces on fire, repeated endlessly, right down into infinity.

The doors slid open and they walked out into a narrow, pulsating room. The walls were pitted concrete, plumbing and ventilation ducts crisscrossed the ceiling, the floor felt as if it were covered in thick rubber. As Daniel's eyes and ears adjusted to the flashing, spinning lights and the thudding dance music, he saw that two or three hundred young people had crowded into this concrete room. There was no dance floor that Daniel could make out. Dancers were everywhere, moving in perfect harmony with each other, some dancing around the tall mushroom-shaped tables scattered about the room, others line dancing on a narrow ledge that ran along the walls, still more—perhaps a dozen—swaying and dipping atop the mirror-surfaced baby grand piano. Four boys in white T-shirts and tattered jeans, hanging from a water pipe that ran diagonally across the room, performed chin-ups above the piano.

Bodies swirled around Daniel and Iggy, all of them making the same perfectly coordinated movements. The heavily amplified female voice coming from the loudspeakers sang a song in English, the principal lyric of which was the word "holiday." At a certain point in the song—Daniel thought it might be the chorus, since the word "holiday" occurred at even closer intervals—all the other dancers raised their arms above their heads and swayed them back and forth to the thumping music. Daniel raised his arms too and thought of rice swaying with the breeze in distant moonlit paddies.

Iggy's face bobbed up close to his. He was laughing. He pounded on Daniel's back with his fist. Pretty soon all the other dancers around them pounded on Daniel's back too.

"Holiday," Daniel sang along with the music, swaying his arms, "holiday, holiday."

Daniel opened his eyes. His small room looked larger in the dark, the picture window's rectangle glowing pale. Daniel lifted his head and the room lurched to the left, but he felt fine. He was still fully dressed, right down to his shoes. His stomach growled. He wondered if it was too early to call room service.

The bathroom door creaked open. Daniel froze. Then he saw that it was Iggy, naked except for a pair of blue boxer shorts printed over with small white sailboats. In the dim light he looked like a little boy, his shoulders thin, his arms almost without musculature, his rib cage so articulated that for a moment Daniel thought he could see his heart pulsing within. Iggy walked slowly over to Daniel's twin bed and without saying a word lay down next to Daniel. They lay like that for a while, staring at the ceiling. He thought Iggy had fallen asleep when abruptly the boy rolled over on his side so that he was facing Daniel. Daniel stared into his black, shining eyes. He smoothed Iggy's sticky hair off his brow and pulled him closer. The boy was shuddering so hard that for a moment Daniel was alarmed. Then he saw that Iggy was silently crying, the tears sliding off his cheeks and wetting the pillow. Daniel held the boy close, feeling him cry, until the sun came up, until Iggy fell asleep.

.   .   .

The tram rocked gently from side to side. Daniel rocked with it, feeling not so much hungover as incorporeal. For long stretches of the journey he forgot he was a passenger on a tram: he felt like a character in a movie. The interior of the car was painted a soft pale green, its length accentuated by the strip of windows running uninterrupted along either side. Only two other passengers made the ascent with him—a young woman, dressed in a frilly white needlepoint blouse, lime-green capri pants and patent leather Mary Janes, and her tiny dolllike daughter, lustrous hair bowl-cut around her plump face, pink sweatshirt and pink corduroy trousers carefully coordinated with the pink Snoopy appliqués on her tiny frilly socks.

When Daniel had finally awakened this morning, Iggy was gone. He had left a note on the vanity, carefully hand printed on Miyako letterhead. "HAPPY SUNDAY," the note read. "DAY OFF TODAY. NO SPEECH NO DINNER. YOU SEE MORE DISGUSTING TEMPLE? I MAKE YOU MAP. UNTIL WE MEET AGAIN, IGGY." An arrow led to the edge of the sheet of letterhead. Daniel turned it over. A thick line showed him how to make his way to a train station not far from the Miyako. A broken line indicated the tramline he should take northward to reach "MOUNTAIN KURAMA." Underneath these two printed words Iggy had sketched a high-gabled temple. A small sign stood to one side of the temple. It bore two Japanese characters; in parenthesis underneath the characters Iggy had printed in tiny letters, "DISGUSTING."

The train rose gently skyward, the ugly cast-concrete apartment buildings—narrow balcony rails fluttering with airing futons and drying Sunday wash—gradually giving way to terraces of handkerchief-sized rice paddies running up the mountainside and traditional wooden houses with slate-blue roof tiles. A feeble sun slipped in and out between the elongated clouds that layered the sky, sliding across the frame of the tram's long windows like flats across a proscenium stage. Daniel hoped it would rain so he could better appreciate "MOUNTAIN KURAMA."

After an hour or so the tram crept into its final station. Daniel and the young mother and her daughter got off. A cobblestone road tilted sharply upward. On either side were souvenir stands selling cheap-looking demon masks and fans and three or four rustic restaurants or taverns resembling German *Bierstuben*. The restaurants were crowded with avidly eating and drinking Japanese—Daniel thought he might wait and have lunch after visiting the temple.

At the top of the street stood an imposing wooden arch—a *torii,* Iggy had explained to him the day before. Daniel passed through it and climbed a steep stone staircase leading to a small wooden temple nestled among tall pines. A narrow stream ran alongside the stone stair—he was beginning to realize how essential the sound of rushing water was to Japanese gardens and other sacred sites.

He passed two ancient women in olive-green kimonos, wooden sandals on their cotton-stockinged feet. At the rate they were going it would be sunset before they reached the temple. In addition to the strong balsam smell of the surrounding forest, he detected something muskier and more exotic—an odor he couldn't at once place.

The air was thinner here. He was gasping for breath when he reached the temple. Water ran into a small, constantly overflowing cistern. Two wooden ladles hung from the cistern rim. Recalling what he had seen Japanese tourists do outside Nanzen-ji temple, Daniel took one of the ladles, dipped it into the cistern's churning water and poured the cool liquid over first one hand, then the other. He dipped the ladle once more and drank the cold, crystalline water. The tourists yesterday had also clapped their hands once, sharply, either before or after drinking, he couldn't remember which—Iggy said it was to summon the spirits—but he thought such a gesture might be presumptuous on his part.

The temple itself was much like the ones they had seen yesterday—thick timbered, the wood weathered and dark, almost oily black in places. On a wooden altar stood various bronze pots and porcelain bowls, some empty, some filled with wilting flowers. Previous visitors had left small paper scrolls tied with red satin ribbon. The musky odor was stronger here. Off to one side Daniel saw a small niche set into a stone retaining wall. Arrayed on the niche shelf were a small wooden box full of cinnamon-colored incense sticks, a green metal coin box and two red-and-blue-striped boxes of kitchen matches. Small piles of gray ash dotted the niche shelf. Daniel dropped a hundred-yen coin into the slot of the metal box and lit an incense stick, setting it carefully on end. It burned slowly, clouds of white smoke drifting up into the cool, gray air. The sky had lost its layers and was descending over the treetops like a lid.

He turned to make his way back down the steep stairs, feeling disappointed at having come so far for just another "DISGUST-ING" temple, when he saw that another stone staircase led on up the steep mountainside. A stream poured down alongside the staircase, at one point spilling twenty feet or so in a slender waterfall and filling a moss-covered cistern that overflowed to create another, smaller waterfall.

He climbed and climbed, passing middle-aged businessmen in ill-fitting gray or navy suits and down-at-heel shoes; more ancient kimonoed women, toiling ever upward; a trio of sweatshirted teenage girls, two of them slender Japanese, the third a plump Western girl with braces on her teeth who spoke what sounded to Daniel like effortless Japanese with her giggling companions. For a moment Daniel envied the girl her fluency, but at the same time he recognized that what he liked so much about Japan was not being able to understand. He liked having at every moment to figure out what was going on around him, by trying to divine the subtlest gestures, nuances, emotional atmospheres, of the people he encountered. He was, most of the time, baffled, but now and then he caught a glimmer of what was going on. Especially when he was with Iggy. All at once Daniel's entire body was suffused with warmth. In his mind he saw, as clearly as if it were a Renaissance painting hanging in a museum, an image of himself cradling Iggy in his arms, a tiny, naked baby Iggy, and Daniel was naked too.

Near the crest of the mountain the staircase opened out onto a broad stone terrace with a stone balustrade. Daniel looked out over the wide green valley and the valleys beyond it, all made somber and remote by the low gray sky. Inlaid at the terrace's center was a large stone disc, itself inlaid with bronze

Japanese characters and hieroglyphic designs. Daniel stared at the disc for a moment and was about to turn away when an old man carrying a straw broom scurried up to him, thrust a glossy, green-bordered brochure into Daniel's hand and scurried away again. Daniel studied the brochure carefully. It opened out into a map of Mount Kurama, detailing the various temples scattered across the mountainside. Like the temples he and Iggy had visited yesterday, this was evidently a monastery of some sort, but he couldn't figure out whether it was Buddhist or Shinto. Certainly he had seen no Buddhas during his climb—did this automatically indicate a Shinto shrine? He turned the brochure over to read the printed text. Part of it explained, in English, that Mount Kurama was the site where two billion years ago the great Sonten had come down to earth from Venus. The brochure omitted to explain who the great Sonten was. Instead it offered a prayer:

A Prayer for Happiness to Sonten of Mt. Kurama
(Sonten of Mt. Kurama is the trinity of love, light and strength)

For the purpose of elevating humanity
And for the purpose of increasing wealth and glory.

Beautiful like the moon
Warm like the sun
Emboldening like the earth
O Sonten! Bestow upon us Your affluent blessing.

By the mercy of Sonten, let it be realized that peace
surmounts hostility,
freedom from avarice overcomes greed, sincerity replaces
    falsehood,
and respect wins over contempt.

Bestow joy upon our hearts
Elevate our spirit
Bestow glory upon our flesh.

Sonten, the great soul of the Universe
and the great light as well as the great activity!

Bestow renewed strength and glorious light
upon those who come toward Your will
by gathering around and praying to You.

Everything belongs to You.

> *(We are grateful to a Japanese consul to New Zealand,*
> *Mr. Tanaka, for kind translation.)*

Daniel looked down at the stone disc he was standing on. He
wondered if the brass-inlaid disc could be the great Sonten's
landing pad. He stepped off the disc and wandered across the
terrace, looking to see if there might be yet another stone staircase
leading to yet another temple or overlook.

Past a low stone wall he discovered an earthen path leading
down into the darkening woods. The path wound up and down
among the thickly planted pines, passing an assortment of small
wooden or stone shrines as well as the occasional small temple.
From time to time he came upon incense sticks burning in stone
niches although he encountered no other pilgrims in this remote
area of the mountain.

He came to a small clearing. The ground was covered with
copper-colored pine needles, the sandy soil threaded with hairy
tree roots. At the center of the clearing a rusted copper pipe
sprang out of the earth like a cobra rising from its coils. Daniel
turned the spigot and rusty water gushed out of the tap, clarifying
as it poured. He cupped his hands and drank. Next to the tap
grew a small deciduous tree, twisted branches fanning out to
form a wide canopy of green. Each branch was hung with scores
of tiny prayer scrolls, each one tied with a red or pink satin
ribbon. Beyond the tree, precariously set into the mountainside,
were five or six of the gray tombstonelike objects he had stumbled
across on the mountainside above his hotel. The narrow stones
were surrounded by a low stone wall, and three of the stones
sported small crimson aprons that rose and fell on the breeze.

Daniel shivered and pulled his linen jacket more tightly about
him. It smelled of smoke. He smiled at the thought of dancing in
that smoky, crowded club, his arms waving high, singing along

to the music. He turned to go and nearly bumped into a Japanese woman laboring up the path he was about to descend. Startled, she lost her footing—her pink plastic sandals offered little traction—and started to slide back down the path. Daniel reached out and caught onto the sleeve of her bulky cardigan sweater, pulling her toward him. She grabbed onto his arm and then his shoulder, clinging to him, breathing hard and murmuring, *"Domo arigato. Arigato domo, domo arigato,"* over and over again, like a chant.

He led her over to a low stone bench, just beyond the little tombstone enclosure. She sat quietly for a moment, fanning herself with one hand. She looked about fifty, stocky from the waist down, a stockiness emphasized by ill-cut brown trousers of some cheap synthetic fabric. Her torso, half hidden by the sagging hand-knit sweater, looked more delicate. There was something peculiar about her face. At first he couldn't say what—it seemed cockeyed somehow. Then he realized that it was her hair—her black, densely piled hair was askew. She was wearing a wig. The woman noticed Daniel's gaze. A wide clownlike smile transformed her face. With both hands she readjusted the wig. There was nothing self-conscious about the action—she did it matter-of-factly, as one would resettle a sweater or a coat. The proper adjustments made, she put her hands together in her lap and, rocking slightly back and forth, smiled at Daniel. Daniel smiled back. The dark down on her upper lip reminded him of someone, he couldn't think who. She lifted her hands and held them in front of her, as if she were grasping the steering wheel of a car. Daniel looked at her, uncomprehending. She turned the invisible steering wheel this way and that, smiling contentedly. Abruptly her eyes rolled upward, her head fell forward, her shoulders slumped, her hands dropped onto the stone bench. Daniel feared she was either mad, or experiencing an epileptic seizure or some sort of stroke. He moved to put his arms about her, hoping that would in some way calm her, when she sat up straight and giggled.

"Are you all right?" he said.

She nodded her wig-heavy head.

"You're sure you're all right?" Daniel said, rising from the bench.

She nodded again, giggling.

"Then I should probably be on my way." He glanced at his wristwatch. He started to move off, but she gestured for him to return.

He was beginning to find her mercurial pantomime a bit tiring. She opened her black shoulder bag and rummaged about in it.

"Really, there's no need . . ." Daniel said. "I'm the one who almost knocked you down."

The woman shook her head, indicating that he should stay exactly where he was until she found what she was looking for.

Exultantly she pulled her hand from her bag and held it out, palm up. Two mandarin oranges nestled in her lined and slightly grimy palm, their skin rich and startling as newly unearthed gold in the murky forest light.

Daniel took one of the small oranges. The peeling came off smoothly, in one piece. He divided the small fruit in half and gave half back to the woman. He split off one tiny section and put it in his mouth. It released its flavor in a single burst, the juice so sweet it burned his throat. He stood, slowly savoring his half of the orange, section by golden section. The woman made quicker work of hers. When he had finished, she dug into her shoulder bag again and produced a small white handkerchief with a bright pink cherry blossom embroidered in one corner. Daniel took the handkerchief and wiped his sticky fingers. He started to hand the handkerchief back, but the woman held up her hand to indicate he was to keep it. She dropped the other orange back into her shoulder bag and zipped it shut.

"Thank you very much." Daniel bowed again and again and then uttered his first words in Japanese: *"Domo arigato, arigato domo."* He backed slowly down the path.

The woman sat on the stone bench, gently rocking, her clown-like mouth broadly smiling, thick-layered wig bobbing, until Daniel disappeared from sight.

The earthen path led Daniel down to a blacktop road that followed the course of a wide rushing stream. He thought he would walk along the road until it came to a village where he could have lunch. Somebody there could surely tell him how to get back to the Kurama tramway.

At regular intervals along the road he saw more stone staircases angling up to temples high in the woods, some with orange-painted *torii*, others consisting of a single rough-hewn structure. He felt too tired to climb anymore.

Eventually he came to a brightly varnished building with alternating blue and white rectangles of cloth fluttering over its entrance. As Daniel was passing, an old woman emerged from the building, carrying a round gold-lacquer serving tray.

"Excuse me," Daniel said. "Could I have lunch here?"

The old woman, who was wearing a purple-and-green-striped kimono, looked up at Daniel, squinting her eyes. She shook her head rapidly and, indicating Daniel was to wait, tottered back inside.

She returned in a few minutes, pushing an adolescent boy before her. He was wearing a white T-shirt, damp jodhpurlike gray pants, blue canvas gauntlets and heavy wooden clogs. He grinned at Daniel. "I speak English. You American?"

"Canadian," Daniel said. "From Montreal."

"Ah, Canada," the boy said.

"Montreal Olympic," Daniel offered. "May I eat lunch here?"

The boy turned and said something to the old woman. She answered him with a torrent of words, tapping his bare forearm with a gnarled index finger.

The boy turned to Daniel. "My grandmother say it cost a lot to eat here. Two thousand yen."

"That's fine," Daniel said, smiling to himself at the unworldliness of these simple country folk. Two thousand yen was only twelve or thirteen Canadian dollars.

"Sorry," the boy said, bowing quickly. "I make mistake. Twenty thousand yen."

"Twenty thousand?" Daniel said.

The grandmother grinned up at him, showing two rows of perfect bonelike teeth. She said something to her grandson.

"Very special," the boy said to Daniel. "*Kaiseki.*"

"*Kaiseki?*" Daniel said.

The boy held up his fist and opened it three times. "Fifteen courses."

"Really?" Daniel said. Well, why not? He hadn't eaten since breakfast and it was almost three. "That's fine," he said to the boy and turned to enter the building. The grandmother blocked his way.

"Excuse me," the boy said, bowing even lower. He looked embarrassed. "My grandmother want to see money."

"Oh," Daniel said, laughing, and pulled out his wallet. He opened it and realized he had only a few thousand yen. He pulled out his American Express card. The grandmother smiled broadly and nodded her head.

"Don't leave homes without it," the boy said, waving.

The grandmother took Daniel's arm and led him inside.

Daniel sat in a cramped, overfurnished lounge, feeling cheated. He could hear the rushing stream somewhere outside, but he seemed condemned to sit on this vinyl-covered sofa, a bowl of green tea, a colorfully wrapped sweet and a white face flannel on a black lacquer tray set before him.

He pressed the warm face flannel against his brow and held it there a few moments. Then he unwrapped the sweet. It was bright pink. He popped it in his mouth. It tasted, and chewed, like bubble gum. It seemed to adhere to every surface of his mouth. Finally he succeeded in swallowing it—wondering, too late, if it was indeed bubble gum. He drank the bitter green tea in three gulps, impatient to be led to the dining room for his expensive lunch.

The grandmother bustled into the lounge, bidding Daniel to rise. Forgetting his feet were wedged into too-small slippers, he nearly fell over the Formica coffee table.

He followed the old woman through a low doorway, down a flight of stone stairs and along a stretch of stepping stones that ran between two high stucco walls. The rushing stream seemed louder now but remained unseen. He hoped the dining room overlooked the stream. He couldn't imagine that it wouldn't, but then maybe there was something Zen about turning one's back on beauty.

He had to duck his head to pass under a series of small vine-covered wooden arches, rather like a pergola. He looked down: the stepping stones were surrounded by water. Long gold-spotted carp followed the passage of his slippers with interest. He looked up: ahead of him lay a wide tentlike room. The ceiling was rushwork interwoven with vines, the opposite wall, a bamboo curtain. At either end of the platform the wide stream roared along over a sparkling stony bed. The "room" was actually a wooden platform suspended over the stream. Perhaps twenty low black-lacquer tables were arranged in neat rows across the tatami mats. Plum lacquer screens, no more than three feet high, had been placed in front of and behind each table. A young couple—who avoided looking up as Daniel stepped out of his slippers and crossed the narrow stone bridge to the dining platform—were the only other customers.

The old woman led him to a table at the platform's edge, diagonal to that of the young couple. Daniel was about to protest—he didn't want the distraction of eavesdropping on an incomprehensible conversation. Then he realized that the roar of the stream was so great that he could hear nothing above it.

Sun filtered through the rush ceiling, turning the vine leaves translucent. He sat cross-legged on a hard straw cushion as the old woman poured him another cup of green tea. She padded away, only to return immediately with the first of his fifteen courses: a silver ceramic bowl containing five tiny brown carcasses in a pool of brown sauce. Daniel thought they might be sea creatures of some sort, or perhaps baby birds. In any case he couldn't ask what they were, so he popped one into his mouth. It was delicious—tender, juicy, crunchy. He figured the crunchiness must be bones.

The old woman came and went at carefully spaced intervals, one trip bringing three courses at once, stacked in a lacquer tower like an old-fashioned bric-a-brac shelf, other times bearing a single dish, intricate in its simplicity. Daniel ate sweet custardlike cubes nestled in a hollowed-out nettle. He wolfed down sharp-tasting cabbage shaved and spun into filigree. He sat for a long time staring at a silver fish on an elliptical porcelain plate: the fish had been bent to suggest the undulations it would have made swimming down the stream that ran beneath the dining platform. When he finally opened the fish with uncertain chopsticks, its belly yielded up vermillion roe on a bed of cooked egg yolk.

Taking his cue from the nearby couple—who were either lovers or only recently married, they stared so deep and long into each other's eyes—after the last course Daniel reclined like a diner in ancient Rome, one elbow on the tatami mat. He trailed one hand in the clear, cold water. He thought once more of Iggy, coming to his bed this morning, near-naked, crying. Daniel felt a surge of love and then a stirring along his thigh. Elation, shame, confusion swept over him in waves. He wondered how it was that vulnerability could call forth tenderness and hunger all at once. He wished that what he felt for Iggy were simple fatherly affection. It occurred to him that fatherly affection would never be simple for him. Then he saw that the last thing Iggy needed was another father. And calm that felt like serenity descended on him.

It was after dark when he got back to the Miyako. A girl waved to him from the reception desk and hurried over to meet him, holding a brown cardboard mailing tube.

"This came for you this afternoon, Mr. Kenning," the girl said, bowing twice and backing away.

Daniel opened one end of the tube in the elevator. It contained a poster. He unrolled it and studied the large color photograph, which showed a model house, a traditional Japanese house with wooden walls, rice-paper windows and doors and a tile roof, except these were all in the process of flying or falling away to reveal another structure rising from within, a structure with glass walls and metallic tubelike columns enameled in vivid crimson, yellow and violet. At the very center of this structure, enclosed in a red-ribbed glass-and-metal cage, was the tiny plastic figure of a middle-aged Japanese man in a gray business suit, angrily shaking his fist.

A line of bold Japanese characters ran down the right-hand edge of the photograph. Along the bottom, in fainter lettering, EXPLODE HOUSES: ARCHITECTURE BOMBS BY IGGY SATO.

The message light was blinking on the telephone when Daniel

entered his room. He laid the poster aside and rang the operator.

"Room 607?" the operator said. "I'm sorry. No message for Mr. McCaverty."

"My name is Kenning," Daniel said. "K-E-N-N-I-N-G."

"One moment, please." The operator put him on hold. Daniel listened to several verses of a synthesizer rendition of "Home on the Range."

The operator came back on the line. "We are very sorry, Mr. Kenning. Please phone home."

"Could you connect me, operator?" Daniel said, and gave the number.

"Hello?"

"Leslie?"

"Hello?"

"Hello."

"Daniel?"

"Hi, you sound sleepy."

"I am sleepy. I just got up. It's 8:00 A.M. What time is it there?"

"Nine o'clock. At night. Sunday night. How are you? I was so glad to get your message."

He thought for a moment that Leslie had gone away. Then she said, "I didn't phone you. Your mother phoned here and I gave her your number. She . . ."

"All the operator said was that I should phone home."

"Your father's ill, Daniel. Your mother sounded quite upset. She said she thought it would be a good idea if you could come as soon as you can."

Daniel sat down on the edge of the bed.

"Daniel, are you there?"

"I'm here."

"Are you all right?"

"I'm all right."

"What are you going to do?"

"I guess I should call the airline."

"I'm sorry it's interrupted your vacation like this."

"Well," Daniel said slowly, "what can you do?"

"You sound funny."

"I feel funny."

"I shouldn't wonder. It was quite a shock to me too."

"I don't know if 'shock' is the word," Daniel said, putting a finger to his throat to check his pulse. It was remarkably slow. "Listen, I should probably get moving, call the airline and all that."

"Yes. Call me when you get to Vancouver. Or whenever."

"Yes," Daniel said, standing up again.

"I love you," Leslie said. "You understand that, don't you?"

"Yes, I think I do. I love you too," Daniel said. "Give my love to the boys." He rang off.

It took him another hour of phoning to get a flight back to Tokyo and another to Vancouver. He would call the conference office in the morning and relay his apologies to Mr. Kawabata.

After hanging up the phone, he sat down at the vanity and wrote a short note to Iggy, thanking him for the poster and explaining his sudden departure. At the end he included his address and telephone number in Montreal, adding, "I hope you will come visit sometime. Your friendship means a lot to me." As he signed the letter, a drop of moisture ran from his eye. He reached into his pocket for a tissue and pulled out the crumpled white handkerchief with the embroidered cherry blossom in one corner. He dried his cheek.

Folding the sheet of letterhead, he slipped it into an envelope and sealed it. He got up and went to the window. He looked out at the dark sky and the darker mountainside beneath it. Life, he felt, was about to intensify.

PART FIVE

The Country of Your Catastrophe

*I*t would have been a made-for-TV movie, except for his eyes. All the props were in place in the small private room within the ICU: the beeping, blipping machine attached by wires to arms and chest; transparent green tubes running into nostrils; electronically modified voices calling softly in the distance, the squeak of nurses' shoes across freshly buffed tile. And at the center of the quiet, urgent bustle, a pair of eyes so large and startled they might have been eyes on stalks in a sci-fi movie, half watched, half derided at a drive-in, disembodied, swiveling, blue irises surrounded by white, the glinting pupils black points. He seemed to be breathing through his eyes.

Daniel went to the bed and kissed his father's gray cheek. "How are you doing?"

"You didn't have to interrupt your vacation for this." His father's voice was weak, wheezy. "I don't know why Margaret bothered you."

His mother got up from her chair on the other side of the bed and laid her hands on her husband's shoulder. "We didn't expect you until tomorrow."

"That was the first flight I could get, but when I told them why I had to leave, the people at the conference pulled some strings. Got me a seat on JAL out of Osaka so I didn't have to go back to Tokyo."

"And all for nothing," his father said. "Margaret just panicked. You know how she is. I'm fine now. Touch and go yesterday, but I'm fine now. Isn't that right, Margaret?"

Daniel watched his mother nod her head.

"You should have seen me yesterday. It was like my lungs had turned into two sandbags. I just couldn't get any air." Daniel remained standing, looking down at his father. His words seemed almost beside the point, the eyes poured out so much.

. . .

Daniel tossed the two small bags into the trunk. "I can't believe this is all you brought."

"It's my new philosophy," Elspeth said, watching as a jet swept up into low-hanging clouds. "Traveling light. How's he doing?"

"Back from the dead, I think. They've moved him out of the ICU and into a private room." He opened the door of the Jaguar and deactivated the alarm before it could go off. "I've never seen him like this. It's hard to explain. He looks human."

Elspeth yawned. "Sorry."

"Did you sleep on the plane?"

"Sleep?"

"You know, close your eyes, perchance to dream."

She opened the passenger door. "Maybe it's part of traveling light. I stopped sleeping about a week ago."

"You're kidding."

"Wish I were."

"But how do you keep going?"

"Adrenaline. Anxiety. Fear."

"You really don't sleep at all?"

"I lie in bed, washed over by waves of anger."

"Anger at what?"

"If I knew that I might be able to sleep."

Daniel glanced at his sister in the rearview mirror. She didn't look as though she hadn't slept in a week. Then she met his eyes in the mirror and he saw he was wrong. "Has this ever happened before?"

"Every now and then. Not for this long. Oh, when I was in grade four I had insomnia the whole year."

"Did Mum and Dad know?"

She nodded. "They fixed me warm milk every night. Had no effect."

"They didn't take you to see anyone?"

"They never offered, and I didn't have the sense to ask. I had the feeling they were ashamed. By not sleeping I was somehow letting them down, I'm not sure how."

"Do you want to go to the hotel first, or straight to the hospital? You could take a warm bath, have a nap and then come to the hospital tonight."

Elspeth switched on the radio, heard a CBC voice declaiming the news and turned it off again. "If one more person counsels a warm bath, I'm buying a gun. Let's go to the hospital. There's no point in taking a nap. I won't sleep. I've transcended sleep. Think of me as a rung up on the evolutionary ladder."

"Have you tried pills?" Traffic had slowed to a standstill. Large drops of rain burst on the windshield.

"Daniel, can it, okay? I don't need your brotherly concern. I've tried pills, malt whiskey. A kindly model slipped me some opium during a shoot. That was the nicest—I didn't sleep but I didn't care. I'd made an appointment at the South London Sleep Lab, but then Mother called." She pressed a button and her window glided down. "I can smell the sea. He really does seem different?"

"It could just be me. Wishful thinking. But he looks as though he's back from a long journey and is seeing the world with new eyes."

"That makes two of us," Elspeth said, laying her head on Daniel's shoulder.

"Maybe he'd know of a sleep clinic here."

She sat up straight. "If you mention one word . . . I couldn't stand the warm milk treatment all over again."

He was sitting up in bed. The oxygen tubes and monitor wires were gone, although a tube ran from his left arm to the IV drip. Daniel stood at the door as Elspeth went to her father's side.

"Hello, Daddy."

He grinned up at her. "So, did you come back to collect your inheritance?"

Elspeth looked dismayed. "Daddy . . ."

"Sorry to disappoint you."

Mrs. Kenning laid aside her magazine and came round the bed to embrace Elspeth. "Did you have a good flight? You look tired."

"Rough week at work." She turned back to her father. "That's a fine way to greet me after I swim the Atlantic to see you."

"I'm sorry, Elspeth." Tears spilled out of the great staring eyes. "I don't understand."

"Don't understand what?" Daniel said.

"Why you've both come so far to see me."

"Because you're our father," Elspeth said. "Why wouldn't we come?"

"I didn't think I was worth the trip."

Mrs. Kenning went to his side. "You're just worn out, that's the problem." She took a tissue from a box on the bedside table and dried his cheeks. Turning to Elspeth and Daniel, she said, "Dr. Smythe told us the anticoagulants along with sedatives can leave some people pretty emotional the first few days."

"What you've been through in the last few days would make anyone emotional," Daniel said, looking into his father's eyes.

"I think they'd run all the time if I let them," his father said.

The door swung open and an orderly came in carrying a plastic jug. "Hey, Doc, how's it going?"

"Couldn't be better, Keith," Dr. Kenning said, rubbing his eyes with his free hand. "Got the whole family here now."

"That's good, Doc." Keith held up the plastic jug. "You think you could get me some urine when you've got a moment?" He glanced at Elspeth and Daniel. "No hurry, but the chart says every two hours, so every two hours it is."

"I think I can spare a few drops," Dr. Kenning said.

Keith placed the jug on the bedside table. "You take your time and visit with your family. I'll be back in a little while." The door swung open and Keith was gone.

Dr. Kenning reached for the jug, raising his knees so that his bedcovers made a tent. He slipped the jug under the sheet, between his legs, grimaced and then sighed. Daniel heard the hollow sound of his father's urine streaming into the plastic jug. His mother gazed out the window, Elspeth gnawed at her thumb.

Daniel tipped the bellboy and closed the door behind him. Crossing the room, he tapped on the door. "Breakfast's here."

"Be right out."

He wheeled the room-service cart closer to the wall of windows looking onto the water. Picking up the folded newspaper, he glanced at the headlines and then laid it aside.

The door opened and Elspeth came in, wrapped in a big white terry robe with the hotel crest embroidered on the breast pocket. Her short hair was wet and tufted.

He looked at her closely.

"Don't even ask," she said.

"I won't." He lifted the silver domes to reveal waffles covered with strawberries and blueberries. "You hungry?"

"I'm always hungry." She pulled an armchair closer to the cart.

"Coffee?" Daniel said.

Elspeth nodded, picking up the newspaper.

"Can I ask one thing?"

"What?"

"If you don't sleep, what do you do all night?"

"Depends on how frustrated I am. Sometimes I read, sometimes I get up and clean the flat. Most of the time I haven't the energy to do anything, so I just lie in bed cursing myself."

"That's terrible."

She shrugged.

"If you're going to read at table, could I have the arts section?" She passed it to him. "Is that what you did last night?"

"Until about four, when it started getting light. Then I got out of bed and watched the sun creep over the horizon—that was lovely until the rain started up again. Where's Mum?"

"When I got up I knocked at her door to see if she wanted breakfast, but she'd already gone. She'd even made the bed."

Elspeth rustled through the editorial section. "How long do you think you'll stay?"

"I don't know. Mum said the doctors told her last night that he could go home within the week if he keeps making progress. I thought I'd wait till then, help her get him settled at home."

Elspeth poured them both more coffee. "I can stay till then too."

He scanned the movie page. "Not a lot on. Hey, they're showing *The Funeral* at the College Rep."

"What a brilliant idea, Daniel. Just the thing for the whole family."

"It's a comedy. From Japan. Supposed to be very funny."

"I'm sure." She trickled more syrup onto her waffles. "It would be nice to do something besides go to the hospital. You can watch someone recover only so many hours in a day."

Daniel turned the page. "My God."

She looked up. "What?"

He held the paper out. Elspeth stared at a photograph of a woman wearing black-framed octagonal eyeglasses. "It's Meredith McCrory," he said. "She's a big deal in architectural theory. I met her, oh, about a year ago in Montreal. When McGill gave me that award? She's designed the sets for a play they're putting on here at the Firehall."

"She looks intimidating."

"Yes, she is a bit. You want to go see it?" He skimmed the accompanying article. "Oh, she's not here. Or she was here but now she's gone."

"What's the play?"

"*Ajax.*"

"The foaming cleanser?"

"I'm relieved to see that years at Oxford beat the philistine right out of you."

"I don't know, Daniel. Greek tragedy? I never feel I'm quite up to it, even at the best of times."

"I can go alone. I want to see what she's done. If it's really tedious we could sneak out at intermission."

Elspeth ran a hand through her hair. "If I remember the Firehall, they don't do intermissions. That's the first rule when you're doing experimental theater: no escape hatch."

"How do you know that?"

"Graham—the bloke I'm seeing?—is a director."

Daniel reached for the phone. "I'm going to find out if they have any tickets left. You coming or not?"

"Yes, I'm coming. What else is there to do? I've already memorized the bedroom ceiling."

. . .

He walked at his father's side down the long corridor, holding on
to his elbow. With his free hand his father held on to the chrome
IV stand and the attached electronic monitor rolling along on
casters at his side.

"Good to be up and around," his father said.

"I bet."

"Lungs hardly bother me at all. Only when I cough—then it's
like somebody sandpapering in there."

They reached the nurse's station at the center of the crossing
corridors. Daniel looked at the bright rectangle at the far end of
the hallway. "You want to keep going, or should we head
back?"

"Keep going," his father said. His maroon dressing gown had
fallen open, revealing the pale green hospital gown underneath.
The gown was twisted to one side so that one of his hairless legs
was exposed almost to the hip.

"Here, Dad, your gown has ridden up." Daniel crouched down
to pull the hem straight. His father's hand came down heavy on
his shoulder. Daniel paused, lost his breath. He looked up. His
father's eyes were full of tears. High electronic beeps gave Daniel
back his wind.

"What's that?" he said.

"The goddam machine." His father let go of Daniel's shoulder
and untangled the tube running from his arm to the IV drip.
"When the tube gets twisted, the alarm goes off."

A nurse came rushing along the corridor. "It's all right," Dr.
Kenning called to her. "False alarm." More quietly he said to his
son, "Stand up or they'll think something's really wrong."

Daniel retied the sash of his father's dressing gown and stood.
"There."

"It never does want to stay tied. I tell Margaret silk's a waste
of money, but she will have the best." He wheeled the IV stand
in a semicircle.

"Where you going?" Daniel said.

"Back." His father shook his head. "Even a little crisis can
wear you out."

. . .

"Shall we sit or just walk?" Mrs. Kenning said.

"Walk," Elspeth and Daniel said together.

Mrs. Kenning led them along the curving brick path. "Look how heavy the peonies are—heads nearly down on the ground. Too much rain."

Over a hillock, Daniel could see two Asian gardeners in canvas aprons standing on the stone rim of an oval pond.

"It's a beautiful garden," Elspeth said, catching up to her mother. "All the times I've been to the hospital and I never noticed it."

"It's fairly new," Mrs. Kenning said. She pointed past the pond to a line of poplars. "There used to be a school over there. It burned in the late seventies. Where we're walking was the school-yard."

"I remember the school," Daniel said. "Sort of Elizabethan." His mother thought for a moment. "Yes, if you mean windows with all those panes. I imagine they had to have someone on staff just to keep them spotless."

They came to the edge of the pond.

"Look," Elspeth said. "Goldfish. Huge ones."

Daniel clapped his hands twice. A dozen or more carp jostled to the surface, mouths pulsing.

"How'd you do that?" Elspeth said.

"Years of Zen study."

"Good afternoon, Yukio. Hello, Nguyen," Mrs. Kenning said to the gardeners, who were bent over a flowering shrub.

They looked up. "Hello, Mrs. Kenning," the younger one said. He pointed at the shrub. "Bad roots." The older, who was completely bald, gave a gold-rimmed smile.

"You must come here a lot," Elspeth said after they had left the pond.

"I've been involved from the beginning—I even chose some of the flowering trees. It was your father and some of the other doctors who clubbed together on the design and planting costs—they set up a trust fund to cover upkeep too. The hospital bought the land with an eye to expansion, but then with all the cut-backs . . ."

"I didn't know Dad was interested in gardens," Daniel said.

Mrs. Kenning laughed. "Since the ribbon cutting I don't think he has visited it once. I wondered about having you wheel him over in a chair, Daniel, but I don't imagine he'd want to be seen in one. It's hard enough being a patient at your own hospital."

"He's improved so much since I arrived," Elspeth said, fingering the waxy leaves of a magnolia.

"He's still so distressed," Mrs. Kenning said. "He can't seem to get himself under control—they've got him pumped full of so many different things."

"You think it's just the medication?" Daniel said.

His mother looked at him over the top of her glasses. "I'm not sure I follow."

"Well, he's been through a lot, Mother. You wouldn't have called us home if he hadn't been in real danger."

"But look how quickly he bounced back," Mrs. Kenning said.

"It is amazing," Elspeth said.

"Yes, it is," Daniel said. "But don't you think, when you've had an experience like that, it's bound to change you?"

Mrs. Kenning brushed a fleck of lint from the sleeve of her pale suit. "We had a scare . . ."

"He seems different to me," Daniel said quietly.

"To me too," Elspeth said, covering her mouth with one hand.

"More open," Daniel said.

"You can see it in his eyes," Elspeth said.

Mrs. Kenning turned from them and looked back over the pond to the hospital.

"This is the first time," Daniel said, a tremor in his voice, "that I've felt hopeful about us as a family."

Mrs. Kenning glanced back at him, her mouth set in a line. "I think I'd better be getting back now—they'll be bringing his tray. You two stay here and enjoy the sun while you can," she said, and walked away.

Elspeth tapped Daniel on the wrist with her rolled-up program. "If this doesn't put me out, nothing will."

They sat huddled together on bleachers with fifty or sixty other spectators—the gutted firehouse, hung with catwalks and tier upon tier of lights, could have held four times that many.

"It looked like you nodded off this afternoon," Daniel said. "At the hospital."

"Everybody assures me I must sleep during the night as well, otherwise I couldn't keep upright day after day. If that's true, why do I feel like this?"

"Like what?"

"Flayed."

"I wish there was something I could do," Daniel said.

"I do too. I wish—" The houselights went down and the enormous tarpaulin that nearly covered the elliptical playing area began to stir. Portions of it jutted up, then flopped to the ground again, raising clouds of dust. Soon the whole expanse of rust-colored canvas roiled like a sea. The sound of stampeding hooves came from overhead speakers, mixed in with strange animal bellowing and high-pitched inhuman shrieks.

Elspeth whispered to Daniel, "You didn't tell me it was a comedy."

A trumpet sounded, and the entire tarp heaved up into a mis-shapen three-crested tent. Through a gaping triangular hole in the tent's front wall, Daniel glimpsed close-set pairs of yellow lights that flickered and darted in the dark like animal eyes. Two wooden columns topped by a rustic pediment glided out of the tent until they filled the triangular opening.

A spotlight picked out a woman in a white military tunic who seemed to hover in midair above the tent. "Ajax," she said in a high, clear voice, "I call you once again!"

As she spoke, the vast tent glowed from within, dark canvas lightening to scrim. At first Daniel could make out only humped shapes, glinting golden poles angling across the tent interior. Then he saw it was a broken circus carousel. Polychrome plaster of paris horses, lions, zebras sprawled on their backs and sides, bellies cracked open to reveal hollowness within. And at their center a man in a ringmaster's jodhpurs, boots and scarlet long-tailed coat, flicking a two-thonged leather whip.

. . .

"Take the long way back to the hotel," Elspeth said as Daniel pulled out of the Firehall parking lot.

"Which long way?"

"Any one."

They drove along quiet residential streets, windows down, humid, sweet-scented air pouring in.

Elspeth pleated her program into a fan. "You know, I really didn't get it. I didn't get him."

"Ajax?"

"It's just so weird. So foreign. I got the part about humiliation—the rivalry with Achilles and all that. I can understand how Ajax would feel ashamed because Achilles is the better fighter. But I don't see the connection—why does Ajax turn around and slaughter all the animals?"

"I'm not sure there is a connection."

"Why couldn't he do something straightforward, like sleep with his mother and gouge out his eyes?"

"We should probably have read it before we went." Daniel turned onto a narrow street that curved down toward the water.

"Do you think it would have made any difference?"

"No." Wisps of fog eddied toward them over the glistening asphalt. "It must have been clearer for the Greeks."

"I hope so." Elspeth slumped down in her seat, biting at her thumb. "And why'd he drag the animals into the tent to torture and kill them? Why not do it outside?"

Daniel flicked on the high beams, the fog became a white tunnel. He switched back to low beams. "It was a shameful act—he didn't want anyone to see, so he took them inside."

"It still doesn't make sense that everyone would be so upset. Ajax just spent ten years in Troy killing people right and left. And now everyone's up in arms because he kills animals in his tent?"

Daniel pulled into a scenic overlook. He turned off the engine but left the headlights on. "If there weren't so much fog we could see the sea."

"If wishes were horses . . ."

". . . Ajax would kill them too."

"Please," Elspeth said. He saw she was shredding her program and stuffing the confetti in the ashtray.

"I'm sorry you didn't like it."

"I didn't say I didn't like it. I didn't get it. Your friend's sets were amazing."

"Meredith McCrory knows her stuff. Did you notice that whenever somebody had the upper hand, he stood in the doorway?"

"No, I guess I didn't," Elspeth said. "I liked the way the chorus sort of wafted back and forth when everyone was gathered on the beach. Like waves."

"You know what my favorite part was?" Daniel turned in his seat so he was facing his sister.

"What?"

"When the messenger rushes in with the bad news and he's so overwrought he's not making a lot of sense. To calm him down the chorus says, 'You don't know where you are in the country of your catastrophe.' "

"Yeah, that's a good line. It reminded me of you."

"It reminded me of me too."

Elspeth reached over and put her cool hand on his. "You seem a lot less lost than the last time I saw you."

"At Christmas?"

Elspeth nodded, shivering.

"Cold?"

"Tired. I think I'd like to go back."

He turned on the engine and pressed the buttons set into the armrest. The windows glided shut.

"You know the part I liked best?" Elspeth said.

"What?"

"When Ajax puts his uniform on his son. The poor kid—riding boots up to his armpits, coattails dragging in the dust, just his head peeking out the top."

"Sins of the fathers," Daniel said, gunning the engine.

• • •

The door swung open and the orderly came in, bearing a plastic jug. Daniel and Elspeth looked up from their playing cards.

"Hey, Doc," the orderly said, "it's that time again."

"How you doing, Keith?" Dr. Kenning said.

"Hello, Keith," Mrs. Kenning said.

"Hi, Mrs. Kenning. Say, he's looking pretty good, isn't he?"

Mrs. Kenning smiled. "He certainly has more color."

"You can't keep an old dog down," Dr. Kenning said. "I'm starting to feel like my old self again."

"That's great," Keith said, placing the jug on the bedside table.

"How's the tennis?" Dr. Kenning said.

"Wet," Keith said.

"I bet." Dr. Kenning looked at Elspeth and Daniel. "Keith's on the team at UBC."

"It's supposed to clear this afternoon," Keith said, glancing at the window.

"You're off at three?" Dr. Kenning said.

"I've also got my last final on Friday," Keith said, turning to go. "I'll be back for that in a while. Take your time."

"Okay, Keith."

The door swung open and shut.

"He's quite a kid," Dr. Kenning said. "I don't know how he does it. He's half-time here, full time at the university."

"What did he say he was studying?" Mrs. Kenning said.

"Gin," Elspeth said, laying out her cards.

"Marine biology," Dr. Kenning said, reaching for the plastic jug.

"That's it for me," Daniel said, putting down his hand.

"I don't think anyone would mistake you for a cardsharp," Elspeth said.

"No," Daniel said. His father raised his knees. The sheet rode up to expose his bare legs. Daniel and Elspeth sat motionless, watching their father maneuver his sex into the mouth of the jug.

"Dad," Elspeth said.

"Just a minute, Elspeth. I'm concentrating," Dr. Kenning said.

"Dad," Elspeth said, "when you do that, I think you should let us know so we can leave the room."

Dr. Kenning looked up. Mrs. Kenning laid her magazine aside. "Oh," Dr. Kenning said, putting the jug back on the table and smoothing down the sheet. He looked at his wife. "I think I've offended our daughter's delicate sensibilities."

"Mine too," Daniel said.

Dr. Kenning looked out the window. "Well, that goes without saying. Everything I do offends you."

Elspeth stood. "I need some air."

"I'll come with you." Daniel got up from his chair.

"I don't see what all the uproar's about," Dr. Kenning said, his face going red. "Do you, Margaret?"

Mrs. Kenning folded her arms and watched silently as Daniel followed Elspeth out the door.

The next morning Daniel and Elspeth rode the elevator to their father's floor.

"If you can make it to New York," Daniel said, "half the battle's won. You know you can always pick up a cheap flight to London this time of year."

"I might even spend a few days in New York," Elspeth said. "Hit the museums and galleries, get in some shopping. It's not as though the comic will miss me that much."

"I thought this was their busy season."

"It is. I've been thinking about chucking it in any case."

"Really?"

"You can only work in fashion so long. It's probably time to make the leap to something superficial."

The elevator doors slid open on a phalanx of white-coated doctors. Daniel and Elspeth elbowed their way through. A small boy in a yellow terry robe clung to the railing of the unoccupied nurse's station. On the wall above, a unicorn knelt within a circle of silver-barked trees.

"This doesn't look right," Daniel said.

"Wrong floor," Elspeth said as two little girls in shorts and brightly printed T-shirts raced past.

Daniel pushed the elevator button. "I thought it smelled different."

They got off at the next floor and walked down the corridor to their father's room.

Elspeth pushed on the door. She pushed again. "It's locked."

Daniel pushed on the door. "Should we knock?"

"I don't know," Elspeth said.

They heard the lock turning. The door opened narrowly. Their mother slipped into the corridor, letting the door swing shut behind her.

"What's wrong?" Daniel said.

"Your father's sleeping," Mrs. Kenning whispered.

"Oh," Daniel said.

"We could go and grab some lunch," Elspeth said. "You want us to bring you something?"

Mrs. Kenning leaned against the door, hands behind her. "I'm fine."

Daniel turned to go. "We'll be back in a while."

"I'm not sure that's such a good idea."

He turned to look at his mother.

"Mother, what's wrong?" Elspeth said.

Mrs. Kenning looked at Daniel. "I don't think your father wants to see you."

"Did he say that?" Daniel said.

"I think he's had about enough. We both have," Mrs. Kenning said.

"Mom," Daniel said, "what happened yesterday . . . surely you can understand . . ."

Mrs. Kenning's voice was hoarse. "I'm not talking about what happened yesterday. It's the things you said at Christmas that did the damage. Yesterday was only the most recent example."

"Mother," Elspeth said, "come have lunch with us. You're in that room all day long . . ."

Mrs. Kenning's eyes remained fixed on Daniel. "Do you know how he's been since Christmas? What it's been like for him? There were times it was so bad I worried . . . I thought he was going to kill himself."

"I had to talk about what happened," Daniel said. "We've never talked about anything. I'm sorry if I—"

" 'I, I, I,' " Mrs. Kenning said, her chin trembling. "Did you

ever for a moment think about your father? These are supposed
to be our golden years. We've worked all our lives, doing everything we knew how to give you all you needed and more. Now
that it's our turn to relax and enjoy life a little, you come along
and destroy it all."

"But what about Daniel and what it's been like for him?"
Elspeth said. "With something like this, you have to deal with
it—I don't see that there's any choice. You can't just forget it,
pretend it never happened."

Mrs. Kenning turned to Elspeth for the first time. "I don't
believe it did happen. Any of it." She turned back to Daniel. "I
don't believe you. I don't believe a word you've said."

"But why would I make something like that up?" Daniel said.

"Because you've always hated your father. Always. You won't
be happy until he's dead."

"Mother . . ." Elspeth said.

"You're no better than he is. You parrot everything he says.
What happened yesterday is just about par for the course."

"That's not fair," Elspeth said. "I was the one who objected
yesterday. Daniel only agreed."

"Oh, fair," Mrs. Kenning said. She took off her glasses and
with her fingertips slowly massaged the marbled lids of her eyes.
"Is it fair that your brother drove your father to this? He
wouldn't be in hospital if it weren't for the things Daniel said. I've
watched in silence all this time, but I won't have any more of it.
You do have a problem," she said to Daniel. "I can see that now.
You're selfish—selfish almost beyond belief."

"I don't know what else to say," Daniel said.

"I would have thought you had said enough," Mrs. Kenning
said.

"You may be right," Daniel said and walked away.

Elspeth stayed where she was, looking at her mother, hearing
Daniel's steps fading down the hall.

"I'm sorry to leave you like this," Daniel said as Elspeth pulled
the car up to the curb. "But I don't know what else to do."

"You're apologizing for leaving," Elspeth said, "I'm apologizing for staying."

"Guilty, guilty, guilty."

"It's not as though I'm stuck here that long. If all goes well they'll release him in the morning. I'll drive them home, see them settled in, then drive back into the city and get the red-eye for New York tomorrow night."

"I wish you luck," Daniel said.

"Thanks." She looked into his eyes. "Are you okay?"

He thought for a moment. "Yeah. What she said yesterday really shook me up. Today it feels more like a relief. At least now I know where everyone stands."

"Notice how gracefully I straddle both sides," Elspeth said.

He leaned over and kissed her cheek.

She helped him haul his bags out of the trunk. "I have the feeling you're never going to travel light."

"I don't think it's part of my character," Daniel said.

"I don't think it's part of your heritage."

He kissed her again. "I love you, Elspeth."

"I love you too."

They embraced, heads together, bodies arching apart.

The driver helped him lug his bags up to the door. *"C'était un long voyage?"*

"Plus ou moins," Daniel said. He paid the driver and unlocked the front door.

The house was quiet. Beaver should have been at the door, barking. Leaving his bags in the entry hall, Daniel walked through the living and dining rooms and into the kitchen. He looked out the screen door, but the garden was empty.

Standing at the bottom of the stairs, he called, "Anybody home?" He thought he heard a muffled woof from the top of the house.

He took the two flights of stairs to his workroom two steps at a time.

Porter sat on the daybed, holding Beaver by the collar. "Hey,

Daniel." He let go the collar, and Beaver ran to Daniel's side, tags chinging.

"What are you doing up here?" Daniel said, bending to kiss Beaver's muzzle. "Where are Leslie and Alex?"

Porter pointed toward the far end of the workroom.

Daniel spun around. French doors had been set into the wall next to his drawing table. Through the beveled panes he could see Leslie and Alex, disjointed flames.

"Don't let Beaver out." Porter jumped up from the daybed and grabbed the dog's collar. "It's not finished."

Daniel opened one door wide enough to slip out. "What's this?" he said, walking across the wide deck suspended above the treetops.

"Surprise," Leslie said, taking him in her arms and kissing him.

"Welcome back, Daniel," Alex said, kneeling beside the flaming hibachi. "I think I used too much lighter fluid."

"You always use too much lighter fluid." Daniel ran his hand over Alex's close-cropped hair. Walking to the edge of the deck, he looked out over the rooftops. "This is amazing."

"Don't fall off," Leslie said. "The contractor promised to install the railing yesterday. Today he's not returning my calls. Do you really like it?"

"Like it? When there was nobody downstairs I thought you'd moved while I was away."

"We wouldn't do that to you, Daniel," Alex said, peeling the salmon steaks apart.

"We would have just changed the locks," Leslie said, kissing him on the cheek. "I'm glad you're back."

"Me too."

Porter opened one of the doors. "Stay, Beaver. Stay. Good boy." He shut the door behind him. Beaver pressed his nose against the glass.

"Couldn't he come out?" Alex said to Leslie. "We could hold on to him."

"Absolutely not," Leslie said. "Somebody would forget. Beaver doesn't know he can't fly."

Through the bright panes they could see that Beaver had stretched out on the floor, head between his paws.

"I bet you're ready for a drink," Leslie said. "Porter, will you do the honors?"

Porter went over to the shady corner of the deck and picked up the ice bucket.

"Champagne?" Daniel said.

Porter lifted the bottle out of the bucket and looked at the gold label. "Veuve Clicquot."

Daniel crouched down and helped Alex fit the hibachi grill into place.

"How's your father doing?" Alex said.

Porter held the neck of the bottle away from him and unscrewed the tiny wires, Leslie standing by with a glass.

"He's doing much better," Daniel said. "He'll be out of hospital tomorrow."

A small gaseous pop, and the cork bounced off the French doors. Beaver leapt to his feet, sniffing at the beveled panes.

"You must feel relieved," Alex said, laying out the salmon steaks on the grill.

Foam poured down the side of the champagne bottle. Leslie tried to catch it in her glass, but Porter put his thumb over the opening and began shaking the bottle.

"Actually, I have mixed feelings," Daniel said.

"Porter, stop that right now," Leslie said as Porter chased her around the deck, champagne squirting across her shirt and trousers.

"I think I can understand that," Alex said.

Flames burst up through the grill, singeing the salmon steaks. The sun was almost level with the horizon. As shadows lengthened, the deck seemed to float above the trees. Beaver stood on guard on the wrong side of the door, muzzle pressing against the panes. The siren wail of a distant fire truck or ambulance, and Beaver began to howl, as sparks rose into the darkening air.